THIEF
MAGE
BEGGAR
MAGE

A novel of magic and treachery, of love and freedom, and the
many faces of truth

THIEF MAGE BEGGAR MAGE

CAT HELLISEN

A CIP catalogue record is available from the British Library

www.ghostmothpress.com

ISBN-13: 978-1-7396851-3-3

For all the people who need to slip their skins and find new shapes

I

THIEF MAGE

The thief mage walked into the traveller's camp with the dark at his heels, night falling with a flash of final bloody red. He greeted the People of the Dogs like old friends, one arm raised. The other was an empty sleeve, pinned up at the elbow.

From the shadows on the guest side of the caravan's great fire, Tet watched the mage. He massaged his scarred right knee, tamping down his pain like tobacco into an old pipe as he listened to the mage talk. The wound was not a lie, even if the rest of Tet's identity was a stitchery of half-truths and suggestions. Once, he had been a powerful priest-mage; now he was nothing more than another worn-out soldier with a worn-out soldier's pension to his name, and a limp to match his current identity. No one paid attention to one more war-crippled man, barely more than a beggar. Broken veterans were thick as corpse-maggots in Deniah.

The mage told the People he was selling witchery for an evening's safety. 'Even mages need protection in the mountains,' he said, and they laughed, their wrinkled eyes flashing at this rare guest filled with promises.

He'd woken Tet's interest like the smell of meat wakes a monster. The mage was barely inconvenienced by his deformity. An accident, Tet supposed. Some fall or fight that had sliced his right arm off at the elbow. They were a match – the mage's right arm a thing of memory, and Tet's right leg a thing of nightmare.

The mage sat casual as a prince on the family side of the fire. A rare honour.

It was not this that intrigued Tet. Not his lazy sprawl or his smooth dark face like a statue of a god cut from stone, the long black hair held loosely back from his face with two thin braids.

No.

The travellers' honoured guest was rotten with magic, seething with it.

Most mages were little more than pretenders, weaklings with barely enough spark to light a match. They liked to call themselves something they were not, and Tet half-pitied them for it. But here was a true mage. One that Tet had never seen in the temples – and he'd grown up surrounded by magic, knew every mage worthy of the title. There were few true mages and fewer still who left the mountain temples of Nanak, Vitash, and Epsi, and the austerity of their training and libraries. Here was a man not from the temples, and power swirled around him in an oily blanket.

It could not be a coincidence that this brash princeling had turned up when the caravan was drawing closer to the central city of Pal-em-Rasha. He was not here to beg protection, or pass on news, whatever he'd told the travellers.

The mage had to be the contact Tet had been waiting for, carrying a message from the Monkey. A flicker of hope warmed in Tet's chest, and he pinched harder at his ruined leg, using the screaming pain to douse that hope.

The Monkey was Tet's only route to the *ritual-oresh*. To his promise of salvation. He was the only one who claimed to know the ancient ritual magic that would hide a man from the gods. And with the pain growing daily, Tet would do and say anything to get the *ritual-oresh*. Even put up with feints and schemes clearly designed to annoy him.

Smoke drifted across the circle of the camps as the wind changed, stinging Tet's eyes and making them squint and water. The mage was wavery with tears, but Tet could still sense the oiliness of his magic.

Tet blinked, and rubbed at his smoke-seared eyes. The mage didn't wear the traditional mage-knots. Instead, his hair was left loose, the same as Tet kept his own now. He'd been made to cut his knots when the temple banished him and stripped his power.

Perhaps all might have been better if he'd died the night those mountain bandits had killed his family, and no nameless orphan baby had been left on the temple steps. Tet grinned mirthlessly. He'd become self-pitying in his pain, and he hated it. He wanted his old self back; a torrent of silent rage.

Soon.

He clenched his fists and tried to hold on to that slight flicker of anger. It gave him back something of himself. If his own magic weren't so limited these days Tet wouldn't be wondering if some show-off brat was his contact with the Monkey. He wouldn't be ready to put all his meagre faith in a Southern sorcerer's trick.

The sorcerers of Utt Dih were not true mages. They were cooks. The sorcerers worked with bodily humours and herbs, mixing them like wives preparing a stew. And despite his contempt for them, here Tet was, waiting on one. The Monkey in his turn thumbed his nose by sending a rogue mage as a contact. *Look, see what we think of mages – errand boys and tricksters, maket pieces to move around the Grand Board.*

The young mage rolled a cigarette one-handed and lit the tip from the headsman's offered coal, then leaned back on the stump of his right elbow and blew out apple-scented smoke. As though he had finally noticed Tet's observation, the mage slowly turned his head and stared back over the fire. His magic rasped against Tet's own.

He probably thinks me weak, and he is not far wrong. I am weak. For now. Fate had stolen his name, the gods had cursed

Tet and placed limitations on what he was capable of. They did not want another *accident.*

The mage grinned straight at him, his teeth orange in the dancing light. A moment later he angled his head to the tribesmen, pretending that Tet was no one.

Irritation spiked in Tet's chest. The easy dismissal was a calculated insult. A mockery – *you like what you see? You are intrigued? How pathetic you are.*

'You have seen the magicians of Pal-em-Rasha?' asked one of the bearded older men of the caravans. 'They are fine, in their way, though of course they cannot compare with men such as yourself. Still, I have heard of one turn a horse into a swan and ride off on it.'

'Clockwork,' said the mage dismissively. His accent was faintly Deniahn, though he was trying to hide it. To anyone in the caravan he would sound just like any other Vaeyane-born, but Tet had been a spy in the White Prince's army; he was trained in accents and in the art of mimicking them and could hear the smallest flaw in the mage's vowels, the little tells that gave him away. Under his competent Vaeyane lay the wide flat tones of the city of Pal-em-Rasha.

Tet frowned and wrapped his cloak tighter.

A girl, her decorated arms bright with silver and turquoise, leaned closer to the mage. 'My grandmother told me the marketplaces there are filled shoulder to shoulder with men and women who can charm birds right into their hands, and rabbits from the fields.' Her voice was high and worldly and she wore even more jewellery on her brow and down the curve of her ears. She was a walking treasury, bright as a full moon rising over the snow-faced mountains. Tet tended to pay women little attention, but he had seen enough of her to know she ranked high. A chieftain's daughter. 'She said Pal-em-Rasha crawls with magic.'

It was not exactly true, though mages always argued the distinctions.

The mage shrugged and took a deep drag on his apple-tobacco. 'So it's said.'

The older women were watching him with amusement, chewing at the ends of their carved pipes. One of them pulled her pipe stem free with a wet pop and coughed, fluid rattling in her lungs.

Everyone kept silent, waiting for her to speak. When her coughing fit had finally sputtered to an end, she added, 'It's said, indeed. The White Prince has a clockwork-mage who crafts beasts so fine that they are more real than living animals. I saw one myself once, a little thing shaped like a mountain dragon, but no bigger than a hare. The prince used it to disembowel a traitor in the temple square.'

'Toys for a spoiled child,' replied the mage, and there was a muttering of unease and nervous respect. A spoiled child. A very powerful one. The White Prince was a mythic figure who flaunted his clockwork beasts, his army vast, the lioness god at his back. He was not a good man to have as an enemy, and he made for a cruel friend. Some of his appetites were more subtle and quiet and human, but Tet had spent enough time following his army's tracks through the snow to know how the prince grasped at innocence, playing with it before tearing it apart, like a cat trying to understand the workings of a cricket.

The mage's lack of respect for the prince's city of delights and mazements had quickened the crowd. They were eager to see what he could do that made him so dismissive of the demon prince and his toymaker.

Tet was curious himself, but content to let the travelling girls with their sweeping skirts talk the mage's tricks from him with their lips and lashes. They would convince him to display his little wonders, and Tet would keep his silence.

The mage didn't say much, but when he spoke, the crowd lapped forward. He would eventually give something away. An audience could be a terrible thing for a mage's ego.

'Where are you going?' The moon-bright girl's head was wrapped in the double-coned dressing of a virgin, but Tet figured that for a little lie.

Her sisters had already asked the mage where he came from and he had winked their questions away. He had a thief's manner, devilish and appealing in equal measure. The world was easily seduced by boys with sly eyes and fox-smiles.

'Wherever the world takes me,' he answered, which was no answer at all. 'Have you more tea?'

They poured for him, and their silver turban beads clashed and sang in their eagerness, and even the old women who shook their heads at his insolence did not stop them.

If he was any good at performing, he'd wait just a little longer. But not too long. One needed to judge the audience, reel them in, but not exhaust them. That was the way of the dance. Tet snorted. He was beginning to think like a priest-mage again.

'You said you would show us magic,' said the moon-bright girl.

'I did, but even the greatest of mages must digest first. A full stomach is not good for trickery.'

The old women laughed. They'd already seen him for what he was, but he winked at them and they knew they were all part of his show, and that he knew it too. It was a comfortable exchange. Only the girls were fooled, or willing to let themselves pretend so.

'Drink, then.' The girl's annoyance was inches from boredom; the mage had to strike soon and impress them all with his flash and spark, or all his swagger would be wasted.

He set his tea bowl down between his feet and leaned forward. The flames patterned shadows across his black hair and his copper, wide-cheeked face. Under the cold stars, with the fire-light spilling over him, he had the eyes of a devil or a cat.

The travellers leaned forward with him; the signal given for their entertainment to begin.

'Watch,' he said, and dropped his voice. 'Here, then.' He flung out his one good hand, a sparkle of bright ash flying from his fingers, and a surge of magic slid over Tet's skin, leaving him shuddering.

The flames jumped higher and turned a bright jewel-green. In that moment, as he cast the dust, the mage shifted. Or at least, he appeared to shift – true shifting was too rare and powerful a magic for some city-born gutter mage to actually use. At best this was trickery – *oreshamin*. He'd laid a shadow over his skin like an actor donning a mask of painted paper. Even so, this was real magery and Tet could almost smell it, sweet and cloying.

The travellers shrieked and drew back. The free-dogs howled and barked in their high voices.

There was no youth sitting by the fire, only the sinuous and familiar shape of one of the mountain dragons, its back arched, the fine filaments of its frill and whiskers flaring outward. The malachite scales flashed in the firelight and the illusion was so strong that Tet could hear the rumble of its breathing. Smell sulphur and burned millet, cinnamon, ash. The coiling dragon snarled once. It bared long yellow teeth, breathed out curling ribbons of smoke, and then was gone.

The mage opened his eyes wide, guileless as an infant. 'There,' he said. 'Did I not say?'

The crowd clapped and laughed, and Tet took his pipe from his robe jacket, filled it with the dregs of his tobacco, and lit it.

Across the fires, the mage turned to glance at Tet again. The moment was a silver flash in the stream of time, frozen. The wind dropped, and the silence that followed was immense and black.

In all the universe, Tet was the only living thing. With a mutter of the old tongue, he coaxed a small flame, breathing a flutter of time into it, and drew on his pipe, tasting dead smoke, bitter and black.

The stars had stopped flickering and the threads of the faint clouds were still as rocks cast into the heavens. The sparks of the fire were frozen in place in a whirl of tiny embers. Tet wasn't alarmed, though he knew he probably should be. Or, if not alarmed, perhaps terrified.

He'd become too tired for terror.

It had been happening more often, and Tet swallowed down the sickness that rose in his throat. There was nothing for him to do but sit and wait in the infinite stillness, feeling the darkness inside him spread, pushing at the stone door he held in his head to keep it at bay. Crack by crack, the void widened.

Soon the gods would come and restart the world, but until then there was only the emptiness of a universe without time. A reminder of what he'd done, and how it grew worse with every passing year. The stalls in time came more frequently these days and it took the gods longer each time to fix it.

Until then, there was only Tet and the well-black eyes of the mage staring into his own. Tet stood carefully, untangling his cloak from his legs, and limped around the sculpted column of fire, stepping between the skirts of women, over the free-dogs, until he was in front of the mage. The young man stared blankly ahead, motionless as a carving. Tet crouched, his ruined knee screaming pain through his entire body.

The two mages were close enough that the younger one could have felt Tet's breath across his cheeks. Up close, the mage still looked young, but there was a strange ageless quality about him that made Tet suspicious.

If Tet knew the mage's name, he could control him like a jointed puppet on silk strings. Could strip any disguises and spells from his skin to reveal the truth beneath. Could make him stand, tell Tet all his secrets like water spilling from a broken jug. Could make him dance through the still flames, perhaps even push him into another time and place. If Tet knew his name, and if he were powerful again.

Tet laughed softly at all his stupid, bitter regrets over the things he'd lost. With the very tip of his index finger, he touched the soft skin of the mage's neck and traced up to the curve of his left ear. There was a tiny mark behind his earlobe, a smudge of oily white cream such as actors wore for the stage, and Tet wiped it away. This was the closest to intimacy he'd been in years, and it was nothing. It had been a very long time since he had trusted himself to more than a casual fuck with a stranger who would forget him as soon as the sun rose.

A flicker of shapes slid across the heavens, casting strange lights and shadows across the frozen landscape. Tet glanced up to see the vast, bright forms of Nanak, Epsi, and Vitash, joined by a host of other gods from all corners of the worshipping world. Magic tugged against his skin and bones as the gods worked at stitching the universe together again, layering second on intricate second, like a spider slowly rebuilding a web torn by a thrashing moth.

The great hound Nanak stared down with empty eyes bigger than moons, but she said nothing to Tet, and after a while, the gods faded, and the air felt lighter.

Time would begin soon. Tet left the frozen mage and returned to his place, wrapped his cloak around him as before and picked up his abandoned pipe. Without magic to keep the flame going, it had died again. *'Vlam,'* Tet whispered, and the spark caught long enough for him to take another pull on the ox-horn stem.

He breathed out, and time restarted.

II

THE FLINT POUCH

The **nomadic tribes** of the mountains of Vaeyane put their faith in the roadside gods, all of whom demand charity and hospitality. They were not people to turn away a guest. Even one as apparently useless as Tet they allowed to set a bedroll near their dying fire.

The mage overnighted in one of their painted caravans.

Left with the night-sentries and the lazy, shifting little oxen, Tet lay on his back as the fire dimmed to embers, and watched the sky spread out her stars. The chief's pony whickered a few times, and fell silent. The red cattle stamped and stilled. The laughter and the songs faded. The free-dogs ended their moon chorus. Finally, sleep rolled over the camp, and the sentries leaning on their old guns began to nod in their places. Although they were a rich people who carried all their valuables around the arms and throats and temples of their wives and daughters, they were not often robbed. They had a habit of beheading thieves. Tet doubted their guns could even fire, it had probably been so long since they were used. They were the artefacts of some long-ago trade; symbols rather than weapons.

Their gods – Nanak, Epsi, Vitash – would protect them.

My gods.

The stars pulsed and winked, and Tet could see all of his future laid out in their complicated geometry. His death-curse was there, waiting. Eventually, Tet found her star-shape among the gleam. Closer now. 'Ah, Nanak,' he whispered. 'Another night, if you please.' Nanak had turned her back on him. They hadn't spoken in years. Any help Tet wanted these days had to come from himself alone. Another reason to shake off his faith and turn to the tricks of infidels and pot-stirrers.

It had been comforting walking with the travellers, doing what little magics he could hide from them. But their caravan moved too slowly, and Tet's death snapped at his heels. In the morning he would take his leave. He'd stayed too long, trying to cling to something he could never have. Tet could tell himself he was waiting for the Monkey's contact to reach him, but the truth was infinitely more pitiable. He was pretending. And he didn't have time for that, not yet.

In the temple they had a saying: *There is no point trying to light a candle that has no wick*. Were Tet a good priest, then he would accept that this dream of his was simply a wickless candle and that he was doing nothing more than whining about a life lost, clutching at something that never was.

The *ritual-oresh* was his wick now. If he was hidden from the gods and his curse lifted, then Tet would be a free man with access to his own magic. He could do as he pleased.

Clouds drifted in, thick lines across the darkness, and the smell of rain-in-waiting bit cold in his nostrils. A squall was coming, and Tet had little desire to wake wet and shivering, his clothes pasted to his body and his bones aching from the damp and cold.

Tet closed his eyes and whispered the name of the wind that lives in the east. It didn't take a great mage to control the weather, but it did take a great one to do it so that the weather didn't notice. Better to nudge and hope that the winds did what one wanted than to give an outright command. Tet was lucky tonight. The stretch of his constrained magic, bone-deep and tendon-tight, pulled through him with a fierce ache. The breeze changed against his face, coming from the east and pushing the clouds back a little. He opened one eye to check. The sky was glittered again, clear of their low rolling bellies.

He was getting weak when such a small thing could make his bones feel hollowed and his muscles leaden. *Hah, only thirty-four and already broken. No more magics for a while, Tet.* Carefully, so as to make no sound, he rolled to his side so that his useless knee could be warmed by the embers. Like this, Tet fell asleep while waiting for the Monkey's pet mage to leave his message.

*

There was no peace for Tet, dreaming in fragments. Here: his earliest memory; curled in the blood-soaked snow while bandits looted his family's caravans. Hunger, cold and sharp, followed by hands, warm and rough. Tet was too young to remember the secret name his mother had whispered to him while Tet drank at her breast. That had died with his family, and Tet was not and never would be strong enough to go to the lands of the dead and reclaim his true name like a long-lost prize. There was no one alive who could do that. Even the gods had no command over the dead.

The dreams jolted, and Tet was at the foundling gate of the Temple of Nanak. Another tribe had found him in the snow, the priests had told him later. They brought him to Nanak, as was the way of his people. The foundling child filled with rage and darkness, given to the gods.

Tet grew up as a temple servant, working the small patches of fertile valley-land or herding the oxen when he grew older. His favourite days were the ones where he was left to tend the goats or the oxen on the high slopes, where he sometimes met with the small mountain dragon of the temple pass and listened to her sing.

That was supposed to be his life. Surrounded by snow and mountain peaks, mages and temple hounds, Tet didn't speak for years. But he listened. And he watched. The sticky rasp of magic was all around him. Women and men of power, changing the weather and the world with words.

Inside him the emptiness grew, eclipsing everything. It kept him silent, kept him wakeful. Alone, he learned to hide from that darkness inside him. Slowly closing the void behind a door of stone, until he could ignore it. Pretend it never existed.

The tone shifted, the dream turning deep and dark. The priests of Nanak did not like the foundling Tet, so strange and silent and nameless. They brought him to temple meetings, prodding at him like a sickling calf, trying to find what it was about him that was so peculiar.

'He is powerful.' The abbess was a small hard woman like the heart of an apricot. Tet had always been afraid of her, never more so when she was deciding his fate. 'There's no doubting that.'

'You can feel it too,' said brother Jayim, a gentle priest who tended the novice boys. 'It is...unpleasant.'

'The boy's cursed,' said the abbess. 'Who knows what games the gods play with him. Better perhaps that he go work with the herds where he can do no harm.'

They talked as though Tet was deaf as well as mute, talked of curses and wrongness, strangeness. Without a name to control him, the abbess was wary of training the boy in any of the mages' arts, despite the flicker of power she could sense. Instead, Tet was given over to the servants' quarters, and learned to read the weather and the silent language of the animals.

And always, Tet listened. Slowly, he made friends with the other servants and they coaxed his voice free, soft and uncertain. When he said things, the power in him danced across his tongue. He would mouth the words he overheard from the mages' lessons while he swept, made fire spring from his palm, turned the weather to suit himself, called lost animals home again.

When Tet was caught using magic to change the path of a storm and keep the day bright, Jayim brought him once again before the abbess.

The priests had no idea what to do with him. Nameless, motherless little *tet*. In the old ceremonies, a mage gave their birth-name to the gods and devoted themself to the gods' service. In return the gods renamed the mage as their own and gave their protection.

There could be no such binding for Tet. But he was too dangerous to be left untrained.

The voices discussed him, like an insect in the room.

Finally, a decision was made. Tet was renamed Tet-Nanak – child of Nanak – and given to the gods. He was taken from the sunlight and the open air, and trained under hard, cold priest-mages who did not trust this alien creature. They were determined to make something of him, teach him to be a scribe or a priest-servant. The gift of languages was beaten into him and Tet spent hours each day learning to speak the various dialects of Deniah, of Ganys to the south-east, and even Imradian.

And slowly, Tet taught himself the speech of dragons until it was as natural to him as though he were born to it.

It was here where Tet's dreams blackened. Here, where the door opened a crack. He tore himself awake, clawing, gasping at the nightmare of the day he ended the world.

His face was wet, his sleep-shirt stuck to his skin with sweat. The rising black terror faded, breath by breath, as Tet came back to the present, leaving the dream behind.

Soft laughter and shushes drifted from the closest caravan. The rest of the camp was still. The guards snored.

'Ah,' said the mage, his whisper carrying in the dark. 'But I need to leave.'

That damn boy had left him to wait long enough. Tet turned, easing cramps from his cold muscles. Each movement sent a serrated blade tearing through his cursed knee. *Gods damn the little fool.*

'Oh.' The girl teased. 'Oh, my father, he's drunk. He will never wake.'

'And I am to trust my life to millet beer and ox-meat? No, I think not.' But the mage didn't leave. The words gave way to sighs. The girl moaned softly.

Tet's knee had locked in place, the muscles tense, and angry resentment at the two lovers filled him as he slowly shifted so that the knee could finally bend. In his irritation, he took the mage's dalliance to be an insult, carefully calculated.

The knee cracked, and Tet released a breath through gritted teeth. Perhaps it was simply youthful oversight, he thought. Or perhaps the Monkey's pet mage was kept on a looser leash than Tet had previously supposed. That, or he knew how to slip it. Messages to crippled mages were afterthoughts to someone young and free to do as he pleased.

'Hush now, I have to go,' said the mage. *Finally.*

One of the free-dogs woke, raising its long red jaws. The pack slept close to the fire pit for warmth against the turning season, and soon this one would rouse the others. The mage was walking on shifting ground if he thought he would be forgiven. Tet willed the hound silent, soothing the animal with whispered magic. The dog blinked, then tucked its head back under its tail.

'Take this, then. A gift.' From the caravan, silver beads clinked. *Hah. A fortune to pay for a night's entertainment.* Tet could not help being amused at what the mage was getting away with. Annoyed as he might be, there was a feeling of admiration, or perhaps jealousy.

'I cannot.'

'Oh. And how then will you remember me?' asked the chieftain's daughter.

The mage laughed. 'Indeed. Your argument is strong.'

Tet shook his head. The mage had best be about his business before the drunken headsman woke and made him a son-in-law. Or a corpse.

A while later the caravan door opened and a shadow slipped down, crossing the darkness toward the fire pit. He walked like a ghost-cat, feet picking between sound.

Lying still, watching, Tet began to wonder if he had miscalculated, and that the mage was no messenger sent by the evasive Monkey, merely some chancing thief, when his feet stopped at Tet's head. The soft material of the mage's well-cut trousers brushed against Tet's face.

The mage's knees sunk down into Tet's line of vision. Something brushed a strand of hair back from Tet's face, plucking it free from where it had stuck to the outside corner of his eye. The mage's hand, his fingers still warm from the girl. The scent of her clung like a perfume of musk and thick temple incense. Under that was the mage's own scent, sharp with magic, cold and clean as stars.

His fingers trailed to Tet's chin and still Tet didn't move. Magic prickled at his skin, a desperate itch that tugged like seven-petal. Perhaps, Tet though, perhaps he was wrong about the mage being the Monkey's pet, wrong about everything.

He was just a rake, a man who sowed his maize in his neighbours' fields. And Tet was not too proud to turn him down. The mage was beautiful, and he had the kind of cruel power that Tet had always been drawn to, despite his best intentions. Tet shifted onto his back, blinking up into starlight and the carved face, hoping that the mage would see something reflected in him that would draw him like to like.

'Awake, old man?'

Old man. Tet's amorous moment was short lived. That was an insult designed to cut. With two words he was sliced down to a thing past its prime, worthless and ill-used. Tet gritted his teeth. 'Not awake, as such,' he replied. 'Right now I am dreaming a most interesting dream.'

'And what happens in this dream?' The mage's voice was full of lovely mockery. He brought his face closer.

'Nothing much. I dreamed a monkey held a man on a leash like a pet and the man slipped his leash to indulge in some rather dangerous love-play—'

'Enjoyed that, did you? Or were you jealous?'

'—and some exchanges of treasures. I hope you took only what was freely given; the People of the Dogs do not forgive thieves easily or kindly.'

'Really.' The mage stood. 'Forget your dream.'

'It's easier to forget when I have reason.' *And a message.*

'You talk like a priest,' said the mage. 'Here: *Oh, Tet-Epsi, take this then thy offering.*' He dropped a small object before Tet's nose. It flashed bright as his laugh. Then, in barely more than a whisper. 'Your monkey wishes to meet a merchant named Ohtet Maynim in a lime grove, and his pet wishes that you keep your mouth shut about the treasures.' He stood, and shadow-stepped into the night, pulling his magic around him like a cloak so that even the free-dogs did not bark at his passing.

When the mage had vanished, Tet picked up the thing he had dropped. In the pre-dawn greyness he couldn't see much, but his fingers traced whorls of beading and beaten metal, a soft leather satchel. A commonplace thing – a flint pouch. A pointless, archaic gift when matches had become commonplace even in the northern reaches. And an insult if one were a mage.

'Tet-Nanak, actually,' Tet said, though the mage was long gone and would never hear his correction. The beads dug into his palm. Something skittered beneath Tet's skin, as though the pouch were a live thing, but when he opened his hand to look at it again, it was just metal and glass and leather. Perhaps it was nothing more than the last fading trace of the mage's touch.

Still smarting from the humiliation of the encounter, Tet tucked the offering into his shirt and curled closer to the dying fire, his right knee cracking like a snapped twig. Tet felt wound-up like a clockwork manikin – a coiled energy of springs and wires and cogs.

The discomfiture of the brief exchange aside, Tet finally had his message. He was a step closer to being free. For now, the gods still thought he belonged to them, and that he travelled to Pal-em-Rasha only to fulfil the curse-contract Nanak had placed on him. Keeping secrets from gods was never easy, but Tet had spent so many years of his life lying that misdirection was second nature.

There was time to sleep before the camp roused but Tet lay awake, watching the horizon slowly changing colour. The Monkey's riddle was no riddle at all. The garden-houses for travellers were always named after fruit and flowers, and the Lime Grove was one he remembered from past visits to the city.

The Monkey had told Tet what to call himself, and what fiction to wear: Ohtet Maynim, the merchant. The disguise would be easily assumed, though it meant spending the last of Tet's meagre pension to buy the correct clothes and accoutrements. *Damn it all.*

Tet had no idea what the Monkey planned to charge him for using the *ritual-oresh*. While he could lie to himself and say he would spend any amount of coin to buy his freedom, it was meaningless when Tet had no coin to spend.

He scowled. The Monkey assumed Tet would dance like a toymaker's clockwork monster. And he was mostly right. For now, Tet had to play as the Monkey wanted. The Monkey held out the promise of freedom like grain in his palm. He knew Tet was a desperate man, while all Tet knew was that this Monkey was arrogant and thought himself clever. Perhaps he was, but a cleverer man would not have brought it to Tet's attention. Especially when Tet would soon be free, and more powerful than he had been in many years. Powerful enough to begin looking for something he had only dreamed it possible to have. Tet shook himself, pushing the thought of his lost name out of his head. It was an idiot's fancy.

Instead, he made lists of what needed to be done before he reached Pal-em-Rasha. Ohtet Maynim would need a mount, and clothes, and a history, or his identity would be flimsy as cobwebs. While he planned, Tet twisted his pack open and slipped the little flint pouch in under his change of clothes. At the bottom of the pack lay all his worldly wealth, and Tet pressed the leather pouch of coins between his fingers, as though somehow, they might have multiplied while he was sleeping. No such luck. *The gods don't even bless a pious man like that, and I have had all the piousness torn out of me.*

A horse wouldn't come cheap, and so far, Tet had managed to avoid becoming a thief. A mount, and suitable clothes. Already Tet could picture his coins slipping through his fingers. Just a few nights lodging at The Lime Grove would relieve Tet of a fair bit of his pension. Tet wondered why the Monkey had chosen the place, and not one of the less ostentatious inns. What plans was he making on Tet's behalf? Tet shoved the pack back under his head and waited through the cold dawn, for the last star to fade into the pinking sky.

*

The People rose at dawn, and this group of travellers was no exception. The free-dogs were gnawing at their bones and the first birds were singing; the ponies were dancing under their ornate saddles, and the men were harnessing the shaggy red oxen to their caravans. Everything appeared normal. No mention was made of the mage's disappearance, until one of the old women went to wake him with bowls of buttered millet and strong tea.

Tet glanced at his pack, and the little leather flint pouch buried at the bottom, under his pouch of coins. He should return it. But explaining how he'd come in possession of the girl's little treasure would only make him look like the mage's accomplice, and his story a weak falsehood. Better for now to keep silent and see what happened. It was a tactic that had served him best in the past.

At the very least, the morning promised to be interesting. Tet filled the bowl of his horn-pipe with the fragrant tobacco of the south, plucked a small coal from the dead fire, and coaxed it awake with magic. *Vlam;* it was almost all he could do these days. The first word of power any temple-child learned after years of training in breathing patterns and meditation.

'Ai,' said the old woman, standing in the doorway with her steaming bowls. 'And where has he got to, I wonder?'

The tribe paused as one, all looking to the moon-bright girl's caravan. It was a fine thing, the sides painted with the little fire-throated birds sacred to her family tribe, and it glowed in the bright dawn light.

Tet sucked on the stem of his pipe and waited.

'Yoh!' The girl yelled from inside. The sound of clattering followed, and she flung the door open. Her hair was loose, the fine dark curtain of it swinging almost to her knees. 'Robbed!' she screamed.

There was a distinct lack of silver on her person. She raised her hands, and the wide sleeves of her blue sleep-dress fell back to reveal naked arms. Every bangle was gone. Her necklaces too. Even her lobes, stretched from the weight of hoops and hanging beads, were denuded.

Tet blew out twin flowers of smoke. *What a thief, indeed.* And what magic he must have used for her to not notice as he stripped her of her wealth. Even Tet hadn't realised the extent of his thievery. He'd moved without a single clink of silver. A good mage.

An excellent thief.

'I was robbed!' she cried again, and pulled at her hair. 'The mage, where is he?'

The travellers muttered, some of them turning to look at Tet with hard eyes. *Ah, it was time I was leaving them anyway.* He lifted one shoulder in a shrug and took the pipe from his mouth. 'He was no friend of mine.'

'So says a thief protecting a brother.'

The headsman had never liked him. 'I have travelled with you for five and three days, and not once have I taken anything that was not freely offered. Has Nanak changed her laws of hospitality?'

'Hospitality?' The chieftain stalked nearer.

The girl had begun to wail. A wordless howling noise the likes of which Tet hadn't heard in many years. It was a temple cant, and he winced.

'Even a guest can outstay their welcome,' said the headsman.

Tet raised his hands. 'Indeed. As have I. My apologies. But I stole nothing.'

'He's right,' said one of the younger men. 'We cannot blame the acts of one on another. Besides,' he glanced at the girl, 'Tet-Vitash invokes the penalty on thieves.'

Tet-Vitash. Tet shivered. The girl was much more than just a headsman's virgin daughter, she was also the witch of their tribe. Given to the gods. No wonder she had a caravan to herself. While it was true that she was far weaker than either the mage or Tet, he still should have seen it earlier. Distracted, that was his problem. First by pain, and then by black eyes and darker magic.

Her howls had taken on a more familiar tone. She was speaking to the gods, and most specifically to her own – the silver-moon dog Vitash. What a curse it was too. Perhaps if the mage had known what she was, he would not have been so quick to choose her as his victim.

'Leave,' said the headsman.

There would be no morning millet and tea for Tet. He bowed to the chieftain and collected his satchel, bedroll and his painted lute. The free-dogs and the red oxen were the only ones who watched him leave.

The flint-pouch weighed heavy. Tet's price for silence. Against all the treasures the mage stole from the girl, he doubted this was anything more than a trinket, but he was still burdened with it. His time with the people was over; Pal-em-Rasha and freedom waited.

III

MARKED

Dawn light streaked red and gold through the trees and across the dead grass, slowly warming the frosty air. The caravan fell behind Tet as he limped, swinging his right leg, his hand guiding the twisted thigh. He could keep this pace for an hour, perhaps, before he would be in too much pain to walk further.

Along the Green Road to Pal-em-Rasha there were always a few hostelries and Tet hoped to see one before sunset. He'd saved enough coin while guesting with the travellers to pay for a bed and buy a horse.

Tet smoked while he walked, musing as thin grey streams billowed from his nostrils.

Perhaps not a horse. A dun hill-pony. After that, he would have little enough coin left from his soldier's pension, and now the Monkey expected to meet him in a rich merchant's inn. He had already made oblique mention of Tet's ability to slip free of his name and remake himself as occasion demanded it. It was a curious thing for a complete stranger to know about Tet, and it prickled the edge of his sleeping fear.

His game of shifting name and occupation, and even his entire appearance, was one Tet had learned after the gods cursed him. He was bound by them to return the Temple's stolen Eyes of Nanak, now in the possession of the White Prince himself. Cast out from the temple, he could no longer be Tet-Nanak, priest and nameless orphan. Instead, Tet had to shoulder new identities, picking and discarding them as they were needed. Sektet Am when he had played soldier, and other names besides. Mostly these days he went simply by Tet.

Temple mages were uncommon outside of the mountains and there was no way Tet could have tracked the White Prince anonymously had he not cloaked himself in a new identity. The prince's mistrust of mages was legendary. The White Prince had time only for toymakers, and in his seat of power, all other magics were forbidden. So, while Tet had been many things, the last and longest of them was a soldier in the prince's massive army,

Not that he was much of a soldier. Just a man who could make maps, a man with a talent for languages who ended up in the wrong place at an inconvenient time. And now he was to be a merchant, it seemed. Tet spoke his new name out loud: 'Ohtet Maynim.' A southern Vaeyane family name – neither common nor uncommon. And there in the first name, the ubiquitous *tet*. The Monkey had a sense of humour.

All priests were *tet*, but so were all children.

The sun rose at his left, spilling long morning shadows across the road and Tet ticked through the things he would need to do. Whether he could afford it or not, the pony was a must; no merchant walked into the city of Pal-em-Rasha. Tet gritted his teeth. For now, let the Monkey think he had him on a leash. Tet could play the part of a patient man. Once he was free of the gods he would have time enough to deal with the Monkey, to reset the board in his favour.

The gods were the lords of the game-board, and men were nothing more than their pieces. And if Tet was not willing to follow the moves that the gods had decreed, what made this monkey think Tet would bow to a man?

It was past midday and Tet's right leg was beyond agony when the low roof of the hostelry came wavering into view between the pine-sloped hills. If he stopped with so short a distance still to go, he knew he might very well never start again. 'Come, come, Tet. You can walk and smoke at the same time.' There was his little reward – a pipe from his dwindling tobacco to tide him over until he reached the inn.

While it did not kill the pain completely, Tet added a meagre pinch of seven-petal to the pipe-bowl and drew deeply on that while stumbling the worst of the downhill into the little valley. His supply of the drug was almost up; another reason Pal-em-Rasha called so sweetly; the voices of the seven-petal dens were rich as choirs.

The hostel was made of packed slate, grey with roadside dust. A few ponies in their winter coats huddled by one low wall. Tet glanced over them – thin, rangy, but they looked well-tempered enough.

A girl of fourteen or fifteen came to greet him at the door. Her face was slightly sulky behind her precise mask of hospitality.

'You have beds free?' Tet asked out of politeness, for the courtyard was empty.

The girl nodded and beckoned him to follow her in. A few minutes haggling, and Tet found himself in a small plain room, furnished with a pallet bed. It was a luxury. A cotton mattress after weeks on the ground was a blessing for his leg. The walls were white-washed, and the only bit of opulence was a brass lamp on a small, red-painted bench that also served as a table, and a travel-board of maket with half the pieces missing.

Tet stowed his lute and bag under the bench, washed his hands and face in the wooden bowl, and went to find the inn's shrine. He still had a part to play, after all.

His performance as Ohtet began now. Tet made mental lists of figures, of market grain prices. He switched over to thinking in Deniahn, like a good little merchant belonging to the White Prince. Soon he would pretend a new religion, a whole new way of looking at the world. But before his transformation was complete, he had a final supplication to make.

The inn-mother was eager to show off and lead him to a small room near the entrance. The doorway was covered with a thick hanging carpet to keep out dust, and she lifted one corner and ushered him in.

'Pray,' she said. 'And may all good things come to you.' She left Tet alone with his gods, with the dust and the acrid taste of failure.

Unsurprisingly, it was a shrine to Nanak – the oldest of the gods, mother and hearth-warmer. A bronze statue of a sleeping hound rested on a stone plinth. Peace. She had one useless eye open, one ear cocked, though she was curled small, nose buried under her tail.

There were rituals to be followed, incense and lamps lit, prayers to be said in thanks and greeting. Instead, Tet shuffled to take a seat on an offering pillow and stretched his leg out so he could massage the aching knee. The muscles were leather strips wound on iron rods. He would not kneel before any gods now.

'Ah,' Tet said conversationally to the sleeping statue. 'It has been a while. I have nothing to give, but I came to say my thanks for keeping me alive this long at least.'

Nanak was still not speaking to him. Tet decided on a little honesty. 'I can't do it, you know.' He had begged free of this duty-curse a thousand times, but the gods didn't care. Still, he thought, might as well try one last time before taking the last steps toward the Monkey and his *ritual-oresh*. After Tet went that way, he would never be welcome as a mage of the temple again.

If anything, he was more likely to be burned for a heretic.

The muscle began to ease under his ministrations, or perhaps the seven-petal had finally done its work. 'Find someone else,' Tet said to the sleeping dog-idol. 'Someone younger and stronger. How am I to even have a conversation with a demon-prince, let alone persuade him to give back your eyes?'

His previous attempts to get close to the prince had failed. The White Prince was protected on all sides; not only by his army, but by his court clockworker and their beasts, by a labyrinthine system of unmapped passageways, and – the rumours went – by a magical breastplate that kept him safe from all physical harm. Even if Tet were to get close, he would not be able to use magery against him, and his mapmaker's skill was of little use in a palace guarded by machine monsters.

The shrine room was dark, windowless, and filled with the hanging smoke of old incense. 'I can't do it,' Tet said again, softer. *Set me free, take my burden away, forgive me.*

The gods had punished him for his part in their loss – they had ravaged Tet's magic and body, and set him an impossible task. They expected him to fail. *All the begging probably only amuses them*, Tet thought, though it didn't stop him.

The shadows around Nanak shifted and thickened and Tet couldn't help the momentary leap of hope. Perhaps now, finally, so many years after she charged him to bring back her eyes, and after all his failure, perhaps now Nanak would finally speak and erase his pain.

'Tet-Nanak,' said the shadows. Echoing and empty.

And Tet frowned.

This was not the voice of the stars, of the great mother hound who suckled the first priests of men. Nor was it the bright-sun voice of Epsi – the hunting dog who had taught the People to bring down the great mountain antelope with their golden pelts and coiled horns.

Shit. Tet grimaced, and bowed his head.

'Fortuitous,' said Vitash, and threaded through the dog-god's voice was the howling of the virgin priestess Tet had left far behind him. A possession-sending. He shivered. This was not what he needed now.

'Oh, priest of my sister-wife,' Vitash said. 'There is a boy of your type – a mage – and he has stolen my bounty.'

This Tet knew, and as far as he was concerned, it had nothing to do with him. But it was not wise to tell gods their business.

'I set you now to his trail. Bring me back his head and I will reward you a thousand-fold.'

The howling faded, and the shadows blurred at the edges.

Damn it all. Warily. Tet raised his head. He kept his tone respectful. 'I am no longer much of a mage.' If a man who had never had a name could ever be a true mage, which he doubted. Instead, he had been an approximation. And now he was even less than that. *Not for long.*

'So? You have the mind of a mage, all tricks and slyness. You have done impossible things before. You will find him.' The voice curled and echoed, chasing itself about the small room.

'I cannot.'

The smoke grew heavy, the air crushing. The shadows lengthened, turning the room as dark as the inner depths of a cave. 'You...can...not?'

Carefully, Tet edged backwards, feeling his way along the floor. 'I am already cursed by Nanak,' he pointed out. 'I must complete her order before I can start a new path – surely you must understand?' Even as the words spilled, Tet cursed his stupidity. Never try and bargain with gods; he knew better than that. They were far stronger than mages, and unlike men, they had no room for subtlety and deceit. They were powerful and simple. And that made them incredibly dangerous. One did not argue with beings who saw the world only in black and white, and could crush a man like a screaming infant beneath the wheels of a caravan.

Vitash growled, and the sound throbbed through Tet, turning his gut watery with fear. 'Do as I have asked, little mage, or I will turn your other leg beneath you, and you will crawl on your belly like a serpent.'

Tet's left knee blazed as though someone had just thrust a fire-heated needle through the cartilage, before the pain went out, as quickly as it came. He didn't need to look to know there would be a mark like a crescent moon branded onto the skin.

Vitash had never been Tet's favourite of the three. Tet's breath hissed between his clenched teeth as he struggled to keep calm. The gods were powerful, but they could also be manipulated, he had learned. It just needed to be done very, very carefully. 'As you say, I will do as you ask.'

The sending emanated smug satisfaction.

The gods had answered Tet whether he liked it or not, and set him on his final path. Whatever regret he might have had about going against them was snuffed out like a wick pinched between thumb and forefinger.

Tet had no intention whatsoever of hunting down the mage for Vitash, and less still of cutting off his head and bringing it back to the temple in offering. *Let Vitash think I'm just his little game-piece, brainless and compliant.* 'However,' Tet bowed his head in humility, and dropped his voice to the pathetic wheedle of a broken man, 'Pal-em-Rasha is a vast city and a den of thieves. I would find him sooner for you if I have coin to cross the palms of informers.'

'Men and their lust for money,' said the god. 'So be it.'

The shadows lifted, and the room lightened as Vitash departed back to whatever realm gods came from. The statue of Nanak remained motionless, fast asleep.

Useless.

The sooner Tet shifted the gods from his back, the better it would go for him. Let the Monkey name his price, Tet thought. It could never be as high.

*

Tet might have been pious once when he was still young enough to believe the gods had saved him. He wasn't like most priest-mages who were taken to the temples as soon as it became clear to their families and village priests that they had power. Tet was merely the brat survivor of a hill-tribe caught and annihilated in the northern war. Some traders had found him orphaned among the corpses of his clan and brought him to the nearest temple. They'd given him as an offering. That was why Tet was not a priest of Epsi like most men. He was one of Nanak's: a god of foundlings and old women.

He owed her. Her temple had fed and clothed and trained him, and in return one of his jobs as a young priest-mage had been to guard the great hound statues that were set high above the temples. It was never a task anyone took seriously. Even when Tet still believed Nanak had spared him from an early death so that he might one day do great things, he'd known the job of guarding the statues was merely make-work, something to keep the young men and women of the Temple from having the time to wander down to the camps of the travellers and indulge in a little sin.

The statues of the Temple of the Three Dogs stood higher than the buildings of the temple compounds. They were painted yellow-gold and silver-white and copper-red – another job that fell yearly to the young priests – and were adorned with precious and semi-precious stones. Each of the three statues had eyes as big as wagon wheels, made from a thousand jewels. Green-eyed Epsi of the hunt, with her flashing emeralds and topaz; Vitash, black onyx and garnet; and finally, blind Nanak with her opals and pearls.

At the centre of each of Nanak's eyes was an opal a hand-span long, which flashed and shifted with all the colours of the snow. Scratched into the opals were the blessings of a priest-mage a thousand years dead. The runes were in the tongue of dragons, and they held that as long as Nanak watched over the temple, it would never fall.

No one knew who had built the statues, or who had brought such jewels to adorn them. In all the centuries of centuries that they'd stood, encrusted with riches, no one had actually attempted to steal anything from the statues. The guard duty was a temple formality. The students who had to serve their duty tended to do it drunk. At least millet beer passed the time.

Tet was not a creature touched by good fortune. He'd been twenty-five, and used to the task, and had given it as much thought as any of his fellows would. While he'd slept off several bowls of millet beer, dozing between the great paws of his god Nanak, a thief as soft as the mountain wind had climbed the back of the statue and taken the centre jewels from her eyes. The blind dog was made blinder, and in the morning the first of the outer walls of the temple compound began to soften, the stones crumbling into dust.

Tet had woken to find the opals robbed from Nanak's eyes, and the walls falling around him, heard the wailing of the high priests. They had dragged him trembling and weak-kneed before the great abbess of Temple Nanak.

The abbess's wrinkled face was sterner and sadder than Tet had ever seen it and he was still half-drunk and terrified at what he'd let happen. A sobbing drunkard, half a mage.

Perhaps it would have been better for both Tet and the universe if he'd pissed himself like a coward soldier, but instead, his fear woke in him that strange unnatural power that had so worried the abbess and Jayim when he'd been given to the temple.

The stone door in his head had widened, raining dust. Behind it, the nothingness had gibbered and called, pulling like a great sucking vortex.

Tet couldn't remember what word he'd said – if he'd even spoken at all. The only thing that remained in his memory of that moment was the monstrous rushing of power, black and swift as a river running underground. Uncontrolled, raging, a child's tantrum; his unleashed magic had spilled out of him, fed fat on panic and drunken stupidity.

*

And time stopped.

*

No human should have had the power to do something so counter to the laws of time and natural order. The abbess and the priest-mages and the priestess-mages, the servants and the orphans, the guests and the free-dogs and the birds in the sky; everything around him was frozen in place. Tet had wanted everything to stop, for just a moment, and everything had.

At first, he hadn't believed or understood what he had done. It was impossible. In stunned silence, Tet had reached out to touch the faces of the mages, the folds of their robes.

Everything was hard and cold. He'd walked out through the stillness, down to the courtyard where a swirl of dust had paused in mid-dance. He'd run his hands over the immovable grains. The air had pressed down on him, crushing in from all sides.

It was a nightmare. He'd walked through a world without time, alone, aimless. The only sound had been his heart beating ragged. In that endless, stretched-out infinite now, Tet could have done anything – he could have set and rearranged the people in the world, moved them about like maket pieces.

The frozen tableau had finally been broken by a cacophony of howling and screeching and roaring, the rush of wings bigger than ritual canopies, as the gods had come roaring to this temple in the mountains. And Tet had fallen, senseless.

He'd spent two weeks in a fever, sweating his body thin and wretched, and when Tet woke, he found himself marked and cursed and set to return Nanak's eyes before the temples were entirely gone.

The other gods should have killed him for the damage he'd done to the fabric of the universe, but Tet hazarded a guess that the hounds had argued for his life. Perhaps he'd been too powerful a pawn in their game to simply destroy. Tet doubted it was sentiment that kept him alive, but rather, a god's childlike cruelty. The gods had limited and ravaged his power, crippling it as surely as they twisted his right knee. A punishment, and a measure of security.

Tet left the temples a man thoroughly broken, limping down the stony path that would lead him eventually to the Green Road. His mage-knots had been cut and burned, his hair clipped right down to his skull. He wore only a peasant's shirt and loose trousers, cheap, crude boots. There was nothing left that marked him as mage or priest.

Though the other mages had not watched him go, Tet had not been entirely alone. The local dragon had come down from her peak when Tet walked away from the temples with his satchels and his lute slung over his shoulder.

The dragon was a small beast, no longer than a man, and with the curious large human-like eyes that all dragons had. She was very beautiful, she'd told him, and Tet had not been stupid enough to argue. In better times, they had played many strategic games of maket together, and Tet knew she liked the taste of goats washed down with millet beer. Sometimes she would get drunk and maudlin and sing songs about her ancestors and their doomed loves.

She was yellow and grey like the clouds before a storm, and her long filaments and whiskers and crest were a warm ivory that matched her wicked curved talons. She'd talked to Tet in the common Vaeyane tongue of the mountain tribes, and asked him how he had stopped time.

'The other dragons are very interested in you,' she'd said. It wasn't altogether surprising. They were, after all, creatures of time. 'The twenty-one spirits in the caverns of the dead shrieked and clamoured so when you stopped the rivers of time.'

'Did they?' Tet had still been ill and nervous, his head cold and light. He fumbled with his newly limited power, trying to call up enough magic to light the tobacco in his pipe. Even such a simple thing as summoning fire – the easiest of spells to perform – had seemed as awkward and uncoordinated as a child's first steps. The word had become the wrong shape in his mouth.

'The twenty-one spirits had never been trapped in time before,' she'd told him. 'It burned them right down to their *oresh*.'

'Ah.' It had taken a few tries before the flames sparked between Tet's fingers.

'So how did you do it?'

He'd told her that he didn't know, even though that was almost a lie. Tet remembered the twist and crack inside his chest, the way he'd simply wanted the world to stop, and how it had obeyed him. A terrifying concept, and too dark and strange to face. Much better to run as far from his old life as Tet-Nanak as he could. All he'd wanted to do was find the opals and return them, and never be a priest again. Give up magic, trade for a little caravan, perhaps meet some like-minded soul and live a simple life. Never again let fear ride his back like a little demonic ape.

'It took all the gods to start it again,' the dragon had explained as she padded alongside him.

That had stopped Tet in his tracks, fingers paused mid-click. 'All?'

'Oh yes.' The dragon maiden had smiled and her teeth were very sharp and beast-like below her human eyes. 'All. It was quite the event. They do not like working together.'

He'd started walking again.

'Come back soon, Lord of Time,' the dragon had called to him. 'Bring me rare jewels and fanciful paintings and statues carved from the ivory of elephants.'

In answer, Tet had raised one hand and left the dragon of the mountain behind. For the next few years, he'd followed rumours of the Eyes of Nanak, little hints and secrets, until he'd come to the end of the trail and to the demon-prince of Pal-em-Rasha. Tet had joined the prince's army in an attempt to get closer to him, surrounded as he was by captains and advisers and armed guards. And all that happened was he'd been sent to war and killed a boy who did not deserve to die.

Another layer of guilt, of self-loathing and fear at what he could do just by wishing it. And with every passing year, the god's curse burned deeper.

Nanak, I cannot do what you want me to. Take back your temple name and let me go. The time of gods and mages has passed.

IV

A CHARGER AND A KING'S RANSOM

That night Tet smoked a generous pinch of seven-petal, enough to numb the pain a little, but not enough to send him visions and delights. The evening's plan was to use his time at the inn to rest and gather himself before he began the final leg to reach Pal-em-Rasha. The petal did its job, and Tet fell into a deep black sleep.

Hands filled his dreams.

A hand. Singular. A hand that made up for all other hands, that hummed with magic and power. Tet could smell fragrant oil, the heavy musk of raw silk. The hand ran down his naked chest. He concentrated. An arm materialised, as though the darkness was a coat of smoke slipping away. Piece by piece, the body emerged from the black of the dream. The mage knelt next to Tet, his head bowed so that his face was hidden. So that Tet could not fall into starless eyes. A tiny, rational part of his mind whispered to wake up, that he should shake himself out of this useless dream. To not let himself be distracted. His mind struggled toward the surface of sleep, a wounded fish going to gasp for air.

The mage's voice pulled Tet back, calling him like a lover, telling him to lie down. To stay. His fingers were hot against Tet's skin, tracing archaic patterns between nipples and navel and the few scattered moles. He wrote on Tet in a language older than men and whispered his name in clouds of seven-petal smoke.

His true name.

Tet heard it. Like all things in dreams, he both heard and did-not, understood and grew more confused at the same time. Tet moved his mouth, but the question unfurled in transparent leaves, the words formed by the struts of veins.

What is my name? Before they could reach the mage, the leaves faded, withered into dust.

The mage did not call Tet's true name again, but he took Tet's hand in his and pulled him down to his mouth and devoured him. Teeth long like a dog's, his breath reeking of meat.

And then there was no mage in his dream, no voice telling him his true name. Only howling. Endless howling.

Instead of the night of good sleep Tet had hoped for, he was hunted by giant dogs, their eyes glowing in the darkness. They tore at his legs, ripping the meat from his bones. His tongue was torn from his mouth by a brutal canine kiss, and he was mute again, as he'd been in childhood

Tet woke to find himself on the floor with the blankets twisted around his ankles. Sweat soaked the back of his sleep tunic and his unbound hair was matted and tangled in thick knots.

He lay, heart beating savagely, his jagged breath rasping at his lungs. It was a dream, nothing more, he repeated, over and over until the fleeting pain faded away, and he found his voice again. 'It was a dream.' The words were half-choked and rough, but they were said aloud. He closed his eyes briefly and thrust the last drifts of the nightmare away.

He needed to get up. There'd be no more sleep now. Besides, he thought, *if I look the way I feel, I'll be terrifying every soul from here to Pal-em-Rasha.*

It was nothing a bath and a comb and a smoke wouldn't fix. Tet had suffered through worse nights. And it was morning, at least.

The bantams in the hostel yard were crowing, the piping barbets were laughing liquid, the sound tumbling from the thin trees. Wood smoke and tea and morning incense drifted upstairs. The bright smell curled into Tet's rented room, driving away the last trailing fog of nightmares.

A knock sounded against the door frame and Tet untangled the blankets that hobbled him, and slowly clambered to his feet. His right leg was shaking, barely able to support his weight, and he clung to the wall for a few moments, waiting for the worst to pass.

Another knock, a little fiercer this time.

'I'm awake.'

The innkeepers' daughter poked her head around the door-tapestry, her face dark against the bright reds and blues of the wool. 'Good morning.'

I suppose for some it is. Teeth clenched, Tet nodded. He tried to keep his balance as casually as possible and erased any sign of pain from his face. Features smoothed out into genial welcome. A muscle quiver was twitching up his left calf; his newly-cursed leg joining in the morning amusements. He ignored it as best he could.

'And a good morning to you.' At least his voice held no trace of the whine that sometimes crept into it on exceptionally bad days. Behind his pleasant facade, Tet seethed. He wanted the girl to leave before he fell down.

'My mothers wish to know if you would like breakfast?'

The thought of food was nauseating. He could still taste blood in his mouth from where the dream hounds had ripped his tongue free. 'Perhaps.' He shifted his weight as slowly as possible. 'Your horses?'

'You would like to buy one?' Her face was guileless. 'You should talk to my mothers then.'

'What would they sell one for, do you think?'

She shrugged. 'Thirty fives, maybe more. I cannot say.'

Gods, Tet thought of his rapidly shrinking purse. V*itash better make good on his promise of coin.* 'There was an older mare.'

'Hast, you don't want her. She has the temper of a mountain lion.' The girl held one arm out to him. 'Just yesterday she bit me.' There was a large, reddened mark above her wrist. 'And she kicks.'

Foul-tempered and not afraid to show it. Perfect. Tet could hopefully charm the innkeepers down on her price. It was more suggestion than true magic so he wouldn't feel remorseful about it. 'Breakfast sounds good,' he lied. He would need to eat. And since the gods only knew when he'd get the chance to ease his legs, Tet decided on one luxury. 'And hot water, if you can spare.'

The girl wrinkled her nose. 'There's a wash house. I'll show you where it is and bring you hot water.'

Tet followed her from the room, grimacing with every shuffling step.

'There's something wrong with your leg?' She looked back over her shoulder.

The wall was the only thing keeping Tet upright, one hand pressed to the dusty slate. 'Something,' he said, and forced a smile. 'There were men who came out worse from the war.' She didn't need to know that this had nothing to do with fighting. No one liked to harbour a cursed guest.

'And some who did not come out at all.'

'There's that.' In one respect, Tet thought, people might consider him lucky. He still lived. And somewhere at the bottom of his meagre satchel was even a little medal. Nothing much, but he had been released from service with honour, rather than delivered with a note to a widow.

'My father fought for the White Prince.' She didn't need to tell him the rest of the story.

'I'm sorry.'

She walked off, faster this time. 'It was nothing.' Her words bounced down the passage. 'Watch the steps.' The girl paused as Tet tackled the narrow stairwell. When he was almost at the bottom, she said. 'I do not remember his face.'

It had been a very long war.

*

The girl showed him to the washhouse and brought a pail of heated water and rags, before leaving Tet finally alone. The stone floor was set with polished river pebbles of greenish-brown, and the air tasted of moss. He undressed carefully, folding his worn tunic on the bench.

Right leg first; wrapping the disfigured knee in warm wet cloths and stretching it out as much as he could. The night had left it cramped, the muscles shortened and unyielding.

It took some time before the heat and the massaging of his thumbs did any good. Tet whispered a few words of healing, trying to soothe the ache. Magery would usually work on minor wounds, but this was a god-mark, and Tet's little magics were no match for their power.

When the right knee was feeling a little less awful Tet drew a deep breath, readying himself to look at what Vitash had done to him. He'd avoided looking properly, keeping it covered, but there was no point now in pretending the dog god hadn't cursed him.

The left knee was still whole, but now a thin mark ran along the edge of the knee cap. A sliver of red, a wicked little moon. It pulsed, just a small pain in comparison to the right, but it was a warning of what would come if Tet did not do as Vitash commanded. He pictured the mage's head, held up by the hair like a trophy, blood pooling around Tet's feet.

'Dammit!' He punched the bench. If the Monkey's *ritual-oresh* ended up being a failure, then Tet had bound himself tighter to the whim of the gods. They would make him a murderer, a tool to use whenever they wanted blood spilled.

He needed to reach Pal-em-Rasha sooner rather than later. Tet washed quickly, and hobbled off to eat his breakfast and haggle with the innkeeper women for their ill-tempered mare.

*

Hast turned out to cost Tet more than he had wanted to spend, but at least the women gave him saddle and bridle, feed bags and grain. The girl held Hast's patterned bridle while Tet mounted. She said nothing at his struggles but patted the roan pony's nose when Tet was finally in place, the stirrups left long so he could keep his ruined legs straight.

'That's a strange way to ride,' she said. 'Did you learn that from the Deniahn?'

'That and many other things beside.' It was with the Deniahn army Tet had learned not only to ride a horse in their style, but to memorise city streets, to make maps, and to pretend worship of their bloodthirsty god Nyangist.

'It looks stupid.'

'Yes, it does, rather.' With his aching leg, the Deniahn position was more comfortable than the Vaeyane style, crouched high at the pony's withers. Tet didn't mind the Deniahn seat as much as he minded their murderous religion. While Vaeyane and Deniah were still allies, it was only because the Vaeyane were always too weak and scattered a nation to stand against the prince's armies. Better to join him than to be slaughtered, the Vaeyane had thought. Tet often wondered if they'd been right.

Hast tossed her head, pulling herself free from the girl's loose fingers. Unperturbed, the girl continued quizzing Tet, although she stepped out of reach of the mare's teeth. 'Did they teach you to fire a gun?'

'They were fond of their pistols. The White Prince puts all his faith in machines.'

The girl snorted in mild disgust. 'You look after Hast. She's a mother many times.'

Tet touched his fingers to his head in a salute. Another thing the Deniahn had taught him to do. 'I'll respect her as much as she respects me.'

'Good luck with that.' But she smiled. 'Go then, the Three watch you.'

Tet preferred they didn't, but he was not so churlish as to dismiss the girl's blessing. 'And you.' He tapped the pony lightly with his heels and the mare grunted, before deciding she was in the mood for a journey and ambling off to the road.

'Should I just cut the reins off right now?' Tet asked the mare and she answered him by shitting on the dirt track. 'Ah, yes. I can see we are going to have a most rewarding friendship.' He let the reins hang slack, and trusted the old mare to walk until she felt like stopping. He already knew he was not going to be the one who changed her mind.

The track between the mare's ears was empty, slowly bouncing with each plodding step. It had been a while since Tet had ridden, and before long his arse and thighs were aching. But it was a good, real pain, one that distracted him from his cursed knees.

The scenery changed so slowly that it felt as though they were riding past the same clump of trees over and over. It could even be that they were, Tet thought.

For the last ten years, time had been full of strange little repetitions and stumbles; moments where the last few seconds were replayed like a scene in a rehearsal where the actors had forgotten their lines and must start again from the beginning.

Tet couldn't decide if the repetitive scenery was a problem with time or just the boredom of travelling. *Let it be nothing more than my exhaustion playing tricks.*

It was long past midday when a figure appeared in the middle of the road ahead. Spectral and silver, but still recognisable as the witch-girl of the travellers. Her hair was bound up again in twin cones and looped earrings ran up the curve of her ears, but she had a wiser look to her face. True wisdom, not just little-girl-pretend.

The sending was weak and Tet could see the wavering trees and the long winding trail of the Green Road through the sending's body.

Hast came to a halt and shook her neck, setting the bridle jangling. Tet's left knee twinged, and he rubbed at it automatically. *You will crawl on your belly like serpent,* Vitash had said. But he'd also said, '*So be it,*' when Tet had pleaded for coin.

And gods kept their promises, good or ill. Tet smiled thinly.

The witch's sending was unable to speak – not this far from the traveller's camp – but it beckoned with its white hands, then darted off the road and into the bush. The trees there were stunted and grey, the few blooming rhododendrons smearing pink and white. Tet could just make out the sending's shimmer between the branches for a few moments before she disappeared.

'It's up to you,' he told Hast. 'But I for one would prefer that you follow. It won't take long.'

The mare didn't budge.

Tet grimaced and swung his leg over her rump, and slid down to the ground. Everything felt shaky beneath him for a moment. 'You stay here,' he told her with a pat to her neck. The little roan snorted, swished her tail, and cocked one hoof. Tet chose to translate that as agreement.

Thorn branches slapped at his cheeks, scratched his hands, and all the while the sending glimmered just out of reach. It became clear that Hast was wiser than she looked: any trail that might have wound its way through the thick underbrush had disappeared and Tet was left to bash and hack his way through thickly tangled branches. The sending slipped through them with all the ease of a ghost, careless and single-minded.

When he finally caught up to her, the witch-sending was standing in a clearing before the remains of a vast tree. A wild fig had grown around the corpse, squeezing it into a lace-work web of crushing trunks and branches. The sending drifted her hands through the sprays of leaves and rambling vines. A few birds flickered through the upper boughs like feathered mice, their long tails dancing.

She drifted her hands again, then looked at him in something that was probably exasperation. She meant for him to copy her.

Tet shoved the curtain of overgrown branches aside, half-digging through the foliage to get to the desiccated remains of the dead tree. There was a slit in the side of the rotted bole, hidden by the fig. It was narrow and tall, and a man could fit through if he held his breath and didn't mind losing some skin.

The sending knelt before the crack, her hands fluttering in the darkness, pointing into the dark heart of the tree.

Tet sighed and took out his tobacco pouch. His few matches were in a strip of thin, oiled leather, and he unrolled them slowly, took one, and struck it against a rock. The light flared and he leaned forward, squinting. *Trust the gods to make any gift they give seem hardly worth taking.*

The crack led down to a pit dug under the trees, between the tangled roots, ancient and new. On the largest uncovered sections of root were white painted markings. The language was foreign and not one Tet had bothered to study. It was one of the spindly alphabets from the west; all hatch marks and dots. He couldn't read it but recognised a few symbols here and there. He had not always kept good company while working for the prince as one of his spies and mapmakers.

The light sputtered out and he glanced up at the sending. 'A thief's cache?'

She nodded, spread her hands wide.

So Vitash kept his word and here was the proof of it, but Tet would be a fool to accept. The gifts of gods never come without their own set of problems. *Don't I at least deserve this, though, for all my years of suffering?* The thought of what treasures might be left in the thieves' cache quickly overwhelmed any doubt. Tet inched sideways and pressed himself through the narrow hole in the tree.

Branches scraped at his face, catching in his hair, his hands were stabbed and gouged, but finally, he worked his way in, and dropped into the small cavern beneath the trees. The landing sent needles of pain shooting through his knees, and Tet leaned against the crumbling mud walls, panting until it passed. Lights flashed behind his eyelids, like the fireworks on the grand Rasha festivals and ceremonies when they marched their lioness-headed god through the city, flames flowering behind her like the end of the world.

At least his pain could be entertaining, Tet thought.

The place stank of rotting leaves and damp earth and old piss. The thieves had clearly not been too troubled about using their cache as a toilet. Tet wasted another precious match to get his bearings. In one corner, half-buried under decaying leaves, he spotted the edge of a leather bag, well-worn, the stitching cracked. He hauled it out to find it disappointingly small and not terribly heavy.

The gifts of gods did not come freely and were touched with ill-luck, and here the gift was so meagre Tet wondered what it could possibly bring him that would make following Vitash's witch-sending worth the trouble.   He breathed life back into the spent match, forcing the black twist of wood to catch fire again, then planted it in the wet earth and commanded it to stay bright. The little light grew greater than it had any natural right to do, leaping and spitting, casting Tet's misshapen shadow across the scraped walls. He looked like a monster digging through a graveyard for corpses to eat, hunched and malformed.

The satchel's thin straps were swollen, and Tet tugged at them until they finally shifted under his fingers, the rust of the buckles flaking down like dried blood. Inside was a handful of five and one coins – enough to pay for a few days' food and lodgings if Tet was careful. He hefted the satchel and the coins fell to one side, revealing beneath them a trove of star-bright stones, red and green and white and yellow, some small as pinpricks, a few big as the nail on his littlest finger.

A tight squeeze of panic and elation pulsed through his chest. Now *this* was a thief's cache, sure enough; their winter store of berries and nuts. The light fluttered in the stillness of the cavern, threatening to go out. Tet couldn't pretend that the money and jewels would not make his life easier for the moment, especially when facing the uncertainty of his upcoming meeting with the Monkey.

It was too much. 'Put it back,' he whispered to himself. The words hissed around the roots, and earth fell in a soft answering patter. The flame died, soft and sudden.

The sending flashed before him once more, bright as a lamp in the darkness of the cavern. Her hands closed around Tet's and though he could see his fingers through hers, she was still strong enough to push the leather satchel toward his chest. *Take it,* she mouthed.

Tet was a fool, and he knew it. He should throw the satchel down right here and leave it in the darkness. It was stolen riches, and it was tainted with blood. Instead, he did not move, torn between conflicting desires. *Gods. First they curse you with pain, then curse you with kindness.*

'Forgive me,' Tet whispered to the air, to whatever dead still haunted the treasure, and slung the satchel over one shoulder. Soon he would have no need of wealth, and then, he promised himself, he would donate the remains of these stolen riches to the poor.

He was Tet-Nanak, and needed only magic.

V

THE RICH MAN'S DREAM

Tet rode into Pal-em-Rasha on a roan pony, his saddlebags weighted with bronze five-and-ones, with fallen stars. His stained travel clothes were folded away in his pack, and he'd arrayed himself in a clean formal robe-jacket, with his winter riding coat over that. The riding coat was too hot, but it was finely embroidered, and Tet had cleaned the pale leather of his boots and brightened the old stitching with the word *ferrog*. He was richer than he had ever been, and he could barely enjoy it. There was a small problem with using his weakened magery on a god-curse, and why he almost never bothered. Small was relative. The thing with curses was that gods didn't take kindly to people trying to get out of them. When Tet's magic wore off, the pain returned triple-fold to make up for the ease of the last few days.

He was bent over Hast's withers, one hand clinging to the scruff of her mane for balance, the other clutching his thigh. His nails dug into the muscle, as though trying to make a new pain would somehow lessen the one in his knee. Even though the air coming down from the mountains was crisp with snow, his body was slick with sweat.

The entrance gates to the city loomed above, the road lined with watchful guards. Tet followed the slow huddle of merchant wagons bringing in the meagre winter crops from the outlying farms. The meat wagons from the front at least had their corpses covered, though the flies were already thick as a crawling blanket. Soldiers limped along the side of the road, their uniforms black and tattered. There were missing arms and eyes. Even those who seemed whole had an empty look to their faces. They had lost a generation to the White Prince's expansion, and still they fought. Tet had to hope that soon the promises of honour and glory and wealth beyond measure, and the threat of enemies who would destroy everything their people stood for, would not be enough to keep the armies supplied. There were always rumours of dissenters and protesters, but the prince had an uncommon cruel hand with them, and those rumours faded as fast as they flowered.

The arch swallowed Tet, the shadow passing over his face, and he was inside the White Prince's city. Pal-em-Rasha was filled with laughing doves, and their throbbing good humour cooed around him. They erupted in surprised flocks from under the hooves of horses and oxen, only to settle in brown and lilac drifts over the walls and roofs.

Hast paused in the middle of the packed thoroughfare, and a half-dozen merchants and drivers cursed Tet in the rapid sing-song languages of the Rasha: northern Deniahn, some Imradian here and there like a thrush trying to out-sing a forest of sparrows, and less frequently, the southern clatter of Utt Dih.

Tet had been speaking Vaeyane for far too long. He'd have to retrain his ears and tongue. It had always been his weak point when assuming a new identity, and something he'd had to work hardest on. He was always slow when he first shifted languages, his brain insisting on translating rather than simply dropping into a new sea of sound. Years of practice had made the transition smoother and Tet knew that within a day or two he'd be better. By the end of the week no one would believe he'd been born anywhere else.

It wasn't magery. If there were two skills Tet could call truly his own, then it was his grasp of languages and maps. It had made him a decent spy and a terrible soldier. Start speaking someone else's tongue and learn their city like the palm of your own hand and it becomes hard to keep separate from their dreams. Cities and speech were the symbols of humanity's imagination – towers to rival the gods, myths made manifest.

But Tet had been speaking the mountain languages, and Deniahn was a crackle of noise. It didn't help that he was cold with sweat and his ears were ringing. Tet clutched at Hast's mane, swaying in his saddle, and made a sound that was half-laugh, half-sobbing whine.

'Get out of the way,' an old man spat through broken teeth, and slapped a short whip across Hast's rear. She jerked forward and Tet almost fell to the ground. He didn't have time to dawdle here, he needed to find a place now.

Concentrate, damn you. Tet emptied his mind, as though he was once again just a boy in training, listening to the voices of the priests as they taught him to centre himself, to find the calm within, and to *remember*. He grasped onto the old rhythms of breath, the first cycles all the temple spawn were taught.

Peace settled over him, and the sound of the city faded.

Tet had spent many years memorising every part of all the major cities in Deniah, and Pal-em-Rasha was the greatest of these. He had studied maps centuries old, kept in the temples, and modern war maps in the army. His knowledge was both ancient and new. He knew the traceries of tunnels long-collapsed as well as the scrawl of new roads and tracks and suburbs laid over them like a palimpsest.

A map unfurled in his head, a new road with each breath. *Focus.* Pal-em-Rasha was laid out in a spiked circle, every suburb a petal of an immense lotus. The palace sat at the heart, like a jutting pistil. There were eight gates into the city, and this was the North-East. The best area for Garden-Houses was further to the western side, but still close to the Pistil. That's where the Lime Grove would be; though Tet had never had the money or occasion to stay there, he remembered the name well enough. He visualised the city and set it fast in his mind, gathered Hast's reins, and bit down on his pain. *Soon. Soon.*

They passed several open market courts before reaching the edge of the Silk and Spice, the grandest court of all the merchants. Women and men were thick within its low walls, like lentils in a bowl. The air was rich and heavy. Tamarind from the south, dried peppercorns in red and white and black, shimmering hills of pale green cardamom pods and gold-dust turmeric and bright red threads of saffron. Silks and rugs and polished brass pots like small fallen suns.

The chatter and hum of the crowd was bright and sweet as a song plucked on a zither. Tet didn't enter the court of merchants, but he rode past the soldiers at her low arched gates. The crowd buzzed brighter, louder, and then, as though a giant hand had clipped the zither strings, everything fell silent.

The hush spread out from the market, and around him, the street crowds slowed, stopped, and all heads turned in clockwork precision. Tet followed their gaze.

It was a simple procession, hardly large or gaudy enough to warrant this eerie silence. Not a procession at all, in fact. A single small grey donkey, almost as white as the ash of a long-dead fire. It clopped down the street, the only sound the hollow clap of its hooves against the packed dry mud, the faint echo of its passing.

The rider jolted in his seat, head hanging awkwardly to one side.

Hast danced beneath Tet, and some of her fear itched up his hands and into his heart.

The little donkey drew closer, its rider jerking now to one side. The rider's eyes had been stitched open, and what was left of his limbs were lashed to the saddle with the remains of his own intestines.

The crowd was silent. Tet had seen this before. A traitor in the White Prince's army had met a similar end. But that man had fallen to the swords and spears of soldiers who used to share a pipe and a bedroll with him.

This one had been ravaged by beasts. There were claw marks black with clotted blood down one side of his face. Or hers. It was hard to tell what this corpse used to be.

'What happened?' Tet asked a small, round woman nearest him after the donkey had moved on and the throng closed behind it like the wake of a slow boat.

'New to the city, are you?' she said, one eye squinted against the sun as she peered up at him.

'Arrived today.'

'You missed the game, then. Seems there's always some poor fool who thinks they can sneak past the prince – may his name be blessed and his enemies devoured – and steal his power.' She snorted. 'The White Prince let this one try for his life in the cage.'

'The cage?'

'To fight against the clockwork animals.' The woman shook her head. 'Sometimes he has them crucified, or lets them try their luck with a hunt and rides after them in the old palace grounds. Once one even escaped.'

'Lucky,' Tet murmured. He knew of the prince's beasts, but this penchant for setting them on traitors must be some new game of his. Perhaps he was growing bored.

'But the cages are outside the palace, and you can't get near the front of the crowd for love nor money.' She picked up the bags she set down while the donkey passed, and hefted them back onto her shoulders. 'All we get is the dregs.' The woman took her leave, disappearing through the crowd.

Vile as they were, the Prince's entertainments were not Tet's concern. *Let him do as he pleases with his mechanical animals and his other vices – the petal and the girls being two that marked him as human and not actually a reborn monster.* Tet had his own problems to attend to.

The Monkey, the ritual, the price, and then he would be free.

A row of rippling lemon-green flags raised on high poles was the first indication that Tet was in the right place. The name was inscribed in small, neat lettering on a gate of old and blackened wood: The Lime Grove. The walls were hidden behind thick groves of varying citrus trees and though the fruit had not set, the air seemed sweeter here, promising ripeness.

Pal-em-Rasha was already many degrees warmer than the surrounding hills, and even the icy black river that bisected her couldn't cool the city.

So: Ohtet Maynim. It was time. Tet's final reinvention would be in place before his feet touched the ground. He gathered the voice of the Deniahn people in his head, let the rhythm of it flood his blood and brain and when he opened his mouth he would sound like a merchant-prince down from the mountains. His accent would be rough and raw, which suited just fine for this particular lie. A lucky border merchant, to have avoided the prince's draft. Perhaps he was so rich that had bought his way free, perhaps his farm fed the armies that waited at the walls of the fortress cities of Damak, Aza, and Jora. Either way, a man to be respected. Tet had no intention of being mistaken for a traitor or deserter.

He dusted the panels of his riding coat, and dismounted at the gates. Garden-house servants in cream and gold shifts came padding up to him, their faces supercilious masks.

The trick was to make them believe that he was so wealthy that he didn't care what they thought. Tet handed the reins to the closest servant. 'She'll want grain.' He turned to the next, who was still frowning. 'Bring those.' He pointed at his saddlebags and walked off to the entrance. Looking back would break the illusion, and Tet kept his head straight like a blinkered horse. This was the first part of his transformation.

The rich never explained, and they never asked.

He gave his name to the garden-house mother as Ohtet Maynim.

She frowned. The house-mother was tall and broad, and although she was older than him by a decade at least, she was carefully made up to look younger, and her robes were very fine.

Even Tet's best robe was a little stained and travel-worn, and he'd arrived riding a mountain pony and carrying a lute like a common entertainer. He stood straighter, wearing a look of irritation and disdain.

Her mouth was pulled in a sour moue. 'Ohtet Maynim?' she repeated, as though she must possibly have misheard.

'You're expecting me,' he said. 'A suite of rooms should be ready.' So it began. Tet cast the first anchoring silk of his new identity. Playing the game once more tasted like sour metal – half fear and half excitement. It had been a long time since Tet last changed himself into a new man, and though this was not his own doing, he couldn't help but find a certain enjoyment in the gamble.

'Indeed.' Her gaze fell on the pouches Tet carried. 'Your rooms are waiting.'

'And a visitor?' He was hopeful now. The Monkey must be waiting for him – here, or close by. His freedom brushed against him like a cat.

'There have been no visitors,' she said. 'And no messages.' She motioned for a porter to carry Tet's meagre packs and led him toward a set of grand stairs strung with red prayer bunting, the carved wood gilded here and there with whorls of beaten metal.

In an alcove just before the stairs sat the house-idol of Nyangist, the lioness-headed god. Tet bowed to it as though it were the most natural thing in the world, and gave no indication that he despised her blood-stained religion and the war she had brought down.

Pal-em-Rasha just barely tolerated followers of the Three Dogs, and he was not about to draw unwanted attention to his origins. For the moment, he was just another borderlands merchant-prince, and his only power was money.

Tet dropped coins like autumn leaves. He ate and drank and hired the services of the garden-house masseuse, before collapsing onto a bed stuffed with down. His room sumptuous, more decadent than anything he had ever allowed himself, but there was nothing and no one waiting for him. Tet began to feel a prickle of unease.

The servants had left him a tray of pastries and flagons of wine and well-water. They had opened the window panels at his command, and from outside drifted the cold, and the citrus smell of the lime groves, and under it the hay and manure smell of the garden-house's distant stables.

Night was beginning to fall, and with it came the reek of the city's cookfires, the rich incense burned to Nyangist, and the sounds of the temple bells.

It did not bring Tet what he wanted: word about the ritual. He was so close now that every minute spent waiting felt like a sharpened bit in a cut mouth. He passed the time pouring himself sweet wine, pink as blood-blushed water, and drank it without enjoyment. Maudlin drinking only made him reconsider his brief exchange with the Monkey's pet mage. Tet didn't know his name, but he could see his face clearly, proud under starlight, and remember the way his cheek felt like the softest leather of a rich man's riding gloves, the oily little fleck of white behind his ear, like a stage dancer's greasepaint. The mocking sound of his voice as he called Tet *old man*.

Ha! Vitash take his head.

Tet was not interested in nameless men he could never have. His goal was only to meet with the Monkey. If he didn't show himself soon, Tet would find some way to track him down. He had no talent with findings, but there were clockwork magicians who – for a very high price – could fashion a toy that would hunt down a single man in a city. Tet was wondering exactly what such a trinket would cost him, and what they would need to use to set the toy on the Monkey's trail, when a faint scrabbling came from the window.

A small white and black monkey sat on the ledge of the open window, its tail flicking. The creature's eyes were round and amber, and a tuft of golden bright fur crowned its head. It held out a grey tube in its tiny hand, like a parody of some pompous city official. The monkey dropped the tube to the floor and disappeared as quickly as it arrived.

Slowly, his knees protesting the movement despite the coin spent on massages and oils, Tet went to gather the fallen object.

It was a scrolled letter tied shut with fine thread.

The light was going and Tet used a weak flicker of magic to set the hearth and candles blazing before opening the message with trembling fingers.

A smaller scrap of paper fell out as he unrolled the dove-grey scroll. Tet scanned the scroll – an elegant script cordially invited him to attend the event of a newly appointed brigadier at the end of the following week. Or rather, invited Ohtet Maynim to attend. He clenched his jaw and crouched down to pick up the fallen scrap. This one was written on cheap paper, the calligraphy a careless scrawl; was *this* his first true contact with the Monkey?

It was a set of instructions on the persona of Ohtet Maynim. Maynim was a merchant-prince with a daughter named Anestra. His board and lodging were paid for, and tailors would come to suitably outfit him.

We will meet soon, the letter told him. *Trust, and be patient.*

Tet destroyed it with a vicious twist of magic that flared in his palm, and dropped ash as pale as snow onto the carpeted floor. The Monkey made plans in plans for him, and all on a promise. But even cursed, Tet was not completely without his own means and he disliked being trotted about like a game-piece. There was no need to bother with toymakers and their little monsters when there were other, less-magical means to fish out the truth. If the Monkey was as powerful as he seemed, then he would leave traces. Powerful men needed money. Powerful men who wished to hide in the shadows would make that money not in legal trade, but in a more interesting sort altogether.

Tomorrow Tet would pay a visit to those places he liked best, and in doing so, might turn up a little news. At the same time, he would carefully reveal a flaw by looking like a man who could be easily manipulated with promises of drugs and pleasure. Let the Monkey watch and let him think he had a hold on Tet. He finished the wine in his glass. The sweetness had turned sour and sharp.

VI

A CLOCKWORK PRINCESS

The promised tailor had Tet standing in little more than an underwrap so that he could take Tet's measurements. The cold didn't bother him, not when his entire suite of rooms was heated every minute of the day at the Monkey's expense, but having his leg exposed did. A professional, the tailor made no mention of the hideous scarring and warped flesh as he bent to run his tape measure from hip to floor. He scribbled down notes and nodded to himself. 'And sai would like how many sets of robes and trousers?'

It all depended on how long this little play would last. Tet was hoping for it to be done quickly, but he was too used to the vagaries of fate to expect that what he wanted was what he'd get. And he wasn't paying for this, yet.

'As many as necessary for the season,' Tet told him. It was still longer than he would've liked.

Per the Monkey's message, Tet had instructed the tailor to wardrobe him in the fashions of the city. He had titled himself and given himself a set of imaginary estates far to the north, close to the border. This was the first time Ohtet Maynim had made an excursion from his vast holdings down to the city. He had spoken of his dead wife and his young daughter.

'Very good, Sai Maynim.' The tailor scurried to write down some more measurements.

Maynim. It was his name now, and already it no longer felt like wearing the shoes of a dead man. This new personality had been easy to slip on, and Tet felt it settling into his pores, staining the way he thought, the way he viewed the world.

When he'd been in the White Prince's army, he'd called himself Sektet Am; an appropriate enough name for a spy and maker of maps, for a man who fought in no great battles and killed only once.

Tet did not want to remember that. The boy's face took a while to fade, his soundless scream and surprise imprinted behind Tet's eyelids. The snap of his breaking neck an echo only he could hear.

His leg twitched.

Now, if sai would not mind, I can recommend a cobbler who will be able to make a boot that will balance sai.'

Tet frowned in confusion.

The tailor handed him a robe, then stepped away from him. 'To compensate for the right leg.'

The robe served as a convenient distraction, and Tet avoided the tailor's gaze as he knotted the belt. Confirmation then that his destroyed and weakened muscles were shortening the right leg. The limp had become more pronounced in the last few years, but it had happened so gradually that Tet had allowed himself to believe that the change was not so drastic. 'Yes, fine.' Tet waved him away. 'Send for him to come here.' He snapped, trying to sound commanding, but fear pushed through and made his voice tremble.

The cost of the tailored clothes would have made a sizeable bite in any man's fortune, but Tet insisted on only the finest materials, silk from the south, and the richest dyes and wools. And he doubled the price by expecting them to deliver the complete new wardrobe by the end of the week. The tailor would probably have half the needle district working from dawn 'til twelfth candle. Tet grinned without humour as he dressed back in his familiar old riding gear.

While he was preparing to go out into the city, Tet rediscovered the leather and metal pouch that the mage had given him to keep his mouth shut. The 'gift' had turned out to be nothing more than a fire-starter's pouch with flint and tinder, and Tet had packed it away and mostly forgotten about it. The metal was cold under his fingertips, and Tet contemplated packing the useless thing back into his saddlebags.

It had still been a gift, however. Was it a thoughtless gesture; simply the first thing the thief mage had taken, or was it something more? The mage had known Tet for a fellow magician, and even so he'd given Tet a layman's tool to start fires.

While Tet also kept a little oiled skin with matches from the south, it was merely part of the tricks he used when he was pretending not to be a mage, or when the pain made using his weakened magic near impossible. Even with his magic depleted, he rarely had an actual need for matches.

Perhaps this throw-away trinket was meant to humiliate him.

Or there was a message to it, one Tet was too blinkered to read? With a grimace, he closed his fist on the flint pouch. He'd keep it to remind himself that there were others playing on this Grand Board and that he had no idea what their motives might be. In Pal-em-Rasha, Tet was not the only one the Monkey kept on a leash.

To what purpose does he gather mages, I wonder.

*

Downstairs the garden-house mother was eager to give Tet a list of places to visit, and a servant to accompany him.

'I prefer to do my walking alone.' After all, he was going to seek information, not take in the sights like a tourist. And he already knew the best places to go, where men talked as freely as they dreamed.

She glanced at his leg and Tet pretended not to notice her look. Several days of rest and heated baths and massage had brought the pain to a tolerable level. More than tolerable. He could get used to being a wealthy man.

'Alone? You are certain?' The house-mother's face crinkled in confusion.

'I will be quite safe, I assure you.' Tet knew he sounded like a pompous fool, but she had no idea that he could snap the neck of a man with a word, should he choose.

I do not choose.

'My women know all the places you might like to see, where a man such as yourself will be safe.'

It wasn't safety Tet was looking for. 'Do not worry yourself,' Tet reassured her, though he doubted she was as worried for him as she was for his coin-purse. He did not need her servants to show him the way. It had been more than two years since he was last in Pal-em-Rasha but he could call up a map as if it were a painting he'd made himself.

With more fanfare than he'd wanted, Tet took his leave of the garden-house. The city streets twined together in sinuous loops and turns, and the walled compounds with their fruit tree orchards and wells grew cramped as the avenues narrowed. In the finest parts of the city vast high trees shaded the roads, and in summer dropped garlands of pale lilac flowers over the traffic.

There were no trees where Tet was going. A few stunted shrubs that some earnest and well-meaning fools had planted to try and brighten the lanes, but even these had mostly withered.

The houses were backed against one another, doors snarling. They were painted in the colourful style of the city – each house with its own bright signature and no care that it might clash with its neighbour. Lime against lavender against pink against ochre, but the paint was worn and greyed. Small black bantams scratched in the cold dust, and their shit patterned the narrow sidewalks.

Men and women with rheumy eyes slumped against the walls, begging bowls at their feet, sometimes with their polished medals set alongside to prove that they once had some value, that they were not born to the street. A few had the energy to rattle their begging bowls as Tet passed. He dropped a few coins here and there, even though the futility of it made his head hurt. He avoided their faces, half-worried that he might recognise someone he had served with.

The smell in the air was changing. Incense warred with shit and urine. Under it all was another scent. One that had him pick up his pace. Twinges shot up from his knee and Tet willed himself to ignore them. The smell was heady, ugly, tempting. It left an after-taste like chalk and milk in the back of his throat. And yet it was sweeter than honey dripping off a comb. Tet shared his vice with dragons and beggars, and rumour had it the prince himself had a penchant for its twisted visions.

The Dream of the Seven Petals was a small house painted in the royal colours of red-ochre and yellow. The yellow had faded to a creamy butter and the lower walls were dirt-dark, but the sign was freshly painted.

Two people lounged on either side of the door. One read a small book while the other picked at his teeth. He was muscled, watchful. A doorman for the petal house.

A woman in layers of multi-coloured robes chatted with the teeth-picker. Her dress was fine, but as Tet drew closer, he could see it was stained at the hem, the sleeves mended. 'Do you have a smoke?' she said as he hobbled nearer.

It was a typical approach. Tet shook his head. 'Not today.'

She snorted and turned her attention back to the bouncer. 'This is the problem with petal,' she said to him. 'It makes men impotent.'

The person reading their book looked up and grinned. 'Some more impotent than others.' They were sharp-featured, striking, and Tet looked to the ground. He'd not come here for whatever they sold, even if he might have desired it.

It was not strictly true that he no longer wanted what they offered. Petal did eat away desire, though, if one over-indulged, and that was a price Tet had no problem paying. Desire was a waste. He nodded to the two at the door and limped into the shadowed house. Inside it was rich with the overwhelming smoke of seven-petal.

No one asked him what he wanted. The people who came here had only one goal, and so long as they had the coin to pay for it, there was no judgement. Many years ago, the White Prince's grandfather had tried to eradicate the petal-houses, but his own generals stood against him. It was a vice, to be sure, but a pleasurable vice. If only the poor enjoyed it, Tet was sure the old Prince would have succeeded, but when the rich indulge, well, they liked their pleasures without penalty.

The house was filled with many small rooms, each painted in a different shade, decorated with murals and folding screens. Long low couches and beds were covered in raw silks and plush velvets, slippery brocades subtle with tiny intricate patterns. Seven-petal enhanced the eyes and touch, and the management kept their customers longer by ensnaring them with colour and texture. It was not unusual for a man to spend a day wrapping soft shawls of goat wool around his hands, over and over, winding and unwinding, lost in a rapture of fuzz and fingers and dye.

Tet found himself a room painted in a soothing grey-green, with beaten copper bowls and a screen of the hill countries decorating one corner. It was mostly empty. A young man lay stretched out on a low divan, his head tilted back so that he could stare at the painted ceiling. He smoked leisurely, the water pipe bubbling like the lungs of a dying child. The sound was soothing, and Tet's insides relaxed. He hadn't realised how much he missed that sound. That smell. He took a seat on the opposite long couch, and the servant who had been padding after him crouched down by his feet, one hand held out. Tet gave the servant coin enough to keep him here for a day, and he scampered off to prepare the pipe.

The room's other occupant angled his head. He looked like a sculpture charmed to life. His skin was smooth. When he smiled, he revealed teeth white as the most expensive rice. A rich youth, his days given over to lassitude and the ash taste of ecstasy. Rich enough not to go to war, or to choose to chase after other highs.

The man's smile reminded Tet of the thief mage, and his slight grin, his air of imperious contempt. Try as he might, he couldn't seem to shake the mage from his head. No matter what he did or where he went, something always brought Tet's thoughts back around to the one-armed mage, his dragon shift, his magic.

Perhaps I should simply give in and let my imagination do what it wants. Like the man in the room, the mage was handsome too, despite his arm. Mocking and sly and beautiful – a combination Tet had always found particularly intriguing. Men like that were not often worth the chase, but he followed at their heels, nonetheless.

Tet shook his head in exasperation. Vitash hadn't asked him to seduce a mage, but to saw off his head. And of course, Tet planned to do neither. He was here for word of another, and he wouldn't allow himself to be distracted by things he couldn't have. Instead Tet turned his focus back to the man on the divan and considered if it would be worth his time to try.

He wondered what the man saw when he looked back at him. Tet had the straight-cut features of his mountain people, the fine black hair, the thick eyebrows. His face was still smooth. Nanak had once called him pretty, but that was ten years ago and no one else had ever said anything similar since. Gods have strange ideas of beauty. And back then he'd stood tall and didn't limp.

Tet looked away from the man, and stared at the floor instead, following the twists and curls of the carpet design while he waited for his pipe. A serving of humiliation and rejection could be saved for a day when he was better equipped to deal with it. For now, he'd smooth out his worries and guilts with the dream of seven-petal.

The young man didn't speak until Tet was settled and the twin sounds of their water pipes were bubbling in complacent harmony. The taste of seven-petal was acrid and rich in Tet's lungs, and he relaxed, enjoying the pull of the drug, content. It would hit sooner or later and there was no rushing it.

The man turned his head very slowly and gazed at him with leaf-dark eyes. His hair was loose, and it fell from the edge of the couch in a russet curtain. Tet wanted to reach out and touch it, run his fingers through the flames.

'You're not a regular,' the russet man said. His voice was higher than Tet had expected, but soft and throaty from smoke.

Tet shook his head. 'Just got into the city.' And already he had confronted the White Prince's peculiar brand of madness. His dreams were rotten with the image of the eviscerated corpse clopping along on a little ash-grey donkey.

The russet man leaned his head back and sighed. 'Ah, have you seen the princess yet?'

Princess? This was news to him. The White Prince had no living siblings, and as far as Tet was aware, was still unmarried – he didn't need to be when he could take a mistress whenever he wanted. He had a host of them, like floating lilies on a jade pool.

'No, I have not.' Tet's head was beginning to swim, and his well-favoured companion was fox-eyed, green and red and gold in the fluttering candlelight. He curled his fingers into his palms, concentrating on speech instead of the crimson thread of desire. 'I did not know there was one.'

'She's from the west; a kingdom called Sinal.'

Tet knew Sinal from maps. It was far to the west, so far that he doubted many people in the city had been there. In the temple, the priests and nuns had sacred illustrated books that talked of the fabulous creatures of the country – long-legged birds taller than men, with the heads of serpents, brindle camels that could walk for months without food or water, wingless dragons that swam through the rivers and could neither speak nor breathe fire. Not terribly much about princesses, though. 'What was she doing here?'

The man laughed thick grey smoke into the air. 'What do all princesses want?' He closed his eyes and was silent for so long that Tet assumed he'd fallen asleep.

The conversation over, Tet lost himself in reverie. His limbs grew looser, heavier, the pain seeped away from his legs and from across his back. Slow as ferns, his fingers uncurled. Deep in the haze of petal, Tet dreamed of touching the man – a safe congress, mouths that never met, slick and sweet, but without meaning. And if he found curves and softness where he expected harder planes and angles, that too was fine. He dreamed of red hair between his fingers, skin shifting against skin, their sighs pressed silent against palms.

Just a fantasy. Nothing he would act on.

He hadn't realised how much agony he was truly in until the seven-petal worked its relief. Tet sighed, slow and languorous as the pain was softly erased. Colours throbbed across the wall and the shadows from the lamps chased each other over the canvas of the room, acting out a story he could almost understand. Deep in his head, the void turned, dust hissed down from the edges of the sealed door.

The man turned his head very slowly and gazed at him with leaf-dark eyes. His hair was loose, and it fell from the edge of the couch in a russet curtain. He smiled.

Tet's stomach jolted. Time flickering back again, and he waited for the conversation they'd just had to repeat itself. His innards twisted and tightened. *I did this, I did this.* Sweat gathered at his temples and with it his recurring fear that even if he was able to slip the gods and their curses, he would still have this at his back – the fractured time. He'd caused it, but Tet knew no way to fix it. And he really didn't want to think about what it meant that the gods themselves were not able to set his little mistake right.

Little mistake. Tet almost laughed; a sick, choking feeling tightening his throat.

'You're not a regular,' the red-haired man said, and Tet clenched his fists again. It was not desire flooding through him now, but fear.

He was back to waiting for the pipe to be brought to him. Tet wasn't high, or perhaps he was or would be. It was so hard to tell where he stood when time skipped back. For safety, Tet kept to the script that played before. 'Just got into the city.' The words tasted stale and bitter, like a coating of ash on old food.

The man told Tet about the princess. The shadows seemed deeper and darker and Tet had no idea if this was true or just a trick of his memory. It was such an imperfect thing. He frowned in concentration, trying to see something he hadn't last time. The man told him the princess was from Sinal, before the scene flicked forward again, and Tet was stranded back in the right time, with no idea how long he'd been lying in this den of petals. *It was nothing, just the drug.* There was nothing to be afraid of. It was just the drug. It had to be.

'She wants a powerful king for a husband,' said the fox-faced man, his eyes closed in pleasure.

'The prince has no need of a wife,' Tet replied. Not when he had his harem, his innocents. Besides, Tet didn't care about the prince and his future. He cared only about his own. This princess was nothing but grist for the gossips.

'Oh, indeed.' The man stretched, syrup-slow. He smiled at the ceiling, lost in dreams of smoke.

Thoughts of foreign princesses and cruel white princes were packed away, folded smooth. It was time to get to business. 'I'm looking for a man,' Tet said. 'Though I do not know his name.'

'How do you know you look for a man, then?'

Tet laughed the bitter ash taste from his mouth, blew it out and away. 'True. Perhaps I look instead for a monkey.'

The man started, lurching up on one elbow so that he could stare Tet full in the face. 'I wouldn't speak of such in this city,' he said. 'Be careful, stranger.'

After that, he had no more words, and all Tet's attempts to draw him out again fell on silence. Rebuffed, Tet smoked the last of the petal and pondered the lines of the web. An underground figure, as he'd suspected, with his grip on the dens and the seven-petal. Probably on the thieves too. And any of the clockwork mages who needed patronage. The web was vast and delicate. The Monkey was a shadow, with his claws wound in threads.

Tet would have to walk warily if he wanted to bargain well and come out of it with freedom on his own terms.

VII

THE MONKEY'S INVITATION

Hast was growing bored and fat in the stables. In the time Tet had stayed at the garden-house, the mare had unlatched her gate and wandered off almost every day. Twice she'd released all the other horses stabled there. The garden-house servants had just brought her back again after catching her in the neighbouring house's orchard.

Tet leaned over the stable half-door and scratched her ears, which she allowed. 'I'm sorry I've upset you.'

The reason for her current temper stood gleaming in the stable-yard, polished white metal catching the sun and burning in reds and oranges and blues like the surface of an opal. A gift Tet had given himself, bought with his own spoils. Word would reach his benefactor soon. *Let him think about what it might mean.*

'No one will believe I was a merchant-prince if I go riding to invitations on a hill pony, even one as undoubtedly fine as yourself.'

She nipped desultorily, barely missing Tet's hand.

The clockwork horse standing in the yard was a masterwork of the toymaker's combined magery and engineering, made of metal and wood and cogs and silk hair. The clockworkers and the mages had always been at odds. The mages were people of sacred power, blessed by their gods. Tet's mouth twisted at one corner at the thought of being *blessed*.

Perhaps, perhaps not, I prefer to think the gods flock to those of us with power, like bumbling moths to paper lanterns, but that's an unacceptable viewpoint.

The clockworkers were men and women of more limited power; with the minds of engineers, with nimble fingers and an artist's eye. Perhaps that was why the mages hated them so much, Tet mused. They created a mimicry of life out of machinery, made it beautiful, fed it their life force, and pronounced that magic.

Maybe we are scared of their art. In return, they fear us because we remind them of their lack.

Whatever centuries-old reason had driven a wedge between mages and clockworkers, and whatever the priests and nuns had taught Tet, it suited him better to ride to the round of season's parties on a toymaker's mechanical beast than to use Hast.

His invitation was tucked into his shirt. The time had come for Tet to play his first act, and to hunt down this little monkey and end his game of hide and seek. The splintered wood of the stable door dug into his arms as he bent his head closer to Hast's so that no one could possibly overhear him. Tet spoke in the tongue animals understood, the language of magic and mystery. 'Please would you stay in the stables, at least for a while? The servants are beginning to grumble a little too loudly.' Although these were words of command and power, it had been a long time since Tet had used them to do anything more than ask. Being under his own compulsion had softened him.

Hast flicked her ears back and turned her head. The stare was considering. It was unusual for men to ask beasts. After a moment's contemplation, she snorted in gentle agreement.

Tet nodded gravely. 'Thank you, and when this is over, I will sell the abomination, I promise you.'

The clockwork horse ran by winding a key hidden under the fall of its mane. As much as Tet found the automatic beast unsettling, he admired the skill of the clockwork mages. The animal was finely built and richly decorated. The one who crafted it may not have been on the same level as the White Prince's court toymaker, but she'd made tiny additions to emulate a real animal, and the beast did more than merely walk and trot and canter. Occasionally it flicked its head or gave a playful half-buck. Not just machinery, it had the tang of craft under the metal skin. If the Moneky's mage were to ride this beast, Tet suspected even he would have some grudging admiration.

Any other wealthy man would have sold Hast, but as beautiful as Tet's new mount was, as cunningly made, she was cold and hard, and perhaps his training went too deep for he did not like the Pal-em-Rasha mockery of flesh for machine.

There had been more to the intervening days than showing off his wealth, and Tet's hunt for the Monkey had so far not brought any fruit. He had spent his nights dressed in simple travelling clothes, walking among the beggars and the street-workers, dropping coin in the right hands, sharing a petal pipe with gossips and snitches, and not one person had admitted to knowing of the Monkey. Eventually, Tet had altered his approach and asked instead about the hired mage, and again, no one had seen a thief with his right arm cut short at the elbow. Tet had described him as best he could, but either he was a ghost in this city, or the people of Pal-em-Rasha were terrified of what the Monkey might do to them.

While his private search for the Monkey might have come to nothing, Tet had heard unexpected rumours. Some about the princess that wished to become a wife to the White Prince, but also other chatter. The tales had the taste of legends and myths, the sort of thing they collected in the Temple – scrolls and scrolls of prophecy and stories.

But Tet had never heard these ones before.

The beggars waited until the temple women handing out alms left before they would tell Tet stories of a great prince who would turn the whole world to his whim, who would rise from the Underpalace on the back of a dragon, ride into Pal-em-

Rasha and overthrow the White Prince and bring peace to the divided kingdoms. A thief-prince to end the never-ending war. They talked of a secret army of assassins who would rid the city of bloated bureaucrats and war-mad generals.

Even the veteran soldiers seemed to cling to this fancy, desperate for a saviour. They had invented this new myth to give them hope. It was a sign of the slowly turning tide, that the people would cling to the dream of an Underpalace prince to replace the demon that they had now.

Tet had spent many years studying in the temple libraries, whether he wanted to or not. The Temple of Nanak had many records of the White Prince; the words of seers who foretold his pale skin and clockwork armies, who said that he would never fall, even after death.

Of this Underpalace pretender, there were no records.

From what he had gathered, The Underpalace was a city-below to rival the White Prince's city-above, but peopled with thieves and assassins, all of them loyal to the serpent god of thieves, Sinastrillia. Tet snorted. He suspected that to be nothing more than an exaggeration. The Underpalace was likely a loose collection of petty crooks and beggars living off what they could scrape out of the city sewers. And Sinastrillia? Her worship was so discreet that sometimes Tet wondered if she wasn't simply a fabrication. Some idol that thieves had taken in desperation. A man-made god.

He'd heard whispers of how she grew in power, how in the last decade the unwanted children that were meant to go to Nyangist's altars were offered to Sinastrillia instead. If that part was true, Tet definitely wanted no part in it.

When Nyangist stopped playing with the prince's soldiers and turned her attention to the city instead, she would tear the worshippers of Sinastrillia limb from limb. Tet had seen what was done in the name of Nyangist, had seen her great lioness-headed form in the sky, and felt the murderous pulse of her. He was not stupid enough to want to attract her attention.

Whatever rumours the Underpalace spread, it would be foolishness to give them any credit.

*

Vitash's curse had taken a firm hold, adding its agony to Nanak's own festering malediction. By the end of each night, Tet needed all the comfort his seven-petal pipe could bring him. It leavened the pain, but it also served another, more blissful purpose. It made him forget. It smoothed over the black emptiness inside him, covering it away in shrouds of smoke so that Tet could almost forget that he was broken. More than once, he wished he'd been a rich man's son, with an endless supply of seven-petal, and only a passing association with gods.

The masseuse at the garden-house had made herself a tidy sum working at his legs. It hardly made a difference. Each morning he woke, crippled again in his sleep. Until now his pride had kept him from buying a walking stick, but that pride had begun to falter. It wouldn't be long before Tet needed not one stick, but two.

This night, however, he would dance. Tet commanded his legs in the mage tongue and forced them strong and whole for the evening. He would deal with the backlash of pain later.

He refused to face the Monkey limping.

The clockwork horse cantered up to the mansion gates, its metal hooves striking sparks against the cobblestones. Even the jaded servants clustered about it as Tet drew on the reins and brought the machine to a halt. He beat their hands away with his switch. 'You'll leave no finger marks,' he warned them. 'Or I'll have your thumbs as trophies.' He was Ohtet Maynim now, and in his new formal robes of scarlet and black, was ushered into the entrance hall. Tet flashed the invitation to the house-guards, who led him to the humming courtyard.

A flock of bright green parakeets with heads the colour of bruised plums took flight overhead, and the night followed the shape of their wings.

A servant in a short robe plucked Tet's invitation from his fingers and cleared his throat, announcing to no one in particular: 'Ohtet Maynim, of the Maynim family of southern Vaeyane.'

Tet had chosen to seat his fictional home in his own land, near the Deniahn border. That way he technically didn't fall under the rule of the prince, and few would question any minor slips in his accent. No one paid his introduction much notice. A few heads turned with bored disinterest, before going back to their conversations. Nobles and other men and women of rank gathered in clumps, discussing whatever it was that interested them. Money, Tet supposed. Politics, the war.

The White Prince would not be here. The evening's host was a one-time brigadier with a newly-awarded title for his years of service. He was a duke now, of some settlement closer to the border with Vaeyane than he would perhaps have liked. His new lands were in a county rife with highwaymen and other bandits. The White Prince was using him as a buffer, and everyone here knew it. *Doesn't stop them from being jealous at his new rank.*

Tet settled his fiction into his veins and let it flow through him, infusing his personality. He was Ohtet Maynim. A tribe-prince in his own lands, with a beautiful and marriageable daughter. With his head raised and his legs spelled strong, Tet watched the crowd around him pulse and seethe, as it worked its way through the opening moves on the Grand Board. Maket, the game of all players, was repurposed here by nobles, turned intricate and formalised, and so bloodthirsty under its pretty skin. Tet kept a wary eye open for anyone who watched him too long, who perhaps knew there was nothing more to his name than fabrication and borrowed wealth.

A serving girl brought him wine, which he accepted, and food, which he declined. Tet wanted at least one hand free and no chance of crumbs or grease on his clothes. Magic crackled in the spaces of his bones, hummed through his blood. Behind the stone door inside him, the void hissed and seethed, a flood held behind a dam wall.

'Ohtet Maynim?' said a small portly man wearing a deep blue jacket and trousers. His head was smooth-shaven and tattooed with indigo swirls. A sash of emerald announced him as a city-speaker, one of the men who held council with the White Prince and offered him their guidance. A man close to the prince was too exposed to be seen conversing with, and Tet wanted no reasons for the house-guards and secret agents to start paying him careful attention. He would pretend distant civility and hope the bureaucrat moved on soon.

Tet bowed, his heart singing shrill, blood throbbing. He felt too bright, like a rare creature on display. The Monkey or any of his spies could be watching him now, and thinking that he made deals with royal cronies. That Ohtet Maynim was untrustworthy down to his bones. Which he was, but Tet didn't need the Monkey to know that quite yet.

'Ymat Shoom.' The small man held out a hand. Inside his sleeve blinked two round eyes, coin-bright. A tiny monkey peered out, the golden tuft of its head like a fluff of winter grass seeds. 'Saw your beast when you arrived. Marvellous thing. Have always wanted one myself.'

It was him. The promised sorcerer. The Monkey. Tet doused all his previous irritation – he needed to court the man. The Monkey was the key to his emancipation. He grasped the proffered hand, and the monkey scampered out the sleeve, running over their clasped hands to peer at Tet's face before darting back to the safety of its owner's robe. The dry skitter of its little hands and feet was oddly intimate. Tet wondered what it would be like to sit down and converse with it in mage speech.

He wasn't here to have conversations with monkeys, and Shoom was more interested in Tet's metal horse than his own fascinating pet. For now, Tet let him lead the conversation, deep in his pretence of being the rural merchant-prince with more money than sense. This was a dangerous game they played. Monkey or not, Tet still did not want to attract the attention of either gods or court spies.

'It is a marvel,' Tet said of his horse. 'I had heard stories of the clockwork animals, and have always wanted to see them. When fate brought me to Pal-em-Rasha, I decided that fate must also have wanted me to own one.' He shrugged as though the vast expense were only a trifle. 'So it goes.'

'Ah, fate. There's a fickle bitch if ever there was one. Not a religious type, I take it?'

Tet shook his head. Tet-Nanak may have been a priest-mage, but it wouldn't do to follow the wrong god in Pal-em-Rasha. There was only one true god as far as the White Prince was concerned. A god of war, a bloodthirsty image of fang and tawny fur. As Ohtet Maynim, Tet had forsaken his own gods. And he hoped desperately to never have to go back to them. 'Not particularly,' he said carefully, 'though I begrudge no one their beliefs.'

Ymat snorted in amusement. 'No need to pussy-foot here, this may be a temple city, but she is riddled with godless people.' He was laughing, but his eyes were hard, careful.

'And you, Sai Shoom, are you also godless?'

'No sais, please, you can call me Ymat. Call me that fat bastard behind my back though, I find it hurtful when people use it to my face.' He didn't sound particularly hurt. 'And no, I'm not. But parties are no place to discuss religion, unless we are celebrating the start of war, in which case it is the perfect venue.'

'No war. I think we have had enough of that.'

'Certainly.' Ymat Shoom grabbed a pastry from a serving girl's passing tray. A commotion had begun at the far side of the courtyard, an expectant hiss and chatter. 'Ah, I wondered.'

'What's that?'

'It looks like our elusive princess had deigned to come to this little shindig. Marghas will be crowing about it for weeks, the plebeian.'

The head servant's strident tones announced her to the waiting nobles. 'Princess Kani Roiyant of Sinal, and attendants.'

Tet couldn't see the princess, not with the normally uninterested crowd suddenly discovering previously untapped wells of curiosity. Small groups clumped forward to get a better view of this guest. Tet told himself he was not interested in her spectacle. All he wanted was to speak to Ymat plainly, to make their plans for the *ritual-oresh*. However, Ohtet Maynim would have been most fascinated by a foreign princess. With a grimace on his face, Tet turned with the crowd to pretend interest in this new distraction.

From the centre of the circle of nobles rose six elaborate headdresses of red-dyed fur sculpted into obscene crests. The crowd parted for the entourage, and six men strode forward. They were taller and darker than anyone else in the room, and their robes were not the Pal-em-Rasha cut; they were longer, looser, with wide round necks heavily decorated with beading and mirrors. The men's expressions were proud and grim: servants with the faces of emperors. The leading man gave the room a last disdainful glance, then turned and stepped aside so that the princess might walk forward.

Her arms were black, almost shadows against her side, until Tet realised she was wearing long leather gloves that disappeared under the wide sleeves of her dress. The gown was deep emerald, and unlike her servants' clothing, it was cut in the current fashions with some minor changes; the sleeves were short and loose to display her long graceful arms, and instead of the baggy look of the short jackets and loose tunics that the women of Pal-em-Rasha currently favoured, she had belted her robe with a wide sash. Her black hair flowed loosely to her waist.

He took in these details – the donning of the city's style, but repossessed to her individual taste; the unbound hair, scraped back with an assortment of foreign combs and jewels; the leather gloves; the amusement in her mask-white face – and found himself grinning. There was some uncanniness about her that charged the air, as though a mountain thunderstorm was about to tear the heavens apart.

She would certainly get the White Prince's attention, but Tet wondered how long she would be able to keep it. The prince would endure the amusement of her individuality for only so long. And he liked young women, innocent little doves that he could claw at. As far as Tet could see, this princess had left her girlhood behind. She was still lean and coltish, but she would be harder for the White Prince to break. Whatever she offered him as a wife it wouldn't be the same gifts he looked for in the flock of mistresses he kept. Her lean figure best come complimented by vast tracts of land and pits of yellow diamonds.

'Don't even think you'll get the chance to talk to our mysterious princess of Sinal,' said Ymat quietly at his side.

Tet turned from her. 'Eh?'

'So far she's spoken to no one. She has a Voice – a man who talks for her, repeats whatever it was she whispers to him – but that's all. And even then, she doesn't exactly hold conversations with the likes of us.'

'Perhaps her real voice is as hideous as her looks are not.'

Ymat laughed softly. 'Perhaps. A flaw in our heartless diamond, yes, I should like that.'

'You're not impressed by her?'

'Oh, I am very impressed.' His fingers darted forward, pecking a handful of snacks off a passing tray. He popped one of the rice balls down his sleeve. 'But, there is something a little *unusual* about our princess.'

Tet knew what he meant. That storm-prickle, that oily buzz that made the hairs on his skin stand up. He was familiar with it, coming as he did from the temples, but common people wouldn't recognise it. Wouldn't even realise it was there: the taint of heavy magery; of old, old power.

Ymat was a small round man, the type easily dismissed, but he was perceptive and smart, and with no little power despite his apparent status as a simple spokesperson, who would be forbidden by law to accumulate land or titles. He was a sorcerer of Utt Dih, however, or a student of one. Even so, he was not a mage. He would not feel what Tet did.

'Unusual. Yes. Now that you mention it, I feel a certain...' Tet narrowed his eyes. 'Perhaps it is only my imagination.'

Ymat returned his thoughtful stare. 'Imagination and magic. Funny how they should have such similar roots.'

'Funny, yes.'

When they both looked at the princess again, Tet could almost see the threads of magery dancing about her, holding her together. *What was she?* Whatever her truth, she was like him, and the only ones who would recognise it were true mages. In Pal-em-Rasha the toymakers might be thicker than drifts of dirty feathers in a chicken coop and their Floating University might hold all the power, but they had no understanding of Temple magery.

She's one of us, and I have never seen her before. How interesting, this sudden proliferation of mages who should have trained at my own temples, and who have sprung like cicadas from the ground, fully-formed and with no history.

Interesting, and a little unnerving.

The princess took a long-stemmed glass from a servant and her mouth crinkled in amusement. For a brief moment she looked Tet's way, and he wondered if she could see in him the faint traces of his remaining power. Their gazes met, and there was a pull unlike any Tet had encountered before. It was like staring into a reflection and being trapped by his own eyes. Drowning in power.

In the west, they had a story of such a god who fell in love with himself, died staring at the one thing he could not have. And while the princess looked nothing like Tet there was something about her that made Tet think that they were two fictions shadowing each other. They stared because they could sense each other's truths below, like ghost carp moving in flickers and flashes under the mud-dark surface of a mountain river.

Or a more reasonable explanation: Tet had finally and rather unexpectedly gone completely mad.

He stepped back, out of her sight, and wondered what to do – if anything – about this new development. The princess was a flame, and she drew him, but Tet had long ago had his fill of playing at being a moth. Singed wings and broken legs were not worth a dalliance.

'Allow me to buy you a drink, Sai Ohtet,' Ymat said.

Tet glanced around at the milling servants and their trays of wine. 'Buy?'

Ymat snorted. 'Not here. Come, I know a lovely quiet little bar not very far. I think you'll like it. And we have much we should discuss.'

'Do we?' *Finally, the way was clear.*

When Ymat smiled, the monkey mimicked him, and the moon-sliver of its bared fangs flashed in the darkness of Ymat's sleeve.

Tet glanced back once to the Princess Kani. She was watching him leave, her face cold and white, her magic rich and heavy as perfume around her. Even when the gates closed behind them, Tet could still feel her, prickling against his skin. She was a magnet and he was an iron filing, fighting to escape her pull. The longer he stayed in Pal-em-Rasha, the harder it would be to walk away. He needed to get this over with and leave the city as soon as possible.

She was a dangerous woman, and worse: a mystery.

VIII

BARGAINS AND MAGICS

The wine bar Ymat took them to was a small grotto tucked away down a winding little lane hemmed in with high buildings spilling ivy leaves and flowering vines down their walls like writhing waterfalls. The night air was damp and green and touched with ice.

The bar lay down a small flight of stairs. The masks of various minor Pal-em-Rasha house-gods lined the walls and spat water into stone bowls. The splashing followed them, echoing through the narrow pathways. The air was heavy with the smells of strong tea, wine and beer, and seven-petal.

A small boy in simple robes of sky blue led them to their table. The bar was a maze of nooks and sheltered crannies, separated by fountains and swinging paper lanterns in every colour one could think of. Between the dancing light and the competing shadows and the walls of greenery, each little table was given privacy. Conversations were kept secret under the laughter of the water.

'An interesting place,' Tet remarked as they took their seats.

'It's something of a hidden jewel. You can bring us a pipe, and a number-two selection, and tea,' Ymat said to the boy, then raised an eyebrow at Tet. 'You'll take tea? Or something else.'

'Tea suits.'

They waited in wary silence, marked only by the spill of water, the bubble of the pipes and the soft exhale of petal smoke.

The little tufted monkey finally braved its way out of Ymat's sleeve and sat on the table, plucking dainties from the food trays and tasting them with tiny bites.

'A strange pet,' Tet said and thought of Ymat's other pet. A mage. He did not intend to become another one in the Monkey's menagerie.

Ymat took the proffered pipe from the server. 'A thief,' he said. 'Like all my pets.'

'Oh?' The monkey had taken hold of one of Tet's fingers, grasping with its tiny black hand. It looked up at him with owlish eyes that seemed both doleful and hopeful. The wizened face with its ruff of white and black fur was so oddly human in its expressions.

'Don't trust the little monster,' said Ymat. 'It will steal anything not nailed down.' He set the pipe on the table, indicating to Tet that it was his turn. 'Please, relax. Consider me a friend.'

Tet was careful to eat from the platters Ymat had ordered – little finger foods and oily breads peculiar to the city – so that he would not be completely overwhelmed by the drug. Contained like this, seven-petal worked in harmony with his magic, and he had never felt better. A false sense, if ever there was one. Tet was aware of this, and yet he found it hard to hold the thought; it beat between his fingers like a trapped moth, and he let it go. 'So,' Tet said after his mind had stretched comfortably, and the laziness peculiar to seven-petal had eased its way through his limbs. There was no more point in being circumspect. 'The *ritual-oresh*.'

'So plain-spoken.' Ymat looked almost offended.

'I was never one for the Grand Dance.' Let Ymat think him a boor, it suited Tet to guide the man down a coiled path. And he had long since lost patience with Ymat's manoeuvring. Either the man helped him soon, or Tet began to look once again for some other sorcerer. This time he would cross the border into Utt Dih, if he had to. Tet would have to make the choice to leave before he was forced to crawl all the way there.

'I see.' Ymat burbled on the pipe and blew two thoughtful lilies of smoke that drooped slowly above his eyebrows. 'Fine. Then let me speak without veils. We have, I believe, something in common.'

'Do we.' Tet curled his hands into his sleeves and willed away the first faint tracing of pain growing in his knees.

The monkey, which had been dozily grooming itself, started at the small movement but Ymat continued as though he had not noticed. 'The thing you want me to do is rare knowledge, and not to be attempted lightly. I have the means to help you, and in return, I ask for your promise that you will help me.'

Ah, we come to our price at last. 'Speak,' Tet said. 'I would hear what you think you can do before I agree.' A desperate voice railed at him, telling him to shut up and accept the offer. It was a voice borne of a decade of suffering and it took all his will to drown it out. Tet leaned forward. 'Speak,' he commanded again, louder, over the voice in his head, over the slow grating of stone, and the pulse of darkness.

'There is something that the White Prince possesses – a treasure. And I wish to own it.'

'A treasure.' And Ymat wanted him to steal it from the demon himself.

The same damn task his own gods had set for him. He wanted to laugh. Or cry. This was madness. Everyone knew the prince's coffers were guarded by his court toymaker's beasts. There was no chance to get past them, even if his power was back in full force. Shoom's price was as bad as Nanak's. On the other hand, Tet could at least bargain with men. 'You wish for me to steal from the prince?'

The Monkey nodded.

'I think you've come to the wrong man. I am no thief.' *There, let him counter.*

Ymat set the pipe down between them and steepled his fingers. Intensity made him lean forward, his eyes yellow gleams in the dancing lamplight. 'Let me be as clear as I can. Your name is Tet-Nanak, your magic is ruined and you are a cripple. What your god has asked you to do, you cannot, and will never complete on your own. In a few years, maybe more if you are lucky, you will be a withered-up man crawling in the filth, screaming out his agony and shitting himself when the end comes. There is no magic that will keep you from death.'

The light flickered, and all Tet could hear in the following silence was the splash of the fountains. Even the murmur of conversations had died down. Either they were alone in the grotto, or everyone was trying to eavesdrop. A shout sounded from the distant kitchen, followed by a smash of crockery, and then the raised babble of an argument.

'Unless...' Ymat leaned back, and the corners of his mouth shifted minutely. 'Unless I help you.'

Tet's heart was racing and the sweat gathered along his back in slick rivulets.

Ymat pressed on. 'You were once a mage of some considerable skill—'

'No.'

He cocked his head. 'No?' Fat fingers darted forward to reclaim the abandoned pipe, and Ymat and Tet examined each other across the shifting haze of smoke.

One of us is the predator, the other the hunter. We are armed with gun and claw and cunning. We wait for the other to make their move.

A sigh escaped Ymat, like the soft whistle of air from a punctured lung. 'Time is limited, Tet, and I am not a man prone to wasting it. Let me make this simple for you.' He was not smiling. Instead, he looked almost saddened, as though this work pained him on a deep level. His monkey was also giving Tet mournful looks. 'I can give you back your magic and free you from your curse. In return, you will give me your name, and your word as a mage that you will complete this one task for me. I am not unreasonable; I will not keep you tied to servitude.'

Of course, once he had Tet's name, Ymat could do whatever he wanted with him. Not that it mattered either way. The Monkey was not as all-knowing as he believed. He had offered an impossible bargain. But Tet could pretend to be willing. 'One thing. That's all?'

Ymat nodded, his bald, tattooed head shining in the light of the many candles and lanterns.

This time when Ymat dropped the pipe between them, Tet took it. His fingers trembled, but the soothing rush of the seven-petal stroked down his skin, easing shivering muscles. Tet leaned back, warily. 'And I am to trust that you would not turn me over to his Royal Highness the moment the deed is done?' Let Ymat Shoom think he had Tet, at least until Tet had his magic back.

'I do not like to put myself in precarious positions,' Ymat said. 'And I do not like to waste men.' The man would not turn him over, not unless he wanted to be named as a conspirator. Ymat Shoom would not like to be disembowelled and paraded through Pal-em-Rasha on a donkey.

Laughter – insane, manic laughter – sat in Tet's chest like a case of hiccoughs, jarring against his sternum. It was time to find out what ridiculous treasure Ymat would risk himself for. 'And what would this item be?'

'The prince wears a magic breastplate, said to protect him from all enemies. It is this that I need. It cannot be removed, so instead one must find a way to make him take it off, of course.'

'Of course,' Tet murmured. He knew of the breastplate – had almost seen it in person as the White Prince inspected his troops along the border, flashes of pearl brightness under his crimson cloak. He bit down on the manic laughter. 'And how would you like me to accomplish this. Even with my magic returned, the prince is warded and protected by the very thing you wish me to steal. And I do not think he will obey any request I make.' He imagined cordially requesting the prince to strip for him, and almost laughed again.

'Oh, there will be no attack.' Ymat pressed his steepled fingers to his chin. 'I have my own ways of getting to the prince, and of removing his breastplate. You can trust me to oversee the details and provide the means. That is not your concern. Your job is truly a simple one. I need you to do one thing and one thing only.'

'And what is that?'

'It is said, Sai Ohtet, that you have a most singular gift.' Ymat smiled, and around them the night thickened, the sounds of crickets rising to a deafening pitch. 'That you can step into the river of time and hold it still for a few moments.'

Tet froze. 'You are mistaken.'

'I do not think I am,' Ymat said. 'When your magic is returned to you in full strength, you will wait until the prince is suitably un-armoured, and at my command, you will stop time for me, and bring me the breastplate before the gods restart the world.'

An impossible prospect. Tet swallowed. His escape route was being filled in, stone by stone, and despair washed up over him like a river in flood. There was no point in continuing the charade. Someone had told Ymat this thing, and there was no one human who knew it. The gods? But why would they have told Ymat such a thing – unless this was a move on their Great Board. He grimaced, and wished he knew which gods played against which, and who moved the pieces now. 'Your intelligence was not without flaw, *Ymat*.'

'And how is that?'

'I have no name to give you, and so any bargain we make must be built on trust alone.' Tet decided not to mention to Shoom how stopping time had almost killed him, left him raging in a fever for weeks after. He'd been awake for only minutes before he'd been struck down by the backlash. Even with time stopped there would not be time enough for Tet to escape the prince's reach.

'An honest mage.' Ymat smiled. 'How unexpected. Let me return the favour. I already knew as much, I merely wanted to see if you would confess it. Here is my counter; the *ritual-oresh* that frees you from the gods will also bind you to me until I choose to release you. I have no need of your name.' He plucked a sugared plum from the tray and fed it to the monkey. 'There is your dilemma then – you merely need to choose the kinder lord. Men, or gods?'

The sentence was on him, whichever way Tet chose to look. His magic was wearing thin and the pain was spiking up his legs. A fierce and brutal reminder of what was to come. Either Tet could die for the gods, or he would live for Ymat. He would accept, and when he had his power, Tet would find a way to wriggle out of this foolish bargain.

Not all help came in the form of gold and gems. Sometimes it was a sly man with a thankless, forgettable job, who kept thieves as pets.

'Fine.' Tet stood and tossed a handful of coins on the table.

'I have already paid,' Ymat said. 'Fine, what?'

'Let the table servant take it as a tip.'

It was a week's wages for a respectable artisan – possibly more than a month's for the boy. Even Ymat eyed it and flicked his tongue to his upper lip. The monkey darted his hands out to grab one of the coins, less constrained by propriety than his owner.

'We will need to discuss some items,' Ymat said, 'before we may begin the ritual. Though I must inform you that I will need something else from you.'

Of course he does. 'Spit it out.'

'Blood. Not much, of course. A bit of hair and skin, a fingernail paring. See, a very small price.'

Tet narrowed his eyes. *No better than alchemy, like mixing soup from human souls.* 'When do you plan to do this working?'

'I can do it now.' Ymat pulled a small dagger from his sash and handed him the hilt. 'The first part, at least.' Once Tet had taken the blade, Ymat fished inside his robe and withdrew a small leather pouch. From it, he produced a rounded bottle of blue glass, no bigger than two thumbs. 'In here if you please.'

The blade was sharp, and Tet nicked his thumb, squeezing blood into the bottle.

Ymat held it beneath Tet's dripping hand, his own hands steady, a small tight smile crouched in the corners of his mouth. 'Skin.'

Pain was nothing new to Tet, and he pared off a little section of flesh and added it to the mix. The fingernail scrap followed. His hair had not been cut since that day he was shorn and told to leave the temple, and the little lock he sliced off felt oddly liberating. It was a symbol of Tet's defiance of the gods. A sharp pain throbbed through both knees as he cut, but Tet gritted his teeth and did not scream. 'Is that all?

'You will need to be pure in body. Fasted and empty.'

'I will see to it.' He wanted out, away from this damp labyrinth. He wanted clear air, a clear head. His knees were shrieking at him. 'Tomorrow, then?'

'I will send you a message. Make no moves until I do.'

Tet jerked his head once in agreement. He didn't really care anymore. He needed to get somewhere alone so he could howl and sob without witnesses. The magic that had kept him from feeling the full effects of the curses was fading fast and the returning pain was cold and hot, alternating spikes through his bones. *Please. Just ten minutes, Nanak. Vitash. Ten minutes. I need my dignity.*

*

The message arrived after three days. Three days in which Tet devoted himself to spending more money on seven-petal to try and kill the mounting pain, on massages for his ruined knees, and fasting in preparation.

He drank only water. He even, briefly, considered praying – begging the gods for relief with tears rolling down his face. *I am not the mage Ymat wants. My power is broken. My body is broken, please, please, let me be.*

Instead, he dressed with trembling hands in traveller's grey and rode Hast through the city, with his eyes opened now to another world in Pal-em-Rasha. Ymat Shoom had spies, that much was certain, but they were good ones and Tet could not spot who might be following him and who knew his identity. He rode poor reluctant Hast all the way to the grand temple of Nyangist, trying to sort through the jumble in his head.

The bells rang out, dolorous as screaming crows, and the bronze lions that guarded the temple square mocked him with their smiling snarls.

Perhaps it was good fortune that he'd been handed to Nanak's temple. If Tet had been further south when the raid came to his family's caravan, he might have ended up being given to Nyangist. She was not a god with time for orphans, and unwanted children were still ritually sacrificed on her hidden altars at the solstices. Or they had been. Tet frowned and wondered what the god of thieves did with her orphan sacrifices.

He may have been crippled by his gods, but at least they hadn't eaten him.

The thought was not as warming as it should be. *If the path I'm on keeps winding like this, soon I may wish I had been eaten.* Tet sighed and wheeled Hast around and headed to his meeting with Ymat Shoom.

IX

A HIGH PRICE FOR A TRINKET

'**O**nce all this** nonsense is done, we'll travel north, to the mountains,' Tet assured Hast as they passed through the darkened city. 'I think you'd like it there. The trees blossom when we tell them to, and there are dragons in the caves. Sometimes, when they're extremely bored, they come down and talk to us. There's one who is very fond of playing strategy games. Thank the gods that dragons don't gamble with coin or she'd have wiped out all the temple coffers by now.'

Hast picked up the pace, breaking into a spine-rattling trot.

'They don't eat horses.' Tet guided her down a latticework of alleys and streets until he reached the address Ymat's hireling had given him. There was no stabling in this area, so he knotted Hast's reins to a suitable post. 'Sorry, old girl. Not ideal. I hope this doesn't take longer than it has to.'

And what would I know about how long Southern ritual-magic takes? He understood little enough, and had always dismissed it as chicanery. But it was other mages who'd told him that the Southern methods were useless.

Am I scared? Yes. I think so. Fear and stupid hope combined in a fizzing sickness that sat under his diaphragm. A disconcerting feeling of joy and illness. As for the price –

stopping time and stealing from the prince – Tet had put it from his mind. That was a problem for another day.

He stood outside the narrow door of a three-storey building. The door was made of planks roughly hammered together and painted white. The edges of the planks were worn to black wood, and large splinters stood at jagged angles

A distant howl cut through the evening. It was not the familiar singing of the city's slave-dogs, but something wilder, older. Something hunting.

Sudden pain cramped along Tet's right leg, making him stagger forward, gasping. He clutched at the door handle, using it to keep himself upright while bright needles of pain lanced through his muscles, radiating out from the bone. The left leg joined in and Tet almost wept out loud. This was an agony unlike any he had felt before; the worst of his bad days multiplied a thousand times. It was as though someone had taken a jagged-tooth saw to Tet's knees and was severing his legs as slowly as they could. If there were anything left in him to throw up, Tet would have vomited then and there. As it was, all he managed was a little yellow frothy bile. He forced himself to look down, expecting to see blood soaking his trousers, bone pushing clean through raw meat.

Nothing, although his legs were shaking. They crumpled beneath him, twisting and spasming, and Tet fell, split his lip between his teeth, tasted copper and salt.

I will not scream.

The high door screeched open, and Ymat looked down, his eyes hooded by the darkness. 'I was hoping to get this done before your gods noticed.' He sighed. 'We'll have to work fast.' He leaned down and grabbed Tet's arm just under the shoulder, and with a strength Tet had not expected from the little bureaucrat, hauled him bodily across the threshold and dumped him on the cold stone floor.

The door shut, and Tet heard Ymat locking the bolt. 'Can you stand?'

He shook his head. His breath whistled, fingers clawed the cold slabs of rough stone.

'How annoying. I'd already prepared the other room.' Ymat's feet slapped past Tet's face. 'I'll be back, do try and hang on till then.'

Ymat left Tet alone, his sweat-slicked cheek pressed against the floor, fingers curling and clutching blindly. The lower half of his body was consumed in a furnace of pain on pain on pain. He fought to control his breathing, to fall into temple patterns that would centre and calm him, but the pain ripped the air out of his lungs, leaving him gasping.

*

By the time Ymat returned, Tet was close to blacking out.

Something hissed against the wood like a stream of sand grains. Tet tilted his head to see Ymat pour a fortune in rose-pink salt about him, and as the last grain fell into place, the pain lessened, releasing Tet's body like a clamp taken from a wooden beam. He sucked in a deep breath of ice-sweet air.

It worked. Salt. It was not magic or incantations that had hidden Tet from his gods, but salt. A cook's trick. Tet's body loosened, every limb turned floppy and weak as a suckling's. He groaned and rolled over onto his back. The movements were slow and carefully precise; he didn't want to stir up the pain again.

Ymat peered, leaning over him. 'Better?'

Tet nodded in stunned disbelief and raised one shaking hand to wipe away the blood from his mouth, and swallowed coppery spittle.

'It won't last long, I'm afraid. Although if this goes as planned, that won't be a problem you need to worry about for a while.'

'If?' Even though the little trick with the salt had worked, Tet was still not totally convinced of the veracity of southern magic. And what did Ymat mean by "a while?"

'When. Now, don't distract me. I've prepared your essences.' Ymat held out a jar as though Tet could understand what he had done. 'You need to lie absolutely still for this part.'

Tet was about to ask him if it would hurt. And then he laughed.

So what if it does?

Ymat stepped into the salt ring and held the jar over him. He was speaking in an unfamiliar language. Though the words and rhythms were not ones Tet knew, here and there a fragment sparked some forgotten memory, enough to know that Ymat was probably speaking one of the tribal tongues of the hill people of Utt Dih. Ymat Shoom was no Pal-em-Rasha native, that was certain. He'd hidden it well, so well that even Tet had taken him for a native of the city. And the southerner had carved himself a place in her courts, had the ear of her prince. He was an enemy wearing the face of a friend, hidden in plain sight. Tet's respect and wariness grew in equal measure.

Ymat tipped the jar and poured a steady trickle of a viscous liquid down Tet's body, from temple to feet. Some of it ran into the corners of his mouth, and Tet tasted oil, salt, bitter herbs. Despite the tickling itch as the liquid ran down his skin, he did not flinch.

A pulling sensation began in his sternum, as though something large and wet was slowly being tugged loose from his body. Tet swallowed convulsively. *Stay still, stay still.* The tug grew harder. More insistent. A meaty force pushed against Tet's ribs, spreading the bones apart from the inside.

The urge to scream built, and sweat ran down from his temples as Tet gritted his teeth. Cold nausea rushed through him. The pain was different from the spiking, rusty ache of his legs. This was deep and solid, as though Tet was giving birth to something terrible. The thought made him bare his teeth like a frightened dog, and he could feel laughter pushing alongside the pain. Insane laughter. Nothing about this was the slightest bit amusing.

'Not much longer,' Ymat said.

Oily writhing smoke burst from Tet's chest. It twisted up toward the ceiling before curling in on itself. A moment later the pain snapped, with the sound of a heavy stone door being smashed shut, leaving him empty and dizzy. The smoke-thing lurched this way and that, battering at the walls of its invisible prison, unable to move beyond the salt lines.

Tet was hollowed out, a melon scooped clean down to the bitter rind. He felt battered, pulpy, and small and insignificant and for a moment he wanted to scream at Ymat to stop, to reverse it all but he couldn't even summon the energy for that.

One year when he had still been a priest-mage, one of the temple bitches had whelped in Tet's bed. He'd woken to a litter of blind and squirming bloodied things lying at his feet. They were helpless as maggots. He felt like them now – soft and weak and faintly repulsive. Anyone could crush his skull if they chose.

Ymat barked at the smoke in his foreign tongue, his tone obviously ordering, and held out the little jar. After a few wavering moments, the smoke-thing flowed into the jar. Tet had no idea how it crammed itself into such a minute vessel, but on it poured and poured until there was no trace of it left. Ymat sniffed and shook the jar. It rattled, a pebble-rattle, small and empty and unexpected.

'Oh very good,' Ymat said to himself, smiling in soft pleasure. Then to Tet, 'You can move now.'

'What exactly did you do?' Tet thought he already knew, and he didn't like it. His emptied body quivered, little spasming aftershocks. He knew what he'd lost. What he'd given away.

'So many questions, Sai Maynim.' Shoom clicked his tongue against his teeth and spared Tet a twisted smile. 'Does it matter, considering the gift I've given you?'

'Of course it does.'

He sighed, rattled the vessel again. 'It's your *oresh*. And such a grand one you have.'

Tet's stomach convulsed. *Oresh*. 'I do not know the meaning of the word,' he said to Ymat, who simply looked at him and shrugged.

'And here I thought you a lettered man.'

The pain was still under control – no, better than that, negligible – but that could be down to Ymat's circle of salt. Tet ignored his little dig and pulled one leg up, catching his knee and hugging it to his chest. Then he eased it down and repeated the process with the other. It had been years since he could do that, could get his knee even halfway to his chest without his whole face twisting from the agony, breath coming short and sharp.

It was easy. There was no strain, no *wrenching twisting cracking* running through his bones and muscles. *Please, please, let this be real. Let this not be a trick.* 'It's done?'

'So it seems.' Ymat tipped the jar over his left hand and caught something small in his palm.

A knock sounded at the door and Tet staggered to his feet.

'Ah, just in time.' Ymat curled his fist tight around the thing he'd taken from the jar

oresh

and stepped past him.

'Make yourself presentable. We have a guest.' He didn't seem in the least worried, so Tet brushed the stone dust from his trousers and boots, and eyed the ring of salt crystals. *It's either do this now or spend the rest of my presumably short life hiding behind a line of salt.* He drew a deep breath and stepped over it, expecting to be struck down in incomparable agony as Vitash and Nanak realised what he'd done.

Nothing happened. His legs stayed strong and firm. He was whole. Quickly, Tet untucked his right trouser leg from his high boots and rolled the loose material up to check the curse scar. The mark was still there and the twisted mass of scars was still gouged deep into his flesh, but the constant gnawing curse-pain had stopped.

All that was left was the tight ache of healed muscle. Tet flexed his leg. *Unbelievable. For this, I will steal Ymat a thousand magic breastplates.*

'Through here,' said Ymat, and returned with a wiry little man behind him. The man was short and carried himself with an arrogant grace. His dark eyes were sharp as he glanced this way and that, taking in the room. He sported a fine, neat moustache, carefully shaped with marrow. Finally, his gaze settled on Tet, and he nodded, just the smallest acknowledgement.

'Sai Tiger,' Ymat said, waving one hand at the newcomer. 'And Sai Hound.'

'We are enemies then,' said the Tiger, curling his top lip in wry amusement. It made his little moustache look even more ridiculous.

'Sai Hound was until very recently a priest-mage of the dog-temple.'

'Ah,' said the Tiger. 'I take it you've had a crisis of faith?'

Tet canted his head. 'Something like that. And you are?'

'A man of little sentiment.' He bowed, a mocking dip. 'I am my own god, and a maker of clockwork beasts and curiosities.'

Ymat coughed. 'Sai Tiger is here to perform a mechanical binding for us.' He held out his closed hand, opened it like a flower.

In response, the Tiger craned his neck, his eyebrows rising just the slightest. 'Fascinating.' He plucked the thing between forefinger and thumb and brought it up to one eye. 'I take it you've performed the *ritual-oresh*? I thought it was impossible, not to mention illegal.'

'I was curious.'

The Tiger flicked a glance toward Tet. 'Well, he's still alive, and more than that, still standing. Is he sane?'

'Perfectly,' Tet interrupted, before glaring at Ymat. He would not give in to terror. Perhaps it was safer tied to the gods. Sweat dampened his skin, but Tet held his head high and pretended to feel no fear. 'You never mentioned exactly how risky this was supposed to be.'

Ymat tried to look contrite, then gave it up as a waste of time. 'You never asked.' He grinned, and Tet was reminded of his little monkey, how it bared its teeth in a parody of a human smile. 'You were a man blinded by pain.'

And pain could make a man choose terrible futures.

'So,' the Tiger continued. 'His magic is now completely gone?'

Tet froze, his insides turning to churning river water. The relief from pain had so overwhelmed him, he hadn't even realised exactly what price he'd truly paid.

Oresh, the Monkey had called it, a southern word for something so much a part of Tet that it was sometimes the only thing about himself he considered real.

Oresh. He had initially thought it little more than a corruption of the word *oreshamin* – trickery – a way of fooling the gods. And he'd let himself be blinkered by his own desperate hope. What one man calls trickery, another calls power, and still others call *soul*. It was this power that flowed through all human lives, and in the end, was finally reborn in a new skin with a new name. That was what magic was. Power and eternity and the flame of life force. And Tet had handed his over to Ymat Shoom.

There was nothing inside him. Instead of the flow of potential running along the power lines of his body, Tet was solid, mundane, utterly, utterly human in his nothingness. Less than that, even, because even the mundane still had souls. When he died, he would not be sent to the cavern of shades where the twenty-one spirits of the dragon ancestors waited to guide the dead who were ready to leave the after-world and be reborn.

If he died without a soul, he was doomed to nothingness.

'What—' Tet's voice was weak, broken. He swallowed past the horror and tried again. 'What have you done?'

'Would you like to see?' Ymat said, and he held out the vessel to Tet like a temple offering.

X

ORESH

Tet rolled the small black pebble gently back and forth in his cupped hands. The surface glimmered with an oily shimmer. This was his magic.

'The *oresh* spell-working forces the incorporeal to take a physical aspect,' Ymat explained. His voice seemed to come from very far away. 'What you hold there is a solid manifestation of your soul. Interesting, don't you think?'

'Why?' Tet managed.

'It's simple. Surely you understand?'

Tet shook his head. Truthfully, Tet had spent all his years growing up learning and believing that what priest-mages did was the only true power. Magic ran through them. They used it to change themselves, change the natural world. They had never had much time for the machinery of the toymakers, or the blood and bodily parts and esoteric chanting of the south. Foolish, maybe, but mages were still human.

'You have great power contained within your soul and your name. That is why you are important – not because you have done anything worthy of praise, but rather because the gods have noticed you. The gods don't see humans as physical beings. Our little flesh shells are of no interest to them. What they concentrate on is the thing inside. The soul. Mages like yourself use your souls for magic.'

Tet had heard similar philosophies before, but he kept quiet, letting Ymat Shoom talk.

'When the soul is vast you have more power to use, but eventually you wear that power thin and you become like the rest of us, and then you die. Gods are only interested in you because for the moment you burn brighter than other men, they see you better.'

'A likely tale.'

The Tiger smiled. 'If that's what you choose to believe, dog-priest. What Sai Monkey has done is remove your soul. I will use my art to hide it in metal and stone. Think of it as covering a lamp with a shade. The gods cannot see you now.'

'And what they can't see,' added Shoom, 'they cannot toy with. For the moment, little mouse, you are safe from the claws of bored cats.'

Tet curled the stone close and held it to his chest. It was his heart, and Tet willed it to beat. To be alive. 'This is blasphemous.'

'Perhaps,' said Ymat. 'But you walk. Sai Tiger will give you the means to access your magic without alerting the gods. You'll need to keep the stone against your skin at all times.'

'Why?'

'Think of it as a temporarily amputated limb. We can reattach it, but not if it dies first.'

'I don't understand.' Here Tet had thought he was a priest-mage, that the world was as he understood it and ran on the rules he had learned, and now his entire universe was rearranging itself around him without a thought to how Tet might feel about it. Tet was like a child discovering that everything he knew was wrong. 'Re-attach.'

'Eventually the soul will need to be returned,' said the Tiger. 'A separation can only be temporary. The longer your soul is kept from you, the further away it is kept, the sooner your death will come knocking.'

Tet closed his eyes briefly. All he had bought from his alliance with Ymat was a momentary respite and a cage to spend it in. He was a fool. Now that the pain had dropped from him like a shed skin, Tet was thinking clearly for the first time in ten years. It was easy now to see how he had been manipulated and lied to. He'd thought himself so clever, but he'd been caught, and the only thing he could do now was manoeuvre a path through this prison he had caught himself in. To use the time Ymat had given him to free himself. On his own terms.

His breath was cold in his chest but Tet stayed calm, willed his heartbeat slower as though he were once again a boy in the temples learning to meditate. 'I'm certain I don't want to hear why it must be temporary, but tell me.'

'Have you ever watched a soulless man slowly dying?' said Ymat. 'I have. Trust me, you want to do the things you have promised, and return to normal.' He spread his hands. 'And do not think of using your power against me. If you think once Sai Tiger finishes the working that you can strike at him like a snake, you would be wrong. I have bound you close.'

Tet nodded, numb. 'Fine.' There was no point in being angry or scared now. It was too late. Focus, that's what he needed. 'How are you planning to let me use my magic?'

The Tiger held out his hand. 'I'll need the soul and some privacy. Give me an hour.'

Tet released his soul into a stranger's care, a stranger's manipulations.

'Come.' Ymat clapped one hand on his shoulder. 'You'll be feeling drained. There's food waiting for you. Eat, drink. Sai Tiger will not have it long.'

*

Alone with Ymat, Tet sat silent while the man busied himself with tea. The house was ramshackle and poorly furnished, but the roughly plastered kitchen walls were lined with shelves and glinting pots, and for a moment it seemed like any other home in the city.

There was no cooking fire burning, no family gathered, but Ymat lit a small fire at the hearth and set a kettle to boil. Moonlight fell through the rows of small windows, and Ymat's shadow danced and bulged across the walls as the flames guttered a little in the droughts.

It was only a little magic to make the fire flare brighter. A child mage could do it. *Vlam*, Tet whispered under his breath. *Vlam!* Though he willed it until his temples were slicked with cold sweat, the flames did as they pleased. Tet felt emptier than ever, a sick man woken from a week's fever dreams. He'd last felt this terrified and drained ten years ago, when he'd done the impossible and almost burnt himself out by fracturing time.

Then, he'd been sick from the sheer amount of magic he'd used. Now he was soulless, a demonic thing. Cursed. Nothing the gods could ever do to him was as bad as what he had allowed others to do now in this house.

If I die...

'Here,' said Ymat, his voice almost kindly. 'You look as colourless as the prince himself. Drink.' He held out a bowl of tea, in the eastern style. It was red and fragrant.

'Thank you,' Tet said dully, by rote.

'Forgive me, Ohtet,' Ymat said, very softly. 'I assure you we will not keep you and your soul parted for longer than is necessary. The prince's war must end, and this was the only way we could see it. There are greater stakes here than the life of one rogue mage.'

His last traces of anger fizzled out like a candlewick clamped between a spit-wet forefinger and thumb. It was not Ymat's fault that Tet hadn't questioned what exactly the man was planning on doing. His hubris had led him here. Hubris, and a little bit of hope.

A terrible combination.

His hands were still clamped around his bowl of hot tea when the door swung open and the Tiger sauntered in, grinning, and swinging a glittering beetle from a fine chain like a pendulum. Tet slopped burning tea across his knees as he stood, and set the bowl down.

'And?' Ymat drawled.

'It is done.' The Tiger tossed the beetle toward Tet, who caught it instinctively. 'Put it on.'

The *oresh*-pebble was different now. It had been set in wire and slivers of beaten metal so that it mimicked one of the copper-brown chafers that set summer groaning with their buzz and bustle. The stone itself was undamaged, as far as he could tell, but it had been harnessed to machinery.

Tet shuddered, but he slipped the chain over his neck and let the stone settle against his chest. It was hidden under the neck of his shirt, throbbing against his skin. The beetle flinched and Tet yelped as it dug its spike-ended claws in deep, connecting the two of them.

The joining brought him back his soul. Almost. The magic was in there. Oily, squashed, wanting to be free. But it was his. All of it.

'Can you feel it?' The Tiger asked.

Yes, there. The Tiger had harnessed the stone and added tiny gears, clockwork and metal and springs to the body around it. 'I can feel...something.'

Ymat snorted. 'Perform us a trick, Sai Hound.'

A trick. Like a performing monkey. Tet glanced over to him and wondered just how many people and pets he owned. 'What would you have me do?' Though his voice was steady as he could keep it, inside he trembled. If he failed, then all of this would be for nothing. Tet would have had one evening without the gods' cruelty, an evening tempered only by fear and the capriciousness of mages.

'Light more candles. This room is too dark.'

Tet nodded and took a deep breath, gathering the magic inside him. The feeling of power shifting within was gone. The stone doors and their great void were still there, but unreachable, like a vision that kept moving into the distance. No. This was not how it worked any more. He focused instead on the thing at his chest, the deep claws. The power throbbed, and *there*, he pulled it down the six tiny channels of its legs, sucking it into the emptiness. The power was strangled, but pure. It was his magic and it was untainted by the curses of gods.

The room flared, every unlit candle shooting from its wick a flame a foot high. The light supernovaed, casting the two men as small burnt shapes before the flames settled.

They may have been standing in a plain kitchen room, the walls streaked with dirt, the dust thick on the floor, but the Tiger and Ymat were dressed in their finery, two princes in exile. They looked at each other. Ymat clapped his hands in a slow applause, while the Tiger smiled thin and sly.

'And now,' Ymat said, 'you will not speak again.'

'Wh— ' The numbness hit him, heavy as a mallet to the back of his skull, spreading down through his bones. Tet's stomach twisted in on itself like a snake in its death throes. He staggered forward, catching at the edge of the kitchen table, rocking it and sending the empty tea bowl flying to the floor where it shattered. He gagged, but he was empty – both in soul and body. Words blanked from his head and he choked, spittle hanging from his mouth in fine silver threads.

'Enough,' said Ymat. 'I merely wanted to prove a point.' He crouched down to gather the broken bowl, balancing the shards in the palm of his hand. 'You may have your voice back.'

Tet coughed. Glared.

'Come now, Sai Hound, I could not set you free into the night without at least making certain you knew the length of your chain.' He took the broken pieces to the table where he dropped them in a small pile. 'The bowl is like a man,' he said. 'Once it is broken, it is good for nothing. I don't intend to waste you, but I need you to understand that I can break you as easily as you broke this.'

His speech was coming back to him now. Tet swallowed hard to clear his throat, which still felt as though it had been stoppered with a clot of dirty wool. 'I gave you my word that I would help you. There was no need for this.'

'Oh, on the contrary. There was every need. This way you will not waste your time trying to devise ridiculous attempts to move without my order. I hold you, Sai Hound. Do not forget it.'

As if Tet could. Ymat couldn't take his will from Tet, but he could curb that will with no more than a simple command. For the moment, Tet was completely at his mercy. Any steps Tet took against the Monkey now would have to be small and careful.

'Go home,' said Ymat. 'Rest, and in the morning, we will introduce you to your daughter and give you further instructions.'

His daughter. Tet had almost forgotten that part of the fiction Ymat bade him create. He'd dismissed it as detail, an afterthought. But now it seemed there were other acts to play before he reached the prince and

stopped time.

Tet let himself be directed by Ymat's guiding hand. The door closed on them, and he felt nothing but a dull emptiness.

No pain.

Nothing.

*

Hast was skittish all the way back to the garden house, shying at shadows and dancing sideways at every gust of wind. She felt the wrongness in her rider, but couldn't understand what had happened. Tet patted her neck. 'It's all right, girl,' he said as The Lime Grove drew into view.

She responded with a nervous buck.

Even the servants looked at him strangely when Tet dismounted and handed them the reins. Or perhaps it was simply because he'd chosen to ride a ragged old mountain mare instead of his shining clockwork monster. Or maybe it was the clothes.

Stop being so paranoid, Tet. He stopped in his silent conversation with himself. Was he really still Tet-Nanak? Cut

111

off from his gods, he had become less than nameless. And besides, hadn't he agreed on a new fiction?

'My name is Ohtet Maynim,' Tet whispered to himself as he climbed the stairs, but the words were dry and papery, and the name would not stick.

He shoved open the door to his suite, pulled at the magic trapped in the beetle amulet, and with a flick of his fingers, lit the room's hanging lanterns. 'I am Sai Ohtet Maynim,' he said out loud.

'Well met,' answered a girl, her voice soft as the down lining of a nest. A figure about a head shorter than Tet, lithe and thin as an acrobat, came lashing through the space between them.

It's said that time slows before one dies. Time does not slow. Tet saw only a flash of brightness, the lamplight dancing off a blade, the whip of the girl's hair as she turned her head, and he moved, the stone door in his mind swinging half-open, the rage and fear behind it seething out.

The spikes in his skin bit deeper, pulling into the meat and bone of his sternum. Magic hissed down invisible lines. Tet opened his mouth, and the word rolled out like a wall of power. '*Stil.*'

The girl stopped so fast Tet heard the crack as her neck broke. She dangled for one moment. A puppet. Her expression was confused, as if the meat had not yet realised it was dead.

She dropped. Her corpse thumped on the soft carpet, sinking a little into the thick wool pile. Her hand released its grip on the silver dagger.

Tet stepped back and the scene crystallised, the shadows shifted around him, and, 'Well met,' said a soft girlish voice.

Gods, it's happening again, and just as he thought *this time, oh gods this time I will not kill her* the spikes of his soul-beetle slid through his skin sharp as needles, flooding him with fear and magery, and his mouth opened of its own accord and he couldn't stop it from happening.

'*Stil.*' His voice echoed.

The bones in her neck cracked.

The dagger fell from her hand.

The stone door rolled shut.

The room was very quiet. Outside a cricket restarted its chirping song. Tet could hear his breath, soft and measured. He had not even broken a sweat.

Another time skip.

Carefully, slowly, he edged towards the corpse and knelt down. Tet knew she was dead, but even so, he checked her breathing, hoping for some flicker beneath her eyelids. Nothing, naturally. He had killed her twice.

She was small and olive-skinned, her hair braided in many fine thin whips each no wider than a mouse's tail. Instead of the usual loose over-robe tucked into wide pants that was the city fashion, she wore a plain dark grey tunic and leggings, simple and close-fitting. The uniform, if one wanted to call it that, of an Underpalace assassin. The uniform of rumours and shadows.

Tet pressed his fingers to the hollow of the girl's throat. There would be enquiries. Explanations. Why would a woman from an organisation that didn't exist want to kill a bumbling drug-addled merchant? An over-fed merchant-prince might be robbed in the streets – but assassinated? *Oh no.* His fingers trembled, a whisper away from the bell chord.

The body needed to go.

Tet knew of only one quick and quiet method of disposal, one that would leave no traces. It was a death ritual sacred to the priest-mages; reserved only for the holy dead. Tet snorted. What was one more act of blasphemy now?

Quickly, he stripped the girl, folding her clothes in a small, neat pile. She'd been born a boy, and her back and belly were pocked and disfigured with scars from some childhood disease. He tried to look past her as he touched the cooling flesh. Tet couldn't even ask her for her forgiveness. She'd meant to murder him, he knew, but he had never been a killer.

Liar.

Liar.

Liar.

It was hard to argue with one's own inner voice.

'Fine,' Tet said the words out loud, softly into the room. 'I have not been a killer for a very long time, and then only once.' When the girl was naked, he rolled her onto her back. 'I'm sorry,' he said to her. 'At least it will be quick.' And it was a ritual with dignity. Perhaps the only time the girl had been shown any honour.

Tet sat back on his haunches and touched his fingers to the magic trapped in the stone. It pulsed, warmed.

This should be safe enough, at any rate. Tet was not going to talk to the gods. Instead, he was going to talk to the dead. Dead dragons. They had names; the nine fathers, the twelve mothers, and he knew them all, had spent years chanting their names in time with his breathing, invoking them. He began with Mil, firstborn, and ran through them in order. The names of all the original world-serpents, the first to walk the cooling surface of the planet. The first speakers, the first hunters, the twenty-one first men from which all men come.

The race of dragons had fallen now – no greater and no lesser than any other – but these twenty-one spirits still ruled the caverns of the dead. They passed judgement and guided the spirits on to their next lives when they were ready to return again to the flesh. Mages could call them briefly into this world, but had no control over them, and no mage could trespass into the world of the dead. Not if they wished to live. There were some that believed it possible to step briefly across the border between worlds and speak with the spirits, but no mage who attempted such a journey had ever returned.

Speaking to the dead was magic even the temple-mages did not possess, no matter what half-truths common men believed.

One by one, the twenty-one dragon spirits slipped into the room, materialising from the walls and floor and ceiling. Grey shadows, flashes of coloured scales. Their great yellow eyes like floating gas lights. They coiled around the corpse.

Tet gave her to them, as the ritual demanded, and in moments her body was shrouded under the shifting layers of their smoke coils. The minutes passed slowly, but finally the dragon-spirits returned to their realm. They left nothing of the girl assassin behind them. Not a hair nor a fingernail. Nothing but the small and pathetic crumple of her clothes on Tet's lap to show that she had ever existed.

But body or no body, the girl's attack raised a serious problem. His fiction as Ohtet Maynim must be wearing thin if someone already wanted him dead.

XI

LAKETRI

Sleep, when it finally came, was fitful and uneasy. Tet was not attacked again, and time didn't skip about like a child set free from its lessons. Both were worrying in their way. They loomed over him like bad promises.

Tet fumbled instead with his magic, learning to use it unhampered. He was stronger than he'd been in a decade, but accessing the magic through the *oresh*-beetle was awkward and slow, like relearning how to walk. He spent the next few days flexing his power, lighting and relighting candles with a word, moving the pillows in his suite across the room, tossing them back and forth, and finally abandoning them on the bed in a pile. The actions of a child just learning to control his strength.

While Tet waited impatiently for Ymat Shoom to send word again, he made careful plans, redoubling his efforts to track down Ymat's pet mage without drawing Ymat's attention. That's what Tet was now – another pet. The thought rankled. But it was not the only reason he stayed away from his suite of rooms at the Lime Grove. As Tet wound his way through Palem-Rasha's narrow streets, her bustling markets and shaded alleys shrouded in the heavy smoke of the petal dens, he kept a watchful eye open. People were following him.

Or at least, he thought they were. Perhaps he was becoming paranoid.

Tet took a seat on the upper balcony at an open-air tea shop with small square tables; only a few of which didn't already have maket boards set out, the pieces ready for play. Most of the other tables were taken by old men, women, and those who were neither and both, the round bowls of their pipes stuffed with tobacco and mint, their eyes narrowed in seams of wrinkles as they stared at the boards and moved the ivory tiles in an arrhythmic clack under the roof of stretched yellow silk.

It had been years since Tet had played a proper game of maket. In the army, they'd played a modified version using no board and only a handful of the major tiles, but these were full sets, with the elaborate boards marked out and finely illustrated. Some even had gold edging and inlaid mother-of-pearl.

It made him think of his years in the temple, playing against the dragon. Like all dragons, she'd been a master of strategy and almost always won every game she played against human mages. He didn't learn strategy from her. He'd learned how to lose gracefully. And she'd taught him songs. The soft click of the tiles made him long for the taste of millet beer and the feel of his lute strings under his fingers, the resonance of his body with the correct notes, losing himself in learning the songs the dragon sang.

It also reminded him that the game they played was an approximation of a far longer and greater game – men as ivory pieces, the world as the board, gods as players.

Tet was just another maket piece. But which one? Not the Emperor, not a prince or a dragon, certainly. He'd like to think himself more than one of the pieces in the four suits of arrows and cups and coins and caravans. That left only the middle-rank tiles, each with its own movement and ability and strength.

A wind tile, he thought; unpredictable and powerful only in certain limited attacks. A useless tile unless one held the correct accompaniments. *And then. Oh, and then, you could take out an entire army with it.* Tet watched the nearest game, absorbed, and he only noticed the girl when she took the seat opposite him.

'Ohtet Maynim,' she said.

Tet jerked back, spilling expensive imported southern tea from the Ten Thousand Island Heaven Kingdom over the table. A waitress appeared at the table so quickly and silently it was almost magic, blotted the spill, then whisked away his empty bowl.

The girl opposite him smiled patiently while the waitress brought Tet a fresh bowl of tea and the same order for her.

They sat in silence, Tet's heart hammering against his ribs. *Was this another assassin?* She didn't look the part, and they were in broad daylight, in a public place. Whoever had sent the Underpalace girl would be insane to have him killed here. Even though Tet knew this, and he had the full power of his magic back, it took a few moments before he'd slowed his heart, his breathing.

He stared at her – a pretty enough girl, with a wide-cheeked, innocent face, red as a copper kettle, and her dark hair unbound in the manner of common girls of Pal-em-Rasha.

'Don't look so terrified,' she said.

'Who are you?'

The girl sighed and tapped her fingernails against the side of her porcelain tea bowl.

'One of the Monkey's spies?' Tet raised an eyebrow.

'And what a dreadful spy I would make,' she said. 'No. Though I am one of his pets.'

'Ah.' Tet leaned back in his chair and scanned the little balcony, the tables of elderly men and women. No one seemed to be paying them any attention. The tiles shifted, moved into place by wizened hands.

The girl tipped her head forward and said, very softly, 'We are, of course, being spied upon right this moment.'

'Of course.'

'But every pair of those eyes belongs to our mutual friend.'

Every pair – as in, more than one spy. He was outplayed in this city.

'I'm Laketri,' said the girl, 'though you may call me Anestra.'

'Anestra.' Tet turned his tea bowl, uncertain exactly what she wanted.

'Or daughter, if you prefer.' Her smile was very beautiful. It put him in mind of the grinning thief mage at the traveller's camp, though softer and sweeter. Her smile turned her already pretty, round face into a lamp in the darkness. 'I'm afraid that our mutual friend can make no more open movements right now. You must trust me, and do exactly as I say until he can contact us again.'

'And what an idiot you must take me for, Daughter dearest, if you think I will dance to the tune sung by a complete stranger.'

Her smile grew thinner, more brittle. 'I too am on a leash, Father. Do not think otherwise. I have my own debts to pay. Now, we should go back to your suite where it will be easier for us to talk.'

Easier, and safer. Laketri – Anestra – might think that the only spies around them were those belonging to Shoom, but even she could not be certain of it. Tet made no move to leave, sipping his black tea spiced with cinnamon, and watching her carefully over the steam. He nodded to the boards. 'Do you play?' He wanted a single game against her. A short one, just to get some measure of who it was he was dealing with.

The girl scowled. 'I learned maket.'

It didn't answer his question, but they were already playing, she just hadn't realised it. 'I do. I was taught by a dragon,' he told her. 'She was an excellent teacher. I never won a game.'

Laketri peered at him. 'How does that make her a good teacher?'

'She never let me for one moment forget that I was no one in the grand scheme of things – that there were always better players on the board, and sometimes that the best player appears to not even be playing.'

'Gods.' She rolled her eyes. 'You sound like Sinastrillia— '
Her mouth snapped shut. 'I've no time for games, Sai Maynim.
I was told that should you prove reluctant, I had only to say
oresh, and you would listen.'

Tet wanted to start laughing. He set down his unfinished tea
and left a handful of coins next to the bowl. 'You're right, our
talk will be pleasanter in more comfortable surroundings.' He
stood. 'Besides, I grow bored of watching others play maket.'

*

Anestra explained what Tet was to do. Ymat's instructions were
simple enough, though it seemed like the plan of a mad man.

'This is ridiculous,' Tet told her. 'It has never been my skill
to rework people's memories. Ymat knows this, and besides, it
was not the task we agreed on.'

Anestra shrugged.

'And you should not be willing to let me do this to you – it's
abominable to even think of it.'

'I have my own reasons, Maynim, and I don't need your
judgement or advice,' she snapped back at him. 'Trust me when
I say that I'm no actor and that the memory charms are for my
protection as well as yours. It's the only convincing way I'll play
your daughter.'

This was Ymat's plan to get close to the prince, then. Tet was
to pose as the father of a little dove – another toy for the White
Prince's harem. It was the prince's one weakness that Ymat felt
he could exploit. They would get this daughter into the prince's
bed chamber, while Tet waited, like a dutiful father, for his
liege to deflower her.

And then he would stop time.

Anestra didn't know that last part; she had merely been
informed that when Tet rewrote her memories, he was to
ensure she was to give a prearranged signal when the prince
was suitably under-dressed, and Ymat and Tet would take care
of the rest.

'Idiocy,' Tet said. 'And what if it goes wrong?' *As if it could go any other way.* The sound of donkey hooves echoed in his memory – the mutilated body that had been all that remained of the prince's entertainment. That mangled corpse had tried to steal the prince's power and failed. Had they been another of Ymat's pets – a trial run to gather information? Sweat dried cold on Tet's skin, and he shivered. 'We will die.'

Anestra's face was hard and scared. 'I would prefer we not think like that. Ymat assures me that you are very powerful and that you will be able to do this. That you will do as he had ordered.'

He was right about that last – thanks to the *ritual-oresh* Tet was finally powerful. And controlled. 'Gods damn them all,' he whispered. 'He cannot want me to remake your memories. It's abominable.'

She sighed. 'And I do not want it either, but it's a necessity to get past the guards on the prince's wing.' She was right about that much – the prince's chambers were guarded by the strange beasts made by his toymaker. The machines would not be fooled by humans nor magic tricks. If Anestra was to get safely past them, she would need to truly believe she was the daughter of a merchant-prince, a girl destined for the bed of the ruler of Pal-am-Rasha.

His head had begun to ache. *Fine, fine.* Tet breathed in deeply. He could do this; he had to. Anestra's step into the prince's rooms was also his chance to recover the opals that Nanak wanted. When the Monkey finally released him from the *ritual-oresh*, Tet knew he would have to be ready to face his own gods and fulfil the terms of his curse. Or one of them, at least.

Tet needed to look at his time with Ymat as a blessing, not a cage. 'I will do it,' he said. There was no point in telling Anestra what exactly he planned to plant in her head. She certainly didn't need to know that he would make Ymat's puppet girl dance for two masters.

*

Giving Anestra a series of false memories was delicate work, but once Tet focused, the time passed quickly.

She lay on her back on the bed. Tet sat alongside her, close enough to hear the soft wing-beat of her breathing, count the flickers of fear in her trembling eyelids. Her temples were warm under his palms.

His strengths had never been in memory and dream – there were mages who specialised in this kind of thing, and for all his raw power Tet had never been skilled enough to be one of them. Still, he'd had sufficient training to do this, though it would take him all night and more power than Tet would like to think about.

'A small cost,' Tet told himself, to assure that Anestra would be the perfect actor in this drama. Her pulse slowed, began to match his own, and as the rhythm of their heartbeats synched, he let the power pull through from the *oresh*-beetle dug into his chest. The magic came through stilted, stale, like water kept too long in a leather pouch. Despite that, it was still more than he'd had access to in years.

Carefully, he built a little wall in her head, using bones and flowers and soft red earth – the fragments of dreams. The river of her thoughts slowed, the trickle stoppered. Here and there images flicked into Tet's head like snow-trout dancing upstream. Once, he was certain he saw the thief mage's face, but he closed his mind against the memories, refused to look. Even if Tet had wanted to, he was concentrating too hard now on the dam wall than to pay attention to the stream.

The work was painstaking, and dimly, he felt his back crunched up with tension, his neck aching, the jagged knife blade of a headache tearing up his temples.

His magic stuttered, faltered, and Tet tugged again, reeling it out of the *oresh*-beetle like a skein of yellow silk eased from a cocoon.

Hours later, his interlocking dam of symbols had completely stemmed Laketri's memories. It was a simple thing; not designed to hold for more than a few weeks. He'd used the traditional symbols of man; repeated motifs from stories: the red heart and the white bone, the starling feathers and the pure snow, the golden fish and the black storm, eyeless skulls and earthen jars and silver crowns. These were the commonalities of human minds, children's fables. It was the easiest way to do this trick. Not subtle, but about all he was capable of. Tet had no mastery here.

The rare mages with the talent and training for this kind of thing could step into the tales of others and rewrite them, could dream their way into other minds. All Tet could create was a thin blank swathe of mud on which to tip his new jumble of stories. Soon Laketri's real memories would wash them away.

Anestra would drown.

He opened his eyes. Anestra's face was still, her breath so shallow and soft that for a moment Tet's heart missed a beat in fear. But she was still alive. His skin was cold with drying sweat, his stomach a knot around an empty bag. Tet got up to stretch the ache out of his muscles, twisting so his spine cracked

The sound reminded him too much of the assassin's death, and he rubbed his hands fiercely together, not so much to warm them as to hear something different. His throat was parched, his head pounding like the start of a fever. He'd used too much magic too quickly and unskillfully.

There was no food here and he didn't want to wake the house-kitchen now; instead Tet drank from a small carafe of rhododendron wine, just to take the taste of his fear out of his dry mouth. The old candles had burned down to stumps, so he replaced them with fresh ones set into the melted wax of the dying.

Fortified, the darkness driven away a little, Tet returned to the bed and continued the process of building Anestra over the temporarily obliterated Laketri. He flowed the false memories through, layering them over the old. He dandled her new childhood over the buried one; little fragments of growing up the pampered only daughter of a wealthy landowner. He flooded her brain with laughter and young sorrows – giving her depth, but not making her too dour nor too flighty. To keep the illusion realistic, he invented interests and hobbies, suitable for a girl in her position. Tet wiped away Laketri, and he made Anestra.

Tet knew little enough about the childhood of a girl grown up on a wealthy man's estate, but he wove his own small moments of youth in the temple into the story, altering it here and there to keep the fiction stable. A game of ball with a stuffed leather pouch, roughly stitched, kicked between dusty bare feet. The laughter, the jostling. The smell of a young ox-calf, born in the night and already staggering about its dam. The sound of stories at star-rise and the touch of fingers quick and shy in the dark while soft words curled around lover's heads. As a kind of gift or an apology – Tet gave her more joy, more ease, more little luxuries he wished to have experienced. His meagre happiness multiplied and gifted to her. Tet invented for her the father and mother he never had. Reinvented himself as his own perfect father.

Tet had never mourned the parents he'd never known, but he took his yearning emptiness and folded that over and over, turning it into a tight core of private grief for Anestra; the loss of her mother a few years ago. They'd been close.

He built up her hopes that a union with the prince would save her family from the deprivations of the long-running war; garner them some breathing space on the borders. Safety. Security. A childish naivety that princes – even men of war like the White Prince – were the heroes of stories. That she would save what was left of her family, the prince would favour her.

Weaving through her dreams of the prince were Tet's own. Threads of black silk hair, skin that smelled of musk and incense and magic, eyes glittering with stars. Though her prince had icicle fingers, Tet made her want them on her face, touching her cheeks like the wingtips of mountain moths. Guilt thick in his mouth, Tet made her crave the length of the prince's throat, the sinews of his wrists, the strange landscape of his spine.

The thief mage's face flickered in his mind, and Tet took in a deep breath. He drew on the mage's form, overlaid it with the

White Prince's features, turned the dark hair golden, gave him two whole arms, an eye like a cloud-occluded moon. But even under this mask, Tet felt the pull of the thief mage and his strange power.

The fiction took on a depth and authenticity that surprised him. *Perhaps it was easier to be honest when building a lie for someone else.* Tet drew back from her, shivering and sweating, and wiped his brow. Gathered his magic for a final assault.

She would remember nothing of the plans they had made as Laketri and Tet; all she knew now was the truth he'd built for her – that she was the daughter of a wealthy and widowed merchant-prince, Ohtet Maynim, that they hoped to raise their standing significantly when she was one of the prince's mistresses.

Deeper under the false memories, Tet planted the idea that when the prince was naked, stripped of his armour, she would go to the windows and open them for fresh air. He made her think of how beautiful opals were, how fascinated she was by their changing beauty. There was little more that Tet could suggest without risking triggering the suspicion of the clockwork beasts. It was a wild chance, but perhaps luck would be on Tet's side, and once he'd stopped time, he'd stay sane and strong enough to not only gather the breastplate for the Monkey, but likewise the opals for his god. It was a weak trick, but the best Tet could think of.

'You can open your eyes now.' Tet pulled his hands away from her clammy skin, and her eyelids flickered, rose. The irises were dark puddles, brown and amber, and flecks of green. She squinted, then, 'Father, did my dresses arrive? I know you said you ordered them, but surely they should have been here already?' She started, eyes widening. 'Oh, *Nyangist*! What if he doesn't like me – what if he thinks I'm too common, or ill-educated?' Her face was a mask of worry. 'I can't go back if he doesn't choose me.'

Tet was left saddened. 'The White Prince will adore you,' he said. The word *daughter* stuck in his craw. It would take some practice.

'Oh.' Her mouth puckered. 'Dresses,' she said again. 'You promised me robes for this party.'

'So I did.' He did not want to leave her alone in case something went wrong with his magic, and if more assassins should come prowling. 'You sleep here, your old father will take the divan. We will worry about dresses and jewels and other things in the morning.'

'Jewels?'

'Sleep.' His chest ached like a healing bruise where the magic had pulled through from the stone and into him. *What a strange and complicated way to do things.* Ymat had explained that, as long as his magic wasn't a part of him, Tet would stay unnoticed by the gods. While Tet remained hidden from them, he was safe from their curses. The damage to his legs was, unfortunately, permanent, but at least while the gods couldn't see him, there was no constant increasing pain. That would have to be salve enough.

The gods would not be happy at having lost him. Tet wondered if even now, Nanak and Vitash had taken form and were searching through the city streets. The thought chilled.

Anestra clambered under the layers of woven blankets, and blinked sleepily. 'Good night, Father.'

'Good night,' Tet said. *Daughter – I don't even know who this is.* They'd been thrown together by their debts and were not friends, let alone family. He shuddered and sat down cross-legged on the divan, one hand clutching at the stone around his neck. Tet had no intention of sleeping.

XII

VOICE TO VOICE

Ymat didn't give Tet time to fret at his new situation. Half a day only; half a day filled with deliveries of embroidered dresses, visits from hairdressers who set Anestra's long black hair into the elaborate cones of virgin daughters and decorated it with beaten coins and silver wards against demons. It was a good thing the prince liked his mistresses young, and Tet looked older than he was, otherwise the fiction would have been so much harder to sell.

Nerves made it difficult to eat more than plain rice. Every mouthful made Tet feel like throwing up.

'Are you ill, Father?' Anestra asked him in concern.

'No.' Tet wiped his brow with a pale blue silk handkerchief. 'Perhaps I have eaten something that disagrees with me.'

'You always were terrible with parties,' said Anestra, drawing on memories Tet had given her, her own imagination filling in the blanks. 'Mother said that before your wedding, you didn't eat for a week!'

'We are not preparing for a wedding,' Tet pointed out, and Anestra's face fell. He cursed himself. It was hardly the girl's fault that he was a fool.

Before Tet could say something to try to comfort her, a disturbance broke the flat calm of late afternoon. A house servant had flushed a cobra out of one of the ground-floor rooms and there was much screeching and leaping and to-doing while the snake-handlers were summoned to pin the thing down and take it away. They spoke a minor dialect, so thick with cant that it took Tet a while to follow the gist of their conversation. It was a welcome distraction, pitting his mind to the course of language.

Finally, they disappeared into the house, only to pop out a half-hour later bearing their treasure before them. A bronze beast, coiling and writhing from where the handler held it pinched and tight behind the head. Tet leaned from his window to watch the spectacle. From up high it looked like burnished metal, the sun catching on its scales. For all he knew, it could have been a toymaker's little machine.

'What will they do with it?' Anestra asked. She was leaning sleepily alongside Tet, nibbling at the out-of-season fruits he had bought for them.

Laketri would have known. 'I have no idea,' Tet said sharply.

A jabbering argument had erupted between the two rival handlers, and he listened.

'They're debating whether or not to bring it as an offering to Nyangist, or to turn it over to one of the toymakers for study.'

'Ah?' Anestra opened her eyes and leaned forward over the windowsill to peer at them. 'What's the difference?'

'The reward. They argue whether blessings are worth more than coins.'

'Silly things,' said Anestra. 'We must always respect our god. Nyangist will provide for those that worship faithfully.'

Tet swallowed. 'She will indeed.'

'Oh look.' Anestra pointed to an outlying building linked to the main house by a low pitched roof. 'A monkey,' she said. 'There must be more of them. They've probably come to see the excitement, curious things.'

There was only one. A small black and white wizened creature with a gold tuft like a tiny wig. No troop came into sight.

'Come away from the window,' Tet said to Anestra, and tugged her gently by her sleeve.

It made no difference. The monkey had spotted them, and it darted along the ridge of the roof and scampered nimbly up to the windowsill.

Anestra backed away from the window. The monkey sat on the ledge, grinning its mimicking grin. 'Shoo!' she said. 'Oh, make it go— What if it bites?'

'Then it bites. I'll take care of it.' Tet motioned for her to withdraw, and she did, hurrying out of the room and shutting the door behind her.

The monkey and Tet stared at each other in the sudden silence. Outside the snake handlers had stopped arguing, though he did not know their resolution. Evening fell in ribbons of indigo and orange, and the bird songs had grown muted and occasional. Only the jungle fowl screamed harshly as they clattered up to the low limbs of trees to roost.

The little creature had a small white fur pouch harnessed to its front, carefully camouflaged.

Tet tugged at the magic in his *oresh*-beetle in readiness. 'Sai Monkey.' He gave the messenger a vaguely mocking bow. 'And what brings you here this time?'

The monkey cocked its head and blinked once, slowly, as though reconsidering any previous assumptions it had made about Tet's stupidity. Then with a flash it produced a small red scroll from its pouch, bound with silk in a deep blue that was almost black, and offered it to him.

The paper was velvet-thick with a rich nap. Expensive, and the indigo silk had been skilfully knotted into the shape of a tiny dragon strangled by its own tail.

The monkey waited while Tet unpicked the knots, helping itself to handfuls of over-priced fruit and sweets. The tiny mouth chomped as Tet read the fine golden calligraphy.

So. Ymat is done with setting his maket board. This evening he would move the first of his pieces and Ohtet Maynim and his daughter were invited to the Pistil to attend one of the White Prince's evening *entertainments*.

*

Anestra and Tet arrived at the carved gates of the Pistil in a hired carriage – the very best he could afford. Even after eating up most of his remaining ill-gained money, it did not stand out among the display of pomp and wealth gathered outside the White Prince's palace.

Huge caravans almost as high as two-storey buildings stood in the streets, festooned with gilt and flags, and pulled by black wetlands horses or slope-backed sets of giraffes. One vast red and gold tent-like ship was drawn by the revered elephant of Utt Dih. Up close, the beast was rheumy-eyed and ill, dripping a steady stream of snot from its long trunk. The sawn-off tusks were capped with gold and silver and studded with topaz. Underneath the gilt, the creature looked to be dying. It wheezed sadly as they passed. Without pausing, Tet whispered a few words in beast tongue; for strength and health, and another to clear its lungs. It answered with a blast of trumpet cacophony. Tet cast a backward glance just in time to see the animal slap at its handler in irritation, its small eyes glinting.

There, Ymat. Not every trick I do is at your command. The pinch of his magic left his chest feeling raw and bloody, and an involuntary tremor ran through him as Tet considered the immensity of his task. *Stopping time. Again. Madness.* His throat was too dry to let him swallow, and a feverish fear bit behind his eyes, making them water. He had to do this. Tet was no longer a foolish young man with no understanding of his own power. He needed to be strong. Tet closed his eyes briefly and breathed in the circular pattern that was the first step in walking meditations. This was how all great magics should begin. With preparation and calm, not unbridled fear.

He could do this. The magic pulsed at his chest, the *oresh-*beetle thrumming in anticipation, the claws punching deeper into his skin.

'This is so exciting!' Anestra whispered, clutching at his arm. She stared around her in wide-eyed wonder. Her beautiful hair was hidden away under layers of turquoise turban wrappings, with matching robe and trouser-skirts, and a short jacket of emerald and jade stripes. The edges of her sleeves and hems were trimmed in silver embroidery, and a double layer of tiny silver beading curled up the edges of her ears. Bracelets and silver collars of coins danced and sang as she moved. Her eyes had been carefully rimmed in olive dust.

They pushed through the massive throng of seething humanity. People wore clothes of every known hue, jewelled and decorated with riches Tet had never dreamed of. His own little stolen fortune was a servant's pittance in comparison.

There was Ymat Shoom, resplendent as a small planet in silken robes of carmine and cream, his speaker's sash, his smooth head painted with white spirals that edged the darker blue of his tattoos and made them appear brighter. He stood with a small group of men, all with the wary, yet oddly smug look of the city speakers. Of the moustachioed clockwork mage who had refitted Tet's soul into a beetle, there was no sign.

Ymat Shoom paid him no attention, and Tet offered him the same courtesy.

The crowd were making their way up the huge steps toward the palace entrance. If Pal-em-Rasha was a many petalled flower, then the White Prince's palace was its pistil, and it was exactly as crude as it sounded. A bulbous tapering tower at the head of a set of golden stairs. There were said to be a thousand steps leading to the gates, but it was an exaggeration – a few hundred, maybe.

That was still enough for Tet to break out into a slight sweat by the time they reached the curlicued gates and their rows of uniformed and armed guards. The men and women of the prince's private army carried short, curved swords that remind him of ceremonial scythes, though there was nothing ceremonial about the amount of damage they could do. Several of the guard had slave-dogs on tight leashes, and the bound animals were vicious, straining at their metal chains, pulling so that they stood on their back legs. Frothy saliva dripped from their teeth.

Tet repressed a shudder of revulsion. Although it was a common enough sight here in the city, it never failed to horrify him whenever Tet saw a slave-dog. In truth, he was surprised they used real dogs. He'd expected clockwork. Perhaps the White Prince was doing it simply to thumb his nose at the gods of Vaeyane.

At *his* gods, Tet supposed.

Anestra shivered next to him and muttered an invocation under her breath. Tet must have accidentally imbued her with some of his own prejudices. 'So cruel,' she said to him in a whisper. 'Are they always like this?'

Tet nodded. 'You'll have to get used to it, if the White Prince chooses you for his company.' It was a polite fiction that the prince had many women who enjoyed his favour, as much as he enjoyed theirs. They walked past the guards to where a liveried servant was manning the gates. Tet handed the woman their invitation, and she scrutinised it, frowning, before passing it back and opening wide the vast iron gates.

They passed into a city within a city, to the White Prince's tower. Tet's skin grew damp and chill, sticking the fine silk to him with fearful sweat. They were walking into the den of lions, and he had to trust his magic to hold fast in Anestra's head, and that Shoom had not set him up for some design of his own.

Magic was no real weapon here in the Pistil, not with the prince protected by his toymaker's beasts and the breastplate, as well as his armed guards.

Tet didn't pray these days, but for a moment he wished he still could.

*

The White Prince had been born to an ageing king and a previously-barren queen. He came from the womb pale as the sands of the western deserts, his hair a golden auburn, with his sister clinging to his heel. 'He is a ghost, already dead,' cried the midwife, who was later beheaded. 'He is the setting sun,' the attendants cried, and soon the rumour sped through the city that this was to be the final king of a falling kingdom. He had one clouded eye and the other dark grey. Some said he was born with the tail of a cat – blessed of the lioness god Nyangist – while others said that the moment he was born, the palace's queen cat had spontaneously aborted her litter and then bled herself to death.

The sister was an abomination even more appalling, and the king had her strangled with her own umbilical cord before she could cry once.

Tet, in his guise of soldier and spy, had stood on a cold dead field, the wind lashing at his frost-bitten cheeks, his lips cracked and bleeding, while around him men died where they stood and the flags stood stiff with ice and watched the prince ride a dark horse up and down the ranks, his hair loose as though the wind and cold meant nothing to him. His shield of rhinoceros hide was decorated with the lioness-head of Pal-em-Rasha. It had grinned at their misery, and Tet had lost all love for lions.

The prince had said nothing to the soldiers. He'd stared at them all with his broken hard eyes, nodded, and sent them off to beat themselves to death against the walls of the Canton of Ys. It was the only time Tet had been close to him before, as the prince had passed him clothed in armour and pride.

The breastplate Ymat Shoom wanted so badly – that the prince had worn hidden under a cloak embroidered with rich designs and tiny mirrors that flashed ice and sunlight. Of course, the breastplate had not been Tet's goal. He had tried to get close to the prince in the hopes he would hear what had become of the stolen opals. Rumour had led him so far and no further. Whatever the prince had done with them, Tet had no idea.

Tet found he had little desire to see the prince again, the deep nothingness that had sat behind the man's strange eyes as he'd ordered his troops off to their deaths. That was a monster, truly, in the form of a human.

Courtiers ushered them through a bannered street and up to the doors of the palace. The Pistil of Pal-em-Rasha was formed of golden-brown rock, pieced together with a magical skill not seen in many generations. Tet couldn't imagine a day would come that the Pistil would give in to the wear of time and begin to crumble. Whatever masters Ymat worked for, they would need to do more than simply steal away the prince's magical protections and hope that he would fall. Any move Tet made under Ymat's command was most likely one of many thin strands, all designed to bring the prince down. The thought was sobering.

With dull resignation, Tet realised that Ymat was truly not going to let him go when this act was done. Not for as long as he could use him.

Curving passages led them to the centre well of the building, where the huge circular garden had been lit with strings of lamps and clockwork birds which flew back and forth, trailing tiny flowers of light from their crooked claws. A raised podium sat in the clear space in the middle of the garden, and a band was playing. The music was foreign to Deniah, and it took Tet a moment to realise that the White Prince had instructed the band to play the folk songs of all the cities fallen in his war. He had taken the souls of a destroyed people and turned them into entertainment.

Men and women dressed as animals, with huge mask-heads, stood higher than any person in the milling crowd, cavorted through the massed people. They ran and danced, playing out some endless complicated ritual.

'It's amazing,' said Anestra, breathless. She clutched tighter at his sleeve. 'Oh, *Father.*' The excitement and wonder skipped and tumbled in her voice.

'Come.' Tet steered her toward a group of men he had made good acquaintance with in the seven-petal houses. 'Gentlemen.' He bowed. 'Allow me to introduce my daughter.'

'Ah, so this was the reason you came to the city,' said the lithe and languid Sai Conor. His eyes had a dull, glazed look, and his clothes reeked of petal. The smell made Tet crave another pipe. He might not need it for the pain, but that didn't mean he couldn't enjoy the visions and the calm. And calm was everything he wanted at this moment. 'You are a blessed man, Sai Maynim,' said Conor.

Anestra turned the dull colour of old stove brick and stared at her feet.

'Come now, flower,' Sai Conor said, and laughed, his long fingers chucking her under her chin. 'No need to be so shy.'

'I think I am too awed for banter,' she said softly, and looked up, eyes wide, guileless. 'I have never seen anything like this.'

The men shared glances and laughter, sipped at their wines. 'The prince does enjoy the innocent ones, Maynim. A bit too much. Maybe you should have let her out of the house once or twice.' But despite his words, Conor hadn't stopped staring; he was already entranced. Anestra's pretty trap worked.

Now to wait on this damned prince, and have Ymat do his introductions as we planned.

It was past midnight when the host finally deigned to arrive at his own celebration. The crowd had simmered away, imbibing wine, smoking the bubbling pipes of seven-petal. Gorging and dancing and making their connections. The Grand Dance had moved on pointed feet.

Anestra's cheeks were flushed and her eyes were liquid and lovely. Men crowded about her, court butterflies trying to steal sips from the same flower. While she danced, Tet leaned against one of the light-strewn trees, taking occasional drags from a communal pipe of seven-petal flavoured with crushed mint, and some other spice he was unfamiliar with. It bit at the sides of his tongue and lent the hazy feeling of the high a hyper-real acuity that was strange and pleasant. *Not too much, just enough to blunt the edge of fear.* When the drug had made everything slow and dream-like, he set down the pipe, focusing instead on his breathing, on emptying his mind of useless terror, of thoughts of the gods and how they would retaliate. He could not even think of running – Ymat's ritual kept him from that. Finally, Tet's mind settled and a peaceful veil fell over him.

Nothing could go wrong, everything had already happened, they were successful. Tet didn't even need to picture the future, he simply made himself believe that the course had run, the game won. A mental trick, but a useful one for calming the cascade of negative thoughts.

Ymat was bobbing through the crowd, bowing and nodding and eating. He had greeted Anestra warmly, admired her robes, the chains and jewels, made risqué jokes about the gloriousness she had hidden away beneath the folds of the turbans. In short, he had paid her the same attention as any of the other beautiful women here tonight.

The only one Ymat had avoided, or indeed, who he could not get near enough to play the expected round of compliments, was the Princess Kani.

She was there, of course. Ever since she arrived, surrounded and barricaded by the tall dark men of her bodyguard, Tet had been aware of her – the air as she passed had a thick oily feel. Most mages were not so obvious unless they were actively using their magic, and Tet could see no reason why this princess was doing so now.

It was a risk to do so. Especially with the toymaker here, as always, at the prince's side like a revolting tumour. Though the toymaker was not a mage, they surely had some skill with magic – perhaps enough to sniff any loose mages out like rabbits on a plain.

The prince, dressed in robes of white and mirror, with his flaming hair a beacon among the oiled black hair of his courtiers, stood like a bright fierce sun. For the first time Tet caught a brief glimpse of the prince's official toymaker; the court clockwork mage who was never allowed to leave the Pistil. They were a formless fluttering of silks, draped from head to toe in white funeral veils. They did not eat or drink, and Tet wondered if under that blank nothing there was even a human, or simply another machine made to look human. A toy who made toys.

A muttering erupted around him and Tet had his first clear view of the Princess Kani as her bodyguard parted to allow her to step near to the prince.

Once again, Kani was wearing full-length black leather gloves, and her hair was loose, not hidden away under wrappings. The deep raven lengths were decorated with loops of starry chains, and she wore her distinctive robes, this time in a white as blinding and many-hued as a fresh-water pearl. A vision that even Tet could not look away from; she drew his magic closer with her own, two snakes twining around each other in a slow dance.

The court toymaker bowed stiffly from the waist, their veils billowing, and Kani smiled smooth as a dark moon. The prince held out one hand for the foreign princess to kneel before and kiss.

'Damn it all.' Tet picked up his pipe again. He blew out a silvery plume of seven-petal smoke. Anestra was beautiful, but she was just a toy to play with. The prince would be a fool to turn to her when there was the mystery of Princess Kani to devour.

He would also be a fool to marry Kani. She was too powerful for him, too sure of her own place in the world. Her magic would battle his myth. Tet sucked viciously at the pipe, let the water burble. The Princess Kani had placed compulsions on herself, that much Tet could read. It was a foolish step when she was in the heart of the prince's Pistil. He narrowed his eyes, trying to split the various spell traces apart. There were the obvious ones – beauty, mystery, lust – but there were also others. They were darker shadows laid along her skin, marks of protection, safety, commands to awe at her, but never wonder.

Our foreign princess is hiding something. Everything.

The White Prince's mouth moved although it was too far for Tet to lip-read and there was no way to hear him over the whispers and hisses and drunken merriness of the party. The Princess Kani did not answer, merely smiled, and waved another of her servants forward. The Voice, it had to be. She covered her mouth with one hand and the Voice listened, frowning, then turned to speak to the prince.

Dammit, I need to find a way to extract the prince from her talons and focus him on Anestra instead. The crowd swelled and heaved about Tet as he moved over to where Anestra was once again in conversation with a group of rapt young men. Standing just outside her circle of admirers was Ymat. He nodded slightly at Tet's approach; a movement that would go unnoticed if one wasn't looking for it.

Together they corralled Anestra. The courting men seem to melt away, and gentle as free-dogs herding a lost ox, Tet and Ymat drove Anestra towards the prince and Kani. The bodyguards had spread out, allowing the crowd to come a little closer, although two tall, muscled men stood on either side of the princess. They were, like everyone else at this party, unarmed, but there was a steel to their eyes that suggested this would hardly be a problem for them should there be a need for violence.

The private conversation appeared to have ended, and the leonine prince was laughing with some court toady, a glass of thick black wine in one hand. His light eye focused on nothing, the pupil dilated, but his other eye was never still. He watched the crowd as he talked.

'Your Majesty,' Ymat said with a bow.

The prince nodded at him. 'Shoom.' His glance slipped past the city speaker and stopped on Anestra, who was standing just behind Ymat, her eyes lowered, the turban chains tinkling in silvery laughter. She glanced up from under her lashes and smiled with a nervous sweetness that Laketri would never have been able to pull off. While Tet regretted the memory charm, it was obvious to him how necessary it had been.

'And this?' said the prince, holding out a hand in greeting. 'A friend of yours, Shoom?'

Ymat inclined his head modestly, knowing that the prince mocked him.

Across from them, Kani seethed, her eyes black stars. She did not move, but there was a sudden stiffness about her back. Despite himself, Tet wanted to laugh. He wondered what the mage princess was like with all her lies and finery stripped, how strange and subtle she might be under all the magic.

'The daughter of a northern land-owner. Anestra, my dear.' Ymat turned to her, guided her with one hand at her elbow. 'This is Prince Lainn.'

Anestra bobbed at the knees, a stilted little bow that managed to convey just the right amount of respect and awe and girlish interest.

Kani turned her head smoothly like a hooded cobra flaring in warning. Her eyes glittered blackly, a night without stars.

The prince bared his teeth and drew back. 'I hope you enjoy your evening, my little Anestra. You truly are a dove; your parents named you well.' But already he was turning his attention away from that dove, back to the glittering Kani.

A game of mages, is it? Tet narrowed his eyes. With the slightest brush of his own magic, hardly enough to stir the seed tufts of plains grasses, he touched Anestra with a soft compulsion, a gentle enticement to interest the prince in her again. Anything more than that and he would give himself away.

Kani's glare deepened, her eyes flashing under the lamps. They had the prince between them, a white flag on a rope in a game of tug-of-war. Tet readied himself. As strong as Kani might be, she would not know who he was. What he was capable of doing.

Instead of responding with more spellwork, Kani whispered to her Voice, and the man coughed delicately for the White Prince's attention. The two conferred, before the prince turned to Ymat, and said, 'What of the girl's father. I should like to meet the man who gave the world such a glorious creature.'

'Of course.' Ymat bowed hurriedly and shuffled away from them, and over to Tet. He bowed again. 'Sai Ohtet Maynim,' he said as if they had met just once. 'The White Prince has requested an audience with you, concerning your daughter.'

Tet's stomach lurched; he tasted sour wine and the acrid burn of seven-petal. This was how the play was meant to go, but something about it felt skewed, subtly wrong.

XIII

PAPER MASKS

Tet played the doting father and watched Anestra hook the prince. She needed to seduce him tonight. Tet wanted this bargain finished with: breastplate to Ymat, and if he was lucky, opals to himself. And then, he supposed, he would find out if Ymat would let him run. It wasn't as though Ymat would be able to publicly use him in the city again after this. Tet was, essentially, disposable.

But Ymat could always find other places where Tet would still be a valuable tool. *Damn it all – this is what happens when you try and play the gods at their own game.* Once again, Tet wished desperately that he knew his true name; to be completely his own, beholden to no one and nothing.

His feet numb, Tet stepped forward to meet the man he'd killed for, almost died for, and now planned to destroy.

'Good evening,' said the prince. His one light eye stared past Tet's shoulder. It was disconcerting. 'I should congratulate you.'

'I— Your Majesty.' Tet bowed, and waited for what he hoped was long enough before standing straight again. 'Thank you.'

'You don't even know what I offer my congratulations for?' the prince asked mildly.

Anestra was looking meekly at Prince Lainn, her eyes on him alone. She was smitten. Tet wondered if the compulsion he'd set worked both ways, or if the daughter he'd created was truly a fool. 'Congratulations on my daughter?' he ventured, 'I thought...'

Prince Lainn's dark eye was hard, amused, and a smile just touched the corners of his thin mouth. 'Naturally, your daughter.' He held out a hand, taking Anestra's in his. 'She is a fine specimen.'

Too fast. Too easy. Strange magic coiled around Tet, prickling at his legs, testing and tasting blindly. This wasn't his. Tet dared a glance at Princess Kani, but her face was a pleasant mask of mild amusement. Neither the toymaker nor the prince seemed to be aware of the two mages' little power struggle. *Good.* The sweat was drying in Tet's long plaited hair, pomaded and done up in the style of the northern border merchants. He was wearing a sash Ymat had sent to him, indicating Ohtet Maynim's position as a third-ranked prince in the merchant guilds, the embroidered peacocks on the outer jacket sleeves hinting at wealth.

This was meant to make Anestra an even more potent lure – a sweetmeat from a moneyed family. The prince would believe he captured two birds with one small trap. *Fine specimens indeed.* 'Thank you, your Majesty. We have always found our daughter to be a blessing.'

The prince laughed softly. 'It seems to be the season for good hunting,' and he looked to Kani, who merely smiled in response to his little jab. 'I shall soon be drowning in courting maids.'

Kani beckoned her Voice closer and whispered to him. The man's brow pinched together slightly, but he nodded and repeated his princess's whispers.

'Or courting mages,' The Voice said. He was well-named. He had a compelling tone – soft and firm and with a low power that forced men to listen. Hearing Kani's thoughts in the man's voice only increased Tet's desire to hear her speak for herself before he realised the full implication of what she'd said. He froze, stomach lurching

Tet perfected an uncertain smile. 'I'm afraid we have no mages in our family.' He opened his hands wide in apology, willing the slight tremble to fade. 'I had no idea your Majesty was interested in a witch for a mistress.'

The last riposte startled a laugh out of Kani. It was harsher than Tet had expected.

After another bout of whispering, The Voice spoke again. 'There is something your Majesty should know,' he said.

'Spit it out then.' Prince Lainn released his grip on Anestra's hand, and she pulled herself back like a flower in the heat of the noonday sun.

'The man pretending to be Ohtet Maynim is an imposter.'

Tet stood firm, though it felt to him as though his chest was caving in. *Keep the confused look, the nervous smile.* 'I'm no such thing.' The prince was looking at him curiously, and Tet resisted the urge to press one hand over the hidden beetle stone and keep it safe. 'I have no idea what the good lady is talking about—' Tet turned, looking for Ymat to vouch for him, but the city speaker was gone, melted back into the crowd. Ymat's name stuck on Tet's tongue, refusing to dislodge. Tet could feel the bounds Ymat had put on him with his southern craft. He was constrained. He would not be able to name Ymat, let alone speak of his part in any plot.

Tet had no idea how to circumvent the spell or break Ymat's control. He was no adept of southern witchcraft and its riddles of skin and blood and bodily humours. *Damn him for this, and damn myself for being fool enough to let it happen.* He had to think fast, find some rabbit-slip out of this, away from the prince's closing jaws. 'The lady is amusing.' Tet licked his dry lips. 'But a mage? I am merely a landowner from Deniah. I have papers.' He nodded at Anestra. 'A daughter. Or does she think I hatched the girl overnight?'

'Father,' Anestra said, her voice breathy with fear. 'What is she saying – such terrible lies.'

'Is this a joke, my dear?' The prince said to Kani. 'The man may be nothing more than a glorified farmer trying to sell his daughter for favours, but calling him a mage and an imposter is surely going a little too far. Or are you that jealous of a little country slut.'

Kani ignored him, and stalked closer to Tet. She sniffed, breathing in deeply as if by doing so she could scent out what he was. She knew Tet was using magic, but not how. Where Tet should be wrapped in power the way she was, there was nothing. Against his chest, the stone throbbed, hot and strange and eager to be free.

For the first time, Kani spoke out loud. She was quiet, meaning only for Tet to hear. 'What are you?' Her voice was not ugly, indeed, there was a certain musical tone to it, like a lute that was almost but not quite in tune, throaty and dark. Her accent was uncertain, shifting.

Ah, so her magery could not quite cover up her roots. Tet bared his teeth. 'I am as much a fabrication as you,' he hissed back.

Kani narrowed her eyes and drew further from him. Another conference, and her Voice said. 'The girl is under memory charms.'

Everyone turned to Anestra, whose eyes widened. Her mouth was open and she stared this way and that, seeking some kind of safety. 'What are they saying?' she squeaked.

Kani didn't show any outward sign of her craft, and her whispered spell was too soft for Tet to hear. One moment, Anestra was a confused and slightly simple merchant farmer's daughter with delusions of bedding a prince, and the next, she was a street girl from Pal-em-Rasha. Tet felt the dam crack, his magic snapping; a brittle twig under the hooves of a clockwork warhorse.

Kani smiled thinly, and her magic pulled back like the tendrils of a vine.

'Shit,' said Laketri. She blinked. 'Where in all the hells was I—' She stopped, seeing for the first time the White Prince standing next to her, all traces of amusement gone from his face.

'What is this?' he said. He touched Laketri's throat. 'Who exactly are you?'

This was Tet's cue to use his legs while he still had them, and run.

Before the thought had passed through his mind, two massive hands clamped down on his arms, just above the elbow. 'Please wait,' said one of Kani's guards, his breath against Tet's ear. 'You should stay.'

Tet opened his mouth, readying his magic. It was too damn late for disguises and subterfuge. He'd come to stop the world, and now it seemed he would do it, no matter that the plan was falling down around him like a collapsing city. Tet managed one syllable but the guard was too fast. A rough cloth was forced into Tet's mouth, and he was gagged. He struggled, trying to wrench free, to twist and wipe the gag from his mouth, but the guards were already tightening another strip of silk over the gag so that he couldn't spit it out. They were men who knew how to deal with mages. Men who had been *informed*.

Laketri wasn't stupid. The game was up, but she still could pull herself out of this mess with the least amount of tarnish. She fell to her knees, knocking her forehead against the short-cut grass. 'A million pardons,' she said. 'Your majesty – I have no idea how I came to be here!'

Actually, she's not a bad actor, Ymat should have given her more credit. Tet moaned against the gag, trying to form the words that would free him.

Nothing. Terror slammed his heart against his ribs. He had no escape route. Laketri and Ymat would save their own skins, and Tet would take the fall. In the prince's palace, that would be a long, slow, and excruciatingly painful fall. Tet thrashed, trying to pull magic into himself and use it subvocally, but the connection between him and his power was broken, fed through that damned *oresh*-beetle. He screamed in rage, the sound muffled behind the silk gags.

The prince crouched down, talking to Laketri as if she were a little beaten dog. 'Hush, girl. Look up.'

Laketri obeyed. The fear in her eyes was not faked. Tet's own spine was slowly turning to a gelatinous mush. Seven days to die in a hanging cage while the White Prince mocked him from his window. Or the quicker death facing one of the court mage's clockwork monsters. Better or worse, he couldn't tell. *Damn the gods, and damn that fickle little shit Ymat.*

'Do you know this man?' The prince said, pointing at Tet, who was still struggling uselessly against the grip of his captor. *Like a rat in a cage before they give it to the dogs.*

'I-I do not know.' Laketri's eyes widened, and her lip began to tremble. 'I've seen him, yes, I think; he bought a copper pot from me, from my stall, and then...and then...' She burst into a round of sobs, her voice choking up. 'I do not know. There is only darkness after that.'

'Arrest him.'

The prince's own guards come slipping from the crowd where they had mingled and hidden among the guests. These men *would* be armed, and there was no longer any point in trying to struggle. It might be easier to slip the trap at a later moment, but not here and now, with the crowd staring.

'Who are you?' the White Prince asked, clearly not expecting him to answer.

Tet was bound in chains, gagged, humiliated. The crowds gathered to see what was happening, and around him, the whispers roared. The musicians faltered, trying to see what the fuss was all about. A girl with the towering head of a deer watched, glass eyes shining in the fluttering lamps that dangled from the clockwork birds that back and forth overhead.

He needed magic, he needed time to stop. Behind Tet's eyes, the great stone door stayed closed, though Tet battered against it like a gnat slamming itself to death against a fortress wall. He focused all his terror and was rewarded when the door seemed to shift a quarter-inch, stone scraping against stone.

A sudden spear of pain lanced through Tet, making him scream again.

The sky went black, all the stars extinguished. It was as though a hand had grabbed Tet's entrails and was pulling him back. A pain that was both intense and agonising while also dull as the ache of an old tooth.

'Who are you?' The White Prince asked, his words the slow booms of an executioner's drum, and Tet realised they had skipped back in time.

Just a few seconds.

It was different now. A red pall covered the city, illuminating the watching faces like creatures from a hellish tableau. Everything moved underwater-slow, dream-slow.

The starless sky filled with vast ethereal shapes as insubstantial as the mist that rises off a morning river. Dog shapes, lion shapes, serpents and horses and men with the heads of birds, women with the heads of deer. *Gods.* They had come, not at Tet's command, but because the broken time had become even more fractured. Whatever he'd done with his warped magic, it had once again summoned all the gods of the world. They moved in slow undulations of light, each form stretched out, the pressure of their presence enough to make Tet's skull and ribs feel as though they were being pulverised.

He was going to die this time, he thought, but just as the pain became too much to bear, the sky lightened, and the gods vanished into the ether.

The sticky feel of damaged time shifted and once again the sky was empty, only spatters of vague pinprick stars against indigo. The red veil had lifted, the gods were gone, clockwork birds whirred their clockwork wings. The gods were gone and all that remained were the people in the gathered crowd, dressed up in paper masks.

The gods were gone and no one had come to save him. Not even Nanak, who had taken Tet as her own, whose name he'd carried for so many years. Tet-Nanak, finally, irrevocably, abandoned.

Who am I?

Even Tet didn't know the answer to that.

'Cut out the mage's tongue,' said Kani, her voice unexpected and dark as palm sugar and coriander sweets. 'Unless you think you can use him.'

XIV

TET

'**C**ut out his tongue?' The White Prince raised an enquiring brow at Kani. 'Why, would you like it as a gift?'

Tet was gagged with a courtier's handkerchief of yellow silk, and his hands bound fast behind him. Magic pulsed at his chest, waiting for him to release it with a word. Kani had been right about that much at least; it was the small flaw in magery that a mage needed their voice to direct it. She'd known when Tet arrived at the prince's stronghold that she would need to find a way to cut him out of her game – expose and gag him before Tet could do the same to her.

She had it planned, damn her. And it wouldn't take much more than a word from her, and Tet would be tongueless, powerless.

Laketri, hauled to her feet and held by impassive soldiers, watched him with a mixture of fear and guilt.

Kani shrugged, then whispered to her Voice, who said to the prince, 'He is dangerous only if he can still speak. As for your offer of a gift, the princess says only if you thread it on a silver chain. She has no need for men's tongues.'

'Says the tongue of a man.'

The Voice bowed his head in acknowledgement.

151

The prince looked long on Kani, eyes narrowed. 'You are surprisingly well-versed in magery, is this common to the women of Sinal?'

Another whispered conference, and the Voice said, 'The courts at Sinal do not have clockwork mages, and must employ men such as this,' he gestured at Tet, 'but they are kept tractable by certain measures.'

'Measures?' The Prince waved the Voice away. 'And stop this nonsense with your man, we know you can speak the language.'

Kani's face remained impassive, but Tet caught a slight flicker of irritation in her black eyes. 'We own their names,' said Kani. 'If you can torture his true name from him, you will have a powerful weapon.'

'Is that so?' The prince smiled thinly at Tet, considering.

'Though it may prove hard to get,' she said. 'The moment he has the chance to open his mouth he could kill you with a word.'

'I won't give him the chance,' said the prince. 'An educated man can write, and I plan to leave him with one hand.'

Kani flinched and drew back.

Tet's stomach roiled as he fought down his fear. Gods only knew what tortures a devotee of Nyangist could come up with. And Tet had no name to give the prince, even to save his own life. It made him harder to own, Tet knew, but it also made him weak, and now it would be his death-sentence.

*

The Pistil had a labyrinthine system of dungeons and empty hallways hidden far below its golden stem. The guards led Tet down to them, down rounds and rounds of spiralling staircases and along endless dark passages, deeper and deeper, until there was no notion that a tower soared above them. Instead, it felt as though the weight of a thousand tons of stone was sitting heavy, weight pressing down through the soils and the beams, threatening to crush them all slowly.

The air was moist and heavy, a stagnant mossy air that sank in cold shrouds to Tet's feet. The guards did not talk as they led him, but whispers followed them. People lived down here, people locked away for gods' only knew how long. What crimes had they committed against the White Prince – were theirs worse than Tet's?

What kind of punishment should he expect for this act of trickery, Tet wondered. He hadn't been caught trying to assassinate the prince, but he was still a mage. In the end, it didn't matter what he'd planned to do. They could wring any confession from Tet except the name of the man who'd brought him here. Ymat had seen to that. They would assume Tet had acted alone in the city – perhaps on the orders of one of the besieged Canton princes.

Worse still, the White Prince had commanded his men to twist out Tet's true name so as to make the mage another weapon in his immense arsenal. If such a thing were possible, Tet would end up simply another clockwork beast, controlled and owned and set to war.

What tools and tortures do they have planned for me, to make me into what they want? Icy sweat poured down his skin, burning his eyes, plastering Tet's robes to his back and stomach. It was not simply the fear of what was to come or the thought that the entire tower could just sink down like a tired old woman and crush him into the mud, but the constriction. Tet was from the mountains. His people travelled over the hills and valleys, free of anchors. They did not live underground. Even when he'd been given to the temple, no one had ever expected him to go and live like a worm under the rocky soil.

'Here.' The first guard stopped before an unmarked door. Tet had no idea what set this cell apart from the others, what made them choose this particular one. Perhaps it was random, they were simply going to shove him in and leave him to the dark.

His breath whistled in his chest.

The walls were lit with sputtering grease lamps – no clockwork birds and orbs of glass filled with curious gases here.

How long would it be before the flames went out? It wasn't that the dark scared him. He had lived through darkness before.

It was the dark that waited inside his head, the yawning emptiness of a soulless mind.

The other guard produced a ring of keys from a chain on his belt, and they clattered in his fingers. There weren't many, and Tet latched on to that tiny bit of hope. The lock might be easier to pick. Or at least easier to charm. There had to be a way for him to get free of this gag, and he would play desperate and weak if it gave him any chance. Tet staggered like an old man.

They shoved him into the cell and untied the bindings from his wrists, though they kept him gagged. He couldn't make a move, not yet.

The guards had their swords drawn. 'You try anything, and I will enjoy separating your head from your body,' said the first, a man with a square proud jaw and trimmed beard, a warrior's watchful squint to his eyes, and coiled calm to his limbs. He held the sword closer to Tet's neck, and the sharpened blade cut like a whisper in a lover's room. Blood ran warm and slow in a fine trickle along his throat.

His shoulders and arms ached from being twisted behind his back and Tet rubbed them carefully, slowly.

'Strip,' said the bearded guard. The weapons were drawn and ready. Any flicker of movement in the wrong direction, and it was clear they would not hesitate. The prince had already told them that Tet was only to be kept alive for as long as it was safe. They would rather a dead mage and no weapon, than allow him a moment's chance at freedom.

Do nothing for now, Tet told himself. He had to angle for time, angle for a moment when their eyes were elsewhere, for a chance to work the gag loose. *Patience. Slowness. Calm the heart, calm the breath, calm the tongue.* The sweat prickled along his spine. Following their command, Tet loosened his belt, his short robe, his trousers. He stepped out of his embroidered leather boots lined with sheep wool. Finally, Tet stood naked, just the dull grey pendant still on its chain around his neck, the sodden silk in his mouth. Before he could do anything, the guards twisted his arms back again, retying the knots, tighter than before.

'And that,' said the guard, pointing at Tet's chest.

They can't have it. As soon as I work my way to get free of this gag I will need my magic. My soul. He tried to twist out of reach but the guard grabbed the chain and pulled, breaking the thin silver loops. The beetle legs tore free from Tet's skin, ripping through the flesh. The sudden agony was excruciating. He coughed, bending half over, choking on the silk and pain, certain that the invisible needles would pierce his lungs, spear right through him.

'What the hells?' The guard looked at the pendant dangling in his fist, then at Tet's chest. A series of six puncture holes were bleeding out over the mage's skin. He turned to the other guard. 'The prince will want to know about this.'

The other guard sputtered in agreement, and backed away. Tet could only hope that the prince was no scholar, that he would not realise exactly what the *oresh*-beetle was. A trinket, a toy. Nothing much. As Tet now was without it. A cavernous despair eclipsed the pain, swallowed him, and he had to fight to stay on his feet instead of crumpling to his knees. Deep in his head, the stone door faded to mist and shreds.

The prison door shut on Tet's face and he leaned against the solid wood, choking coughs clawing through his chest. His eyes streamed, but pulse by pulse, the pain lessened until all that was left was a deep hollow ache. Even that started to fade.

Finally Tet pushed back and stumbled from the door. *Mistake*. The room was lightless, a black so empty and cold that it ate away at Tet's sense of self. He blinked and blinked, hoping that each time his eyes would begin to adapt and that the blackness would be recast in shadows and shades. Nothing. He was deep underground, far from the sun, from candles and oil lamps.

Tet crouched down and shuffled his way about the room, relying on his meagre sense of proprioception. The floor was chilled and damp; ancient stone. Cold gnawed its way up his legs and his bound arms, and he shivered uncontrollably. The guards had left him naked and blind, voiceless and armless. And soulless.

There was nothing left of him in this pit.

Time took on its own rhythms in the underground cell. There was no way to measure the passing minutes or hours, no candles to mark out the day from the night. Tet tried to count his own heartbeat, but after he lost himself in the millions, he realised just how pointless an endeavour it was.

He tried to be more proactive, turning his head to the side in the hopes that perhaps he could work the gag loose by scraping it against the stone. His efforts proved fruitless. Tet twisted his hands, working his wrists in their bindings until they ached. Pain pulsed through the ragged flesh with every heartbeat and the ropes were wet and warm with his blood.

It was useless. Even now, after so many years of weakness, he was too much a man of magic. In truth, Tet had never had to rely totally on himself before. Without power, he was unschooled. Helpless as a child.

The darkness flittered, took on the hallucinogenic pulse and shimmer of seven-petal visions, and Tet leaned back into one corner and watched the light-show in his head. It was that or think. And he did not want to think. When he'd been just a priest-mage in training, the novices would be forced to kneel for hours and sink themselves into deep meditations. Falling back on the familiar comfort, Tet did this now. It was a way to lose himself in the timed breaths and silence.

Silence.

There was so much of it that it was impossible to ignore. High in the mountains, everything had been snow-muffled, but there was still sound: birds, distant voices as his fellows went about their duties, the barks of the free-dogs, the oxen calling to each other in the valley fields, the wind whispering to itself as it wound about the rocks. Even, sometimes, the trill and flute of the dragons speaking to man or monster.

Here the silence was as empty as the dark. It pressed on Tet, squeezing him inside his skin.

His breathing took on an excruciating loudness. Tet coughed, his tongue raw against the material in his mouth, and the earth tremored as though his heartbeat was the sullen drum calling the priest-mages to prayer.

His head throbbed in time.

Hours later he pissed in one corner of the cell, and the sound of it splashing against the cold stone only made his thirst grow greater. His throat slowly dried, tongue growing thicker, too big for his mouth, the silk wicking all moisture away, tasting like stale spit.

Tet's stomach cramped, eating at its own lining. He tried praying.

Nanak, Vitash, Epsi. Words that should be said aloud. *I call on you, watch over me, grant me your protection. From Nanak, I beg comfort, and give my heart in offering.* The dull thuds of his slowing organ were the only answer. The gods only saw men with souls, and Tet had made himself into an empty flesh vessel. That was what Ymat Shoom had turned him into. *And I let him, damn him three times over. Not let – I sold myself into his bargain willingly.*

He swallowed drily. *From Epsi, I beg meat, and give my flesh in offering.* A dying broken body that no god would want. And finally, *From Vitash, I beg rain like stars, and give my water in offering.* He had given them up, these three gods. Tet had given up his soul to be free of them. He supposed it was not un-ironic that now, alone, in the dark, waiting for his death, Tet had turned to them again.

They would not hear his soulless soundless prayer.

Tet slumped further down the cold wall and wondered if it was worth conserving what little energy he had left. There was no bed, not even a scattering of mouldy straw, but despite this, he fell asleep.

The sound of the latch being drawn back woke him from a nightmare of being eaten alive by the twenty-one ghosts of the first dragons, who were men before there were men. He could still feel the residual pain singing through his tendons and flesh, hear the snap of bones, frozen in the paralysis of a nightmare as the guards came for him.

*

The two guards took him to a room bright with grease lamps. Tet's eyes ached after the darkness of his cell. Tears streaked his face, itched against his skin.

Prince Lainn was waiting for him. Cold and gold and white, his expression empty, one clouded eye staring into nothing. The other was bright and predatory as a griffon vulture's. He watched, as though waiting to see if Tet was worth the effort of tearing apart. The White Prince was arrayed in court armour – ornamental, mostly – but there; just under his cloak of lion fur, was the soft clank of the metal panels of a breastplate knotted together with leather. A sound Tet knew well: all of the Deniahn army wore them. Tet remembered his own as heavy and uncomfortable, providing protection only to the chest and groin, kept in place with leather buckles.

The prince's would be of somewhat better make, finer metal, fitted to him alone. Enspelled with protection, and the gods only knew what else. The breastplate Ymat so desperately wanted. So close, so unobtainable, and Tet was just a cowering naked, spineless, useless mockery of a mage, and he hated himself for it.

'Ohtet Maynim,' said the prince in his cat-claw voice, in his ivory and blood voice. He sounded like a thing bred to hunt and devour and dream of hunting and devouring.

He is still just a man. And like all men, he has his weak points, his vices and soft underbelly.

Tet nodded clumsily. His breath was loud, whistling through his bruised nose. The guards had not been careful bringing him here. Blood dried in a thin crust above his upper lip, in the corners of his mouth.

'We can drop the pretence. It's not your given name, I know.' The prince gestured for one of the guards to bring him a chair. He sat down and studied Tet, relaxed, frowning slightly, as though the mage was a puzzle to be solved. 'You are an educated man,' he said. 'You come from the temples, so you can read and write.'

There was no point in trying to pretend otherwise. Tet nodded in resignation.

'You will write down for me your true name.' At a flick of his hand, the guards brought an inkpot and a reed brush, and a rolled paper. An excessive amount, wasteful.

Tet swallowed against the putrefaction in his mouth and tried not to gag. Slowly, he edged toward the table. His hands were still bound. With another silent command, the guards cut the blood-soaked leather at his wrists. A flood of stinging pain filled his hands, and it felt as though they would balloon like leather sacks of water, that they would be too puffy and tight and painful to ever use again. Slowly, slowly, choking all the while, Tet flexed his stiff fingers through the pain until the circulation returned.

His eyes adjusted to the brightness, and he saw the mess of bloody raw skin on his wrists. It stung and throbbed in the open air, and the underlying sweet scent of rot rose from the wounds. *Not good. Not good.* Briefly, he considered trying to rip the gag from his mouth, but Tet already knew that it was too tight and he would be too slow, too weak. The guards watched him intently, their swords drawn. *I'd be dead before I got my hands up. And what can I do without magic?*

All through Tet's slow recovery of the use of his hands, the prince sprawled, one elbow propped on the arm of his chair, his chin against the heel of his hand. His good eye flicked, the only movement. The other was a dull moon, a symbol of death.

It was unsurprising that the people believed him a lord of demons.

'I don't have all day, *tet*,' the prince said softly, and the use of Tet's temple name – however innocent it was – made him shiver. 'Your name. Now.'

The ink smelled damp and black like the wet ashes of a long-dead fire. Tet's fingers shook as he dipped the cheap reed brush provided for him. No antique hollow bone, delicately carved.

Not, Tet supposed, when the prince thought he might try to use it as a weapon. *Were I to try and stab anyone with this, it would be a joke.*

Tet's shaking hand splattered a fine spray of ink drops as he waited, wondering what he could possibly write that the prince would believe. There were options; Tet could write some made-up name and pretend to be under the prince's control. But the man was no fool, and he'd be sure to have some plan to check that Tet wasn't lying, some task it would be impossible for Tet to do unless he was under compulsion. The edges of the paper were beginning to curl back to their rolled state as if they did not want Tet to spoil them with his lies.

Finally, he dropped his hand, and the brush kissed paper, leaving a curved line of scratchy black. Tet wrote in Deniahn, in the temple script of the high priests of Nyangist, a script that hung neat as a line of prayer flags. When he was done, he pushed the paper a little away.

One guard took it to the prince, who stared at the slowly drying ink in silence. The White Prince dropped the scroll onto the ground and stood. 'Amusing.' It was the last thing he said to Tet or anyone else in the room. With a soft clank of metal and the hush of fur, he left all three of them alone.

The smaller of the two guards picked up the scroll and peered at it. 'What's this rubbish then?'

The bearded guard glanced at it for the briefest moment before laughing in a short bark that was less amused than impressed at Tet's gall. 'You are a stupid man,' he told Tet. 'A very, very stupid man.' *Perhaps not impressed.* There was nothing impressive about a man with a death wish, even if he could see no other path to take.

'What's it say?'

The guard who was both warrior and, surprisingly, scholar, said as he hauled Tet's hands behind his back and steered him away from the table: 'It's the first line of the Book of the Lion, in the high script of the priests of Nyangist.'

'What— "Name me, Child."?' The other guard shook his head. 'Fucking idiot.'

It's a joke, of course, one for the prince. Tet had written it with two subtle changes that shifted the meaning. Now it simply said, 'Call me Tet.' He hadn't carried on with the rest of the first verse of the Book of the Lion, no need to talk about how, when the child names the dark, the dark will come for him.

I already know as much.

*

The guards didn't remove the gag, but they held Tet down and poured cold water over his face. He half-drowned, but enough water soaked through the silk and trickled down his throat for Tet to consider the torture a small, painful blessing. The prince intended for him to stay alive, at least for now. His stomach lurched, but his thoughts felt a little clearer now that his raging thirst was somewhat slaked. Tet twisted his head as they pulled him up. The room was empty but for a Y-shaped wooden post, meant to hold a man. A small table with an assortment of thin blades, awls, tools that he didn't recognise.

They started with his knees, splitting open the old scars.

At the end of it, the guards give him back his piece of parchment and the chewed-reed brush and the ink of burned bone and pitch.

Tet wrote nothing. There was nothing to write.

*

Days passed. Pain, lack of food, the water that saved him but was also part of his torture. Tet's cell reeked, but he only noticed it now and again: shit and piss and copper-blood, the stink of unwashed skin. The stink of unanswered prayers and a peculiar wrenching despair he hadn't felt even when he was cursed.

Tet shivered uncontrollably, in bursts and shudders, and he knew that his body was consuming itself for heat.

Mostly, he slept. A deep lethargy had swamped him, and even when he was finally given fresh water, he did not have the energy to look up. After a while, they had found a new way of dealing with him; knocking him out with a sweet-sour drug long enough to change his gag.

He would always wake from these drugged moments to find himself spread on the beams of the Y-shaped cross, his mouth filled with the musk of hemp cloth. They'd stripped skin from his legs and chest, driven hooks through his nipples and the soft meat of his lower lip and mangled the fingers of his left hand, crushing the bones in a vice. Hunger had chewed the marrow out of Tet's bones.

Every night he dreamt of being devoured.

XV

THE RIVER SERPENT

Tet woke from the drug to find himself splayed on the Y-shaped post, only this time, the prince lounged loose-limbed in his chair as though it were a vast throne

By now Tet was ready to give the prince his name. If he had known his true name he would have spat it out and accepted any chains, as long as the torture would finally end. That was the irony of it, that he would have done it, let himself be used as a weapon, do whatever he had to if he only could.

The prince was not alone. The white-draped figure of the toymaker stood just behind him, milky veils fluttering with each soft exhalation.

The toymaker had always seemed more ghost than human, so it took Tet a moment to realise the figure was speaking to him. Their voice was soft and lilting, hypnotic, filled with magic. Perhaps if they'd been born in the mountains, they would have been given to the temple and trained up. They would have been like Tet.

'Mage,' they said. 'You have been cruelly used.'

There was not much to say to that, even if Tet were able to answer.

The prince watched Tet while the toymaker spoke, studying him like a lion considering whether or not to pounce on a little water-snake.

'My lord wants you to know that it does not have to be like this.' They raised their arms toward Tet, lifting the veils so that their hands appeared from the pillar of silk, palms up, like a beggar accepting charity. 'See, there are no marks on me, no chains, no bindings.' Their hands were as white as their veils, moon-bright and slender, pale as the prince beside her.

Tet narrowed his eyes.

'If you only give him your name, then you will be well-treated, will have rooms of your own within the palace, will eat at his table.'

And be his slave-dog. No. On second thoughts, even if I had a name, I'd rather the fucker kill me. I'm done. Done with being pressed into service, into slavery. So the prince's toymaker lived in a vast and gilded cage, perhaps they had even chosen their enslavement – after all, toymakers sold their services like whores and mercenaries, no names were needed to bind them to any cause. Tet couldn't say anything, but he shook his head, once, slowly. Even that small movement was enough to make him dizzy and weak. Weaker.

Let the prince do as he wished; Tet was done with them all. Even were he to say yes, even if he *could*, his magic was gone. His *oresh* lost, a single drop in the treasures the prince used to fuel his war-machine.

A fierce clarity rushed through him. *The prince's war is failing.*

Why else would he care about gaining control of one little mage? Perhaps he saw Tet as a gift from his god, a treasure thrown into his lap. After all, he couldn't go openly against the temples of the dogs and force a weapon that way. The Temple had never come forward to help him or any king in their bloody games. Though Vaeyane had capitulated gently under his will, the mages in the temples had done nothing to change the tide. They were not men of war.

Men of letters and knowledge and power. Wasted power.

Perhaps.

The White Prince had never truly understood the actions and motives of the temple priest-mages. All the prince could see now before him was a fool. A powerful man who would not use that power.

'So far, the prince has been a lenient man,' the toymaker said as they gestured at Tet's wounds with a graceful twist of their wrist. 'His patience wears thin.'

Still the White Prince said nothing, one eye fixed on the mage.

'Think on this,' they said, and their hands withdrew, they bowed stiffly, formally, in a strange gesture of respect.

It caught Tet off guard, and he was blinking in confusion when the prince slipped out of his sprawl and was on his feet, stepping right up to Tet. He was closer than he had ever been before, breath against Tet's face, warm, spiced with cinnamon and cloves and honey. Tet's stomach lurched, thinking of the feast he might have come from. What the prince might have eaten.

Prince Lainn raised one hand and carefully, slowly, pinched the soft leather of his gloves from his fingers, easing the supple white skin away until his hand was bare. It was almost as pale as the glove itself. He pressed this cold white hand to Tet's face, ran a thumb under the gag and into his mouth, sharp nail nicking the soft wet flesh, drawing blood. It was a strange and intimate invasion. Tet was tightly bound in place and could do nothing to stop him.

Tet tasted the traces of honey still on the pad of the prince's thumb before he pulled away. The prince held out his hand, and the toymaker carefully scraped the spittle from his finger into a tiny vial, before he turned his back on Tet, drawing the glove back on.

He had taken from Tet, marked him. The cut inside Tet's lip throbbed out of proportion to all his other, deeper wounds.

The toymaker held up the vial to the flicker-warm glow of the grease-lamp. 'Remember this,' the toymaker said. 'His patience is not infinite.'

*

A healthy man could live a lunar cycle and another half, without food. Tet was not a healthy man. He was a man with a leg that was twisted; naked in a freezing room, wretched of earth.

The guards came for him once every three to four days. It was the only way he had of counting. If Tet's calculations were right, then he had been there almost a full cycle. Seven times he'd been blinded by the lights, and for a moment glimpsed the entirety of despair. Seven times he'd been handed a page on which to write down his name. Seven times he'd wished that he could. The White Prince had not put him in a cage to die or set him to fight one of his toymaker's beasts. Seven times Tet had wished he would.

Tet's death stared him in the face, its white teeth dripping. Hazily, he wondered if he would still be able to call the dragon-ghosts down for himself with no voice. With no soul. They could eat his remains and leave the White Prince an annoying puzzle.

His hearing had grown better alone in the pit. From far away came the soft thud of feet. Only one guard this time. His steps were light, snowfalls on snow. Maybe he came to slit Tet's throat and rid the prince of an annoying and embarrassing failure. He could only hope so.

The lock clicked, though Tet had heard no tell-tale jangle of keys. The bolts slid back, the rust catching rust, making its familiar gritty whine, and the door slowly opened, but there was no comforting glow of the guard's grease-lamp.

It was dark as ever, and for a moment Tet wondered if he had gone completely blind. If worms had swallowed his eyes in this endless night.

'Ohtet Maynim.' A young man's voice, husky-soft as a dove's. 'You will stand, and you will follow me, and you will make no sound. You may trust me; I am in the service of a mutual friend.' He leaned forward and with a whispered word, the knots of Tet's gag untied themselves.

Tet's heart thudded as he spat out the revolting mush of hemp. His bound hands were freed as the man whispered softly. *Ymat Shoom. It can only be – he's sent his pet thief mage to rescue me. No. No, my contact was a youth, and this is a man, his shadow taller, voice deeper.* Tet had to be mistaken. He was ill with hunger, with torture, and he was only dreaming that his rescuer was using magic to slip Tet's bonds.

It was more likely that if Ymat Shoom sent anyone, it was an Underpalace assassin to kill Tet, or if he was lucky, to cut out his tongue before the prince could. After all, what good was Tet to Ymat now – a mage without magic? He crawled to his feet, using the freezing walls to help him stand. A wave of dizziness battered him, leaving him weaker, even more pathetic. He swallowed and swallowed, his tongue shrivelled and rotten in a mouth that felt suddenly cavernous. Tet's teeth felt loose and rancid. 'Kill me now,' he managed, choked the words out like chewed leaves. 'Get it over with.'

'I'm not here to kill you, old man,' his rescuer said. *Old man,* gently mocking. 'But I will be paid only when you are free, so hold your rancid tongue and follow. Here.' He shoved something towards Tet, and the mage smelled musky ox wool. He fumbled until his broken, aching fingers closed on a heavy length of material. A few moments and Tet had covered himself in what felt like a traveller's long cloak. The relief from the cold was enough to make his heart fill. Such simple happiness.

Tet's legs were weak from sitting, from pain, from infection, from lack of food, and although it seemed all he'd done these past weeks was cry or sleep, he'd never felt so weary. The chance of freedom spurred Tet to follow, clinging to the walls for balance, his rescuer's whispers in the dark leading a path away from his incarceration.

They left behind Tet's pit, his stone coffin, his dreams of death, and Tet staggered through a web of underground tunnels so vast that he was certain by the end of it they would come out in the mountains of the gods, where the three spires stood wreathed in perpetual storm, the statues of the Dogs looming over them.

When they were far from the wide passages of the castle and deep into the subterranean network of sneak's tunnels the man seemed to know better than the map of his own hand, Tet ventured to speak again. 'Who are you?'

'A friend,' the man said and laughed. 'A paid friend.'

'The best kind.'

They stopped, and the man handed Tet a leather skin of water, clean and cold as mountain springs, and Tet drank deeply. A distant rushing rumble made him think of waterfalls in the mountains, and the sound worsened his thirst. After Tet handed the water-leather back, slivers of dried and salted meat were pressed into his hands and it took all his strength of will to not just swallow them down and beg for more. Tet chewed slowly, forcing himself to squeeze the meat to mush, to grind and grind every last swallow of flavour from the dried meat. His teeth were loose, the gums soft and swollen with putrefaction. Tet pushed the lump of meat into the hollow of his cheek and sucked at it like a child.

The rescuer offered no more. 'Dozha,' he said.

Tet choked on the lump, coughed. 'Your pardon.'

The man chuckled softly. 'My name. The greatest name in all of Pal-em-Rasha.'

'Ah.' Tet swallowed, his stomach a tight ball of pain. 'Can't say I have heard it.'

'And that's why it is great.'

The man was an excellent thief to know the ways in and out of the White Prince's palace as if it were nothing more to him than taking a stroll in the public gardens. Even Tet, with all his map-knowledge, gleaned from years of study, did not know a quarter of the under-tunnels, and certainly none that would lead him straight to the Pistil dungeons. And if his rescuer was not a master thief, then he was a petty thief with the right knowledge. It didn't matter. *Let the man believe in his own grandeur. What business is it of mine?* 'Ymat Shoom sent you?'

'The fat man with his fingers in all the millet bowls, yes.'

If Ymat Shoom wanted Tet dead, he would have paid for a knife in the dark, not for this. Tet hoped. 'I guess I will owe him,' he said softly.

'Your soul and more, I would say.'

What more could he take from me? Tet supposed now Ymat could tie his loyalty to his schemes, and use him as a servant. Perhaps Ymat thought he would do what the White Prince couldn't and, once his soul was returned, make Tet a pet mage. *If I get my soul back.* Tet couldn't bring himself to ask Dozha if he had recovered that too. He was not ready for the disappointment if the man said no. What had Ymat said about the separation of soul and flesh – that it would bring his death closer. How long would that take?

'Are you rested?' said Dozha, 'We'll reach the crossing soon.'

'Crossing?'

Tet couldn't see the thief smile in the darkness, but he was certain Dozha was laughing at him.

'Where Imal the Black runs under the palace grounds.'

Ah. The White Prince's city was built partly over the river, diverting it underground. Tet had heard whispers that the underground river was sacred to Sinastrillia, the water-serpent god of thieves. A god Tet was half-certain had been invented. He knew little of the cult's practices; they were secretive, and few openly admitted her worship. There were rumours that all thieves and assassins were sacred to her, that the Underpalace was her temple, but Tet had heard only rumours, and nothing more. What he had heard wasn't reassuring.

Sinastrillia took Nyangist's former sacrificial offerings, and while that might mean that the blood of children no longer wet the altar of that murderous lioness-god, it didn't tell Tet what happened to those children instead. Perhaps her temple saved them from sacrifice so they could become thieves and assassins instead. Assassins who died with a word and with the snap of their spine. Tet pushed the thought away. 'To Imal the Black. And what of the serpent god?'

'You will be safe from her,' Dozha told him. 'She does not eat her own kind.'

'Meaning?'

But Dozha only said, 'Keep to me, old man.'

Again, the insult. It was not the first time someone had tried to mock Tet with those very words. But the other had a young man's voice, sly and new, with a different accent, more cultured.

Tet followed the near-silent pad of Dozha's footfalls, keeping to his heels, while around them the rushing sound grew louder. They were coming to Imal. The tunnel widened and a small sphere of light in the distance was enough for Tet to make out the wide stone paving on the banks of the icy blackness of the river. He didn't have the chance to get a glimpse of his rescuer.

Dozha spoke in the language of the dragons and shifted. At the same instant, magic rushed over Tet's skin, and he fell to his belly; arms and legs obliterated, long stomach muscled and ridged with overlapping scales.

His tongue flickered at the air, tasting the million river tastes, the million air tastes, the million skin-and-scale tastes of his serpent-brother in the darkness.

'What have you done?' Tet hissed, and Dozha replied, 'It is the only way to cross,' his forked tongue quivering, moon-and-star eyes blacker even than the river. He had turned them both to water-serpents.

The thief was a powerful mage. These were not illusions spun over skin; both men had been completely remade and at simply a word. And that was certainly not the first time Tet had seen such a trick performed. *Ymat Shoom must have paid a fortune for my rescue. And how many mages lie hidden beneath the stones of Pal-em-Rasha, gathered like woodlice, waiting to be uncovered from the dark?* Ahead of him, Dozha the water-serpent slid into the black, and Tet followed, writhing on his belly.

*

The underground river was colder even than the stones in Tet's cell, and he grew drowsy and slow as he wound through the inky water, following the barbed tail of Dozha. Once, halfway across, something huge arched below him and Tet felt a jolt of recognition.

Dragon.

She brushed his serpent belly with her ridged head, her smooth scales, and then she was gone. The speech of dragons, echoing and full of underwater bells, sounded in his head. Her name, soft as distant songs until it became simply meaningless sounds. *Sinastrillia, sinastrillia, sinastrillia.*

Then she spoke, mind-to-mind. *Swim, Lord of Time,* she said. *Swim.*

It left him shaken. Tet had dismissed her cult, dismissed her as an idol worshipped by scavenging heathens, but Sinastrillia was real. Imal the Black boasted a river-serpent unlike any other. A dragon of the river. The ones from the mountain might never speak of such, but they had never been a race prone to telling truths to men.

Dozha released them from his magery once they had slithered out the water and into another tunnel. When Tet had a human mouth again and all his limbs, he remarked only, 'That was well done.' *One does not ask questions of mages, especially ones who have the skill to transmute flesh and form.* Even his cloak was bone-dry.

Tet's hunger and thirst had dropped away from him as if his body had gorged itself on that magic instead, and the rest of the journey passed in wincing silence. Tet wondered just what he would now owe Ymat Shoom. And how much it would cost him to hire a mage named Dozha, should he need to steal his soul back.

They climbed a flight of steps so narrow that the walls brushed against their sides. Tet limped up, each jerking half-step sending pain grinding between the joints of every bone, rasping raw skin. From above came the smell of tanning leather, pungent and putrid, and the sulphurous light of gas lamps, the stink of sweat, and the chant of leather workers. Tet hugged the cloak tighter to hide any weakness, nakedness. His bare feet were bruised and bloody and aching, but he refused to stumble into freedom.

Dozha's silhouette was narrow and oddly hunched. Tet could make out little except for his wiry slightness and the length of his hair as his plait flicked from side to side with each step. It was only when he stepped out into the light and turned to give Tet a hand over the last crumbling ledges that Tet was able to truly see the man who had saved him. Sly dark eyes and wide bronze cheeks, the narrow nose and arched brows.

One good hand was held out in an offer of assistance.

The other was missing, cut off at the elbow.

XVI

NUMBER SIX CHILD PERSON

The stars were a thin haze through the smoke and sickly yellow lights of the leather-workers' ghetto, but the moon was a silver grin, and Tet could clearly see his rescuer's face. There was no doubting who he was now, not with those black eyes and that missing right hand, the arm that ended in a puckered stump. The mage's face was subtly older, the youthful cast discarded like a worn disguise. But it was him. The thief mage Vitash wanted Tet to kill. The one he'd met at the fireside of the People of the Dogs.

'What?' the mage Dozha said at Tet's continued silence. 'You were a soldier. You've spent how many weeks in Pal-em-Rasha, you speak her tongue like you were born in her gutters, and you've never seen a cripple before?'

Tet shook his head. It couldn't be the same thief who had slipped through the caravan like a shadow, robbing the People blind. Vitash had tasked Tet with bringing him the thief's head, and had burned the mark of his moon-curse into Tet's right knee. Vitash's witch-sending had led him to a fortune so that Tet could do as he commanded. And now the youth – Tet squinted; the man, wiry and stunted by a hard life – had led Tet out of his own hell. Tet owed Dozha a debt, whether he liked it or not. 'Who are you, truly?'

'I told you my name.' Dozha shrugged. 'We have no time to stand here. Shoom waits, and my pockets are empty.' He gave Tet a hollow grin, but his eyes remained black and humourless.

Tet knew he couldn't stand there naked but for a cloak, too weak to run, pondering on the identities of thieves. He was a dead man if he was seen by the wrong people. By now it was certain that the guards had found the cell empty. If his sudden change in luck held, then perhaps Tet might have another day or two before his escape was reported, while the guards tried to find him in order to save their own hides. But soon enough, the palace would know. He could take no chances. For the moment Tet would have to put his trust in this thief, this liar, this rogue mage. 'Lead on, then,' Tet heard himself say, though a small part of his mind was screaming at him that he was letting himself be manoeuvred from trap to trap.

Dozha turned round, shadows cloaking him, and beckoned for Tet to keep pace.

They kept to the flickering shadows of narrow buildings crammed up against each other like oxen at spring dipping. They flitted through the dark, leaving the stink of the leather works behind, turning down a twisting warren of alleyways until Tet began to recognise familiar landmarks.

He oriented himself, pinpointing the place in the large map in his head. They were going to the outer south-eastern petals of the city. If Tet's guess was right, back to the double-storied battered hovel where Ymat had performed the southern witchcraft that took Tet's soul and magic and put it in the form of a stone and clockwork beetle. He clawed one hand uselessly against the mark at his chest, and shuddered at the sudden stabbing pain. Perhaps the thief had done more than steal Tet back for Ymat Shoom – perhaps he had other treasures. *Please. Please let Ymat have my soul.*

Trailing Dozha, Tet hobbled down a familiar street and toward the painted wooden door he remembered from that briefly wonderful, and mostly awful night. There'd been a clockwork mage in Ymat's employ too; a Sai Tiger. If Tet's soul had not been returned, perhaps the clockworker would be able to trace the *oresh*-beetle, since he had fashioned it. Tet clung to the faint wisp of hope as they approached the door.

Dozha rapped against the splintered wood, and after a few moments the stairs creaked under the weight of a solid man.

Ymat's sallow round face greeted them when the door squealed open. He was frowning, sweating despite the chill air. 'In, in,' he whispered, and waved the mages into the hovel, shutting the door quietly behind them after a quick nervous glance at the deserted street.

The front room was lit by a guttering oil lamp with a length of silk thrown over its glass cage so that the room was sunk into deep lake greens. Once he was certain that they had not been followed, Ymat relaxed, the frown smoothing away. He mopped at his forehead with a small red handkerchief that he tucked back into his wide sleeve, then breathed deeply through his nose, puffing up like a mating season pigeon. 'You look better than I had hoped for,' he said. 'Though you will need to see a medical man.'

Tet's scraped skin, the tears from the hooks, his ribs like a starving dog's, the mangled fingers – and that was all Ymat could say? Tet shook his head in disbelief. He wanted to collapse where he stood, but he forced himself to stay upright, swaying slightly. 'You freed me. Why?'

Ymat stared, eyes bulging a little. 'My dear Ohtet,' he said, his voice stiff and slow. 'I am not a disloyal man.' He beckoned for the mages to follow him and showed Tet to a low seat in the back room. 'Sit. You have been grossly ill-treated. I'm afraid I have no servants here to draw you a bath, but I brought food, and wine. I will have clean clothes found for you.' He gestured at a small table next to the seat, where a clay bowl and two jugs waited.

Tet peered into them. One jug of crystal water and the other of sweet rhododendron wine.

He glanced back up at Ymat, who nodded, and waved his hands toward the waiting food. 'Eat, eat.' This time, he had left his simian friend behind. It was a good thing, Tet didn't think he'd have the energy to try snatch his food away from a monkey.

Tet sat, grateful to finally ease the weight from his shaking legs. If he kept trying to hang on to the dregs of his dignity and stay standing out of some kind of stubborn spite, he'd probably end up falling. The rush of exhilaration in escaping the White Prince's dungeons had fled, leaving Tet wrung out and limp as a grey washrag. His hand trembling with the meagre effort, he poured water, spilling drops down his hands and chin. He didn't care. The water was cold as the heart of a winter-night, like the source of Imal the Black.

'My coin, fat man,' said Dozha, from where he was leaning against the door frame, watching Tet with a faint look of pity.

'Ah.' Ymat looked from Tet to Dozha, wringing his hands. The intricate silver rings of rank flashed in the eerie light. His teeth shone like underwater pearls. 'That.'

'Yes,' Dozha drawled. 'That.' His face had gone very hard, almost as lifeless as a clockwork automaton. Even his voice had taken on a mechanical harshness. Tet decided he would not want this mage's dislike turned on him. Pal-em-Rasha might think the Underpalace was a realm of rumour, but Tet was ready to believe that it had its own kings and princes. He was certain now. The mage was a dark prince to mirror the white one above, an anomaly he had not expected to find in this city that hated mages.

The conversation had continued while Tet had pondered, and it took him a moment to realise that Ymat was addressing him about the question of Dozha's fee. 'I am afraid that Sai Dozha's price for rescuing you was rather high,' Ymat said to Tet. 'And while I am responsible for vast wealth, none of it is *technically* mine. With things being as they are right now, I cannot take the risk that an amount of that size would go unnoticed. You must understand.'

'I see.' Though Tet didn't. His brain was furred with decay, with hunger, with waves of pain that rose and crashed over his head. The water had re-awoken that desperate black hunger in him. His stomach growled and tightened. With a steadier hand, Tet poured some wine and watered it down.

'After your arrest, I had your belongings swiftly removed from the garden-house,' Ymat explained. 'There will be enough there to cover Dozha's price.'

'I understand.' And it was a fair enough deal. Wealth that had come easily, and now easily dispersed. He could hardly have expected Ymat to pay for his freedom out of the goodness of his heart. 'Yes, of course.'

Ymat walked out the room, and Tet heard the clattering of dishes before he returned with a covered brass tray. The smell of cold meats and fried battered vegetables seeped out into the room, and Tet's mouth filled with saliva. 'We can discuss our next moves on full stomachs, I think.'

The thought of what Tet might be forced to do next sounded unappealing, but at least there was food. While Tet ate and drank, filling his stomach until it seemed that his skin would burst and he would die a far less glorious death than any he could have imagined for himself, Ymat left the room, off to busy himself with Dozha's reward.

'So,' said Dozha, casually. 'You were a rich man?'

'Am,' Tet told him, and gnawed at the remains of a bantam wing sticky with orange sauce. His chin was wet with grease. The tear in his lip burned, his teeth wobbled in his gums, but the need for food called louder than pain. Whatever Dozha's cost, there would be something left over with which to start again. He'd had so much.

Dozha's laugh was hollow. 'Were, old man. Were.'

Ymat coughed to announce his return, and he handed Dozha a large leather pouch so loaded with five-and-ones that the seams were stretched and it bulged like Tet's stomach.

Tet could see how poor his freedom had made him. The gems had long since been exchanged for coin, and there were likely to be none left now. But he said nothing. He would have paid more if he'd had to. The White Prince would soon have grown bored, and he was a man who took time and pleasure with his cruelties. Tet hadn't yet known true suffering at the

Prince's hand, and he knew it. He shuddered to think what more could have been done to him.

Finally, sated, Tet slowly wiped one side of his mouth with the inside of his sleeve and leaned back. He could taste blood in his mouth where the recently-healed tear had opened again. It mingled with the salty-sweetness of the chicken and his stomach threatened to revolt. But the feeling was distant, dampened as though it was an echo of something that had happened before. It wasn't a time slip, though. Tet frowned, the edges of his vision blurring slightly.

There was something in the wine, he realised belatedly, some medicine or poison that numbed his skin and left him hollow, only half-aware.

'And.' Ymat coughed again, his fist a delicate curl that he peered over. 'There was also the matter of my own reimbursement for certain measures I was forced to take at great risk to my personal safety.'

'Of course,' Tet slurred, but his stomach sank like a sack full of stones. *How much will I have left after this?* Had he been freed from starvation in a pit simply to starve under the stars? How the gods must be howling with laughter, if they could see this. *'Look, you begged for freedom, and we gave it to you. Enjoy it.'*

'The clockwork horse will suffice,' said Ymat, and Tet choked.

'Ah,' he said, once he'd swallowed the blood filling his mouth. 'Shoom, what is that going to leave me?'

Ymat looked uncomfortable. 'There was a hill-pony—'

'Hast, and how am I to afford her stabling?'

'I will keep her with my own herds until such time as you can collect her,' he said.

Tet felt a momentary pity for Ymat's grooms, but at least Hast would be safe and with her kind. *I will go make my apologies to her as soon as I can.*

'You also have a satchel of clothes, including a few of those I had ordered for you as Ohtet Maynim; a seven-string lute in the hill-tribe style, and this.' He held up a small leather pouch like a maiden's limp hand. 'It should see you through until – until your fortunes change.'

Ah well; ill-gotten wealth, gifted by the gods. It was never really mine to hold on to. Despite his priest-mage upbringing, Tet couldn't help the little pang of loss. In a short time, he'd grown accustomed to wealth. It had made everything so easy, painless. No wonder the temples discouraged it.

It was not the wealth that truly concerned him now, but something far more important. Under his ribs, the numbness spread like dead fingers moving through water. Tet avoided the implications with another question. There was something else he'd been worried about. *Someone else.* 'Laketri?'

Ymat closed his eyes as though in pain. 'A waste, that. I won't be able to use her again.'

Tet swallowed down his rising nausea and closed his good hand into a fist. It was true that he'd barely had time to know her, but now she was a victim to the schemes he'd agreed to. Her death lay with Tet as much as it did with Ymat Shoom.

'I am sorry to hear it,' Tet said softly. What else was there to say – condolences from him would be like ashes rubbed into an open cut.

'As am I. She's a smart girl, but the prince knows her face now.'

Wait. 'She's not dead?'

Ymat waved one hand as he frowned. 'The girl has a lucky streak river-wide. No. She's not dead. Gone back to selling pots, whatever good that does me.'

Tet breathed a little easier. That Laketri still clung to life – had *returned* to life – cheered Tet more than he'd like to acknowledge. If she had the chance, perhaps then so did he. And she was a tenuous link to the Underpalace. She'd known things. 'Selling pots?'

'A waste, I know,' Ymat said. 'Though she's remarkably good at it, for all that. Has a shop in Orphan Street now.'

Their conversation ended as Dozha stepped forward to heft his own sack of coin and set to hiding it carefully under his traveller's coat, checking that the weight of it wouldn't hinder him as he returned to whatever dark passages lead him back to his underworld. Tet's time with him was done.

I was supposed to kill him. A useless man like Tet, with no magic, was meant to kill this mage who could turn him into a serpent with a single word. Tet looked away from Dozha and spoke instead to Ymat, 'And my soul – what of it?'

Dozha paused in his fastenings, his quick fingers falling still as he listened.

'We will talk of that later, Ohtet,' Ymat said. 'You must eat, rebuild your strength. I will fill you a pan of water for washing. That is all I can offer, I'm afraid.' He glanced at the thief. 'And you, your work is done, your coin paid. Be off.'

Dozha flashed him a sharp-toothed grin and bowed to Ymat. 'Blessings of Sinastrillia on your house.'

'Thank you very much, I don't think,' Ymat said with a shudder. 'I'll have no god's luck, ill or good. Out with you. Out.' He shook his head when Dozha was gone. 'Sinastrillia indeed. More a curse than a blessing, these damn thieves.'

Tet stared at the closed door for a moment. Dozha was not the only person he'd met in this city who made free with the use of Sinastrillia's name. *Laketri.* He filed the thought away, keeping track of Laketri and Dozha's possible spider-silk connection.

*

Tet was cleaned, his wounds treated with salves and bandaged, and he was dressed in the plainest of his old clothes when Ymat finally reluctantly told him what had happened to Tet's soul. Ymat had splinted the fingers of Tet's left hand and poured him more drugged wine for the pain. It left him drowsy, but the throb was distant, and he was trying not to think on it.

'He gave it to her,' Ymat said from his seat on the low long couch, and held his hands wide in apology.

'He? To who?' The drug was slowly wearing off. The tiredness shed from Tet like papery skin, and he was itching to do something. To have his revenge against the White Prince, to get back his soul...and to make a decision about Dozha. He put that thought from his head. Dozha was a problem that could wait for a brighter day.

'The Princess Kani. Prince Lainn gave it to her as a betrothal gift, or a thank you. One isn't quite sure. He is playing this game in a most guarded manner.'

'He plans to wed her?'

Ymat shrugged. 'Perhaps. Who can say. The prince is not like other mortals—'

'He's just a man,' Tet spat, 'and not even a mage.'

'And more fool you for believing *that*, Sai Maynim.' Ymat scowled and folded his hands in his lap. 'The truth is, for whatever reason, he has given it to that vicious bitch, and no thief in all of Pal-em-Rasha will go up against her.'

'Dozha?'

Ymat shook his head. 'He said she was too skilled a mage for him to make a move against.'

Skilled; she was at that. But so was Dozha. And therein was a puzzle. 'Why does a mage as powerful as Dozha work as your contact?' A stupid question that Tet knew Ymat would not answer, but the drug had loosened his tongue. 'Why is he only a thief?'

'Only?' Ymat raised a brow.

Tet smiled thinly, his pain and good sense still hazed somewhat by the drugs in his food and the wine. 'Fine. You know what I mean. Why has he not gone to the temples to study to be a priest-mage? Why live in the sewers under the city?' *And if he was not a priest-mage, who had taught him his skills?*

'Who can say. It is not my business to enquire after a mage's training.' Ymat stood. 'And now, Sai Maynim, there is the matter of what you will do now before your death.'

That slapped Tet back to sobriety. 'I will die?'

Ymat nodded. 'An unfortunate reality. I can see no way of getting your soul back. But the process is slow – slow enough, and we have some little time. Perhaps circumstances will change, and perhaps the princess will grow bored with her trinket and we will be able to retrieve it. Until then, I am afraid you must reinvent yourself once more.'

Tet had expected as much. The prince knew him by his old name, and it would be an act of idiocy to keep it. 'Give me until noon,' Tet told Shoom, 'and Ohtet Maynim will be as dead as if the White Prince had truly succeeded.'

*

By the time the sun was overhead and the day was as hot as it was going to get, Tet had a new name. He'd washed the cell dirt from his skin and cleaned the badly-healed six-point scar in the centre of his chest, squeezed out the pus, and scraped the wounds raw and healthy. Ymat had given him a paste to keep them clean, and the pine-scented ointment left his chest cold and greasy under its bandages.

Tet pressed his good hand flat against the throbbing mark, and pushed, hoping to feel some remnant of magery dancing under his palm. *Nothing.* The stone door in his head was still and cold, no sign that it had ever been anything but an image of ancient stone, leading to nothing.

Tet's black hair was plaited into a long queue and coiled and knotted at the back of his head, in the military style of the armies of Pal-em-Rasha. It had taken far too long and was messy and badly-done, but his hands remembered the patterns as if it had been only yesterday the last time he'd braided and bound it back. He'd left the shaggy beard he'd grown underground unshaven. Ohtet Maynim, while not exactly a plump merchant, had been healthy and smooth-cheeked. This new man was poorer, gaunter, and the ragged beard made the hollows of his cheeks appear deeper.

Tet's reflection in the polished mirror was unflattering. He'd lost the best of his youth to war and pain. His eyes were as dead as those frozen fields where he'd fought. Tet's clothes were no longer richly brocaded, embroidered, watered silks covered with intricate paintings. Instead, he wore the grey and white of a peasant or soldier. On his belt, he'd pinned the one small medal he'd earned at the front. A red starling pin that was both common and unremarkable. No badges or sashes of rank.

He went back to the name Tet. A small and stupid act, perhaps, but it was the only name he had left to cling to, that made him feel like himself. Besides, it was a simple name. A peasant's name. In all the languages spoken from the northern mountains right to the shining azure seas that beat against the ragged tooth of the southern lands, Tet had always meant child. To balance it, Tet had given himself the unlucky number six – the number of a child a starving family would have signed up into the army. A child who would have no future but to serve and die. Now in the language of the Deniahn he was Sektet Am. Am was was so common a family name as to mean nothing at all. It was the Deniahn word for person.

Tet had reinvented himself again, this time as the Number-six Child Person. A name for a nobody.

It was an acceptable disguise, close to the truth – as the best disguises were. Tet was a man returned from war, crippled and broken. He had no trace of magic to him. No money, no lands, no gods.

Tet attempted a smile at his mirrored face, and the sight of it saddened him. He had grown old as if responding to Dozha's mockery. His lower lip was black and bruised around the tear. It would leave him a scar, of that he was certain. His broken nose had set a little crooked, and his eyes looked permanently bruised. His chances of looking young and handsome were long gone, slipped away while he wasted time praying to gods who used him like a game piece.

'You look a different man than the one I met a few months ago,' said Ymat's reflection over his shoulder.

Without turning, Tet acknowledged the man's presence. 'A different man indeed.' Carefully, he straightened the front of his short robe and shirt, then gripped the heavy edges of the robe's neck. 'Ymat.' His fingers tightened. 'You are certain Dozha will not steal the beetle back?'

'Most certain.'

'Perhaps if I speak with him, he can be persuaded.'

Ymat stared a long time before answering. The lines that bracketed his mouth had deepened these last weeks, and he had not shaved his head. The tattoos were hidden under a fuzz of grey bristle. He wore a long heavy robe of mustard gold, simple and un-embroidered. Perhaps he too felt frail and weak with his plan so gloriously destroyed. 'And with what would you pay him?'

It was a good question. Tet slipped his right hand into his shirt to feel the pouch of coins tucked behind the wide belt. It was depressingly slack, the coins sliding against each other. The little he had would be enough to rent accommodation in the eastern part of the city for a few months, maybe more if Tet found a landlord foolish enough, but even if he sold Hast – a thought he preferred not to contemplate – Tet would still have nothing to offer Dozha. *I know that, so why even bother?*

Perhaps he needed to look into Dozha's face and remember what it was he'd been cursed to do. For now, the gods' curses meant nothing. They could not find him without his soul and Tet was under no compulsion. The ruined left knee still pained him and made him limp, but it did not grow worse with each passing day, and his right knee did little more than twinge in the coldest parts of the night. Nothing he couldn't live with. With the curse lifted for the moment, it gave Tet time to breathe and think. And time was something he'd always been able to use to his advantage. A grim smile pulled one corner of his mouth. *I'm not beaten yet.*

'Dozha,' Tet repeated. 'It's an unusual name.' Tet had to speak with him. Dozha must know something of the foreign mage Kani – if he was afraid of her. Perhaps if Tet asked the right questions, he would learn a way to get his soul back.

'It is rather,' said Ymat. 'I believe it is in the tongue of the Underpalace.'

The cant of thieves and assassins. It was not as if Tet had occasion to learn it. He knew little more than a few thief signs, and that only from years in pursuit of the thief who took the opals. They were not a trusting people by nature.

'It means dragon,' said Ymat. 'And if that is not warning enough, then consider that if the dragon of the Underpalace will not go against the Princess Kani no matter what I might offer him, then you are more foolish than I believed possible. Drop this fancy of yours. Go to your death with some dignity.'

'I will wait.' Tet straightened and turned to face Ymat. 'Perhaps there will be a change in my luck, and I will not need the help of dragons or thieves.'

'Or of old, fat men who have their fingers in all the millet bowls,' sighed Ymat.

'Or them,' Tet agreed, and for the first time he felt a little good humour. He was not dead, not yet, and while his luck had always run strange, that didn't mean it had *always* run ill. He had done terrible things and lived. Dragons spoke to him, gods cursed him, but Tet was still alive.

He would find out everything he could about this Kani. Tet would take a beggar's bowl and limp through the market, play his lute for drunken courtiers, go to the Dream of the Seven-Petals and listen to the visions men had, he would find Dozha and ask him what he knew. Determination straightened Tet's spine and soothed the old pain in his legs. Ymat had given him hope, whether he knew it or not. 'Thank you, Ymat Shoom.'

'I only wanted the clockwork horse,' Ymat said, waving one hand. 'Now. Once you have found a place, you must make no move to contact me. I will send word to you if I hear anything.'

He could have simply taken the horse, and they both know it. This was about having Tet in his debt. If Tet regained his soul, Ymat would have more than just the magic bindings to control him, he would have bought Tet's loyalty. And he knew who Tet was, how powerful he'd been. And whatever had gone wrong in Ymat's plans, Tet was certain that he still wanted to get his hands on the prince's magical armour. 'And the breastplate?'

Ymat smiled tightly. 'There are other snakes in this city, Sai Am, and I will have the White Prince's protection away from him one day. I am a very patient man.'

XVII

BEGGAR MAGE

Tet found a room to rent in the eastern precinct of the city, far from the convenience of the largest trade-markets and the wealthy merchant streets and the moneylenders, and far from any place that the White Prince would ever go. His landlady was a ghost-faced woman with black hair pulled back from a face gone old too early. She was from the southeast of Utt Dih, and her husband was long dead. She still wore the clothes of her country in a kind of silent defiance, and the long robes that wrapped over her body were once brightly coloured and threaded with silver, but they had faded, and dust had sapped all the jewel-bright tones from her silks.

She offered him a dusty, cold room at the top of a narrow building in the southern style. The roof was slanted against the rain and snow, but instead of the high arched openings Tet was used to, she had tried to bring sunshine into her house with wide windows.

Their slatted shutters only brought in the cold and the wind, and with them, the inevitable orange dust. She kept a flock of flightless ducks, and the yard reeked of their shit. The thick chalky stench overlay everything else. The rent was low, but she demanded two months in advance, and after that Tet had almost nothing left.

The woman had led him up a narrow flight of steps, the wood creaking and musty, releasing spores with each footfall, to the very top room of her house. The room itself was large enough only for a simple bed and a place to set Tet's trunk. The sloping roof made it impossible for him to stand straight except in one small area. *This room will turn me into a hunchback.* At least it was high above the ground, and the sun and air came through the holes in the roof. Tet was certain that if he still had a soul he would sell it again not to be underground.

'You were a soldier,' she said to him in her feeble old woman's voice. It came incongruously from her plump mouth.

'Was.' Tet was tempted to roll up one trouser leg and show her the mess of scars on his knee, but she'd already seen him limping up the stairs. She'd seen Tet's bruised face, his bandaged left hand, the little finger taped neatly to the next.

'Hmmm.' Her eyes narrowed. 'You may take the room, but I want no wastrels under my roof. No seven-petal, and no girls. Do you understand?'

Tet nodded gravely. 'I assure you, you will not be disturbed by anything I do, gracious lady.'

'Good. Good.' She fidgeted with her sleeves, fiddled with the combs in her bound hair. She wasn't ready to leave the room, and Tet began to sweat from a nameless fear. Was she about to turn him in – had she seen something in his face that screamed traitor? Tet tried to stand straighter, to present himself as a soldier returned from the front. Noble and destroyed.

'I am just a woman alone,' she began, and Tet gritted his teeth. He wondered if she was going to try to seduce him in the hopes that he'd bring her some respectability. She surprised him. 'And I have no coin to pay a boy to tend the gardens. I can drop your rent by a five-and-one a week if you will rake and trim for me. The garden is small, and you won't need to tend it often.'

It was a pittance, but it meant Tet would be able to eat. His hand ached at the thought of the labour, but he nodded. He was no stranger to garden-work. 'That will suit,' Tet told her. 'Thank you for your generosity.'

Her mouth pinched small as Tet handed her the coin. She did not help him bring his small chest up the stairs.

*

There was a new fiction to be built from the ashes of Ohtet Maynim. But first Tet spent the next few days sleeping like the dead. Proper sleep, not the cold, nightmare-ridden misery of his cell. His body knocked out his brain, desperate for healing. Tet woke knowing that he had dreamed, his brow slick with sweat, night clothes stuck to his back and chest. His memory was fuzzy. A good thing. On his chest the marks from the soul beetle ached deeper, harder. A cold emptiness that spread right into his flesh.

When Tet was well enough, he ventured back out into the autumn sunshine of Pal-em-Rasha, feeling half-real, not himself. He needed something physical to cement him back into the world.

He started with the garden.

Widow Peniki's back garden turned out to be a small wasteland of neglected vines and rhododendrons. Grass grew in wiry clumps from the dry soil and thorny seeds stuck to Tet's shirt. Despite the growing cold, he'd taken off his outer robe, and sweat dampened his shirt as he hoed at the cracked soil, breaking the clumps of hard red ground apart. His left hand had gone through pain and into a kind of dead numbness.

Tet told Peniki she needed some good mulch to bring the soil back from its state of neglect and she merely stared at him before saying, 'It's a good thing you're here to help me, Sai Am,' and went back to her seemingly endless sweeping. She bought long stiff leaves from the markets every morning and plaited them into brooms that she sold to a broom salesman for next to nothing. Her hands were scratched and calloused from the sharp edges of the leaves. When she wasn't making brooms, she was using them to drive the dust from her stoop.

The autumn sun was relentless, beating down against Tet's back, and he paused to drink some water and to sit against a shady patch near one wall so he could stretch out his legs. He massaged the knotted muscle with his good hand, grinding the pads of fingers and thumb deep into the flesh. The pain retreated a little, but Tet couldn't help thinking of the relief he could get from a few petals, or from a whispered word or two.

He was feeling the lack.

Even when he'd barely used his magic, it had always been there. Though he'd told himself that he used his power only infrequently, he'd used it more often than he had realised. Little magics that Tet had done as unthinkingly as blinking. Not all magic was flash and glamour.

Even this gardening would have been made effortless with some power still at his command. How easy it would have been to whisper softness into the ground, to charm the burrs and thorns from his clothes, to turn away scratches and pain with a suggestion.

Tet sipped warm water from the bowl Widow Peniki had left him, and brushed a large blue and scarlet fly away from his face. It buzzed off, indignant. The heat of the wall and the lethargy were driving away any small desire Tet had to get back up and work on the widow's garden. Instead, his thoughts slipped to his escape from the White Prince's palace. A dragon had spoken to him. And not any dragon – Sinastrillia. *A dragon who styled herself as a god.* Tet wondered how he could find out more about this secret god of thieves and murderers. He could probably find his way back to the leather-working area, go underground and walk the dark mazes until he came back to her river.

Probably. But he did not want to go underground any time soon. And what would he find out, anyway – what she did with Nyangist's former sacrifices? Did she eat them? Use them as slaves? Tet had no reason to go to her, yet. And more than that, he really did not like what she'd said. She *knew* him. Knew more about him than he cared for. *Lord of Time,* she'd called him. Tet shivered despite the sweat and the wall's warmth at his back.

Lord of Time, indeed. It was easy to see how that would snare the attention of a powerful dragon; those creatures that lived in and outside time as they wished, that played their games against the gods, while pretending they did not. Sinastrillia's interest in him was far from comforting.

*

The next weeks were spent cementing his new identity into place. With the remnants of his army uniform worn almost to rags and his hair bound up military style, with his limp and his wasted features, it was not hard for people to look past Tet as if he wasn't there.

On one of the last warm days before the season changed, Tet visited Hast in Ymat Shoom's fields. Ymat had sent him no word, but his state-granted holdings were public knowledge and no one would begrudge an old soldier the chance to rest his elbows on a split fence and watch the hill-ponies in their thickening coats as they grazed.

His magic was gone, and Tet could no longer speak to Hast in the language of beasts, but the roan mare recognised him and ambled over. Or perhaps she was simply taking a chance that he'd have something for her. Which Tet did. A few withered carrots stolen from Peniki's kitchen. They were so shrivelled and brown the widow surely wouldn't miss them, but Hast crunched happily, spittle dripping from her bristled velvet lips. The grass in the fields was thin and browning. Summer's rainy season had long since passed.

'Hast.' Tet scratched her head as she crunched and slobbered the meagre treat from his open palm. 'Oh, old girl. Do not hate me for this. I will come and get you, queen of horses.'

She flicked an ear and nipped his sleeve. Tet liked to think that even though he had no magic left, she understood a little. Hast pressed her soft nose against his chest and huffed, pushing at the circle of scars the soul-beetle had left on him. She was insistent, as if she knew something beyond Tet's simple human understanding, and his chest ached. A thin pain arched all down his ribs and faded. 'There now.' Tet pushed her head away and showed her his empty hands.

She rolled her eyes in answer and sidled back to the small herd of ponies that bunched together under the shade of a large tree. The ravens jeered at him from its branches as Tet turned away.

He wandered far from Ymat's fields and back home. Along the way, Tet saw the signs of the prince's war. He'd turned himself blind to it over the years – begun to accept the unacceptable – but now he was looking for a young man, and when one looks, one sees.

There were no young men. Well, there were, but none were healthy. Most were crippled, and the few that seemed hale had the pocks of disease or addiction or madness. Men young and in their prime had lost limbs to the war, to the borderland frost. Their once beautiful faces had blackened and rotted. They sat on the pavements, their legs curled under them, begging bowls seeded with a few ones, sometimes the heavy red shine of a five.

The orphaned children ran wild in the streets in robber-gangs. The women ran the shops, the women lent money, rented out their houses, their oxen, their arms and skins. The women walked together, and here and there Tet saw a pretty young thing with an older woman who had dressed in short robes and trousers and wore her hair tied like a man's. And there were others, neither man nor woman, who walked freely; an idea unthinkable a decade before.

The White Prince had decimated his city and those around it. The only strong, healthy men left were in his palace, or at his borders. His armies were stretched thin, and yet, somehow, he prevailed.

The cantons fell before his tired and ragged army, and he wore his protection always. While no common man had ever seen this mythical breastplate, it was said he'd had the finest clockwork magicians work on it. It was imbued with charms and power, and no arrows could pierce him, no sword cut his flesh, no magic control him.

Closer to Widow Peniki's house there were white scratches gouged on an alley wall, and Tet recognised thief sign. He followed the markings, but they lead him only to a dead end. When he left the narrow mouth of the street, a group of hard-faced boys watched him, and one called out in an unfamiliar language.

Tet took a chance as the boys slipped away into the crowd. 'Dozha!' he yelled.

The oldest boy – he looked no more than twelve – stopped, and walked back to him. He spoke in a rush of gibberish, and Tet shook his head.

'Dozha,' he repeated. 'I'm looking for him, If you could just—'

The boy snorted and walked away. In a moment, he was lost to the heaving, grubby crowd.

*

The days passed. Tet grew colder, emptier, poorer. At the end of his second week with Peniki he took a final look at his remaining coin and picked up his lute again. The carved dragon headstock had dust gathered in the crevices and he wiped this out as best he could. The paint was old and faded. He unwrapped the bandages from his hand and wriggled his fingers experimentally. The little one was still black with bruises and crooked now despite Ymat's ministrations. It couldn't bend, but its companions were almost usable. He tuned the strings, easing the pegs fractionally until the lute sang again.

With his tea bowl and lute, Tet went to the poor market of the eastern quarter and found a spot for himself among the other beggars. With his empty tea bowl at his crossed feet, Tet tried to play his lute for the passers-by. He played until his joints ached and his fingers had deep marks cut into their tips. At first, he played the old war songs he'd learned in the army, but no one paid for those. A woman spat on him, and another kicked his begging bowl over.

'You shouldn't play such here,' said the old beggar next to him. He was blind, his eyes sewn shut, and his hands were gnarled as the trunks of the oldest trees.

'The city is at war. The White Prince himself commissioned these songs.' But Tet fumbled on the notes.

The man chuckled, then coughed up phlegm. 'We are far from the Demon Prince here.'

Tet looked up. It was true. From this dead and dry little market, the Pistil of Pal-em-Rasha could not be seen. There was no wide avenue for the Prince and his royal guard to march down, pennants flapping, trumpets calling.

It had been so long since he'd played anything but what he'd been told to play. He'd forgotten so much, but after some fumbled starts, the old songs began to thread through Tet's fingers, remembering themselves.

When he switched to the poignant love songs of the south, Tet was rewarded, however slightly. He sang in his cracked voice, and when he ran out of love songs, Tet tried his hand at the mountain dragon's old ballads. These earned him curious looks.

The common people didn't care what he was playing as long as it wasn't the war songs of Pal-em-Rasha, but now and again a woman or boy stopped and watched him sing the dragon's songs, and when he was done, they gifted him a brass one. Always a one.

At the end of the day Tet had made barely any coin and he was hoarse and his fingers shook as he packed up his lute and meagre spoils. Of the handful of ones, five were ruined and useless; a deep gash ran through them, with another diagonal gash through that.

It was a thief sign of some kind, but what it meant Tet did not know.

XVIII

TIK-TOK-TIK-TOK

The week was a long one. Full of strange love songs, and half-sightings. The blind man who had become Tet's neighbour against the market wall liked sitting near him. At least when there was no rattle of coin against wood, he could listen to the old songs.

Tet had started trying to use the little finger as best he could, and though it ached by the end of each day and the notes buzzed, it gave him a small feeling of accomplishment. *I can do this. I can rebuild.*

The blind man, Sovhar, asked him to play songs Tet didn't know, and when he told the man he had never heard them, Sovhar sang to him in his wavery old-man voice until Tet got the tune right. The market was meagre for the most part, and the people buying the thin, limp produce and the rough cloth were thin and rough themselves. They didn't have coin to spare for another broken man home from the border but they left what they could, even if it was nothing more than a gourd or a tuber. Still, Tet couldn't risk going to the more affluent areas – not if the palace guards might still be on the lookout for him, or at least for Ohtet Maynim. Tet didn't want to take the chance that someone might recognise him.

When he trudged home each evening with his meagre take, he kept to the alleyways and shadows. It was not just because he hoped to avoid any guard who might be prowling the eastern areas, but in case he caught a glimpse of a one-armed thief flitting through the dark. That day, like all the others, Tet saw nothing but the long moving shadows of the buildings, clawing the streets like black fingers as the sky washed red over the city. Always disappointment. Tet had collected nine more of the ruined one-pieces by playing the love songs of dragons, but after a few days had passed, no one added more. He must have missed some vital thing – a word he was meant to say in answer, or a sign to give them – to let them know he was to be trusted.

Tet's head was heavy and slow, and his wrists and hands ached from playing so much; he planned to take to his bed early. The homeward-bound crowds had thinned, most people were already at their cooking fires, or boiling water for tea. He walked head down, half-asleep on his feet, and didn't notice the dog until it was right before him.

He jerked to a halt. The dog was red-furred, the tail curling over its back like the coil of a new vine. A free-dog. A strange sight in this city where all the hounds were kept as slaves on iron-link chains. It growled, yellow-white teeth curving to points.

Tet's heart hammered slow and painful, fear making his limbs numb. *Have I already been found?* This was an animal sacred to his people, and to Epsi, Vitash, and Nanak.

The dog walked up to him, stiff-legged, growling, its ears pressed back against the skull.

'You are far from your caravan,' Tet said softly, pushing his fear down and away. *I will not let myself be mastered again.* 'Run back to your people, before one of the prince's men puts a slave's collar about your neck.'

The dog paused, the growling stopped. It sniffed once, then, as though Tet was worth no more of its interest than a pissed-on rock, turned about and left him standing alone in the alley.

A coincidence, Tet told himself. A lost animal. Nothing more. He closed his eyes in silent gratitude before shuffling homewards. But it was a sign. He'd need to make other plans to hide. With his *oresh* gone, the gods might not be able to see him, but they had other means of finding a wayward priest. This was just a free-dog from the caravans, the next time he might come face to face with one of the larger hunting hounds, bred to bring down tigers and leopards.

Tet could change his face, his name, he was hidden by his lack of magic. But he couldn't change his scent. How long would it take for someone to find some article of Ohtet Maynim's clothing, of Tet-Nanak's, and set a hound to his trail?

Not that long at all. He shuddered and pulled his threadbare cloak tighter around his shoulders. *No fear,* he told himself. Fear was the master that would break him, and he was not prepared to walk that road again. *I will make plans, I always do.*

He told Widow Peniki that he would be retiring early after a thin supper of boiled millet and rice cooked over her kitchen fire. She allowed him this meal with grim indulgence.

'I could include your meals,' she said, as she watched him stirring at the little cast iron pot.

'Thank you. I think I have spent too many years eating my own slop to have the palate to appreciate anyone else's cooking.' Tet didn't want to tell her that he had barely enough coin to feed himself, let alone pay someone else to cook for him.

She frowned. 'You should at least put some vegetables in that.'

When all Tet did was hum in gentle agreement, and the only sound left between them was the slow scrape of his spoon against the edges of the pot and the occasional slapping plop of cooking millet porridge, she stood and wrung her dry hands in her apron. 'So be it, Sai Am. And don't forget to clean any mess you make, or you'll be out on your ear,' she paused, 'be sure to take a duck egg for yourself after you've done the gardening.'

It was his plan to move, now that the free-dog had seen him near this place. But where was he to go? Tet had spent almost all his remaining coin on the deposit. And more than that; Peniki's house and garden had become a refuge for him. He wondered that she had no other tenants. Her house was draughty, but she had room to spare. She must have been lonely here in Pal-em-Rasha with only the ghost of her husband for company. All she ever seemed to do was sweep and make brooms.

The millet looked cooked, and the damp mush smell of it was making Tet's mouth water. He'd taken to eating only when he truly had to, and then as little as possible. A duck egg would be a good addition to his breakfast tomorrow.

He was restless. No word from Ymat, a dwindling pile of money, a chance and probably meaningless encounter with a dog. Add to that a slow ache in his chest that grew deeper and colder with every day. There might be no curses working against him and twisting his legs useless, but the loss of his soul was wearing him thin and at night he dreamed of the dark, of the cold, of nothingness.

*

His rented bed was very narrow. When Tet went to sleep, he lay on his back like a corpse and counted the threads of a million cracks in the oiled wooden ceiling beams. He counted the knotholes and the shadows. When the dreams came, he would sometimes think he was still awake.

Not for him the pleasant blankness of dreamless sleep, of exhaustion wiped away by night's soft hand. Instead, he was trapped in a void, hung like a mote in a vast darkness. It was immense. Nothing pressed him in on all sides, swallowed his screams, forced him to stay still. If he tried to move, he was crushed smaller. This was what waited for him after death, Tet knew. This and worse.

Sometimes he woke to hear the last echoes of his screams and wondered how long before Widow Peniki threw him out.

That night was no different, Tet had fallen back into his nightmare like a child tripping off a cliff in a game, and the

Nothing clutched him in its hard fist. His mouth was open, lungs crushed breathless, but all he heard was silence. It had given him a horror of growing blind or deaf like the other beggars in the market. Of being kept underground, gagged.

He screamed. And screamed. Even though he knew it was futile, Tet would be damned if he didn't try *something*. Giving in to the Nothing, even if it was just a dream – and priest-mages would be the first to tell you that there was no such thing as *just a dream* – was giving in to an all-encompassing defeat. If he did not fight, Tet was throwing away hope, his soul, any chance at making something out of what was left of his existence.

The silence filled his throat, plugged his ears and nose.

Tik.

In the dream, Tet paused for breath and listened.

Tok.

Impossible. Since losing his *oresh*, all his nights had been given over to the grave's emptiness and now here came sound, tapping into his head with the softest whisper of a dropping pin.

Again. *Tik. Tok.* Then faster *tiktoktiktoktiktiktiktik* until it ran into an almost inaudible scrabble. It drew closer, but there was nothing in the dark, nothing around him. Tet's skin crawled and itched and he wondered if this was some new aspect of the nightmare, that from now on he would lie soundless and sightless and unable to move while grave insects consumed his living corpse.

He felt it. The prickle against his broken littlest finger, a needle-dig as something began to pinch its way up his ruined hand. This time when he screamed, sound replaced silence. Tet's eyes flew open, and he smashed his head against the slanted roof above the bed. Pain blossomed from the top of his skull, folding his head in petals of aching colour. He closed his watering eyes for a moment and grit his teeth.

When he looked again, there was a thing on his wrist the size of a one-piece coin, working slowly upward, little legs jerking it along. Its carapace was a dim grey in the night. Tet jerked his arm hard against the sloping wall of the roof and smashed the thing clinging there. The shells cracked, splintering fragments of dust.

Doubtless, he'd be bruised all the way up his forearm from the force of the blow, but at least he'd killed the thing crawling on him.

'Fool,' Tet whispered to himself. 'A beetle. It could have done you no harm.' He was not one for killing, even the small things, and his reaction had been driven by dream-terror. Always, it was fear that made him destroy.

The crushed beetle had dropped to the ground and rolled under the bed. A flitter of guilt passed through him as Tet shifted on the narrow bed and rubbed at his arm, erasing the little marks of the beetle's journey.

The first birds were already trilling uncertainly at each other, and soon the dark would lift into the silver-grey of morning. He lay back down, eyes open, and when Tet woke again, the sunlight was pink and gold, and the air was bright with the promise of frost.

After dressing in winter trousers and pulling a quilted short robe over his shirt, Tet knelt down to search out the remains of the beetle. The attic room was home to small things like woodlice and spiders, but he'd not seen a beetle that size in Widow Peniki's house before. Even in the gardens, nothing grew that big.

His fingertips touched something hard and cold, and Tet closed his hand around it. It was slippery like a moss-covered stone pulled from a green pond. Not like a beetle at all. The unusual texture made him shiver, made his hand ache. Slowly, he turned it this way and that, staring at the thing that had been crawling on him in the dark.

A beetle, yes. It was bigger than he remembered – a sparrow's egg of a beetle, the carapace shimmering blue and gold. The colours moved across the wing cases like rainbows on oil. The body was crushed, fine cracks splintered through the carapace, and the black spiked legs were twisted at unnatural angles. Warily, Tet pressed a fingertip to the crease along its back, and the case parted; the wings unfurling like glittering sails. Fine wire threaded through the almost translucent material. The wings were dead, but Tet was familiar enough with the concept of clockwork magery to know that they would have been used to recharge the creature's tiny heart. They would have drawn on sun and warmth and body heat to power the magic keeping it alive.

Under the open wings lay the intricate clockwork inners, with cogs small as spiders' eyes, the butterfly proboscis coils of its springs.

Tet's heart stuttered, and he quickly smoothed the creature shut and wrapped it in a scrap of cloth before tucking it into his belt. It could be anything; a mistake, a message from Ymat, or something more sinister.

Clockwork magery was an intricate business – marrying magic and science. And it was no cheap matter to hire a clockwork mage or to buy one of their trinkets. Their work was the realm of rich men.

A handful of months ago Tet could have closed his eyes, breathed into the First Pattern, and known in an instant what this thing was supposed to do; if it came from friend or enemy. But now all he had was the throbbing ache of a remembered organ, long gone. He had a cold stone door in his head, and a space behind his heart that echoed the hollow thumping, that reminded him of everything he'd lost. First, he'd lost his name before he was even old enough to know what it was that he'd lost, and then his magic. And even if Tet found some way to get his *oresh* back, he would always be constrained by his lack. He should have been able to do the things Dozha did seemingly without effort, to shift his skin and walk like a ghost. Instead, all Tet had was brute force, no subtlety, no perfect control.

The things I could have done if I had my name. Tet laughed bitterly. No wonder every damned princeling and spyling wanted his name for themselves. He must look like an expensive toy set just of reach. Tempting and wasted.

And now, there wasn't even the raw power left to have value to anyone. Without magic Tet was half a man, floundering in a sea that other men learned to swim as children. Tet felt papery; creased and thin. His time was running out and the grains of it slid under his skin and through his bones. With each passing hour, he could feel the shadow of his death drawing closer.

Ymat had said not to go to him, that he would contact Tet if he had any news. But the beetle did not feel like something from Ymat Shoom. While it was true that Ymat did have the clockwork mage Sai Tiger on a leash, this work didn't seem like his. In comparison, Sai Tiger's work was crude and simplistic. This was the work of someone else. And the only people who could tell Tet what this beetle was meant to do were the clockwork magicians themselves. None of them kept businesses in this poverty-stricken quarter and it would be madness to walk into their street of wonders, near the Floating University. If one of them had sent this beetle, Tet could be walking straight into the bright jaws of a trap.

Few toymakers were good enough to create something this fine, and their ability would mark the fabric of the thing as clearly as a stamp. It might be worth the chance of going to one of the men or women who had failed their training and been expelled from the University. They would have information, but not skill enough to have set this thing on him.

Tet no longer looked like the man who'd ridden on a clockwork stallion to the gates of the tower, who swaggered about the town, throwing coin like grain for hens. He'd be safe. Beetle tucked away, Tet strapped his lute to his back and slipped downstairs to where Peniki was already sorting through her reeds and leaves, laying them next to each other on her porch in order of length.

'Good morning.'

'Off early today, are we?' she said, without looking up from her work. Her nimble fingers selected a handful of long-bladed narrow leaves and bent them in half to begin her braiding.

'Some things I need to see to.' Tet paused, one hand pressing against his belt, to the dead beetle behind it. 'Are there any clockwork magicians in the eastern precinct?'

She laughed harshly, a donkey bray. 'Are you a fool?'

Tet smiled innocently back, though it took him a moment to remember how to do it. 'It was a fool's question, I admit.'

'There are failed toymakers.' Her hands wove, her fingers pinched and pulled and threaded.

Exactly what he needed. 'Where would I find these tinkers?'

Peniki finally paused, her hands stilling as she glanced up. 'There's only one near here,' she told him. 'You can find them on the Iron Ox road, there's a shop there – it sells junk and broken clockwork. Yulikiya's their name, but they'll be no help to you if you want real clockwork. They can mend a little, but that's all.' Already she was squinting, calculating what coin Tet must have if he was looking for the services of toymakers.

Tet shook his head. 'Thank you, I'm not in the market for trinkets, but I might have some scrap for them to buy. You have been most helpful.' Tet dropped her a half bow and Peniki sniffed and went back to her work, a blush darkening her cheeks.

*

It was easy enough to find Iron Ox way, where the traders of scrap metal shouted and crashed and filled the air with the bright noise of copper and iron. A few even had signs proclaiming they worked with gold and silver, but in this dingy place, Tet found that hard to believe. Yulikiya's shop was painted a deep bright blue like the sky on the hottest day and a sign hung in the open doorway, with a fine border of red around the painted name. The wood showed through the scarred paint on the walls, and the city's dust had dulled the bright colours, but the shutters were propped open, so Tet peered in.

The interior was small, the walls lined floor to ceiling with planks to serve as shelves, cluttered with more dust and cups and platters and cogs and icons and idols and coils of wire and lengths of rusting metals. There was no order to what stood next to what. The only clear place was on the counter, and even that was taken up by a sprawled white cat with black ears and a few cloudy grey patches along its flanks. It gave him a desultory tail-twitch and yellow-eyed glare.

There was no sign of anyone else.

'Yulikiya?' Tet called softly. Perhaps they were in some back room.

The cat flattened its ears.

Tet was about to leave when a narrow door behind the counter opened and a person wrapped in layers of plain robes barrelled out, their arms filled with a mass of various metal artefacts. Their head was uncovered, the hair pulled back away from their sharp face, and over their eyes they wore ground glass lenses held in place with a wireframe.

'What?' they snapped. 'Oh, wait. You're a customer?' They dumped the metal on the already overflowing counter with a crashing clatter. The cat didn't so much as twitch.

'Something like that,' Tet said.

'Well either you are or you aren't. Which is it?'

Tet pulled out the beetle and cradled it in the curve of his palm. 'Would you be able to tell me about this?'

Yulikiya squinted, then shuffled forward to lean across the counter. 'Hmm.' They frowned as they reached out to grasp Tet's wrist to draw his hand closer. Their fingers were bony and metal-cold. 'I could,' they said, eventually. 'But I'm not a charity.'

'All I need is an answer, for that, you can keep the beetle.'

Their frown deepened. 'That's no small fortune you're handing out,' they said.

'I'm not a thief.'

'Never said you were.' They peered at him through the glass, their eyes small behind them.

'But you thought it.' Tet balanced the beetle on the top of a pile of tarnished cogs and nails. 'It came to me in the night, and that is enough to make any man curious.'

'Or fearful.' Yulikiya plucked the beetle up between forefinger and thumb and held it close to their face to examine it. After a few moments, they glanced at him and said, 'What makes you think I know anything about this sort of thing?'

Tet shrugged. 'Rumour.'

'That old cat.' They closed their fist around the beetle. 'I was not weak,' they said. 'Whatever the rumours tell you. I have the skill of joining magic to metal.'

'Your eyes.'

'That.' Yulikiya nodded. 'I can make nothing for I have no skill for the fine work, for the details, and the craft demands an equal skill in both. My parents thought they would make money off me, sending me to the Floating University, but I was never able to keep up with my classmates. A year,' their face twisted, 'a year's training from books I couldn't read, holding tools to trinkets that were hardly more than blurs.'

'A fickle god, fate.'

'I don't believe in gods.' They smiled thinly. 'What exactly do you want to know, Sai—?'

'Am. Can you tell me what it was set to do?'

'Of course.'

'And who sent it?'

Their face was guarded for a moment, but then they sighed and nodded. 'It was sent to hunt you down, *Sai Am*, and it was sent by the finest clockwork magician in all of the city.'

That much he supposed was obvious from the detail of the work. A white-veiled figure bowed in his imagination and Tet breathed through the sudden flare of fear – perhaps he was wrong to be here. Someone was hunting him and here he was, leaving a shining trail. *Damn all the gods*. It could be any number of enemies. 'And there's no way to tell who it was who hired the maker?'

The thin smile fell away from Yulikiya's face. 'No one *hires* the prince's toymaker. I think you know who sent this.' They held out their hand, palm up, fingers like the petals of chrysanthemums. The beetle sat there, broken and gleaming. At the very heart of it was a tiny glass tube, no bigger than a grain of rice. 'This will hold your essence,' they said. 'Some scrap of skin or such like.'

'Saliva?' Tet asked softly.

Yulikiya nodded.

Tet remembered the taste of the prince's fingers in his rotten mouth, the honey and the heat. The prince knew he'd escaped. Of course he would. Those soldiers would have to tell him, even if it meant their death. Or he would finally have come to see Tet again – to offer him some last choice between death and pleasure. Tet drew in a deep shuddering breath. *First the free-dog, and now this.* While he could brush the first aside as a stray encounter, this was not so easy to dismiss.

He was hunted. And the prince would not take kindly to his escape. The trap was closing on him. 'How long does it take a magician of that skill to create something like this?'

Yulikiya frowned, flicked the beetle with one chewed-to-the-quick nail. 'It is fine work, but small. They could make something like this in two days, maybe three. Another day to set the magic in place.' They squinted back up at him. 'It depends on how eager *he* is to find you.'

And how eager was that? Tet did not like to think. The prince wanted a pet mage at court or he wanted him dead on a spike, and Kani wanted him out of the picture so she had no rivals. More than that – Tet had humiliated the White Prince by escaping. The prince did not like humiliation or losing, and he could draw out revenge like honey spooled out on a wooden spoon. He would not be kind.

'You had best leave, Sai Am, and take your beetle with you.'

Tet hurriedly plucked the offending mechanism from Yulikiya's palm. The clockwork beetle shivered as he tucked it back into place behind his belt. Even wrapped in cloth and crushed, Tet could imagine it coming to life again.

Tik-tok-tik-tik-tok.

Dogs and gods and clockwork hunters, and at the end of it all, a grinning death's head.

I need more time. The thought of it had him laughing, softly, quietly, madly. If he had his soul, he could have all the time he wanted, but instead, Tet had nothing but his wits.

XIX

A PROMISE MADE

Tet **was not** going to wait for Ymat Shoom to make a move, or for his soulless body to finally turn to dust and ash. He had to do something. Though he'd already sold his handful of princely clothes and boots, that money was long gone and the pittance he made at the market was hardly enough to pay for meals. His infrequent attempts to work in Widow Peniki's garden left him more tired than it was worth. His time with her would soon be up and he'd need to pay another month's rent. Even when Tet had been a mage he couldn't conjure gold from the air. What chance did he have now?

The White Prince was looking for him, and with his court toymaker at his disposal, it would not be long before some other trinket found Tet and he ended his days in a cage. If he was lucky.

Without Ymat's help and with no way of tracking down Dozha, Tet had only one person in the city he could turn to. He'd avoided her before this – partly for her own safety, and partly out of guilt. Guilt and fear.

Tet packed his remaining bag neatly under the narrow bed and stowed his lute with it. The only things he took with him were the ruined beetle and the handful of useless coins he'd earned from the thieves in the market, and then made his way across the city on foot.

It took Tet a very long time, but he used the pain as a goad. He used it to remind himself that it was his own foolishness that had brought him here. His drunken negligence to his duties, his fear of punishment, his incomplete control on his magery. He'd used his namelessness as an excuse to hide from his own ability. Instead of acknowledging that he was powerful, he had pretended weakness so that he wouldn't have to deal with the consequences of power. Tet snorted. Great things were expected of great mages, and he did not want to be great.

He wanted to be allowed the freedom that came with mediocrity. It wasn't *quite true* that there was no way for Tet to find his true name – he'd used that as an excuse so that he would never have to try. True, no mage had ever returned from the dead.

But no mage had ever stopped time either.

Tet had let fear rule him. His little flaws had made him less than a person – a weak fool. All he had now was a memory for streets and buildings, and a certain touch with languages. As if that was enough to overcome his incompleteness.

Everything came back to fear. His fear had crippled his studies, had stopped time, had killed a boy in the Canton of Ys. Just a boy, not a soldier. A boy who could no more have stopped Tet than caught a wren with one hand. His fear had killed a girl. He could have bound her in place, and instead fear had made him break her neck.

And finally, his fear had kept him from chasing after death and finding the shades of the people who knew his name. It was too late now. He had no power left to do it. The thing that ultimately destroyed him would come dressed in shining scales of terror.

The sun was red and low, the shadows streaming cold, by the time he came to the end of Orphan Street. The buildings were painted white and the pretty sloping roofs hid carvings under their eaves, and the shutters were coloured in bird-brights, in vines and dragons and flying things that seemed to follow him as he walked.

The paint and colours man was packing up shop as Tet limped past him, and the older man paused to stare, narrow-eyed. He was wrinkled as last year's apples, and he closed the lids of his powdered colours with careful slow movements, shutting the azures and crimsons and saffrons away into the dark. He sniffed as Tet walked to the door of the next shop, and went back to his business. The way he'd looked at Tet though... He shivered. *Not every person in Pal-em-Rasha is a spy, not every set of eyes sees only for the prince.*

Or for the gods.

The pot shop where Laketri was supposed to be had already closed up. The shutters were down and the wooden pegs in place to hold them closed. The wooden frames were lacquered with emerald and the shutters were a deep blue like the start of twilight. The paint was still bright and clean as new shoes.

She was not dead. Instead, she had wealth. Perhaps the prince had given her coin to tell him if ever she saw Tet again. And if she did turn him in, Tet supposed he'd deserve it. He'd been ready to run to save his own skin and leave Laketri to her fate. She had every reason to hate him. He tapped nervously at the door, half-hoping, and half-fearing seeing Laketri's face again. After a few moments, someone shuffled behind the door, then opened it up to him. An older woman, not Laketri at all.

Darkness welled behind her, but Tet heard clattering upstairs, and a snatch of song. The air smelled damply of clay and colour. The rich earth taste of the glazes, the slowburn of the kilns. All along the walls were stacked their wares, and they were fine, fine indeed.

'Sai.' Tet swallowed away the slick cold taste of fear, and he bowed. 'I'm looking for a girl called Laketri. Do you know her?'

The woman's face soured. 'What's she done now?'

Relief rushed unexpectedly through Tet. She was alive and getting into trouble. She was still herself. 'Oh nothing, Nothing. I'm an old friend,' he lied. 'And I hoped to see her.'

'My daughter has no soldier friends,' said her mother. 'Not if I can help it. Idiot girl.'

Before he could think of some protest to make, Laketri's mother stepped aside. 'Come in, then, friend-of-my-daughter.'

Tet bowed again and followed her as she shrieked her daughter's name at the top of her voice. Upstairs, the singing faltered, followed by a laugh and a shout. Voices rose. Many voices. The sisters, he supposed.

Laketri hurtled down the stairs, her hair loose and cut to her shoulders, the front of her jacket and shift beaded with water. 'That little shit Jola just threw his bath water at me, mother—' She paused in mid-complaint when she saw Tet.

'Well.' Laketri stopped on the stairs and pressed one hand to the white wall. She was real. Alive. Her feet were bare, but her dress and belt and jacket were all very fine, the stripes of gold and brown and red, the shimmers and embroidery were not the plain weave Tet had met her in. 'It's you,' she said softly, ignoring her mother's curious look. 'Did you rise from the dead?'

'Something like that.'

'Go back to your grave.'

'Laketri!' said her mother.

'Please,' Tet inched forward, his feet heavy and faltering, knees suddenly fiery with renewed pain as though just seeing her had driven heated nails between the joints. 'A word, just one, and then I will go.'

'One word.' Laketri's face was hard and distant. Ymat Shoom and Tet had both wronged her. But this new wealth came from somewhere. From the White Prince, paying her for her inconvenience in Tet's charade. Perhaps he was paying her to stay a spy.

It didn't matter, Tet still needed to ask her what she knew about Dozha. Laketri was no simple innocent, she knew much more than he did. And he was basing this on a slight slip in an apparently innocent conversation. A conversation that had started a game. 'Sinastrillia.'

Laketri's red face, so beautiful, became harder, smoother, and she smiled with one corner of her mouth. Her eyes were dark as the hearts of fires. 'There's a place,' she said. 'Where the water runs loud and the food is good and monkeys like to meet. I think you know it.'

Tet nodded.

'I'll be there in an hour.' Laketri turned her back to him and went up the stairs, the dusty shadows of the slow night swallowing the pattern of her clothes.

Her mother inched closer to him as though she could glean some understanding of this stranger's place in her daughter's secret life by examining his face, his raiment.

'Thank you,' Tet said, holding on to his shield of politeness. 'So sorry to have disturbed your family.'

'It was no trouble,' she said, but she was already opening the door to usher him out.

*

The wine bar where Tet's life-changing meeting with Ymat Shoom had taken place was exactly as he remembered – filled with the rill and ripple of falling water, the splash from spouted mouths, the air sweet and thick with cooking. He sat alone at a hidden table, hoping that no soldier took a turn here, or some merchant-prince, and recognised him as Ohtet Maynim. They shouldn't; he was ragged and thin as one of Peniki's old brooms, a nameless broken soldier in a city that seemed to vomit them out.

Still, he couldn't be too careful. Tet kept his head down, hidden in the hood of his dirty travel cloak. He breathed in the stink of his own despair, the terrible pathetic life of the unwanted child that was Sektet Am; sixth son and another mouth to feed, another cog in the prince's clockwork war machine. Tet was not the only thin and hungry face here, but even so, none looked quite so ill-used.

He relaxed. There was a greater chance of him being thrown out by the management than of some prince's man seeing in him the mage that had been caught at the heart of the Pistil.

Falls of vines turning crisp and red left trailing shadows on the tiled walls. The stone table was empty except for a bowl of the cheapest wine. Made by peasants, drunk by peasants. Tet told the serving boy that he was waiting on someone before he ordered food and flipped him a single copper piece, and the boy left him alone, turning his attention to more profitable tables.

People flickered past Tet's alcove, but if he was hoping to catch a glimpse of Ymat, he was left disappointed. Eventually, a face appeared from out of the flame-lit dark, and Laketri slid onto the seat opposite him.

His shoulders relaxed a little and they sat in silence. The boy returned, and Laketri ordered platters of food Tet could no longer afford. When the serving boy had brought her sweet wine, and water to wash her hands, she finally acknowledged Tet. Until she said his name, it was as though she sat alone at a table with only a ghost for company. 'Maynim,' she said, her voice low as the sound of the wind at night.

He corrected her. 'Sektet,' he said. 'Sektet Am.'

Laketri wrinkled her nose. 'So many lies. So many little names. And what name do you carry carved on your heart?'

'I don't know.' It was probably the most truthful he'd ever been to her. 'You're doing well, I was worried.'

'About what – that I'd been made an example of? Or that I spilled all your secrets?' She smiled thinly before taking a sip of her wine. 'Don't lie to me, May— Am.'

'I worried.' Tet looked down at the stone table, gritty and pocked with tiny holes, at his bony hand resting against the curve of the wine bowl. The rice-wine had loosened something inside him, shifted the complicated clockwork of his heart. 'How much did the prince pay you for news if I ever came to you?'

Her laugh was loud enough to cut over the burbling water, the burbling pipes. 'The prince paid me nothing. I was just another pot-girl, a stupid one caught up in the webs spun by tricksters and mages.'

When Tet said nothing, Laketri revealed the white tips of her teeth and leaned closer. '*She* paid me, though.'

There could only be one *She*. Kani. 'And what did she want to know?'

'Your name. Your *true* name. I was to weasel it out of you if ever I got the chance to speak to you again.' Her smile flickered.

'And I don't remember it. You should lie.'

Laketri shrugged and leaned away from him. She looked like a teenager again, sulky and unspoiled by time. 'Why bother? She would know soon enough if I were to sell her lies, she would read it on my face, she always—' She raised her head to fix Tet with a hard look. 'What is it you want from me?'

The wine tasted sweeter with each sip, the burn less like a stab through the throat. Tet rummaged for his money purse and emptied the pitiful thing onto the table. The coins were dull round holes in the grey stone.

'I'm not for sale,' she said.

'No, that's not— Look.' He tapped one of the marked coins. 'What does this mean?'

Laketri pulled the nearest coin across the table with one fingertip, into the light of the little lamp between them. Her face slackened, and she ran her fingernail down the gash in the metal. 'I do not know what this means,' she said slowly. 'You should not have come to me.'

'You were working for Shoom—'

'Do not say that name here,' she hissed, eyes suddenly black and angry and frightened. She stood, but Tet stopped her, catching at her wrist.

'You, me, and another.'

'So?' She sat back down. 'And another and another and another.'

'Dozha.'

Her eyelids flickered, but her face remained impassive. Eventually, she said, 'It's not a name I recognise.'

Laketri had been his brief hope – that she might know something about Ymat Shoom's other pets – and the disappointment crushed Tet like a cracked nut beneath a boot heel. Unless she was lying. He pressed on, desperate. The need to find Dozha had become a beacon that would save him. His soulless death was waiting like a whip, and behind that stood the white-veiled toymaker and the White Prince. 'Please. It's important I get hold of him, and I can't approach Sh— The Monkey.'

'Do me a favour,' she said. 'One small favour, and I will do one for you.' She smiled flatly, her eyes empty.

Tet had expected Laketri to simply walk off. 'Anything,' Tet said before he could give himself a chance to turn tail like a scared dog. Desperation was a tireless master.

'Burn down a temple for me.' Laketri curled her hand around her empty wine bowl and spun it slowly. She looked into the stain at the bottom, and not at Tet's face. 'Burn the Grand Temple of Nyangist, and I will find whoever it is you want. That's a promise.'

A mad proposal. Insane. Idiotic. Tet pressed his fingers to his ruined chest, to the aching scar and the emptiness behind it. He remembered Nyangist's lioness-head roaring down from the shields and pennants of the prince's army. He remembered the reeking dead, the frostbitten boys, the ruined men in the streets with their begging bowls. He remembered the vast form of Nyangist towering in the heavens, her searing eyes turned on him with focused hatred.

He thought of how little time he had left. 'You *can* find Dozha,' he repeated, needing to be sure.

Her head jerked up. 'Burn the temple, Sai Am.' She stood. 'Eat what you want, and tell the boy to bring the bill to my shop in the morning.'

It was a promise made by someone who was neither Tet's friend nor his enemy – all they had in common was their bondage to Ymat Shoom, but there was something about Laketri that made Tet want to believe her. But trust? That was another story, especially with Kani paying her.

*

It was near midnight when Tet reached the five jutting phallic towers of Nyangist's temple. He was not going to burn it. Not tonight. Tet told himself he was scouting. Like he'd done for so many years, learning the enemy's territory and drawing the maps he kept in his head.

The building was cornered by squat towers, each topped with a high dome, and at the centre of the courtyard stood the final tower, larger, dome-headed, and tiled in red clay. A strange male symbol for the home of a lioness god.

Statues of lions faced the near-empty plaza. They stood sentry on their stone plinths. Or rather, lay there, the bronze green with age, each one so beautifully, so delicately cast that Tet could almost believe the legend that said the lions all roared when a new king was born.

Did they stretch out and raise their muzzles when the White Prince slipped bloodily into this world? Did they roar as he gasped his first breath? There were no myths about the lions doing anything when a queen was born, so Tet suppose they hadn't cared when the prince's sister followed him, her fist tight on his heel, and he supposed they had not so much as flicked their tails when the attendants strangled the abomination.

He walked up to the nearest, high on its plinth above him, and imagined them shaking their metal flanks and rippling into warm-blooded life, the throaty coughing roars. They were not clockwork. They were older than that newfangled science passing as magic. With one hand resting against the weathered stone, he tried to feel for that remembered jolt of magery, that thrum that let him know when something was like him.

There was nothing. Of course. He knew there wouldn't be, but a small part of him had hoped that a god's power would be enough to spark through his dying flesh and touch that empty place where his soul once was, open the stone door and bring him back to himself. He'd wanted to be rekindled.

The lions stayed motionless high above him. The stars shone dimly through the fog of city pollution and smoke. The light from the priests' fires jumped across the lions' flanks, bathing them in a ghastly orange light.

The plaza was a wide empty wasteland of patterned tile work. The priests lit fires in the hanging metal baskets, and they cast a wild brightness about them, deep pools of light that were horrifying rather than welcoming. The bitter smell of ash coated the back of Tet's throat. Under the soot was another taste. Pungent herbs and roasted meat. Ox or goat, he supposed.

They have given up human sacrifice in Pal-em-Rasha. Nyangist must be unhappy.

Even at this hour, there would still be priests awake, Tet knew. Temples never slept, because gods demanded it. Tet snorted, remembering his own long night shifts in the temple of Nanak, the endless prayers, mediations, the spinning of the great wheel that kept the world turning. He pulled the hood of his nondescript jacket higher and was grateful for the cold that gave him an excuse to wrap his face against the bite of the night air. It was only a small measure of safety here in the heart of the White Prince's domain, but it was better than nothing at all.

At least this temple did not bother with immeasurable flights of stairs, and Tet supposed he was grateful for that. He'd spent the day walking the city and his legs were ready to buckle under him. The prince didn't know he limped – he'd caught Ohtet Maynim, who had been held upright and strong with magic. He had seen the scarring on Tet's naked legs, but would he realise how damaged and weak tet was because of it?

The wide temple doors stood open and inside the central round chamber huddled the dull kneeling shapes of men and women at prayer – more than he'd expected at this hour. The air was heavy and rich with incense and sweet oils, and in the very centre of the open space rose the great stone image of Nyangist, proud and noble as any warrior, her breasts bared in defiance, her spear tip glinting in the copper light coming from the lamps.

On her human torso was the lioness head, the sun-crowned, blood-thirsty face Tet was so familiar with from his time in the White Prince's army. The statue had nothing on the horrifying ferocity of the real thing, however.

She'd grinned down at him from countless flags and pennants and shields, her eyes red as the blood she spilled, her teeth long as fingers, sharp as bone needles. But to see her true face looming above him in the star-still sky, her talons picking at the rift in time, clawing it together, and feeling her hatred seethe from her like a physical force. Well, that was enough to make any man weep. Or shit his trousers.

The night-time worshippers were arrayed in a loose circle around her, facing her stone magnificence. Their mumbled prayers were a far-away chant, hardly recognisable as a language at all. The priest was easy to spot in his loincloth of red and his belt of linked bronze. Even with winter approaching, he had to walk barefoot and uncovered, proof that he was worthy to stand for Nyangist, the Goddess Before Whom All The World Trembles.

His ceremonial sword was at his side, and over one shoulder he wore a beaten copper guard – also more symbolic than useful. It didn't matter. Any priest of Nyangist could kill a man with his bare hands and had to fight the temple lioness for the honour of his place in Nyangist's worship. It all sounded very grand, but Tet had grown up in temples and he'd talked to gods and dragons.

Until he saw the temple's lioness, he was going to assume it was a half-starved mangy thing, legs buckled from life in a cage. Gods didn't bother to send their true avatars unless they really wanted to strike fear into someone. Or drive them mad. It was all part of their game.

Tet had played his share of rounds against dragons, and if the only way for him to be free of all his fate was to play with higher stakes, then he would do just that. He rounded his shoulders and drew on his small skills. Thinking himself older and madder, dropping his mask of Sektet Am and drawing on a new one.

The priest saw him standing motionless, and walked silently through the worshippers, light glancing from his skin like blows of a brilliant hammer, shadows pooling in the hollows of his eyes. For a moment, Tet looked to the sword at the priest's hip and wondered just how stupid he could possibly be to come here now, but then the priest was before him and it was too late to simply turn away. Tet had played his opening move.

'You are new to the temple,' the priest said.

Tet stared him down. 'To this one.'

The priest narrowed his eyes. 'Nyangist does not welcome the children of other gods into her most sacred house.'

'Really?' Tet was tired. He was tired physically from a long day with little break from walking, he was tired mentally from trying to think about how he was to appease everyone in this web of curses and compulsions. He was mostly tired of growing thin and unreal, of being a sack of flesh with no soul to make him real. And he was drunk on rich food and strong rice-wine and he was very, very drunk on not caring anymore. *Play, Tet-Nanak, play,* said the mountain dragon from his youth. *Make it a wise move, make it a foolish one, as long as it is unexpected.*

He owed too many people too many things and he was crushed by it. Why was he standing here ready to make plans to burn a temple so he could talk to a single man? Even if he could track Dozha down with Laketri's help, he had no money to pay the thief mage and Dozha had already refused to steal from the Princess Kani. What could Tet offer him that Shoom could not? What did Dozha truly want?

His name.

Tet's throat warmed. If he got his soul back, he would walk into the world of death and tear his name free from the dark with his teeth if he had to. *If* he burned down a temple, *if* Laketri was not lying to him, *if* Dozha would help him, *if* he could offer Dozha a price he liked, *if* he didn't die first.

If, if, if. There was no more time to sit and pretend that things would magic themselves better. He took the chance and he lost, or he did nothing and he lost. Tet gritted his teeth in a warning smile. At least this way he was in some measure of control over how he got there.

Play, Tet Nanak. The weight of Tet's fear fell from him. His voice boomed. 'Why do the people of Nyangist's chosen city no longer offer sacrifices to their god?'

The priest stared, eyes like boiled eggs, then licked his lips, his eyes flitting this way and that. 'Who are you, stranger?'

'A prophet,' Tet told him. He wanted to laugh. The ridiculousness of the lie swelled his chest. Let them behead him, let them give him to their caged lioness for sport. It hardly mattered. 'Sent in from the desert wastes of the west. A lioness appeared to me in a dream.' The lies flowed sweeter and faster, as though he had tapped a well-spring. Stepping forward into the Eternal Game and choosing his own move had freed him a little.

Tet warmed to his role, and his words rang out, louder and louder, as though he were preaching to a thousand wide-eyed zealots. 'A sorry thing, spotted with mange, her ribs showing. She told me to come to her temple here, and to burn out the rot from her heart, from the heart of her weakest people, that she will be strong again.' His voice trembled with rage and fervour, and he felt it lighting him from within, so much so that for a moment he almost believed that he was a prophet blessed by Nyangist, sent from the desert to put her house in order. Tet bared his long teeth in a lion's snarl.

'A sending,' breathed the priest. He reached out to touch Tet's arm. 'You must come with me.'

For all her terrifying splendour, Nyangist was a fool of a god, if her priests were so gullible as to believe any madman who wandered into their temple was a true prophet. A shiver crawled down his shoulders.

A fool of a god, maybe, but she didn't get her reputation as a blood-thirsty murderer because she rocked children to sleep against her breasts. He gave the towering statue a last look, but the goddess's head was crowned with shadow, and he could no longer see her face.

Your move, gods.

XX

SPARKS TO FLAME

Back rooms of temples were never imposing. The detritus of worship gathered in corners: the dust and the cracked offering bowls, the spoiled texts ready to be scraped down and reused, the offerings that had no place, brooms and buckets and mops.

The priest took Tet through a long library, quiet and dark now, the scribes asleep. High narrow windows let in only the silver light of the moon, and it spilled over the cases and tilted tables, the empty chairs, and inkwells. Past this, and past the snoring dormitories, to a simple room furnished with only an unlit hearth and two plain chairs. The priest bid him sit, and lit the fire with flint and kindling. Laborious. Nyangist was known for swords and vicious metal, not magic.

And like any religion unfamiliar with the strangeness of miracles, it lapped them up.

Once the fire was crackling to itself and the edges of the room had warmed, the priest stood. 'If you would wait, please.' He bowed, far too deferential, and a worm of unease nosed blindly in Tet's stomach.

I must keep my mask. A new one on an old face. Poverty and the loss of Tet's soul had left him scraped down, worn and over-used. These days he looked far older than his thirty-four years.

He certainly felt older. It was in its own way useful for his current deception. He felt like a man who had seen visions of gods and wandered barefoot over the biting sands of Sinal. It was the trick of it, to believe his own fictions. That's what made them real.

Alone, Tet unwrapped the scarf from his face and scratched at the rough thatch of beard. It was threaded with silver, to match the one or two strands of grey in his hair. Poverty had aged him. Tet pushed back his hood and undid the soldier's knot to let his hair hang loose.

A prophet, then. He could play that part easily enough. He pulled on the pieces of his history that had brought him here. Prophets were only men who spoke like dragons – without fear – who twisted the truth in ways other men did not. And Tet had been a priest-mage, and he had spoken with beasts and gods. He opened his head to his littered past like a flower unfurling. The memories were smoke and chant, boredom and fear and pride, all poured in equal measures. The stone door hissed, sand sliding between cracks.

When the priest returned with a woman walking behind him, Tet was ready, centred and patient. He had no magic, but he remembered the edges of it, what power felt like. The woman would be the Arch-Lioness of the temple. Behind her padded a vast shadow, not her own, but the avatar of the god she represented.

Damn. Nyangist had been roused enough to send her shade here. She would know that Tet was no prophet. In this form, she could do him no physical harm, but she could command her priestess to decapitate Tet, to gut him, or feed him to the temple lion.

Tet pulled on his fabricated personality and breathed out fear. He had one small trick still in his favour. In this place, his missing soul was a blessing. Gods did not see humans the way people saw each other. That much Tet had learned. Humans saw meat and smiles and skin and eyes and fingers and the expressions of mortal bodies.

Gods saw only souls, how bright they burned.

Sinastrillia saw me – touched me in the waters of Imal. Tet brushed the thought away. She'd seen *something*, perhaps only the traces of Dozha's magery working through his flesh.

The Arch-Lioness stepped into the light of the flames, and shadows and stripes of red-gold bathed her skin. Like her priest, she wore only the loincloth and the linked belt. Unlike him, she carried no sword or shoulder armour, however ceremonial. She was older than Tet by about a decade, and she was harder. Her leanness was from training, not starvation, and her muscles stood out on her arms and legs like twists of rope. Shadows played across her scars. One of her breasts was gone, leaving only a ridged mess of silvered skin. More scars trailed down her side. Perhaps the temple's caged lioness was not as mangy and crippled as Tet might have believed.

He swallowed away the temptation to give in to fear. It wouldn't make a difference now, without magic. The moment stuttered, flicking back and forth like a series of ink drawings flipped under a thumb, before time settled back into place and the image of the Arch-Lioness stilled. Not a jump, just a minor disturbance in the flow of the universal chronology.

'Who are you?' Her voice was scratchy and high, her throat damaged.

Tet did not stand, instead he willed his breathing slower, every muscle to relax, and sunk deeper into his seat. 'The fire come to burn your temple to the ground,' Tet said mildly. 'As it is willed.' Though his voice was as calm as the deepest waters of Imal the Black, Tet's heart was beating so hard it was a physical ache; any moment it was about to burst inside his chest, a spectacle of pulpy meat and jets of blood. At least Nyangist would be amused. If she could see him.

The woman turned her head sharply. 'Leave us,' she told her priest, and he bowed low, and walked out backward, never turning his face away from the Arch-Lioness.

When he was gone, the woman closed the door, and touched her fingers once against the head of the shadow creature that had settled by her side. Tet tried not to look at it. The shade was a facet of a god, and even knowing that she could not see him didn't make the fear any less powerful. 'Willed by who?' There was no threat behind the words, more the promise of violence and an agonising death.

Such was the way of all gods, Tet supposed. Casual torture and a painful ending.

No fear. No fear. Show no fear, feel nothing. 'Ask her yourself.' Tet gestured lazily to the shadow beast, and the woman turned a faint shade of grey.

'I cannot,' she said finally.

The tension that had been twisting around Tet's heart like twine loosened, and the muscle beat freely again. He stood smoothly, pretending no pain. There was no place for weakness in the temples of gods. Even ones that were blind to you.

'You cannot?' He sneered. 'Your god will not talk to you? She talks to me, and she said many interesting things.' The blasphemies slipped from his tongue. His hands shook.

The priestess jerked forward. 'I am the Blessed of the Goddess Before Whom All The World Trembles. She says you are not here, that you are dust and the wings of moths. That she sent no prophets.'

'And I say that you talk to shadows. I have seen the true face of Nyangist.' That, at least, was not a lie. Tet had seen the dead on the battlefields, watched the crows on the corpses, had seen Nyangist's head in profile shining from the prince's shield. He had seen Nyangist when she gathered with the gods to restart time. 'What has become of the sacrifices?' he snapped.

The Arch-Lioness stepped back; a small victory for him.

He couldn't give her time to think. 'The altars are dry, the blood which should feed her is gone. And where to?' Tet grinned and imagined the death's-head he must present. He summoned memories of rumours, of half-spoken things. About the children that went to Sinastrillia, to die as assassins instead of mewling infants. 'The ones who should bleed on my god's altar are sent instead to a god of thieves and murderers.'

'We have a debt—'

'Unacceptable!' Tet roared. If he were a clockwork human, made by nimble fingers and skilled mages, his head would be whirring at that unexpected revelation. Gods didn't strike bargains; they didn't incur debts. And most importantly, they did not do so with other gods. They all liked to pretend that they were the only ones, and their poor worshippers must pretend likewise. It was usually safest that way. 'What debt can the great and mighty Nyangist owe a serpent?'

The woman's eyes hardened. 'You should know, prophet.'

The seconds flicked past, and for a moment Tet wished he could slow the universe enough to give him time to think. Nyangist had wanted something, something she needed to keep her power, and had no way of getting. Something she wanted badly enough to strike a bargain with another god. What? What? *Think, damn you!*

The White Prince. Everywhere he went, he did the goddess's work; sowing steel, harvesting blood. Whatever else the common people might say about their prince, Deniahn reach had never been so wide, her victories so crushing. That was why men like Ymat Shoom, who served other masters, had come to people like Tet and Dozha. The White Prince could not be stopped. And why could the White Prince not be stopped, why would his city never fall?

Because he owned a blessed piece of armour and two opal eyes. Two eyes stolen from mountain gods, from a temple where only the travelling people still worshipped.

Stolen.

'One thief,' Tet said, and his voice was breathless. A god of murderers had made a bargain with a god of thieves. Or, at least, a prince of murderers had made a baragin with a prince of thieves. He held tighter to the walking stick to keep himself steady. 'And two stones no bigger than the palm of a man's hand. These things are not worth the rightful sacrifices of the greatest of all living gods. I am the voice from the west, the prophet of Nyangist, and with her mouth, I say the debt ends.'

The shadow-lion growled, and Tet wondered if she could hear the words spoken by a soulless man. It didn't matter. The Arch-Lioness was like all priests. She was human. She heard him louder than she heard the voice of god.

*

The sun was pinking the sky by the time Tet limped up onto Widow Peniki's wide front stoop. The Arch-Lioness had made no move to stop him when he left, and there was a feeling about Tet that was stronger and deeper than magery. A feeling he had not experienced for so long that he'd almost forgotten it. It came when he completed a map from memory, or when he played his part so well that a man believed Tet was born in the gutters of Pal-em-Rasha, or the streets of Falingad, or the spindle towers of Ys; that he was a priest or a soldier or a minstrel or a beggar or a leather-dyer or a fisherman or a scholar.

Or a prophet.

He had done a job, and done it well. For now. The priests of Nyangist would no longer hand their sacrifices to Sinastrillia. Perhaps they would forget the old king's decree and the blood would flow down the altar channels, the brains of babies would feed the temple's caged lioness. Tet knew now that it would not be for long. His next part was waiting; now there were other ears to whisper into, and soon the temple of Nyangist would burn.

And Laketri would draw Dozha out for him. And if she didn't, then Tet would have to go underground to Imal the Black and the serpent that lived there, fear or no.

Despite the warmth of accomplishment, Tet was tired. There was no chance of rest. The beetle still tucked into his belt was a spiky reminder of what could happen were he to let down his guard. Even if Yulikiya said it would take a few more days for the prince's toymaker to craft another such hunter, Tet didn't know if he believed that enough to trust his life to it.

More mundane than that, he had only enough coin left now to buy tea. Tomorrow he would have to sell his soldier's medal. If it would get any more than a few coins, he'd be lucky. With his stomach growling and aching, Tet went to the kitchen to boil some water and the last of his millet and tea leaves; it had been many hours since Laketri had paid for his meal. The prospect of starvation just seemed to make him hungrier.

Peniki's mouth puckered when she saw him, as if she had just bitten into a hard lime. 'Out all night,' she said. 'What are you – a tom cat?'

Tet smiled wearily and sat down at the table. 'It's not pleasure that calls me, but work.'

She sniffed. 'And what honest work does a man do at night?'

'What the gods tell him to.' It took everything in him to not rest his head on the warm wood of the table. The golden grain looked smooth and soft as silks, and it beckoned, an inviting pillow. Tet struggled against the pull and pressed his hands harder against the wood. If he stayed seated, he'd give in. Best to simply make his tea and take his lute to the market as though this were simply any other day in what had passed for his recent life.

'And did you find Yulikiya?'

It took Tet a moment to remember. The failed clockwork magician. It seemed a lifetime ago that he'd gone to them, only to discover that the prince had set his toymaker to hunt him down. Since then, he had set in motion the last grand maket game he might well play. 'I found her,' he said softly. His fingers wandered to his belt, to the little beetle wrapped so tightly and tucked away, useless. It would be a mistake to throw it away, and who was to say it would not come back to life and tik-tok its way back to its maker. 'Thank you, Yulikiya was most helpful.'

Tik-tok. Clockwork. Time.

Tet had little of it left, and the beetle was not the only thing the prince's toymaker could send after him. They must have felt it die. A piece of their magic ripped from the universe.

*

The day passed in a haze. Tet barely remembered going up the stairs to his room or collecting his lute. The market seethed around him and he played. The songs of dragons and princes grew confused in his head, and his fingers fumbled over notes.

'You're off today,' said his blind friend. 'You should hush. You're scaring the coin away.'

The notes faded as Tet lifted his fingers from the neck of his lute, and from a nearby stall a woman yelled, 'Thank the goddess.'

He twitched. Tet didn't particularly want to be reminded of Nyangist now. 'I've had little sleep.'

'So I can hear.' The man rattled his bowl hopefully at the sound of approaching feet, but the women passed, their faces stern and taut with worry. 'The nightmares getting worse?'

They spent the days alongside each other. Tet had confessed to him a little about his dreams, though he didn't tell the old man what exactly it was he saw. 'Something like that.' At his feet, the begging bowl was empty but for the two coins he'd seeded it with. Not a single person had stopped to give him anything, not even out of pity. He was wasting the day.

'You should go home,' said the blind man. 'Sleep. You'll play better tomorrow.'

'Will I? I could be dead tomorrow.' The laugh he forced was hollow.

Next to him, the man spat into the gutter. 'Hush with your ill-talk. Go home.' His concern was gone, replaced by irritation and hint of fear. 'You are bad luck today, Am. Bad luck. Go sit somewhere else and plague them if you won't go home.'

Tet scraped up the two lonely coins and slipped the bowl into his shirt. His eyes ached, pulsing against the confines of his sockets, and his vision had gone blurry with strain. Everything around him was too loud – the screams of competing vendors, the angry murmur of barter, children thudding through the alleyways, and the distant bells of the towers, timed to excruciating accuracy by cogs and springs.

His companion's voice was grating. He had to sleep. And if the magician's trinkets came for him, then so be it. Tet couldn't stand guard against death every moment left to him. He staggered back home, and fell asleep with the sun still shining redly through the gaps in the slats of the roof and the howls of distant dogs ringing in his ears.

*

Tet woke without screaming. The night was thick as winter blankets, down-heavy and spun from black silk. All sound was tamped down, and even the distant screeching of the city's cats was not enough to have dragged him from sleep. He lay very still, hearing only his own breathing, the faint rustle of the blanket as his chest moved.

Nothing. Not a tok nor a scrattle. The toymaker would send something soon and who was to say it would be another beetle? The prince's tame clockwork mage did not have a place in the court because of any lack of skill or imagination. They were a mystery and a monster. No one even knew what they looked like. For all he knew, Tet was the only living person besides the White Prince who had heard the toymaker speak in their soft, lilting voice. The toymaker made no public appearances without the veil. The White Death, the people whispered, but that was not a name. Tet wondered what the toymaker's mother had called their new-born child, and what life had led them to tie themself to the prince. Were they simply another slave?

If Tet were still a priest-mage, he'd not pay the toymaker any mind. Priest-mages had always considered the toymakers beneath them. But now he was only a man. And the prince's toymaker a dangerous enemy.

The dark was unrelenting. Tet's skin goose-pimpled when he imagined what things prowled the streets looking for him. The toymaker could have sent anything. It would be small, unnoticeable. A moth of silver and silk, a copper snake, a mantis painted with jade enamel.

Fears were always so much larger in the dark. The blackness gave them the room to grow that the sun did not. On a small table at the head of his bed, Tet had an oil lamp – unused for fear of wasting oil he could not afford to replace, but a little light would cast his terror away. Or reveal it.

A man can fight only the enemy he sees. Carefully, Tet eased one hand out from the covers and felt underneath the low bed for the small satchel holding the last of his belongings. The straps slipped free under his fingers, and he tugged them loose. He fumbled until he found the ridged metal of the top of the flint pouch. It had been months since he'd thought of it, that long ago night by the traveller's campfire when the thief mage had tossed him this in exchange for silence. The mage who had another face, one older and warier, one not shaded by magery. Dozha.

Dozha had given this to him. It had once belonged to the girl-priestess of Vitash.

Would his life have been better if he'd grabbed Dozha that night and held him fast, handed him over as captive to the headsman and his no-longer-virginal daughter? Would Tet have enjoyed that brief moment, the shock in Dozha's eyes when the *old man* turned on him? Tet thought he might have, just as long as it took for a heart to beat once.

Perhaps Tet would still have his soul. Though he would not have appreciated that fact. Anger clenched a hot fist around Tet's throat and he choked on his own stupidity. Quickly, he pulled the flint-pouch free and opened it. Although matches and magic were his norm, he'd worked with tinder and stones and kindling since he was a child, and his fingers remembered. He sat up, slowly, moving closer to the little oil lamp.

The dark responded, whispering and closing around him, wreathing and dancing.

He struck.

One spark.

Two.

Three.

And the room filled with light.

XXI

NANAK, VITASH, EPSI

The cramped attic shone bright as morning. Three sets of glowing eyes stared back at Tet from the narrow floor space.

Milk eyes.

Night sky eyes filled with stars.

Emerald eyes.

Tet's heart battered against his ribs, even though the creatures looking back at him were not clockwork automatons made from metals and furs and powered by spit and magic. They were not the long-limbed hounds of the hunt, who brought down their prey like hungry ghosts.

They were neither real nor machine, real nor imaginary. They lit the room like votive candles. *They are not gods*, was all Tet could think, over and over. If they were, he'd be dead.

Three dogs sat watching him patiently, their eyes round as tea bowls. They flickered in and out of sight like a play of lights behind an oiled paper screen, but as Tet's breathing slowed, they grew solid. He could feel the heat of their bodies. They glowed brighter.

Unreal. Sendings, avatars, or neither? He'd never seen the like before. Tet had spoken with the gods, and these were not them. The three dogs were part of a witch's treasure, as unbelievable as that was.

The priest-mages were men and women of power who had learned the ability to speak the tongue of beasts and dragons, the first language of the world. They could command animals and men, turn the weather and dry the rivers. Some few could send ghostlike avatars into the world, or shape the dreams of living things. The most powerful could change their very shape, the shapes of others.

Stop time.

But mages did not set the gods to work, nor make mimicries of life the way the toymakers did with their clockwork machines.

These dogs before him were the work of a mage of considerable power. If Tet were still able to feel the traceries of mage-work, he was sure he'd taste it on the air like iron grit, feel its static energy course through his body.

Three dogs. Three pieces of power, cut loose and given life. They were pieces of a mage's soul living on after death. *Oresh-things.* A strange terrible magic; no temple-trained mage would ever have done something like this. It went against the law of all gods, against everything the priest-mages held sacred. *Abominations.*

And now they are mine.

The smallest dog could have fit into Tet's satchel, though it looked nothing like the little sleeve-dogs that wealthy men like Shoom kept. Instead of the flattened face and the long fur, the dog was a hunting hound in miniature, long legs and whip-thin tail. Its short fur gleamed golden. The little beast blinked green eyes, and raised its muzzle to howl. The sound was thin and distant, a far-away call of another world.

Tet grinned. He would give them names. Mock the gods who hunted him down.

Epsi, for the smallest.

The middle dog was silver as a polished button, his dark eyes filled with constellations. Easy to give this one a name.

Vitash. The hound didn't howl, but he bared his long teeth in a grin that was not altogether friendly.

Such blasphemy was unlikely to go unpunished, though stacked against all Tet's other failings, it seemed minor at best. Childish, perhaps. The spite in him rose. If these were avatars or sendings of the gods, he'd be dead already – what did it matter if he was spiteful about it. Tet looked to the largest of the hounds. *She will be Nanak, after the god of my childhood.*

The dog was the size of a mountain pony and took up half the room, even sitting. Her copper-red fur moved in a wind Tet couldn't feel and her eyes were brilliant as the rising stars. She was solid as a mountain mastiff. The fur at her head darkened almost to black, and her great plumed tail curved over her back. The hound was nothing like the temple statues. Instead, this Nanak was more like something remembered by a child in a nightmare – half comforting, half terrifying.

Nightmares. Visions. Perhaps I truly am going mad. Tet let out his breath slowly, expecting the spectral hounds to disappear like a phantasmagorical remnant of the dream that had woken him. Slowly, he edged his right hand down to the knee where Nanak had left her star-burn. Under his palm, the scars felt as though they were moving, rippling. It was only his imagination, but that didn't stop the burn of awakened pain.

The three dogs watched him.

How did one command abominations? *You name them and make them your own.* It wouldn't take magic to do this. Only the relinquishing of a life-time's training.

'I am Tet,' he said, and the three magic dogs stared, huge eyes unblinking. 'And so I name you, and call you mine. Nanak,' he said, and the largest dog shifted, turning her charcoal-dark head ever so slightly as her claws ticked against the wood floor. Her fur smelled like camp-fires and forests.

'Vitash.' Tet extended his hand, fingertips brushing the second-largest dog and claiming it. 'Epsi.' The third, his hand drifting over its smooth head.

This was human magic. Mountain magic. Old magic. The priestess Tet-Vitash of the Travellers could not have known she owned such a treasure or she would never have allowed herself to be robbed of it. Her little flint-pouch must have been a relic handed down from witch to witch, its power unknown and forgotten. And Dozha – he'd definitely had no idea what *trinket* he'd handed on to Tet. It had been a throw-away gift. A token.

And now it was a secret only Tet knew. 'What can you do?' he whispered. A joyous hammer beat against his ribs. At his darkest, his most hopeless, he had been saved. Magic. Tet wanted to whoop, to shout out, to fill the air with his human voice. The terrible joy spread through his body, and Tet grinned. His chest ached as though it was about to split, so great was his relief. He spoke again, louder this time. 'What can you do for me?'

The dogs did not answer, and their unblinking stare dampened Tet's excitement. A cold sweat prickled along his back, and he waited warily. Perhaps he was wrong and they were just flights of the imagination with no more power than the torn wing of a butterfly.

Tet tried to converse with the hounds again, his voice soft and controlled. 'Do you understand the words of man?'

Nanak, Vitash, and the tiny Epsi nodded together, once.

That at least made this easier. Tet allowed himself a nervous smile. Now to find out the boundaries of their power. Perhaps he'd have no need to burn down a temple in exchange for the whereabouts of one man, or go powerless against a mage princess with a despotic prince on a leash. 'Will you do as I command?'

Instead of answering, the dogs all looked to one another. Finally Nanak gave him a half-nod. An answer with reservations. Tet took it to mean they would do as he asked, provided it was within their power. His spirits sunk a little. What could three ghostly dogs do?

'There's a breastplate which the White Prince wears—'

Nanak barked low and shook her massive head.

It had been a weak chance. If the breastplate could be magicked away then someone would have done it long ago.

Next to her, the smaller Vitash bared his long teeth in a row of skinning knives bright as frost. Silver spittle hung from his black jowls, and he whined deep in his throat. Eager. The moon dog, god of the night hunt. And next to him, bright as the fallen sun, Epsi, the day-hunter. Epsi growled, and small as he was, Tet was certain the dog would tear the throat out of any living thing he could.

Were Tet some other man, he'd ask them to kill.

Three dogs, three names. And perhaps my debts would be settled. The White Prince, Dozha, Kani. Instead, Tet looked to his hands trembling against his thighs, and knew he would not. The prince was kept safe behind his breastplate's wards, but as for the others.... he couldn't.

In cold blood, he could not do it. He might have been a killer, but he was not a murderer. Even now. A feeling of ice water running out of a cracked earthen pot left him, and Tet warmed from the inside out.

The realisation of this moral line that he would not cross was freeing. Even if the god Vitash wanted Dozha's head, Tet would not be able to do it. While it was true that he'd killed before, it had never been a purposeful act. He would not be defined by murder. He was – or had been – a priest of Nanak. Under all the lies and the masks, he was still at heart the boy who'd been named Tet-Nanak, and the priest-mages of Nanak were never bound to kill.

Perhaps if murder were out the question, a conversation was not. Tet shrugged. It couldn't hurt to try. He wouldn't risk a meeting with an outright enemy, but he had been trying to get a message to one particular mage for long enough. 'Bring me Dozha,' he said, expecting nothing.

Nanak flicked out like a fallen star, leaving him alone with the two smaller dogs.

Hah. If Nanak the ghost dog could bring Dozha right to him, then there'd be no need to keep his word to Laketri, after all. No need to burn down temples and make himself more enemies. Finally, things were turning his way. He grinned in anticipation. Now he had other plans to make. He might once have gone to war for the White Prince, but Tet's skill had never been sticking swords into people. He changed his face and learned new languages and he made his maps.

I change my face. That was what it always came back to.

Decision made, Tet nodded to Vitash. 'I'll need money.' He almost laughed out loud. When had he become so much like common men, always greedy for coin? Then again, what good were abominations and blasphemy if they didn't bring some luxuries. 'Coin enough to build a new persona. Can you bring me this?'

The silver hound simply disappeared. Tet hoped he found that reassuring rather than ominous.

To Epsi he gave the command to hunt down the clockwork creatures the prince's toymaker had sent after him. The little dog faded away.

Tet stood alone in the middle of his dark attic room. The light had vanished with the three dogs, and he shivered, wondering what exactly he had set in motion. All the money in the world was not going to buy him passage away from death. A moment passed before Nanak returned as quickly as she had disappeared, warming the room like a circle of candles. His heart sank. She was alone. No sign of Dozha. The great dog sat down and whined. Tet had no idea what she was trying to say to him – perhaps it was beyond her to bring him a person, or perhaps Dozha was so well-hidden by his magery that even abominations couldn't find him.

There was still one more thing he could try. 'Nanak,' Tet said and the name stuck in his throat like dry millet. 'My soul.' He swallowed hard past the lump. If he could do this, he'd be whole again, but he'd also be at the mercy of the gods once more. 'Please, bring me back myself.'

It was a desperate chance. If the dogs could not bring him the White Prince's mage-warded breastplate, what hope was there of this? But perhaps the *oresh-beetle* was nothing more than a discarded trinket, abandoned in the prince's tower.

Tet made a promise; a useless, desperate one. If the hound could do this one thing for him, he swore he would do something this time – something great, something worthy of being a mage. He would hunt down his own name, whatever it took. He'd be greater than the gods had ever dreamed. Tet had no idea who he made his promise to, but he felt the rightness of it. 'Please,' he said, a fierce whisper.

The light vanished, and Tet was alone in the room again, one hand clutched around the stolen flint-pouch. From far away sounded a brief chorus of howls, like a pack of hunting dogs.

*

The night fluttered, filled with the soft silence of owls and the distant songs of the stars. The bells of the hours and the fighting cats. And the howling of Pal-em-Rasha's slave-dogs. The sound deepened, becoming louder and wilder, and Tet filled with spreading doubt. Even on nights when the moon was fat as a basket of fish, the slave-dogs of Pal-em-Rasha didn't make this much noise.

He shivered, pulling his blankets closer around him. The dark had settled deep, catching on his skin like thorns. The howls sounded closer, shrill and insistent. It could be the three dogs he'd called up from the priestess's flint pouch, but this sounded more like the hunts that the mountain travellers had when they chased the great bow-horned antelope of the cliffs down for their meat and fur. As a priest of Nanak's temple Tet had never been on one of the hunts, but the mages of Epsi and Vitash would go, and as a child he'd stood at the gates and watched the free dogs and their men leave, and would meet them when they returned, the men struggling under the weight of one of the mountain antelopes.

The head would dangle on a neck ripped open, the horns useless, eyes glazed over. The priests of Vitash would heap the entrails on the altars and cover them in glistening fat as an offering for the free-dogs.

Tet knew exactly what those hunting hounds were capable of. His hands were stiff with cold, with fear, and he counted down the empty minutes, waiting for the siren song of the hunt to pass by and move to another part of the city. Though the stone door in his mind stayed closed, he found himself whispering the words of passing, they fell off his tongue like useless ash. No magic. No fire, no warding safety.

Finally, finally, the howls began to fade and he unclenched his fists. Too close. If he was to have any chance at all, Tet had to get his soul back.

His skin tightened with a feverish anticipation. His fingers twitched with the need to strike the sparks and call the three dogs again, to assure himself that they really existed and were not part of a cruel dream sent to plague him with hope. Tet twisted the skin on his forearm viciously. Nothing changed. He was wide awake.

*

Epsi returned first, slipping into the room from the shadows of another realm. He brought golden and green light with him and the darkness receded. Tet let out a slow breath. One hound.

Something metallic clattered on the floor and Tet crouched down to see that Epsi had dropped the mangled and crushed remains of what had once been a clockwork mantis made from the thinnest beaten metal, enamelled and jewelled. A priceless trinket. He smiled grimly.

'Thank you.' Tet inclined his head to the waiting hound and retrieved the broken mantis. If anything, it was more beautifully crafted than the beetle that had crawled into his room the previous night. The wings were the finest silk, the threads almost invisible. Tet could only just make out the faint green gauze of them when he turned the mantis just so.

The long grasping front legs were spiked sharp enough to draw blood and the delicate wires of its antennae bent gently under the slightest pressure of a fingertip. The eyes were true masterpieces of the toymakers' craft. They had not been crafted from a single jewel, as any lesser toymaker might have done. Instead, each eye had been built up of a thousand pin-prick jewels, and the graduations of colour as Tet tilted the creature in the dim light were breath-taking. It was dead now, but if it were still infused with magic it would be impossible to see it as anything but a live creature.

This was no simple mechanical toy. Tet pressed the carapace open to find the little glass heart that held his essence and crushed it between finger and thumb.

His hunter liked beauty. The toymaker's work was the most skilled he'd seen and it was no wonder the prince kept them for himself. For all the times Tet had dismissed the clockwork mages as toymakers, it would be churlish to do the same to this new enemy of his. Tet's respect for them had doubled. So had his fear that it would not be long before they caught him.

The nets were closing, and Tet was sorely aware that, for now, the three dogs were the only things left keeping him from a painful death. It turned out that he did have Dozha to thank for something, whether the thief mage realised it or not. The flint pouch was more valuable to Tet now than any riches. The gift had given him a sliver of hope that he would survive this. Tet breathed out, falling into the familiar pattern of Dragon Mountain breath, and his snarl of twisted fear began to unravel. There was hope, a bright flame, three sparks.

Earlier he'd cheered himself with the thought that his luck had at least always run strange, and here was the proof of it. He closed his fist around the mantis and crushed it smaller, the fragile metal crumpling and tiny jewels falling with the sound of sand grains. If he'd never used what he'd been given, had not struck that flint in fear of the dark, Tet would be dead now. Instead a gift that had seemed small and useless to a mage who could start a fire with a word had turned out to be the greatest of treasures.

Epsi sat with him as they waited for the others to return, tail thumping softly against the scarred wood floor. The bells of the city were calling out the second hour of morning when Vitash came back, his silver-white fur brightening the room. On his back was a small chest of carved wood, balanced like an elephant's palanquin, though held with no straps or girths.

Although Vitash seemed to not notice its weight, when Tet stood to retrieve it, his legs almost buckled.

The ornate chest took a moment to open, as Tet struggled with the latches and locks. When he raised the lid, he found it filled with small coin. Perhaps not as much as he'd had when he'd begun his sham as the merchant Ohtet Maynim with his thief's cache of jewelled treasure, but enough to begin making plans. Most of the coins were bronze and there were no diamonds or precious stones to augment it, but it would do. The coins slid through his fingers, chinking softly. He closed the chest again, and stared thoughtfully at the design. On the wood of the chest was carved the lioness-head of Nyangist, surrounded by the sun. The White Prince's emblem.

Tet grinned.

Stolen from the prince's own treasury. Proof that there were ways to get around his guards and wards, as long as one had the right magic. And proof that the prince was just a man, whatever power he held. Ymat Shoom might be underhanded as any thief but Tet agreed with what he wanted done; take away the prince's protection, strip him of his power, of Nyangist's strength, and the wars would end. Or at least, slowly ebb to something a little more manageable. Less devastating. Tet remembered the bodies, the ice, the raw red blood turned to slush. The smoke trails from the cantons, and the starveling hordes.

Just one man.

And I will find a way to bring him down. He could make plans spun out of hope and relief. Once he had his soul back he'd find a way round the prince's enchantments, battle the clockwork monsters, retrieve the opals and the breastplate. Nanak would have her eyes back and Ymat Shoom would have what he wanted. All Tet's debts would be paid but for one.

And he could see the glimmer of a way out of that last. If he could destroy the prince and bring his toymaker to heel, Tet could have her make a simulacrum of Dozha's head so lifelike that even the gods would be fooled.

While he waited for Nanak to return, Tet made his plans in the dark, desire burning like a forest fire on winter-dry wood. All of Tet's lofty ambitions rested on one fine point: a beetle black stone, the clatter of his trapped soul like a pebble dropped down an empty well.

*

The stars were beginning to burn themselves out by the time Nanak finally returned. Tet's dreams shattered, the disappointment bitter in his mouth when he saw what the hound had brought him.

He jolted to his feet, face twisting as a rush of terror dragged him out of his cloud castle. He cursed the day Dozha had dropped the flint pouch.

Perched high on Nanak's back like a hunter on a mountain pony was a woman with hair of falling night and eyes that glimmered with the reflection of stars in snow.

'Ohtet Maynim,' Kani said, from her seat on the dog's back. She slipped down to stand before him. 'You've changed since we last saw one another. There were many who would be interested to know that you still exist, though none have found you yet.'

Nanak had, in her own way, brought Tet his soul. The beetle pendant hung at Kani's throat, the chain wrapped twice around her slender neck. In the eerie light of the three dogs, it moved and flickered.

The shadows in the room and the feeling of unreality cloaked the two of them. Perhaps it was only a nightmare. 'Do I exist?' Tet said mildly, his heart beating bird-fast. 'Or do you speak with a ghost?'

'A ghost?' Kani laughed. 'Or perhaps a dream.'

She could kill him with a word, and yet she hadn't. The princess was almost as unreal as the long-ago sending of Vitash's priestess, and she watched him coolly, waiting for him to make the first move.

Tet glanced across the small room to the wooden walking stick he used on the days when the pain was at its worst, but Kani stood between him and the door. There was no way he'd be able to grab his stick before Kani snapped his neck with a word. And even if he could reach it – what then – bludgeon her to death?

Epsi stilled, tail ceasing its slow thumping. The little hound growled, and Tet faltered, catching the breathing pattern of Dragon Mountain again. *Don't lose your head.* Kani had made no move yet, and he did at least have the dogs, if nothing else. And he had once had some measure of wit, which, if he could be bothered to use it, Tet admonished himself, would be very useful.

He'd try reason. She was, after all, a fellow mage. 'I see you've brought it back to me.' Tet's voice was very soft, and he couldn't draw his eyes from the pendant. It was him, his soul, and she wore it like it was nothing more than a mundane gem.

'This?' One gloved hand touched the beetle lightly. Her fingers were slim and elegant, and as she brushed her skin Tet felt the ghost of that touch against his own throat, soft as a lover's caress, a warning and a promise, and he swallowed.

Even in the darkest hours she was dressed to dance, in her devil's robes and her long gloves. He wondered where she'd come from – had the hound fetched her from the prince's side, stolen her away. Or had she been roaming Pal-em-Rasha like a demon-ghost?

'Why would you want a gift my beloved gave to me when I asked him so sweetly?' She smiled crookedly, and the hand dropped to her side. 'I know what it is, Maynim. I also know you cannot take it from me. Not even if you were to kill me. It must be given freely.' Her half-smile slipped. 'You will know this spell, of course. It is the same one that keeps the little thieves that Shoom hires from parting the prince from his beloved breastplate. It is not a spell you can undo with a word.'

She was warded. And extremely powerful. And Tet did know the spell she spoke of. It was a simple one that was also devastatingly clever. However, for all its apparent simplicity, it took a god's power to charge it. The prince must have petitioned Nyangist to help with the warding that kept the breastplate bound to him, but what god did Kani serve? It was not one of the Sinal ones, whatever lies she told. And it was not his own gods. She could serve one of the eastern deities. Not a southern one – they were little more than house-spirits, barely capable of much more than turning sour milk fresh.

'What temple do you serve?'

Kani snorted in answer as she turned slowly. There was little room for her to move, but she did so with an effortless grace that made Tet growl. She hadn't been broken, crippled. And like all people who were whole and healthy, she thought she was untouchable.

She is. 'Temple,' he repeated.

She ignored his question, flicking it away as though it were an annoying flea. 'What a dreary little place to have ended up, Maynim.'

'That's not my name.'

Kani laughed. The sound tripped down Tet's spine, lingering in the hollows between his bones, and he thought of Dozha's mockery, how it had slid over his skin, igniting each cell it touched. *What have I turned into – a man so desperate for the touch of power that I would let this happen to me?* He should have bought himself a night's entertainment when he'd still had the coin, and fucked the need away.

'Oh, I know that, *Maynim*.' Kani slid the name over her tongue, like a stolen sweet. 'But we were never truly introduced.' She offered him a brief mockery of a bow. 'The Princess Kani, of Sinal. I worship only myself. I am my own temple.' She smiled like a sickle moon. 'And what is your true name, then?'

'You must think me a fool.'

'I know you to be a fool.' She yawned, covering her mouth with the back of her left hand. When she lowered it again, Kani stared at him for a long while, her brow slightly furrowed. 'I am unused to dream-hunting, to think that you would tell me your true name simply because I ask it. Each time I dream you, you will not answer me.' She closed her eyes briefly. 'Still, we have spoken further, this time. Usually, there is little talking between us.'

Tet blinked. The scheming witch actually thought she was dreaming this meeting with him. Or she thought to draw him out with deceit. He would have to tread carefully. 'Do you often dream of me, and hunt me down?'

The thought pooled red-hot gold about his innards, and he cursed himself. This wasn't desire. It was need. Tet wanted what she kept round her neck. But she dreamed of him, and he wanted to know what he did in these night-time meetings, if they played games of maket, or if their fingers met in other ways, using slower strategies, sighs and whispers.

The smile Kani gave him was sly, familiar. 'Perhaps. But they are never true dreams, they are only the after-images of desire.'

Laketri had already told Tet that Kani wanted his true name. She held his soul. Why not simply crush the beetle into dust and destroy him utterly? Perhaps she dreamed of what she could use him for if she owned his name. He'd be a tool in whatever scheme she played with the White Prince. Or against him.

'And what happens in these false dreams of yours?' Despite himself, Tet was curious.

'We dance,' she said. 'Sometimes.'

Tet's throat closed. 'I'm no dancer, I promise you.' Did they press close to each other, like the women in the bars under the paper lanterns. Or was it a formal dance, diagramming alliances? 'I have no time for it.'

'Oh?' Her left hand rose again to play with the *oresh*-beetle at her throat, stroking down its closed wings. Her right was clenched in a fist, betraying her. 'And why is that? Even cripples dance when the song is right, whether their wounds are from swords, or birth, or the random cruelty of little gods.'

She knew who he really was. Ohtet Maynim had never publicly appeared limping. But Tet-Nanak was broken. Sektet Am, this soldier he was pretending to be, was. Tet was cursed by his gods, and she knew it. He was shaking. Like Shoom, like Sinastrillia, Kani knew too much about him for him to ever be safe.

'Don't be so furious, Maynim—'

'Stop calling me that.'

She tilted her head to the side. 'Fine. The dance is over. The game is done. I have your soul, *Tet-Nanak*. If I give it back to you, you will be powerful again and you will want your revenge. I cannot have that. I will return your soul only when you tell me your true name. Consider it a safe-guard.'

Tet wanted to laugh, to spit in her face. *Impossible*. They were back where they began, only this time it was not the White Prince asking for something he did not have.

'I'll think on it,' he said.

'Don't think too long, Tet-Nanak. Even I can grow bored.'

Outside, the first birds were calling in long looping patterns. It would soon be dawn. The dogs were fading, looking more ghostly with each passing moment. 'Your dream is over,' Tet said to the princess, and he nodded to Nanak, as Kani leapt up on her back as easily as if the woman were made of empty cocoons.

The dog and her strange burden vanished and the other two hounds slowly ghosted out of sight as the night turned over in its sleep and welcomed the rising sun.

XXII

THE MONKEY'S STRATAGEM

The three hounds may not have done exactly as Tet wanted, but thanks to them he was no longer a poor soldier starving to death in a garret room. Dozha's gift had bought Tet another night to live, and a chance to not only eat, but to pay for the fall of a temple. And – if Tet could ever find Dozha – a chance to pay the mage enough to steal Tet's soul back for him. It was doubtful Dozha would have been so free with the little gift had he realised what it was.

Tet was almost a rich man. The birds were singing as he dressed in soldier's old rags. and braided back his hair. He left Widow Peniki's house carrying his lute as always, but now his coat was loaded with coin. There was a spring to his step, and even the pain seemed less.

Instead of his usual spot next to the blind beggar Sovhar, Tet found a new place on the opposite end of the market, far from the view of people who might recognise him.

It was time to reset the board in his favour. With the begging bowl placed before him, Tet played the love songs of dragons and watched the crowd. When the first scarred coin fell into his chipped tea bowl, Tet stopped playing and grabbed the wrist of the girl who had dropped it. Her hand was marred, six-fingered.

The girl tried to pull herself free but Tet held tighter, pulling her closer to him until her face was inches from his. With his prey trapped, Tet fished a small pouch of coins from behind his belt and pressed it into her caught palm. 'This,' he hissed between his teeth, soft enough that only the two of them would hear, 'is a down payment.'

The girl's face remained expressionless, but her fingers closed around the pouch, squeezing the coins together so that she could feel the edges of the money sharp against her skin. 'For?' Her voice was low and gave nothing away.

'A fire,' Tet said, and grinned humourlessly. 'This is a spark. Bring me a fire in its place and I will give you a lord's ransom.'

A trickle of sweat cut a thin path through the dust on her face. She answered his smile with one of her own, more a twitch and curled lip than anything else. 'I am not an arsonist.'

'And I am not a soldier.' Tet released her hand, and she drew back but made no motion to leave. Everyone had a price, and at that moment, Tet commanded a small fortune.

The girl narrowed her eyes, considering the job, and the promised offer. It was no small thing to burn down a building, but it was done often enough and for varying reasons. 'How do I know you will pay?'

'You do not.' Tet shrugged a shoulder. 'But by Sinastrillia I swear it.' He hid the shaking in his hands by picking up the lute from his lap and setting his fingers to the familiar lines, calling out the songs the mountain dragon had sung in her deep, echoing voice when she was drunk on millet beer. He had invoked the girl's own god, and this was dangerous ground. Gods, above all else, were jealous.

And murderous. Which is what had brought him to this point in the first place. Tet steeled himself. 'There is a god,' he said, still soft, not singing yet. He let the music drown his words, 'who would consume everything if she were not kept in check.'

The girl glanced up at the sky, as though at any moment the gods might appear, looking down on their playthings. 'We are not the lords of gods.'

'It suits gods to have us think so.' He played a run of notes, a cheerful lilt. 'But with so many gods, it seems it is up to us to choose a master. There is power in that. We keep balance.'

'Hmmm.' She weighed the coin bag in her palm. It was a dangerous job he was asking, Tet knew, but he hoped those who worshipped Sinastrillia would see that as a perk. To tweak the nose of an enemy god, and get good coin for it, that was incentive enough for the thieves and cut-throats of the Underpalace. And there was no love lost – Nyangist had killed too many – and now that Tet had pushed Nyangist's temple into withdrawing from the contract between the two gods, he had another lever to use. 'A god owes a god a debt,' Tet said, conversationally, 'and will no longer pay it. How many who should go to the Underpalace will now die on her altars?'

Tet seemed to have struck a very raw nerve. The girl drew back with a hiss. 'You know this? How?'

He swallowed. The broken contract was still new. 'The Arch Lioness has declared the debt paid,' he said. 'There will be no more. How many of your friends lived because of that debt?' He glanced at her six-fingered hand and raised an eyebrow. 'What is it the White Prince does to those who do not give him what they owe?'

The girl slipped the coin pouch into her short jacket and nodded. 'He burns their houses.'

'He burns their houses.' Tet smiled as the girl walked away. She gave him one backward look before she disappeared into the crowd, their strange transaction passing unnoticed.

Perhaps his music was sweeter or perhaps this side of the market was more lucrative. Tet returned home with his tea bowl filled with small coins and glass beads.

Widow Peniki even remarked on his good humour. 'You're cheerful,' she said as she ladled out dinner.

'I am.' Tet stretched out his legs, ignoring the stabbing pain. 'It was a good day's takings.' He pushed a few coins across the table toward her. 'Enough that I can pay for a fine meal.'

Widow Peniki had cooked a meat stew, rich and oily, root vegetables gone to sweet mush and spiced with southern flavours. She served it with rice like clouds, and Tet ate well, taking pleasure in each mouthful.

'Today brought me music, money, good food, and better company. I would be a sour man to find fault with a beautiful day.' The flint pouch was tucked safely behind Tet's belt, and he kept pressing his hand against it, like a child excited by a new toy. Soon, night would fall and Tet would light the sparks.

Peniki blushed and took his bowl away to give him second helpings.

'So what was it that has brought you such good cheer, Am?' she asked as they rounded off the meal with new-beer she'd brought out.

Tet tipped lazily back in his chair. 'M y gods have smiled on me,' he said and took a deep drink of the new-beer. It was not quite true, but Peniki hardly needed to know that. 'And perhaps, finally, I will get what I want.'

'Gods?' Peniki filled his mug with more sour beer. 'I thought you were a servant of Nyangist.'

That's what Tet had told her. No one wanted to be the fool who harboured some infidel mage, even if he was no mage at all. 'My god,' Tet corrected. 'But is not Nyangist the sum of all gods?' The lie was a weak one. *I should have stopped drinking and shut up.*

Peniki stared at him with narrowed eyes, and his heart thrashed like a moth caught in the inner curve of a grease lamp, the edges of its wings just beginning to char.

He needed to allay her fears. Tet opened his mouth with no real idea of what to say. He was about to ask her how the day's broom sales had been when the bells of Pal-em-Rasha began clamouring.

'What is it?' Peniki set down her bowl of beer. 'Armies?' Fright iced up her voice, spreading silvery cracks like filigree. 'It can't be.'

'No.' With his heart hammering in anticipation, Tet stood from his chair. 'There's no army that can take on Pal-em-Rasha while the White Prince is Nyangist's champion. This must be something else.'

The streets were filled with women and children and old men, and all stood talking in hushed excitement while on the eastern horizon an early dawn turned the sky golden. False sunrise spread over the quarter where Nyangist's great temple stood, where the royal slaughterhouses and the wide empty courtyard and bronze lions waited for worshippers.

A flicker grew in Tet's heart, a little joyful flame.

'A fire,' said one old man. 'I saw the like in '27, back when the Seven-Petals quarter went up in flames. Took four days for the fires to be put out.'

'That's more than fifty years ago,' said a woman near him. 'Your memory is riddled with maggots. That's no fire, that's the coming of Nyangist. All should fall down now, and tremble.'

'You're not,' snapped back the old man, and she smiled terribly in answer.

'I'm right with my god, I have given her soldiers.'

Martyrs, more like. But the man was right; it was a fire. There would be no coming of a goddess tonight, or any other. Her central temple in Pal-em-Rasha had fallen. The thieves and worshippers of Sinastrillia had done as Tet had asked and burned it to the ground. The enormity of the act struck Tet with a sudden cold force, and he took in a sharp breath. He was soulless, he reminded himself. No god, not even Nyangist, could see him here.

The temple burned because of him. Tet bowed his head to hide his elation. He would owe the girl. He'd promised a fortune for the risk. How lucky for him that he could pay for Nyangist's destruction with coin stolen from her sweet prince's own vaults.

'We should go help,' said Peniki weakly, but everyone ignored her. It was some distance to the temple area, and no one wanted to leave their home and what little they had to go and beat out someone else's fires. Another sign of how the city had been divided by the war. The people had lost too much to care what happened to those whose word sent their children to their deaths.

Some of the people in the crowd had seen first-hand what had become of those children. Their friends, their uncles and aunts, their fathers.

A little fire seemed hardly enough of a price for the temple to pay, for those who remembered the Battle of Ys, or of Jora, or any of a hundred skirmishes.

The Canton of Ys had fallen eventually, because of people like Tet and his spying, and because of an army of frost-bitten soldiers. It fell to the low, long sound of Pal-em-Rasha's trumpets, a droning endless cacophony. But Ys had not been enough, and the prince's army was spread thin; a web of half-trained warriors holding all the lands from Pal-em-Rasha to Ys where Imal the Black began, and east to the borders of Imradia where the fortress cities of Damak, Aza, and Jora still stood sentinel, with the White Prince's vast hordes waiting at their feet, hand bells ringing to wake the sun and their red oxen eating the fields down to dust.

Tet did not need to have been at the walls of Damak or the others to know exactly how the armies looked with their shining forests of spears, their ranks of archers, the elites with pearl-handled guns, the billowing pennants of Nyangist, the drums and cymbals, the clockwork machines trundling bones to splinters beneath their spiked wheels.

Noise. So much noise. Even when there was no fighting, the prince's armies kept their slow constant drums, driving fear into their enemies and reminding them what waited outside their walls. Tet's own time in Ys had been set to a drone of endless sonic pressure. The prince's war had used magic and music and toys as weapons, as well as the more usual fare of sword and spear.

In that the prince had shown something of himself; Nyangist was more likely to arm herself with tooth and claw. The human magics that Prince Lainn had brought into his employ must have sat awkwardly with her. But the prince had never been one to bow to anyone. Not to his father, and not to the god who decorated his shield. He had always been a man with the compulsion to use whatever was at his disposal.

That's why he wanted Tet's name. Even if Nyangist balked at the thought of using a priest-mage of Nanak, the prince would see no reason to turn away a perfectly good weapon. Tet would be simply another soldier to command in the White Prince's endless war of expansion.

The night raged on, burning itself out in a pall of smoke and ash.

No one went to put out fires in the eastern quarter, where the temple slowly collapsed to rubble. Tet imagined the beams crumbling, the stones falling, the glass shattering like ice and frost cracking in the first days of spring. The lion in its cage burned to charred flesh and bone.

'Come away.' Tet caught Peniki's sleeve. 'There's nothing we can do.' Despite his fierce joy, he was aching from lack of sleep and one too many bowls of the widow's sour beer. His eyes felt like stone marbles, his feet were made of clay.

Peniki didn't argue, and she said nothing when Tet left her to head up the stairs to his little windowless room. She crouched near the door, watching the strange daylight unfold over the city. From far off came screaming. The city was curled around its pain, the buildings shrieked.

Upstairs, the false day was so bright, light seeping through fine cracks in the wood and the straw roofing, that when Tet struck sparks from his flint all he could see was the vague gauzy outline of the dogs before they faded away completely

So. They were creatures only of the dark. Or maybe Tet had only been allowed one night to see them. The thought made his stomach churn. Perhaps he'd had only a single moment, one chance to make his life right and he'd squandered it on a boxful of coins and one night of freedom from the toymaker's beasts.

'You will be fine,' he told himself. Even if that was all he was to get, it still left him with a treasury under his bed, now hidden by an old cloak too travel-stained and ragged to draw attention.

It would be some time before the toymaker could send another hunter, which meant Tet had at least another night in which to make a new plan. Because one road had led to nothing, did not mean that every street was closed.

He took a band of cloth and bound his eyes to the strange light that had turned night to day, and tried to sleep.

*

Never let it be said that the priest-mage Tet reneged on all his debts. As much as it would have suited him to keep the stolen coins, if word got back to Sinastrillia that Tet had invoked her and then broken his word, he knew it would not go well for him.

Sinastrillia's people knew where he worked. They found him by morning, the smell of smoke wrapped around them. The women in the market took their payment, their eyes hooded. They came to him, one by one, when he played the songs from the mountains, when he sang his off-key renditions of the dragon's ballads.

After a morning spent handing out small pouches to the women who threw useless marked coins into his begging bowl, Tet hired a rickshaw to Laketri's shop. Not because he felt like showing off his meagre fortune. If the dogs didn't come back and these were the last riches Tet would ever see, he wanted to enjoy one day without agony layered on agony. As he'd told his blind friend in the marketplace: he could be dead tomorrow.

Tet carried a bag filled with the best finds he could dig out of the coin chest: bright points of fallen stars, red and green and yellow. It would have to be enough to hire Dozha.

Laketri's pottery shop was open, and a host of round-faced girls with copper cheeks and hair like starlings' wings filled the place. Laketri's sisters, Tet supposed. They had her look, though none was as beautiful or as sly. The girls clamoured about Tet, trying to interest him in their jade green pots, their peacock turquoise pots, their carved and painted pots, their thrown and delicate pots.

'Not today,' Tet said to the one pulling at his sleeve. 'Please, no pots. I'm here to see Laketri.'

'Let him go,' said a familiar voice, and the crowd of girls fell back.

Laketri stepped from the back of the shop, her hands still gloved with clay and dust. Her fingers shone a dull silver-grey. On her arms, the dust had begun to dry the colour of bone ash. This wasn't the local Deniah red clay, but white clay from far to the east, even past the cities of Imradia and over those vast ranges of mountains called the Weeping Ones, because they never end and they wear a man down to nothingness. With the war stretching into its second decade, it must have cost a fortune for the clay alone. Kani's money, Tet presumed. Still waiting for him to slip and tell Laketri his true name.

'You have wealthy clients,' Tet said to Laketri.

She wiped her bare arms clean with a rag. 'This way, Sai, we will discuss pottery far away from the ears of little mice.' She smiled at her sisters and they fell back, leaving him to follow Laketri into the back room where she made her pots.

A half-collapsed vase slumped on her wheel and Laketri sighed glumly at the sight. 'You are most inconvenient, Am.'

'I apologise.'

She covered the ruined pot with a damp rag. 'I have little time to waste, what is it you want?'

'You already know.'

Her face was as implacable as a theatre mask, showing nothing. She could be annoyed, angry, relieved. She might be lying to him about her connection to the thief mage. 'Dozha.'

Tet nodded. 'I did as you asked.'

Laketri looked off to the side before flicking her glance back at him. 'So you did. You burned down her temple. It has always been my one wish. Shoom would always put me off when I asked, saying the time wasn't right.' She sat down on a narrow bench against one wall and pulled a worn pillow onto her lap. The pillow had once been fine, the tassels dyed crimson against the teal silk, but the shine had faded away in places. 'After you were caught, I told Shoom that he still owed me, and he said that it would be foolish to rouse Nyangist now. Not when we had failed so spectacularly and the prince was still protected.'

'He plans to try to steal the breastplate again?' Tet pretended disinterest. He'd like to know what the Monkey was going to do.

She shrugged. 'He tells me nothing.'

'And Kani is still in touch with you?' Tet paced the room. 'She also pays you for things – why not ask her to destroy the temple for you?'

She scowled. 'Perhaps it does not suit hi— Her plans. Do I look like I can control *royalty*?'

'Or perhaps she simply couldn't.'

'She can do whatever she wants, Am. Unlike you, she has power. Magic.'

'Ah, but who was it that burned down the temple as you wanted?'

Laketri fell silent, her fingers threading the frayed ends of her cushion. 'I saw the fires,' she said after Tet sat down. 'I went to the temple courtyard and watched the place burn down.' She bared her teeth. 'I thought it would feel better,' she whispered.

The first of Laketri's lessons in adulthood; that revenge was never as sweet a dish as people promise. 'Dozha,' Tet repeated. 'Tell me how to find him.'

'He cannot be found.' Her fingers worked at the tassels, pulling the threads apart.

'That's not what you promised me.'

Laketri stilled and looked up, her brown eyes wide, glistening with something that was neither fear nor regret. Tet had no idea what she was thinking. 'I can send him a message for you. But no one knows where he is. He is the ghost of the city, and he leaves no trace.'

'He's a man who has barely left his boyhood behind,' Tet said, dryly. 'He's a mage, not a ghost. I know better than anyone that mages are still men.' His head was starting to hurt. All Laketri could give him was a weak promise that a message may or may not reach Dozha. 'Fine, send him a message then.'

He was not going to give Laketri his address, not when she could simply turn him over to Kani or the White Prince. 'Tell him I will wait for him by the house where he was paid for my return, tonight.' Ymat Shoom's hovel. Tet hoped it would be unoccupied. It was a convenient place that they were both familiar with. 'I will wait from the eleventh hour until the first, only.'

And if Dozha didn't come, there would be another way to reach him. Another trap to set. Tet would see his mage again if he had to swim Imal the Black under the city to do it.

XXIII

PRINCE MAGE

Tet **was in** the rickshaw on his way back home, when the traffic drew to a congested halt and the sounds of stamping feet and droning trumpets drifted towards him. He leaned forward to the rickshaw puller, a man wiry with corded muscle, his hair cut close to his skull. 'What's this?'

'The prince,' the rickshaw man said, and wiped the sweat from his forehead.

It had to be one of his gods-damned parades – entertainments Tet had thankfully missed while stuck in the poorer quarter with Widow Peniki. He didn't trust his luck to hold should the prince see him in the midst of a crowd, even with his disguise of beard and poverty. The man had marked Tet; the little ridge of scar tissue on the inside of his lip still throbbed as though calling out to its maker. Tet breathed in sharply through his nose and craned behind him.

The way was blocked by a mass of people pushing forward, jostling all around the stalled rickshaws and wagons and horses. Ahead, the wide thoroughfare was empty, as though anyone who had been there had magically been melted away. Now Tet could see the uniforms of palace guards, scarlet and gold-helmed. Their lion's head helmets glittered down on both sides of the avenue. The faces of the soldiers were blank. They were not looking for him. They were there to stand guard, to raise their swords and pistols to their saviour.

Tet settled back and pulled the cowl of his traveller's cloak a little further down. Who would take notice of one of many minor merchants sitting in a rickshaw, waiting for the show to be over?

The trumpets screamed louder, and the cacophony began; the drums, the metallic droning of the singers. Around the rickshaw, the crowd seethed and whispered and murmured. From further up the road came a triumphant shout, and it slid through the masses, growing louder, brighter.

The first of the White Prince's procession came into view. The clockwork birds with their strings of prayer flags in all the colours of the fallen lands. Bunting dangled from their claws, their wide wings beating against the air. Light glinted off their feathers. Tet tightened his grip on the railing of the rickshaw.

After them, the flag bearers marched, and after them, soldiers mounted on matched black horses, their pistols glinting at their sides. The air was perfumed by girls running down the streets with swinging incense holders. Underneath the heady musk was another smell, older and darker. Burned timber and roast meat. When the wind blew from the mountains, the city could pretend that the temple district was not still smouldering, but every now and again a gust swept up from the south-east, and they were reminded.

For now, though, the crowds were enraptured by the sweet must of incense from the southern plains.

The ground shook, vibrations bouncing through the wheels of Tet's rickshaw and up into the soles of his feet, jarring his spine. Another piercing shriek, so loud that the windows of nearby houses rattled in sympathy.

It approached, huge feet raised slow, slamming down with a *whump*, the trunk raised to shriek again. An elephant. A monstrous elephant greater than any living beast. It was higher than the buildings, golden in the sun, the mechanisms screaming under the weight of its metal plating. It was glorious, studded with topaz jewels to catch the light. The white tusks swept the ground, and they too were strung with prayers.

Whump.

The open palanquin on its back was shaded with rippling cloths of silk, white wings that flared out behind it, and the edges of these were held aloft by more of the clockwork birds. Sunlight struck the elephant and it glared brighter than a fire, so that even behind his cowl Tet had to shade his eyes.

Standing atop this terrifying work of art and magery were two figures. They were a foot apart, yet their hands were joined, raised triumphantly. The White Prince shone bright as his mount, but all in silvers and whites like a cold star. His broken eyes were impossible to see at this distance. A mirrored cloak was pinned across his shoulders, and there was no sign of the gods-damned breastplate. He had to be wearing it. Even here in the heart of his capital, he would not risk a public appearance without protection.

Holding his raised hand in her black-gloved one was the Princess Kani. They were of a height, and her black hair streamed behind her. She was just another of his pennants, there to show the city what he had captured.

Her hair flung forward, and the sky collapsed around the city, falling down on her head like a shattered bowl of azure crystal. The elephant ground into reverse. The people around Tet shoved jerkily, and the chatter took on a bizarre grating sound. They were speaking backwards.

This had never happened before.

Only Tet was living in the right order, moving forward through time, while all around him the world shuddered and heaved. The sun collapsed. The clockwork beasts split their seams. 'Stop,' he said out loud, useless, as the world tore itself apart.

Shifting shapes gathered over the skies, merging and drifting like veils of clouds. The gods. Terror clutched at Tet as Nanak's great blind head swung toward him, her ears pricked.

Tet held himself still while time staggered in reverse. The *whump* of the elephant's great feet made the ground shudder.

He willed time to return to normal and for the gods to pass him by, before Nanak turned her head again, and he was forgotten.

The world froze.

A long moment, an infinite moment, and then, with another ground-shaking *whump* the procession flowed forward again and the gods faded from the resurrected sky.

With his heart beating so fast it hurt, Tet tried to calm himself; practiced breathing slowly through his nose. Perhaps he could pretend that what just happened had been nothing, a minor wobble. It was not as though the little stall in time had changed anything. The day carried on, the world unaware that for one bizarre moment it had done something it shouldn't have. Had never done before.

It was getting worse, and Tet could no longer pretend otherwise. The gods were failing, and time was breaking.

The shouting and trumpeting had risen to an unbelievable din, but the grand procession passed, taking the ululations with it and the sound began to die. Around Tet, the crowd sighed out, and the carriages and rickshaws jerked forward and the rhythm of the city was set in motion again.

'Why was the prince out?' Tet asked.

'Don't you know?' The rickshaw man squinted back at him. 'You live under a rock? ...Sai.'

'Something like it,' Tet said, thinking of Peniki's attic room.

'The prince has finally announced his engagement to the Princess Kani of Sinal; they will be married in a month.'

'That seems a short engagement.'

The runner shrugged and took up his handles. 'Who are we to question the ways of princes and foreign witches?'

'Who indeed,' Tet murmured. A month, and what then – would the White Prince be dead, or would he be even more protected? He'd have his court clockworker, and this fake princess filled with power for his wife. With Kani under his control, there would be even less opportunity to reach him.

And she *was* a fake, Tet was sure of it. She might well be a mage, but she was not a princess. Not of Sinal or any other kingdom. And the White Prince surely knew it. The prince had never shown any interest in expanding his kingdom to the west and crossing the twin deserts and the three seas to reach Sinal.

But Kani came with promises of money and power and that might be enough for the White Prince to overlook her little fictions. His vast armies were not fed by empty coffers. Perhaps he had simply closed his eyes to the lie and taken what he could from his bride-to-be.

Unlikely. The White Prince was many things; mad, cruel, and an egomaniac, but that did not make him a fool. He was calculating. And so was Kani.

Kani had something the prince wanted, just as the prince had something she wanted. She was a witch desperate for power. She already had Tet's soul and now she wanted his name. If there was any way for her to get such a thing he would be under her command.

What was she trying to do by marrying the prince and seeking to control Tet? Was she simply hoarding power, or did she have a greater plan in mind? Tet needed to speak to her again. Firstly to find out exactly what it was she wanted to use this marriage bed for, and, more importantly, see if he could persuade her to trust him enough to return his soul.

But before that, there was the matter of meeting Dozha.

*

Fires had taken root through the entire temple district, and smoke trails clung to the spires and minarets, wreathed about the sloped roofs, and wound through the alleyways like the immense ghosts of cats. The night sky turned a dull yellow-grey. Up in the sanctuary of his attic room, the light crept through the wooden panels. Once again, his sparks brought Tet only wavering shades and an empty, tight feeling in his stomach.

He would have to meet Dozha without the protection of the dogs. Instead of the hoped-for cloak of the dark and the safety of the ghost-hounds, Tet had only his own wits. He slunk in the narrow alleyway of a nearby building on the opposite side of the narrow road, watching the door of the house where Ymat Shoom had taken his soul

The house was abandoned. The windows were dusted dark and the door handle had begun to tarnish. Leaves and dirt gathered on the small front step. No one had been here since he'd last walked through those doors, Tet was almost certain of it. Ymat had no need of this particular house. He had dozens of such places scattered throughout the city.

The Great Mouth of the centre city called out the half-hour once, and Tet shifted, wrapping his cloak tighter about his shoulders. He'd been waiting about ten minutes. His plan had been to set up long before Dozha arrived, so he would know if Dozha came alone. If he deigned to come at all.

'You're early,' said a voice from above and behind him. A dark sly voice that had once led Tet out of darkness and pain.

Tet pretended that he'd not been startled; holding his breath until he could let it out, willing his heart to beat slower. With magic, he could have shrouded himself in shadows and moonlight if he'd wanted, and here he was bumbling about like a blind fool in a cluttered room. Dozha had made an idiot of him. The thief had his magery, and Tet had nothing but a body made weak by its reliance on the same.

When he was certain that no tremble would betray him, Tet glanced back and up to where the voice came from. 'What part of the eleventh hour do you not understand?'

Dozha sat on the overhang of the roof, legs swinging gently. In the false-day he should have been easy to see, but he was blurry, wavery as a daydream. He pushed off from the ledge with his one arm and landed in a neat cat crouch. 'You're looking less pathetic these days,' Dozha said as he became clearer, standing up to grin at Tet's annoyance. 'Sektet Am.'

Tet shrugged. 'So you also know my name. The Underpalace is simply another network of spies.'

Dozha laughed brightly, the sound clear in the flame-lit night. 'The Underpalace *is* the network of spies. So far you've pretended – rather badly, your touch is slipping – to be a beggar musician and one-time soldier, rented an attic room from a widow who sometimes feels she ought to have designs on you, but then changes her mind because she thinks you may be mad. You have played songs never sung in the upper world of Pal-em-Rasha before as if they were nothing more than ballads and lullabies; spoken as a prophet and burned down a temple for a chance to meet with me.' He looked to the flaming horizon. 'A temple, and possibly a good quarter of the city. My people were perhaps a little too enthusiastic about that commission.'

'Your people.'

'Come, Am. You knew that.' He leaned against the wall and crossed his left arm over his chest. Dozha gripped the upper part of his remaining right arm and watched Tet, one eyebrow raised in shrewd amusement.

It was the first time Tet had looked clearly upon Dozha's true face, studied his features. He was handsome, Tet had already known that. His eyebrows were ink sweeps, his nose long and straight. In a city like this, he was a little dark for the current fashion where nobles powdered themselves to look more like their demonic prince. He was the same copper-kettle colouring as Laketri.

Even the middle-classes in Pal-em-Rasha tried to emulate the White Prince, and women sold creams guaranteed to lighten the skin. But Dozha was his own prince, and he had kept his own face in a city filled with masks. 'You went to all the trouble of contacting me through Laketri, so, what do you want of me?' he asked.

'How do you know her?' Tet was curious to see what version of their history Dozha would tell him. Perhaps they were lovers. The thought left Tet feeling nauseated, sweaty with something he couldn't pinpoint. He didn't like to think of their mouths meeting beneath rabbit-white moons, their dark hair tangling like fishermen's nets.

'Is that what you called me for?' Dozha seemed amused. 'To question me about my connection to Laketri?' Tet was no threat to him, and Dozha could humour him as long as it pleased.

Tet shook his head. 'Of course not.' He put one hand to his belt, then hesitated. It was time to speak the truth. 'How much would it cost for you to steal a small stone, no bigger than a beetle, from the Princess Kani?'

The sly grin faltered a little, then slipped from his face completely as Dozha considered. 'You are not the first to ask me to steal that,' he said, after a while. 'And now, as then, I will only say I cannot.'

'Cannot, or will not? Ymat said that you wouldn't because she's too well-warded. But you have power equal to hers, of that, I'm sure. I know magery, even if he does not.'

'Equal?' Dozha raised a brow. 'Is that all?'

Mages and flattery, they go together like dragons and spite. 'From what little I've seen, maybe greater.' Tet shook his head. 'Certainly, you are powerful, and you know the ways in and out of the palace. You are a Prince Thief. One little false princess should be no match for you.'

'How do you know she's false?'

'Because I'm not an idiot.'

He laughed once. 'And you think the White Prince is?'

'Not at all.' Tet stepped closer, could smell Dozha's skin, heady as the incense that burned in the city today, the faintest whisper of musk perfume. Under that clung the fragile chalk smell of seven-petal. So the mage was an addict and a dandy.

Tet leaned his face close enough that he could have torn Dozha's ear off with his teeth, or whispered lover's secrets. His stomach twisted tight as the smallest coil in a clockwork mantis. His heart beat faster. The flutter of it pulsed at wrists, at temple, at groin. 'I think the Princess Kani is playing a dangerous game, but that's not my problem,' Tet whispered, and Dozha shivered and pulled a little away. Not as much as Tet would have expected. 'All I want is my soul back.'

Dozha pressed his cheek near Tet's, and when he answered, Tet felt the coolness of breath like a mountain breeze against his face. 'I will see what I can do.' Dozha stepped back, the momentary intimacy broken.

I'll see what I can do. Not a yes, but also not a no, not exactly. They hadn't spoken of a price. Gods knew Dozha had to realise how important this was to Tet, and he was sure to twist that knife in deep. Tet caught his left sleeve, and Dozha jerked his hand back so that Tet's fingers end up curling around the thief's wrist. It felt thinner than it should, and the faint pulse tremored through his own skin. Tet held on for longer than was suitable, letting that fire heat him.

Dozha said nothing. Then finally he quirked one corner of his mouth just slightly and pulled his hand free.

The night grew colder, wrapping them in a shiver of mist. 'How much will I owe you?' Tet was truly hopeful for the first time since the White Prince had him incarcerated. Even if getting his soul back meant all the gods would find him, at least he would not die soulless, condemned to the black eternity of nothing.

'Oh, nothing, Sai Am.' Dozha raised his hand – the one that Tet had just held trapped for a moment – and revealed the full leather pouch of jewels and coins that Tet had brought with him. 'You have already paid.'

Tet's stomach plummeted. In one instant Dozha had not only stolen his wealth but also stilled his heart to cold black marble. 'I don't trust you,' Tet said.

'You'd be a fool if you did,' Dozha said. 'But I don't think you've a choice.' He grinned and faded back into shadows and mist.

Tet stood alone in the alleyway, cold and captured by a terror he was unable to explain. He slipped one hand behind his belt to make certain that the leather pouch was all Dozha had taken. Cold metal spiked his fingertips. The flint pouch was still there. His heart contracted, and Tet realised with a vague dizzy incomprehension that he was leaning against a freezing alley wall in the dark, body aching for the feather touch of fingers too fast for him to remember. He closed his fist about the flint pouch and tightened his grip. *You're losing your mind, Tet. Not that you'll miss it – it can go join your soul.*

Slowly, Tet forced himself upright and limped home, not certain if he had achieved anything with this meeting, or merely dug a trap for himself and lined it with sharpened ivory spikes. *You are a fool, Dozha told you so himself.*

*

Widow Peniki was still up, the lamps burning in her windows like watchful eyes. The evening skies had begun to darken properly and she was not the only one who had lit candles against the returning night. Tet slowed as he approached the house. It was not just the constant ache of scarred knees, but a lance of wariness. Peniki never stayed up late. She was a woman who liked her sleep – and slept well, judging by all Tet's nightmare screams that had gone unremarked.

The White Prince had found him. Or Nyangist. Or Nanak, Vitash, and Epsi. Any number of men and women and gods who wanted him dead. Or better yet, tied up and ready to pay penance in blood and pain. *I should run. Now. I have the flint-pouch.*

The door swung open and Tet lurched back. From the city came the high-pitched howling of the hunting dogs of the mountains.

A man stepped out from the warmth of the kitchen and said his good-nights to the Widow Peniki, the two of them silhouetted in the glow from the house. He kept his head close to her, and they laughed. She sounded girlish for a moment, like someone had painted the bloom back into her soul.

The clenched feeling inside Tet loosened. It was nothing to be worried about. The hunt passed by, their howls fading, and the man finally left the doorway and walked past, his coat-jacket swinging loose. He paused to clap his hand on Tet's shoulder like they were old friends. Tet had no memory of ever having seen his face, and the fear barrelled back, cold and heavy.

'You must be Pen's tenant,' he said. 'She told me all about you.'

'Oh.' Tet swallowed. 'All?'

'Yes.' He leaned forward, still grinning, and said, just low enough for Tet to hear, his mouth barely moving, his smile fixed. 'Shoom sends his regards.'

'I think you have me confused with someone else,' Tet said around the dry tackiness in his mouth. 'I know no Shoom.'

'Is that so?' He laughed merrily. 'I have no idea why he would send me here then, with a message for you.'

'What a strange thing to do, indeed.'

The smile dropped from the man's face, and in a sudden moment of awakening Tet recognised him. He had trimmed his hair and scraped away his curled moustache; it was the clockwork magician who helped trap Tet's soul inside the beetle-stone. The Tiger. 'You are stepping onto dangerous roads, Sai Am,' the Tiger said. 'This is not a threat, merely a friendly reminder that Shoom will cut all ties with you if he must. If you make it necessary.'

'I have done nothing,' Tet said.

'The fires are out.' The Tiger let go of his shoulder. 'And by dawn the priests will be rebuilding the Great Temple.'

'You think I did that? You know as well as I do that I haven't a shred of power left. You can tell Ymat that he has great faith in my abilities if he thinks I'm responsible for the razing of Nyangist's temple.'

'Shoom knows it was you, and he is not impressed. The temple was to fall, but not now, not with the demon still safe. All you have done is rouse Nyangist. You make life difficult for Shoom, and he will make certain you do not have the chance again.' The Tiger clipped a salute; one soldier to another. 'Step carefully, footman Am.'

'Thank you for the warning,' Tet said drily.

The Tiger's smile returned, thin as an old paring knife. 'Shoom is watching.'

*

'What was that?' said Peniki when Tet walked inside. 'How do you know that man?'

'I do not,' he told her. Weariness scratched deep into his bones, and Tet was disquieted by the conversation with the Tiger. Ymat had too much riding on his plan to break the prince's power. If his guesses were even half true then Ymat had thrown money at Laketri, at Dozha, even perhaps at Kani. Should Ymat take it into his head that Tet was a liability instead of a chance at freedom from the prince's tyranny, he would get rid of him. And while Prince Lainn and his toymaker might not know where Tet was currently hiding, Ymat most certainly did.

Damn that man and his network of spies. Dozha's network of spies. Tet's head began to throb. There were too many tangled threads and Tet had neither the time nor courage now to begin unpicking them to see what he was left with. 'I'm tired,' he told Peniki. 'I think it best if I turn in.'

She gave him a candle to light the way up to his little attic room, and Tet took the steps slowly, feet dragging. Shadows chased at his heels, bouncing along the narrow walls like excited children. The night was back, and Tet needed to see if the dogs would come when he struck the flint.

The candle guttered and Tet readied the flint pouch before pinching the little flame out between his fingers and letting the darkness fall. He took a deep breath, and did not pray to gods who couldn't hear him.

One strike, one spark, two, three, and the dogs filled the attic, their tea bowl eyes bright as suns. Tet's heart flamed with relief and a fierce desire to see Kani again. Perhaps tonight he would be able to convince her to give him what he wanted.

XXIV

NAMELESS, SOULLESS

The dogs did as they were bid; Epsi running off to hunt down more of the palace toymaker's trinkets, Vitash prowling the streets on the look-out for Ymat's men, to warn Tet if any came close, and Nanak....

Nanak might not be able to bring Tet his soul, but she could bring him the woman who held it and thought she dreamed herself into Tet's own dreams.

It was many hours before Nanak returned, with no rider on her back.

'Where is she?' Tet's mouth filled with copper, salt, despair.

Nanak whined, her tail thumping against the wooden boards.

Could Kani have simply disappeared? She might be a fiction, but she was still flesh and blood and bone. 'You must find her,' Tet hissed. 'Bring her to me.'

The vast dog shuffled, turning about in place, her whines loud enough to make the timbers shake.

'Hush.' Tet glanced at the door. Peniki might be asleep but enough noise like this and she would be there soon. Or perhaps not. After all, she had left Tet to his screaming dreams and never came to check on him. It might be that she had written off his nightmares as simply the price of having a ruined soldier under her roof. 'Try again,' he ordered Nanak. 'Kani is out there, and she has my soul. Bring it to me.'

Nanak faded away as slowly as melting ice; her huge eyes woebegone. They were the last things to disappear, and when she had finally left, Tet sat alone, skin turning cold and sweaty. Maybe Dozha had gone after Kani already, and that's why Nanak couldn't find her. Perhaps she was already a corpse. Strangely, Tet could feel no joy at the thought.

The first of the cockerels were calling at the fading stars when Nanak finally returned. This time she was not riderless, though Kani was not dressed in her customary finery. Nor was she dead.

She wore sleep trousers and a jacket in a simple cut made from raw silk and her hair was unbound, falling down past her shoulders. Her face was still immaculately made up with ivory paint, her eyebrows dark swoops inked darker and longer, ending in fine points, coal shadows smudged about them. She was alluring, her face a mask betraying nothing. Perhaps Nanak had caught her after one of the prince's balls, or straight from his bed.

The pendant sat at her breastbone, and she had not yet removed her long black gloves.

'Do you wear these even when you dream?'

Kani smiled slyly. 'Do I dream?'

'You must. For I can think of no way to magic a princess straight to me like a stolen soul.'

Her smile faded. 'Whatever you may think, I am an honourable person. I did not steal your soul. It was given to me.'

True, though Tet doubted the prince would have given it to her so readily had he known exactly what it was. 'But you asked for it.'

Kani slipped elegantly off Nanak's back, then touched the dog with her left hand, stroking her huge ears, running her gloved fingers down the animal's muzzle. 'So I did,' she murmured. 'I knew it was powerful, I could taste your soul inside it, even if Lainn couldn't.'

'You call him by his name?' It had been a long time since Tet had heard anyone call the prince anything but the White Prince, as if he were not a living man, but some great figure of history; a myth, not a mortal.

'We are engaged.'

'I heard. And you one step closer to stealing the breastplate for Ymat Shoom.' Tet threw down the accusation and waited to see if she would respond to the bait.

Kani scowled. 'Tell me your name,' she said, changing tack.

Tet shook his head. 'Even if I wanted to, I cannot. If you work for Ymat, then you know as much.'

'Cannot, or will not?'

The words echoed in his head. Tet had said them himself just this night as the last of the fires lit the horizon, as he'd paid Dozha to bring him this pendant that was now only a hand's breadth away. Tet stepped closer to Kani and rested one hand on Nanak's head, stroking down so that he ghosted past Kani's fingers.

Everyone in this game spoke in innuendoes, in carefully selected half-truths. Perhaps it was time to cut through the webs with an honest blade. 'Believe me or do not believe me, but I do not know my name,' Tet said. 'I was orphaned, and I have only ever known the name the temple gave me: Tet-Nanak. All others are fictions.'

'I cannot rule you with a name like Tet-Nanak,' Kani said sourly, 'and you know it.'

'And I have no name to give you in exchange for my soul. If I had some power, perhaps I could get my name back—'

'How?' she snapped, her eyes slitted. 'Who would know your name when you don't?'

Tet swallowed. 'The ones who named me.'

'And they are dead.'

'There's no need to remind me of that.' Tet steadied himself against the dog's side. 'I have pondered the problem of going to the land of the dead and asking them; after all, when a man is desperate...'

Kani blinked. 'Only the dead go there, *Tet-Nanak*. What use would you be to me dead, or have you found a way to come crawling back from the caves?'

It was not as though Tet had any plan, just a numb hope that he would be the one mage powerful enough to simply smash his way between the worlds of living and dead and return unscathed. His shoulders slumped, and he shook his head. 'Not— Not yet.'

'Then we have no bargain.' She lowered her hand and turned to look at him. Her eyes were slanted and large, her eyebrows like the wings of birds. Her nose was long and narrow. She was a handsome woman, despite the painted pale skin, and Tet wondered what she looked like stripped of all her false faces, her long gloves, and wardings. If she were just a woman and not a mage who held his life in her silken fingers.

'Then I will die anyway.' He was desperate. She had to give him his soul back. All she could do with it was torture him to a slow nameless death. Perhaps Kani was petty enough to think that fitting. She had not corrected him when he had suggested she worked for Shoom, and he gave voice to his fevered suspicions. 'I cannot tell you my name, but I can promise to help you retrieve the breastplate Shoom is paying you for.'

'You think you know everything, Tet-Nanak,' she said softly, and her breath was cold and her hair was fragrant as seven-petals. 'You would be wrong.'

It had been a desperate shot in the dark, and it had not met its target. 'Give me my soul. Please.' It was close enough to grab, and casting all instincts aside, Tet reached up and closed his hand around the *oresh*-beetle, willing the magic out from the stone and back into him.

Kani laughed and caught his wrist with her right hand. It was very cold and hard, and she crushed his grip easily. She was stronger than he could ever have imagined. 'It will not work until it rests around your own neck, and you cannot take it from me by force, you know that. I must give it freely. And for now, you cannot meet my price.'

Tet was unable to see the wards on her skin, not now, but he could still feel himself being shifted back, pushed away. She let go of his hand.

'Please, please.' He'd prostrate himself and beg if he had to. He had no pride left, just the empty prospect of the approaching end. If the hounds didn't find him soon, or the prince's toymaker. It didn't matter which, because the dark was still going to be waiting for him at the end.

Perhaps he could accept death if he knew he would at least go on to the cavern of shades to where his unremembered parents waited. Tet could face it then. But death without a soul would curse him to an eternity of nothing. No mage could face that knowledge and grin into the dark, uncaring.

Eternity was time broken. And broken. And broken again. A million fractured points of nothing.

'Please.' It came out a crushed whisper, and if Tet had still had magic now the whole world would be slowing around them, fumbling to a halt, such was the strength of his despair. 'You are holding my death.'

'And what is death if you cower in the dark, Tet-Nanak?" She stepped back and smiled slowly. 'We should dance.'

She toyed with him. 'I've told you I don't dance.'

'You may enjoy the world more if you did. Forget the confines of priesthood, embrace what small pleasures you have left. Life is shit, life is short, and life is nothing if you don't enjoy the little things that make it worthwhile.' Pal-em-Rasha's market accent flickered below her words like a fish in a muddy stream. The flat vowels of the Deniahn people.

Tet grimaced. 'And if we danced, would you give me back my soul?'

Kani grabbed the fur at Nanak's nape and swung herself back onto her mount. 'I'll think about it.' Her voice was not the haughty, throaty speech of the princess of Sinal. Kani was losing her grip on her fiction. 'But I'm not a sentimental person,' she said as Nanak faded, taking her away.

*

Tet lay on his back, blanket clutched between his fingers, as he tried to think of a way free. Around him, all his paths were narrowing and choking, leading him to an alleyway with a blank wall at the end. Nowhere to go. All his hopes rested on Dozha being able to get that beetle away from Kani, and that the two mages were not working together, opposite sides of the same coin that Ymat Shoom had flicked into the air.

Ymat had seemed annoyed by Kani's existence in the palace, but what if that was all an elaborate act meant to fool anyone watching? Meant to fool Tet, perhaps. Tet knew the city speaker had employed more than one person to steal that damn breastplate and that he was not the first. But Ymat had also seemed adamant he would not be able to get the stolen soul back from Kani if she retrieved it.

And why was Ymat allowing Tet to live when he was nothing more than a thorn in his paw-pad? Perhaps the man meant to get the soul-beetle back and control him again. As long as Tet was still potentially useful to Ymat, the man would keep him in reserve. Just as a good maket player will keep the wind tile in a forgotten corner of the board until he has his arrows and caravans surrounding the towers of his enemies.

Tet's eyes ached and he felt every bone-deep agony and scar burn. He needed sleep, or better, to step back into the smoke-quarter and take seven-petal again. Though the curse-scars were not worsening, the damage had already been done and the pain drove him through each day like a whip braided with bone.

He was tired.

Gods, he was tired. Every time Tet closed his eyes, he could feel the darkness, the *thinness,* closing in, unbearable. It was coming. His death was close enough to fill his mouth with the taste of coins and bitter herbs, sweet brown sugar placed on the tongue of a corpse. The void was waiting for him and he had nowhere left to run.

It might even be better if he simply walked into the White Prince's court and told him everything he was able to, swear fealty to him and his endless war. Perhaps the White Prince could make Kani return Tet's soul.

He laughed hollowly. As if that would happen. Everyone seemed to think they could control Tet's magic if they could control him. Ymat knew what Tet could do. And Sinistrallia in the deep, she knew. Kani knew *something*. She'd seen it in his skin the way a true mage can sense another mage's wardings.

The void swallowed Tet when he finally fell asleep, brain tumbling through the variations of strategies he could use to trick his soul out of Kani's grasp.

*

Tet woke screaming, the dark chewing at his ruined legs while the birds called to each other in the back garden, and from downstairs came Widow Peniki's voice as she berated the broom-seller. His skin was damp, sticky, and Tet sat up carefully, stretching out the twisted muscles that had spent the night clenched and frozen. Even his jaw ached. As the dawn warmed the air, he moved slowly, hunch-backed like an old man, and washed in cold water, wiping nightmares from skin.

A terrible weakness had set into Tet's marrow and the pain was worse than ever. It made his head dizzy and empty and he breathed in sharp whistles through his teeth, willing his limbs to come back under his control. He was not old. In the traveller clans, Tet would be a man in the prime of his life, strong and fit and clever. Instead, he was reduced to this – a shuffling husk of the man he used to be. His future had been lost that night between Nanak's stone paws when the thief stole her eyes. All the things the gods had taken from him battered behind Tet's eye-sockets, and he wanted to weep.

He pressed his head against the wall and leaned there. 'You are not dead,' Tet said softly. 'You know where your soul is, you have a small fortune under your cot, you have a witch's charm unlike any other.' Tet ran through the litany. It all came down to one. *I am not dead. Not yet.*

It would be a lie to say the words strengthened Tet, that they poured healing and power into his trembling legs, but they were enough to goad him into moving forward. Ymat's men were watching him, and he needed to keep up his pretence as Sektet Am.

Until either Dozha returned, or until he could convince Kani to give him back his own soul, Tet would have to keep playing his part. He picked up his lute and gave the carvings a quick polish, tuning the strings just to hear their sweetness, before he shuffled downstairs, knees protesting with every step. He had a job to do, songs to play, plans to make.

*

Night fell in velvet layers as Tet walked back home. He'd watched the crowd as he'd played, trying to see if any spies were around, but it was impossible to tell if a woman who paused to listen to a song, or a boy who tried to steal from a begging bowl, or a nearby market trader, or a beggar man with crooked arms and only one leg was in the employ of Ymat Shoom.

Or someone else.

It gave him a headache, this endless untrusting watchfulness, and now, as he limped toward Peniki's house, he cracked his neck from side to side, trying to drive out the gathering tightness. The season was changing, Tet could feel it in the broken scarring of his bones. Soon it would be cold enough that another layer of pain would be added to the ones he already had.

Tet snorted as he pushed open the door. That was assuming he made it to winter.

Peniki was at her kitchen table, the lamp light smoothing the lines from the corners of her mouth, and she laughed at her guest, before gathering the two bowls and making a show of dishing him more food.

Ymat's pet toymaker nodded at Tet, his mouth half-twitching into a sneer that was gone almost as soon as it arrived. The city-speaker was going to make no secret of having him spied on at all times. Tet greeted them both, turned down Peniki's offer of a bowl of her food, and went up the narrow stairs. The only route in and out of his room was now being watched.

But Ymat couldn't know about the dogs. Only Kani had seen them, and she believed she was part of a dream. At least, she wanted him to think that she did.

Tet had no friends in this city. When death came for him, he would be cast into the void and no one would miss him. He would be nothing more than a thorn, removed. 'Hush your self-pity,' Tet whispered, and opened his door.

Sitting cross-legged on his bed was a shadow, hunched, man-shaped. Tet's first thought was that the White Prince's toymaker had finally tracked him down, then the shadow spoke, and Tet's shoulders slumped in a combination of relief and wariness.

'Don't make a sound,' said Dozha.

Tet shut the door slowly, deliberately, then turned back to him. 'I had no plans to.' A flicker of anticipation shivered under his skin. *Does he have it?* Biting at the heels of that thought came another: *how long has he been here, and what has he found, what has he stolen from me?*

The darkness was thick as old ash and still smelled of the wood-smoke from the burned temple. Dozha had brought a new scent into the room – incense and seven-petal. Tet made no move to light his lamp; all he had to strike a spark was the flint pouch. He forced himself to smile so that Dozha could hear it in his voice. 'Since you're here, I don't think it would be too much trouble to ask you to light the lamps.'

A snap of fingers, the word whispered too fast for Tet to hear properly, and the lamp sputtered into life. The flame rose, casting weaving shadows against the sloped roof. Dozha's face burned out of the darkness, regal, his skin flawless as carved stone..

A trick. I could do this too, once. Though I was never as showy. Tet almost laughed at himself. Why lie, he'd had his moments of playing the game. 'Did anyone see you come in here?'

'Shoom's man?' said Dozha. He shook his head. 'A clockworker, and a third-rate one, at best. He will not see me if I do not wish it.'

'Ah.' Tet down on the edge of his bed. It was that or a seat on the floor. Dozha shifted a little further down to make room, and in the golden dance of light he was beautiful, ethereal, and Tet found himself leaning in a little, just to taste incense, seven-petal.

Perhaps Dozha was enchanting him. Had Tet not set similar charms on Laketri to make the White Prince see her? 'Did you get it?' Tet forced himself to draw away.

Dozha sucked at one tooth, considering the question, then sighed and shook his head. 'Sinastrillia wants to see you.'

That was unexpected. Tet considered how to phrase a response. His doom was at his heels, there were gods and demon-princes looking for him, and now another god bellowed and expected him to come crawling. 'And I do not want to see Sinastrillia.'

Dozha shrugged and leaned back a little on Tet's bed, resting his head awkwardly against the sloped roof. 'Ah, but she has something you may want to hear, Am. And besides, the beds in the Underpalace are softer and warmer than this.'

'I am no friend to gods right now.' The heat of the mage pulsed in the space between them and Tet shifted, trying to widen that gap, to keep from making a fool of himself. It had been too long, and Dozha was too powerful.

'Sinastrillia is neither a god nor a man. She's a dragon, and so she has the best qualities of both.'

'And the worst,' Tet muttered. Dragons were a class unto their own. They saw themselves as neither above or beneath the gods and lived in and out of time, doing only what pleased them. Dragons were no more trustworthy than anyone else. But Tet wouldn't mind a dragon on his side, even if only for the moment, and if she knew something that might help him, Tet would be a fool to turn down the chance. 'Can you take me to her without Shoom's man seeing?'

would be a fool to turn down the chance. 'Can you take me to her without Shoom's man seeing?'

Dozha laughed at him, a sound that was unexpectedly sweet, his amusement almost childish. 'What happened to me being a "powerful mage, greater even the Princess Kani?"'

'I was merely flattering you,' Tet grumbled.

'No.' Dozha stood, the movement fluid, serpentine. He held out his left hand, and Tet found himself taking it, pressing their palms together. 'You were not.'

XXV

OUT OF TIME

Dozha **closed his** eyes in concentration, whispering, and the light in the attic room died. Around them, the darkness began to writhe and twist and although Tet couldn't feel the magic working, he could see the edges of it like the shadow of a passing moth. Dozha pulled the night around them, cloaking them in cold silk.

'Don't let go,' Dozha said when he opened his eyes, his grip tightening on Tet's hand. 'I can't keep us both shadowed if we're separate. Not for long, anyhow.' He smiled crookedly. 'You'll have to open any doors,' he said. 'I need all my magic.'

The heat from Dozha's palm burned into Tet's, boiling up his wrist, along the bones, shooting through nerves and branching out along his body.

Together, the two mages navigated the doorway from the attic, and unearthly silence folded around them. The stairs drifted into darkness, but Tet could hear the light buzz of song. Peniki and her guest were sharing beer or wine, singing and laughing. The Tiger would have one eye on the passage that ran past the open kitchen doorway. Dozha's tricks had better be worth his faith, Tet thought. While the clockworker might not stop him from leaving, he would tell Shoom anything he saw.

Below, the singing stopped, and Peniki laughed, beautiful and bubbling like a mynah. The Tiger said something low, and her laughter dissolved into breathless hiccoughs. Tet's throat grew tighter and he wished for cold water, to drink it, douse himself with it, wash away the clammy sweat prickling along his skin, that made his palm slippery against Dozha's.

The magics shrouding them were so thick that even the wooden stairs didn't so much as make a mouse's song. They passed the rectangle of light and Tet glanced at the two people seated by the kitchen table. Shoom's man had positioned himself so that he could see everything and he stared straight at Tet as he raised his bowl and sipped at the beer Peniki had dished out for him. Their eyes met and the Tiger stared blankly.

Dozha tread on Tet's heels. 'Walk on, old man,' he said, but the insult was gentle, and Tet could hear the laugh behind it. Now that he'd seen Dozha's real face close up in the lamp-light, Tet knew that he'd woven spells about himself that first night at the traveller's fire, to look younger, less threatening. The only thing he hadn't disguised was that half-arm.

Tet swung the front door open and it was soundless as the stairs. The night air slapped at his face, burning his eyes. Stars scattered like fallen petals of peach trees in spring across the fields of night.

Staring at the magicians was a ring of green fireflies. The eyes of the hunting dogs. They were staggered in a loose semi-circle around Peniki's house.

'Gods-damned,' Tet hissed, and Dozha held tighter.

'Walk soft,' he said, and the smell of seven-petal rose thick, unfurling like a night-blooming lily, drowning out the scent of two men. 'They won't follow.'

And perhaps they wouldn't, but they were closing in, and they would track Tet down soon. Next time there would be no thief mage to save him. The dogs shifted and whined in confusion, their white flanks pale slashes in velvet.

Dozha tugged him forward. 'Fear nothing.'

Tet kept to his side as they made their way through the twists and turns of Pal-em-Rasha. When Dozha had helped him escape from the White Prince's dungeons they'd left the Underpalace at the leather-worker's quarters, but this time Dozha took him on a new route, up the side stairs of a little tavern. They swept into the light and laughter unnoticed. It was warm inside, and the small bar was filled with women and a few grizzled survivors sucking at their pipes. It smelled of porridgey beer and mint tobacco and perfumes from market traders – attar of rose, bitter orange oil. They slipped past the grandmother at the tiny counter, and only the clockwork greenfinches in their bamboo cage noticed them. They squeaked and fluttered as the mages opened a small door leading to a deserted room.

This room led on to another, down another flight of stairs, and up another, through a rabbit's warren of passages and rooms. A map Tet had never seen, woven from back rooms and staircases and rooftops and cellars. Finally, when the last doors closed behind them, Dozha slipped his hand free and let the magic fall.

Dozha was sweaty, his skin gone grey about his mouth and in the hollows of his eyes. 'I held that for longer than I should have.' He leaned against a wall of the long room. Barrels were stacked neatly in rows, and Tet could read some of the lettering. Southern script, though he did not know the words of this particular language. Perhaps he'd have to learn one day, if he lived, if he found his name. He would always be running from gods. Would they track him down the Green Road all the way across the border of Imradia and into Utt Dih, to the bay of Utt where Imal tipped her swollen waters into the sea?

Tet had never ventured so far south, though he'd read much about the people and customs. Ymat Shoom's soul magic was southern, and Peniki was from a town in Utt Dih, and her accent sing-songed, reshaping Pal-em-Rasha's sounds to suit her own voice.

There was no point contemplating how far he would run. These were the dreams of a dead man unless this meeting with Sinastrillia was to his benefit, which, knowing what he did of dragons, would only happen if it was also to her benefit. For everything, there was a price.

'Time.' Dozha pushed away from the wall and set off again.

They were underground. Tet knew by the flatness of the air, the way it tasted like stagnant water and smelled like the bottom of old barrels, but other than that, he had no idea where exactly they were in the city. He tried to build a map of the networks and tunnels in his head, but there was little to work with, just an endless procession of lefts and rights and ups and downs. Despite the futility, Tet concentrated on scrawling the map through his mind. Better to find a distraction than to pay attention to the ice-crack aches in his knees, the looming promise of death at his back.

*

The world began to change. It was subtle at first. They were still underground, but the tunnels had become wider, the curved roofs arched higher overhead. Now their way was lit by a soft phosphoresce that Dozha conjured. Fires of eerie green marsh gas floated aimlessly ahead of them, tethered by an unseen force. On the walls were markings in the thieves' tongue. Tet could read only a few simple signs, and certainly none written here. The few times he'd heard it spoken it had reminded him a little of the language of dragons, if it were shorn of everything magical and strange. Slowly the scrawls gave way to intricate carvings of dragons, vines, birds, fruit and flowers. The reliefs seem to ripple above his head.

They were in the Underpalace true, Tet realised, when a girl walked casually past them, her dark hair loose, one hand holding that of a small fat boy who was waddling unconcernedly through the midnight tunnels. They both paused when they saw the two mages, and the girl bowed to Dozha. She jerked at the boy's hand for him to do the same.

'So you truly are a prince?' Tet said after the children were gone.

'Not so much a prince,' Dozha glanced back, waiting for Tet to catch up, and frowned, 'as a favourite son. Your legs.'

'What about them?' Tet didn't want him to stop, nor pay attention to his growing limp.

'I hadn't realised they pained you so much.'

Tet pushed past him. 'I am good at pretending they don't.'

The sound of Dozha's soft padding footsteps came from behind. 'You don't know where you're going,' Dozha said in amusement.

'I don't care.' Tet knew he sounded petulant, but it was or start screaming at him that *I can't stop, I can't, don't you understand?*

Dozha caught up to him and rested his hand on Tet's shoulder. Magic settled under Tet's skin, sinking down to his knees, scrubbing the hurt away from his bones. It lifted the edge of the pain, and he took a shuddery breath. He'd been breathing shallowly, only half aware of it.

'It won't last long, I'm afraid,' Dozha said and he sounded truly apologetic. 'My talent's for shifting and shadows, not for the healing arts.' He kept his hand on Tet's shoulder. 'It's not far now. Another fifteen minutes. Do you think you'll make it?'

'Make it – and then what?' The moment of respite was giving him a chance to think clearly. Tet would need all his wits about him for a conversation with a dragon. 'Talk to your dragon like this?'

'She's not my dragon.' He laughed. 'Keep walking and don't worry. You're here at her invitation. She doesn't eat guests.'

Tet supposed he should find that reassuring, but he remembered her presence below him as he'd crossed Imal the Black in a stolen shape. She'd known exactly who he was. Naturally. Dragons were like that, always knowing more than they should. She wanted something from him: another in a long list of personages who thought he could do something for them when in truth Tet could barely hold himself together. He wanted to close his eyes and for once fall asleep and not dream, to wake anew and have the pain leached from his bones like bitterness from oak berries.

'This way.' Dozha gestured to where a huge arched door bit into the wall. 'You are honoured,' he said. 'Just remember that. There are few allowed near here and fewer still who are invited to talk with her.' He finally took his hand from Tet's shoulder and some of the pain curled back, but it was not as hard to bear as before.

Dozha touched the doors, and they parted, a slow yawning.

Ahead of them was a vast cavern, its corners heaped with dark shapes, and Tet became aware of a sound that had been sliding and growling below his subconscious. The river. They were near Imal again. He oriented himself, piecing his map together. It was calming. Bolstered by his armour of remembered twists and turns, Tet stepped into the dragon's lair.

'The throne room of Sinastrillia,' Dozha called out, his voice echoing against the far ends of the cavern. He called her by name like a wayward dog, and Tet was almost amused. Except that Sinastrillia was no free-dog. 'Your guest is here.'

The cavern was dark and damp and Dozha conjured a few more of the little swamp-lights into being, sending them bobbing about in a rough circle. Treasures glinted from the dark, a thieve's cache to suit even a dragon. Dozha had no need of petty coin if this was his inheritance.

Sinastrillia emerged from the gloom, putrid light glinting off the water sliding from her huge body. She was the colour of blackened silver coins, her long head shaped like a horse's, longer even, the great narrow jaw filled with rows of jagged teeth.

'Tet-Nanak,' she said in Deniahn, her voice managing to make even his hard and angular name sound sibilant and fluid. 'So good of you to come.' As if she had invited him to drink rhododendron wine with her at a party. 'Dozha?' she added, swinging her head in his direction. Her mane of rippled fins flickered in the light, like the sides of flashing fish.

'Mother?'

Mother? Tet looked from one to the other. Even though Dozha could take the shape of a dragon for a moment, he was as human as Tet. It was not unheard of for dragons to adopt foundlings. Or at least it was not unheard of in myths. He had stepped into the unfurling beginnings of a legend, and the thought chilled him. It was a dangerous place to be, so close to the gods' game of maket.

'Will you stay?' said the dragon, her voice soft as falling leaves hissing against the ground.

Dozha shook his head. 'I can't. He's expecting me. If I don't show my face he'll get suspicious. Perhaps I can weasel my way out of staying for more than a few hours.' He turned from her to smile reassuringly at Tet, as though he wasn't actually leaving him alone with the vast dragon. 'I'll send someone to show you a room where you can rest, and we can speak when I return.' With a last word of command at the little swamp lights, he left, and the huge walnut doors slid closed behind him.

Tet was alone with Sinastrillia.

'You can still speak with us?' she said in the tongue of dragons, and Tet nodded. Just barely, and there was no magic to it, but he could still shape the words.

'Good.' She showed him her rows of fangs before she settled her long sinuous body in whirls and curls, like the artwork of a drunk painter or a genius. 'It is tiresome to speak your little language. The others can at least speak that thieves' pidgin, but one does so want to converse in one's own tongue. It is, after all, much more expressive....' She sighed.

'You called me here.' This was part of the problem with dragons, they hated to be direct about anything.

'Called, invited. These are different things. We could discuss the intricacies of meaning contained within—'

'Or you could tell me why?' The pain was starting to gnaw at him again. Tet closed his eyes. 'May I at least sit?'

'For a mage stripped of all that makes you a mage, you are intolerably rude,' she said. 'Yes, of course. Sit.'

Tet settled himself down on the cold floor. The river's proximity made the air and stone here even colder, it would do his bones and scars no good; but Tet was too tired to keep standing while Sinastrillia took five-thousand aeons to get to her point, whatever it was.

'You must wonder why I invited you here, Tet-Nanak. I confess that I thought your current had died, that there was nothing left of you. Until I met you in the river, following my son's shadow.'

'What of it?' She'd called him a Lord of Time. He shivered at the memory, at what it meant. *Her son.* He squirmed at this. Men were not the children of dragons, not anymore.

'My curiosity was piqued. You had lived a mediocre existence, flared bright and brief, then disappeared. I had heard nothing of you since that day you stopped time, and then here you were, swimming like a little trout. Right under my nose. But weak,' she said. 'So weak. I stepped outside of time, and went to see if I could find your currents, see where they led you.'

'And?' Tet couldn't help be curious. Dragons did not often show interest in the paths of men. 'What did you find?'

'Secrets,' the dragon said. 'And mysteries. I know many secrets,' she said to him. 'Perhaps it would surprise you to know the things I hear. All kinds of human things.'

Tet shook his head. 'What secrets, and how do they concern me?'

The dragon arched her neck, pushing her face closer to his. 'You could have been a great mage, you know.'

'*Could have been.*' Tet couldn't help the little kick of anger across his ribs. 'Was.'

'Oh, you were never great,' she said. 'But you could have been. And you could still be.'

'I have no magic,' he told her bitterly, as if she did not know this.

'Do you know that even dragons cannot do what you did?' She blinked, finally, eyelids slipping over huge crystal-black eyes. 'We can swim in and out of time in a way that even gods cannot, and yet even we could never stop the flow of it.' Her voice turned into a rushing hiss. 'You did that.'

His hands were slippery, breath cold fire in his chest. 'And what good did it do? I passed out into a fever that nearly killed me. The world was broken and it took all the gods to set it flowing again, to set time back in place.'

'Is that what they told you?'

He stayed silent, watching her.

'Gods are liars, and they will say anything.'

Much like dragons.

'They did not fix time, Tet-Nanak, they only put it together as best they could, like a child will try set a broken pot together before their parent finds their mistake. The cracks are still there and with every passing heartbeat, the clay weakens.'

She shook herself, uncurling, and wound closer to him. Her body was as long as a giant serpent's, but she did not drag her belly along the ground. Four reptilian legs kept her raised, and her claws scratched against stone. 'Soon, perhaps sooner than we dragons would like, the pot will finally break, and time will stop. Permanently.'

It was as he'd begun to suspect, though been too much a coward to face. It was not only his own time that ran small and finite, but the whole world's. And he had done this. A heavy cold despair settled on him, heavy as a soaked woolen blanket. 'What do you expect me to do about it?' A churning knot of fear was growing in his stomach.

'I want you to become great, Tet-Nanak.'

Tet got to his feet. Sinastrillia was mocking him now, and he should have not been so foolish as to come here. Even for Dozha. 'Without a soul?'

The dragon shrugged. 'A soul is a small thing, easily caught. That will not make you great.' The fading gas light glinted off her teeth. The sound of the river swelled. 'Your name, Tet-Nanak. With your name, oh, the things you would do, the kingdoms you would destroy, the kingdoms you would raise and the princes you would follow. I have watched the gods weaken and men grow stronger, and you were at the crest of it, of the changing of power. I've seen it all, in and out of time, and I know the way your river flows. With your name, you would be great, and I can give it back to you. If you would take the risk.'

XXVI

BLOOD AND SHADES

Dragons did not tell jokes. Oh, they twisted the truth to amuse themselves, but actual humour was beyond them. Or they felt themselves above it. 'How—' Tet cleared his throat. 'And how would you propose to do that? Have dragons suddenly become more powerful than the gods themselves? Are you in the habit of sending mages across the boundaries of worlds and back?' As foolish as it was to provoke her, he was tired of being strung this way and that for another's pleasure, as if he were a wind tile on the grand game between the gods and the dragons.

Sinastrillia's tail flickered in irritation. Around her head, the filaments danced in eerie silver ribbons. 'No.' Her sudden curtness was more than enough warning.

'I cry your pardon,' Tet said stiffly. 'I find with my approaching death, my patience for games has grown thin.'

'I am not a tiger toying with a little crippled fawn.' Her tail swished, the rasp of scale on stone. 'There are few mages who would risk going to the land of the dead. I believe that you will take that chance. My child told me you are arrogant enough to think that you might be able to claw your way back to the living.'

Her child. Tet had spoken only to Kani about the idea of crossing over, retrieving his name from his dead parents – a thought only. As surreptitiously as he could, Tet wiped his hands against his trousers. The Princess Kani was Sinastrillia's piece, and so was Dozha, and this Grand Board was far bigger than he had ever imagined. His mouth was dry. 'Arrogant or not, I have no power now, as you pointed out. I cannot walk into death. Or have you found a way to call the dead back to life from the caverns of shadows? That would be a neat trick indeed.'

When Sinastrillia smiled, her teeth gleamed. Dagger-sweet in the light. 'Not even the fading gods who cling to the last of their power can do that.' She moved quickly, and Tet stumbled uselessly to avoid her. He was caught in her coils, her huge body wrapped around him like a vast scaled prison. A furnace burned below those tarnished scales. 'But you are so very close to death, little mage. So close that I could take you into those caverns, and if you are strong enough, bring you back out. Still living.'

Tet swallowed. The heat from her body made his head swim. He was trapped, a little rat in the coils of a serpent. He imagined Sinastrillia eating him whole, head first. Pushing past the crushing fear, he spoke again. 'And the twenty-one spirits, they would let me leave?'

She loomed her head over him and looked down. 'Probably. They seem to like you. In the caverns, you will summon blood to blood, and ask the shades of your mother and father to call you by name.'

A terrible thought, to finally know his name – his true name – and then have to rely on the *probably* of a dragon to save him. To be alive but caught in the world of the dead. Or worse, if Sinastrillia's magic failed and he was simply snuffed out of existence, and there was no cavern of shadows waiting for him, only a void so empty and immense that he'd be nothing more than a mote of dust trapped in infinity.

He thought of the dark of the White Prince's prisons, those terrible weeks of lonely suffering, and imagined an eternity of it. That was the only other path left. At least what Sinastrillia offered was a spark of hope. 'How will I speak with them?' *Them*. His dead parents, people he did not remember.

'You will need to ask the permission of the twenty-one. Best be polite. If they agree, you will give the shades of your parents some of your own life,' she said. 'Blood, to loan them a voice, for a while.'

More blood magics, though this was nothing like those Southern spells the Monkey had used. But the promise of his name and with it a chance to escape the end waiting for him. Whatever might happen, Tet could not refuse this offer. And when he came back he would have something to promise Kani in exchange for his soul. *Perhaps I will make a good slave.* 'Yes.' His voice cracked. 'I will do it.'

'It will take much out of you,' the dragon warned.

'Still. Better a chance taken and lost than to sit here and wait.'

'You are certain then?'

When Tet nodded, she told him to pluck one of her scales free. 'Go on,' she said when he made no move. 'You will need it.'

Her scales burned, heat clawing through Tet's fingers and palm, but he clenched his teeth and tugged at a single scale. Blood poured down his wrist. Each scale was a sharpened blade. The edges cut his hand down to the bone and he was about to give up when the scale tore free with a wet rasp.

'Good,' said Sinastrillia.

The gas lights went out, plunging him into sudden darkness. The dragon's voice faded, sounding as though she was calling at him from across a vast river. 'Do not let go of my scale.'

*

Tet found himself in a cavern, the walls glowing and pulsing like the skin of a luminous beast. The scale cut deep into Tet's palm, hot and sweet, and the only sound was the steady trickle-plop of his blood as it ran down his wrist and to the floor. He looked down, taking slow, controlled breaths in Dragon

Mountain pattern to stop himself from falling. The floor was white and powdery like a layer of fallen chalk dust. A few strides from him stood a stone no higher than his knees. The top of it was slightly hollowed.

Tet was in the entrance cave to the lands of the dead, and if he lived to walk out of it, he would have done something no mage had ever managed. He bared his teeth. *So what? I have stopped time, and that was also something no one else had done. What good are great deeds if they achieve nothing worthwhile?*

There were no ghosts of dragons waiting for him. No twenty-one First Men who walked between gods and humans, who wrote the world into a new shape with their songs. No spirits of the numberless dead. Unsteadily, he took a step forward and called the first of the dragons. 'Mil,' Tet cried into the empty cave.

Before the last echo had died, a shape began to form in the emptiness before him.

His heart stuttered.

The dragon was still a shade. Tet had expected that here in her own realm, the dragon spirit would be corporeal, but Mil was a vast green-black mist that flowed in and out of shape. One moment Tet saw a dragon, bigger even than Sinastrillia, and the next there was only a ribboning stream of swamp fog, twisting about in the winds of time.

She did not speak.

Tet's blood poured down in a steady stream. He tightened his grip around the scale, cutting deeper, and forced himself to focus. *I was a priest-mage once, I shouldn't be afraid of spirits now.* He dipped his head and bowed low, peering up to watch her reaction. 'Great Mother,' Tet said. 'Forgive me for disturbing your rest, but I come looking for the blood of my blood.'

Mil said nothing.

Tet's heart was beating slower with each drip, stepping closer to death, and now he was certain that there would be no return. Just as he was about to throw himself on his knees and beg, a head-shape appeared from the smoke and she nodded to the stone before Tet, to the little indentation at the top of it.

In a moment, he understood and went to hold his bleeding hand over the stone. The blood dribbled and splashed, black and sticky in this world between worlds.

The little trench filled. The fall of blood was hypnotic. The cavern began to chill, the warmth from the land of the living sucked away, and a freezing ache like ground glass crunched between Tet's joints. Frost rimed the edges of the blood pooling in the hollow stone. His teeth chattered as he looked up from the offering.

The cavern had filled with ghosts. His blood grew slower, colder. 'Blood of my blood,' Tet said to the masses of shapeless grey figures. His hand was shaking and he pulled it back from the bowl. He clasped Sinastrillia's scale against his chest. 'I call the shades of my mother and father, I call them to me, by blood.'

For a moment, nothing happened, and he wondered if they'd already moved on, relinquishing the land of the dead to be born again, their memories wiped.

Finally, two spectres slid forward until they were hovering just behind the stone.

His heart hammered.

They studied his face with blank holes that served them as eyes. They were formless monsters, shadow shapes that might have been his parents, or might not. They were people Tet did not remember, and he felt a sudden pity for the child he'd been. He wanted to have memories of these grey shades, better ones than these. He wanted to remember cradle songs, and mother's milk, and father's hands. Not this.

'Drink,' he said, softly.

The spectres bowed their heads to the blood and lapped at it like dogs, though Tet could see no tongues nor mouths. When they rose, the shapelessness drifted off them like scraps of cloud, and they stood revealed; *mother-mine, father-mine*.

Tet found he had no words he could say to these strangers.

It was his mother who spoke first. She was young. Younger than he would have thought – barely older than Laketri – and it pained him. Had Tet been her first babe, held and suckled and loved before she'd been butchered? And his father, no older than his wife, though he had a stocky mountain man's build, and a face round and sweet and open.

It was his mother Tet looked most like, he realised with a strange shock. Though he had his father's black eyes, straight brows. Both of these familiar strangers dead before they had a chance to raise him, to live their little lives in the caravans of Vaeyane, where Tet should have grown up herding the red oxen and chasing the free-dogs and learning to ride mountain ponies and to draw a bow to shoot shining arrows into the sun.

Tet had not only outlived his parents, he'd grown older than them.

'Speak, voice-of-the-living,' his mother's ghost said. 'What can we dead give you?'

'My name.' It was all he could say. The breath had been punched out of him. He was empty. Before, his parents had been abstractions; a sad story, but distantly unreal. Now they had faces.

'Merithym,' they said together and the name was so right, so right, so right that it filled Tet, syllables became wires dug through his skin and bones, holding him up straighter. It swam in his blood, it dripped on the chalk-powder floor, it beat in his head with each pound of his heart.

'Merithym,' they said again, and Tet dropped the scale from his numb hand and fell backwards out of the light and into the dark.

*

'I almost thought you would not return.' Sinastrillia's hiss-flicker voice curled around Tet's head, and he tasted snow and blood. His hand throbbed, in a dull distant way. 'Did they tell you what you needed to know?'

Carefully, he turned his head and spat blood onto the stone. He'd bitten his tongue as he fell. 'Yes,' Tet said. His voice was weak, ragged. 'They did.'

'Good.'

Now that he was coming back to some kind of life, Tet found himself burning with unexpected heat. Sinastrillia had kept herself coiled about his prone body, her silver-sharp sides making an impenetrable wall of protection or imprisonment.

'I only helped you for one reason,' she said.

Of course. Does she think I'm surprised by this? Tet wanted to laugh. Instead, he sat up and cradled his aching hand against his chest. The wound had healed, the blisters from touching the dragon were gone. But he'd not been left unchanged. The whole of his right hand, from wrist to fingertips, had turned a glowing white like the powder-walls of the caverns of the dead. A faint scar bisected his palm, but even that was fading. Tet flexed his fingers, and an echo of pain sparked across the palm, then died.

'You will set time right, mage,' said Sinastrillia. 'I lay this on you—'

'Please.' He made a hollow sound, an empty-water-pot sound. 'I do not think I can take more curses and compulsions.'

Sinastrillia huffed and uncurled so that Tet was freed, her gas-lamp eyes golden in the greyness. 'I do not curse. I do not lay spells of compulsion. I merely ask, as one who has done you a favour. Set right what you have broken.'

'That's all?' The laughter died. It was not what he'd thought Sinastrillia would ask. Tet had been expecting some other treasure to steal, or to burn some other temple, perhaps poison Shoom, or— *Or I do not know what I thought, but it wasn't this.*

'Such a small task,' Tet said, half-mocking. But the sound of his true name beating in his head was a drum that drowned out arguments. He struggled to his feet. 'I don't even know exactly how I managed to break time in the first place, let alone how to heal it.' If it was even possible – such a huge task that it would take every scrap of magic he'd ever had. Sinastrillia had given him back his name but at an impossible cost. 'I cannot.'

His name screamed through his thoughts: *Merithym, Merithym, Merithym.*

Sinastrillia managed to look as sad and troubled as a dragon could. Which wasn't very, but was still disturbing enough in itself. Her voice lowered. 'You will do it, mage, because in the river of time I have seen the current where you do.'

That was not remotely reassuring. 'What else did you see in this current?'

'Only this, that you will succeed where the White Prince will fail, and join the kingdoms from the Islands of Heaven to the towers of Ys. You will unite Vaeyane, Ganys, Deniah, Utt Dih, and Imradia and all their cantons and cities under one shining emperor.'

Unthinkable. Tet was a mage, not a builder of empires, and he had little time for those who wished such things. He looked down at his ruined white hand, like an after-echo of a ghost, a reminder of the unthinkable things he had done – stopped time, spoken to the dead. What was building an empire to that – men did it all the time. *Still, I'm not one for running cities and kingdoms.* 'Me? I'm no ruler.'

'Of course not,' said the dragon. 'That is for the Emperor who will come. You are the one who will stand at his side, feeding your magery to him until all these lands stand united. A great devil-king waits in the future, and I cannot see the true shape of him. All I know is that the lands will need to be strong to hold against him and that you will be part of that strength. Before that day passes, you must fix what you destroyed, or all the worlds end, and there is only nothingness.'

A strange vision and Tet did not like it. He couldn't see how it was possible to be this mage who built empires if he first had to waste all his power rebuilding time. 'Are there other currents?'

'There are always other currents,' said Sinastrillia. 'But this is the only one where you live.'

XXVII

THIEVES AND MASTERS

A girl barely out of her childhood, narrow and black as a sapling, was waiting for him outside the walnut doors. 'Dozha said you would be tired, and I was to show you to a room where you can rest and make yourself comfortable.' Her eyes flicked from Tet's face and down to his chalk-white hand, his marble and milk hand, then back up to meet his eyes. There was nothing in her expression to show that it startled or disgusted her. *Then again, she lives at the doorway of a dragon.*

'This way.' She offered him no help.

He was glad of it. However feeble and wretched Tet felt, however jellied his bones and twisted his muscles, he did not want anyone's pity. He had his name. Tet tasted it in his mouth, soft as the first bite of new bread. *Merithym.*

His face was wet. He'd been crying and not even known it. With his strange hand, he wiped the salt from his face before following the sapling girl through the corridors of the Underpalace. It was too late for him to return now to Peniki's house; he was too tired and lost to even attempt it.

Let a thief break in and steal every coin and diamond I own. At least he hadn't left the flint-pouch behind. Dozha's little miracle gift. Tet had always assumed Dozha had given it to him as no more than a throw-away item, a minor payment for a moment of silence. But the dragon had called Dozha her child, and the end-game of gods and monsters was a long one. No matter how small and simple it might have appeared, there was more to every little thing Dozha did than Tet could have imagined. Everything was a lie chosen to ensure Tet's passive cooperation.

Tet grimaced at this. *Not everyone is a player using you as a tile-piece.* He was assuming the worst. *And that is how I will survive.*

His guide took him to a large room far more sumptuous than he was used to after all the weeks living in the cramped attic room. It was richer even than the suite of rooms he'd rented in the garden house, though smaller. Despite the opulence, there was no forgetting that this was a cell deep underground. There was no scent of lime and orange sweeping in from tended gardens. No trickling laughter of fountains, nor the calls of geese as they flew overhead.

Instead, a silence soft as a sleeping cat draped over the room. No fires were lit, but the room was warmer than the tunnels outside. A bed wide enough for three stood in the middle, heavy with layers of thick woollen blankets and down-stuffed silk covers. The wool was dyed the scarlet of a sunbird's breast feathers, and the silk was heron-grey.

'Are you hungry?' asked the girl as she turned back the covers, as though Tet were an honoured guest in a great garden house.

His last meal had been steamed bread bought from a woman at a roadside stall and Tet's stomach was tight. Reminded now of its emptiness, it growled in dissatisfaction, and the sapling-girl grinned, her teeth bright as pearls. 'I'll bring you something.' She paused from smoothing her hands over the sheets. 'What was she like?' she asked, her voice feather-drifting, dreaming. 'The Mother.'

'Remarkable,' Tet said. 'Like all dragons.'

She stared. 'You have met many?'

'I used to share beer and songs, and play games of maket with one in the mountains, but there have been others.'

'You did not,' the girl said. 'Liar. Dragons don't drink beer.'

Tet settled into the chair that stood in the corner of the room. It was soft as an old mushroom, and he sighed. 'That one did, but I concede that not all dragons have the taste for it.' He tipped his head back and closed his eyes to a grey shot through with spasms of colours. 'But all of them enjoy strategy games.'

'Hah,' said the girl. A moment later, the door clicked shut, and Tet sank into half-dreams while he waited for her return. It seemed only seconds had passed when a hand shook him awake and the girl pushed her pugnacious face close. 'Here, mage.' She drew back. 'You were snoring.'

'Was I?' Tet shook the sleep from his head. Everything felt blurry; his limbs too leaden and stiff to move.

'Like a great dog,' she said. 'Here. I have brought smoked fish in mustard, and fried bread.'

She was as good as her word and the rich and pungent aromas of Deniahn cooking filled the room. The girl set bowls and utensils down on a small table surrounded by four chairs. There was enough on her tray to feed a legion of starving beggar-men, as well as generous carafes of water and wine to satisfy an inebriate soldier. Everything was precious; carefully blown glass of silvery blue, the bone-white porcelain of the bowl gilded. A peasant's meal served on the plates of kings. Mountain water in priceless patterned crystal.

'I'm grateful,' Tet said. 'This is a feast.'

'It's not just for you,' she pointed out. Then more grudgingly, 'You're most welcome.' She finished setting the last of the dishes – places for two – and Tet wondered if she was to dine with him, if she was another spy, although a slight and sweet one.

He was about to ask her when the door to the room swung open smooth and silent, and Dozha walked in, commanding and sure of himself as any prince. The girl squeaked, then bowed hurriedly before slipping out of the room like a nervous kitten.

'Fish,' said Dozha. 'Good.' He took a seat at the table and gestured for Tet to join him. 'Come, old man, I can see the hunger in your face. You look like a gnawed bone.' Although he was joking, Tet thought Dozha spoke as much about himself as he did his guest. Dozha was wearing his magery thin, using it all the time, and it was beginning to show in the waxiness of his skin, the hollow darkness around his eyes. If he carried on using great amounts of magic, he would soon have none. Burned out with mage-fever, like an empty oil candle.

'She left you a pretty hand,' Dozha said, with a nod at Tet's transformed limb. 'I hope this means the meeting was all you could have dreamed of.'

Merithym. And the shades of people he did not remember from life. 'It was both more and less.' Let Dozha make of that what he would. 'I thought you had much to attend tonight,' Tet said. 'Certainly, you let Sinastrillia think so.'

Dozha chewed on fried bread that was puffed up as a frog's throat. 'I didn't lie.'

'Working on stealing the breastplate for Shoom?'

He closed his eyes. 'Yes.'

'You are not so great a thief if it's giving you so much trouble. Surely you could wrap yourself in shadows and stalk kitten-pawed through his ridiculous tower and slip the damned thing off him before he so much as knows you're there?' Even though Tet knew it was impossible, he was curious to hear Dozha's thoughts. He ladled helpings of the fish and rice into a bowl and poured himself wine instead of water. 'And likewise you should be able to steal a pretty bead from the neck of a vain princess.' He would not, because Dozha and Kani were on the same side, both doing as Sinastrillia commanded.

'Vain?' Dozha laughed, eyes still closed. He looked exhausted. Finally, he pushed up out of his slouch and opened his eyes. In the warm glow of the lamps, they were mottled through with the browny-blues and blacks of forests at night. 'The White Prince has a court toymaker.'

Tet dragged his thoughts away from Dozha's night-forest eyes, his drowning dark eyes, and back to the clockwork beasts sent to hunt him. 'I know this. A clockwork mage – the only kind he trusts. But how can a toymaker stop one such as yourself?'

Dozha took more food with the resigned air of a man who had gone past hunger and was only forcing himself to eat because he knew he must, or die. 'They are a very good clockwork mage.'

That was no lie. Tet had seen their trinkets up close—so perfect and detailed they were more than mere metal simulacrum but had the sheen of life. Even with the protection currently afforded by the flint-pouch dogs, the prince's damn toymaker was turning into more of a problem than Tet had anticipated. No wonder the prince kept them leashed to his courts. They were a symbol of his power, and another weapon. At every turn, their veiled shade blocked Tet's way.

'They've made all kinds of creatures to protect the prince, and the rooms surrounding his suite are mazes defended by traps and monsters. If they were true animals, I could turn them aside, but they're not. Their toys can see through magery and they only answer their maker's command.'

Tet knew this but pretended to consider the problem. 'So, it's a matter of getting past these and into his chambers?'

'No.' Dozha poured himself wine, leaving his half-eaten meal, then leaned forward to top up Tet's drink. The pink wine splashed softly, a sound like fish dancing between air and water. Firelight played over his skin, decorating him with shadows of olive green. 'I have a way in. I even have a way to strip the prince of his armour by his own consent. What I don't have,' he drained his glass and slumped back in his seat, 'is a way out again.' The tiredness had settled under the parchment of his face, drawing histories that Tet wanted to erase with his newly-white palm. He wanted to trace the paths Dozha had taken, a one-finger journey.

Instead, he held his wine glass firmly with both hands and pretended that his thoughts were sane, sensible. *Concentrate on the problem of the clockworker, on the problem of the*

White Prince and the gods hunting you down. There's no time for this. 'You can't use the same route that took you in?'

'Let's pretend it's a path I can walk only once.' He laughed hollowly. 'Leave it. I'll think of something.'

Did Dozha not know what Ymat had wanted Tet for – what the city-speaker knew Tet could do and what Sinastrillia knew likewise? Perhaps the dragon did not tell her precious son everything. 'Ymat is paying you for this contract?'

Dozha leaned forward and rested his left arm on the table. His right, or what there was of it, was hidden under the long sleeve of his gold and blue-striped jacket, the end of the sleeve pinned neatly. 'Yes. And no.'

'And what does that mean?'

He laughed. 'It means exactly what it means. That Shoom pays me for some services, and not for others.'

'You serve two masters?' The wine burned down Tet's throat, tracing a route of bitter-sweet flame, pooling warm as blood in his belly.

'I am, always, for hire, and I serve many masters. Haven't you yourself paid me to get back your little necklace.' It was not a question. He raised one eyebrow and Tet was reminded of Laketri. It was an expression she'd thrown his way – a combination of exasperation and mocking humour.

'But it was Ymat who hired you to retrieve the breastplate.' Tet pressed on, certain that if he simply kept asking questions eventually he'd find the right one and the intricate box of secrets that was Dozha would open, like finding the hidden spring and pressing just so. The thought of Dozha opening made Tet's skin heat with feverish aches. It was past time to put down the wine, go to sleep.

Instead, Tet poured himself more wine and pretended that his hands were not trembling, that he was not aroused by that lingering scent of incense, of the drug, of the trace of honey that had followed Dozha into the room. That smell, almost like magic, oily-sweet.

'Shoom has hired me before, as you know.' A small smile pulled at Dozha's mouth, and he gave Tet a sidelong look. It was, despite the black rings, the fever-cast to his skin, a look that strayed too long and too deliberately.

Perhaps I'm simply a thing to amuse him. Tet was certain he had near a decade on Dozha, and probably looked even older. *He can smell my arousal, my desperation, and he thinks he will toy with me. I think that this time I might not care. That I would only hate him for a little while after he is done and cast me aside.* It had been so long since Tet had let himself fall, and now there was hardly time enough left to him. He should take what scraps he could before it was too late. It didn't need to be love, just a moment's romance.

What did a priest-mage know of seduction? Tet's time in the army as their mapmaker spy had kept him constantly on the move, never tied to a unit, bonding with others. There had been little space for dalliance. Perhaps he was seeing the shadows of things that weren't there, catching the tail end of wishes. His delusion was that he and Dozha were speaking the same language and heading for the same conclusion.

Leave this path now, Merithym. Tet's newly-retrieved name brought him back to himself. It was nothing more than the workings of spells and skin-deep enchantments. Tet had no time to get caught up in these games.

'And what about Kani?' Tet settled back and pushed his thoughts away from where they had been heading. 'Have you any luck there? As you have pointed out, you have other masters, and I have paid well for the privilege of being one of them.'

Guilt – sudden and unexpected – danced over Dozha's face. 'I should never have taken that contract from you,' he admitted.

'She was too powerful for you after all?' Tet crystallised all his sublimated desire into anger, let it sharpen his voice. He wanted to be angry with Dozha, to hate him for his half-truths. It was marginally safer than the alternative. Less humiliating.

'Not that.' Dozha shook his head, and passed his hand over his face, wiping away the momentary tell of his contrition.

'Kani is working for Shoom, whatever the man may tell you. And so am I.'

'I had gathered as much,' Tet said dryly.

'It's a problem. What Sinastrillia calls a conflict of interest.' Dozha smiled thinly. 'Do you want the truth?'

'A version of it would be acceptable. Not that I'm accustomed to candour from mages.' Under Tet's breastbone, wariness flickered its forked tongue. Neither of them were men with any measure of honesty and Tet would be a fool to expect it.

'Perhaps I serve too many masters,' Dozha said. 'All of them connected in ways I do not like.'

'Perhaps.' Did this mean he was in Kani's employ too? It wouldn't be beyond the realm of possibility that she had also hired Dozha to steal the breastplate. Mages and thieves and thieves and mages, all tangled up in a mess of deceits. What a game, what a Grand Dance, the greatest ever played. 'Maybe it's time to choose one master only.'

'Ha.' Dozha swallowed the last of the wine straight from the carafe, his head thrown back, throat long. He set it down and grinned, teeth sharp, eyes narrow-sly. 'I like the money, and I like the game. After all, life is shit, life is short, and life is nothing if you don't enjoy the little things that make it worthwhile.'

Tet jerked forward in his seat. The sudden movement set a wrenching pain through his knee, and he winced. His mind was fogged with wine and lack of sleep, but pain could cut even through that. It obliterated the moment of recognition. Words he'd heard before, somewhere else, spoken by a different tongue.

'Your legs, they still hurt.'

He nodded warily. 'They do. I have curse scars from Nanak and Vitash that twist the flesh all the way from the skin to the bone, that bite into the bones themselves. Since Ymat took my soul, they have at least not grown worse. A blessing.'

'Such strange and vicious little dog gods you follow,' Dozha said.

'And yours is any better?' Tet gestured vaguely at the door, and thought of the huge dragon lying coiled deep underground, what she knew, what she offered. What she asked.

'A fair point,' Dozha conceded, and some of his tiredness seemed to lift as he smiled with one side of his mouth. 'But I'd still trust her further than yours.'

'Why?'

Dozha paused, as though he'd never considered the question before. 'Because,' he said softly, 'she gave me purpose.'

'Is that all?'

'Sometimes,' Dozha said. The moment slipped, and the mask of a prince-mage was back. He grinned. 'And perhaps she promised me the world and I thought it sounded like a pretty prize.'

'Are you that interested in crowns and thrones?' It was disappointing to think Dozha was so much like the White Prince himself, but Dozha answered the question with a one shouldered shrug.

'Hardly,' he said. 'But what's the point of a game if there's no pot to win?'

'A game.' Tet snorted, but the movement made him wince, and Dozha's expression drew concerned, his brow furrowing.

'I'm no good with healing spells, but there are other ways to help. Lie down and I'll do what I can.' Dozha went to a woven cord near the door and tugged at it a few times; long tugs and short in some arcane order.

The food and wine had left Tet sated and sleepy, and it seemed easiest just to obey Dozha. He unbuckled his battered leather boots, washed his feet in a bowl of cold water put aside for this, and changed into the pyjamas the girl had left for him. With a quick glance to be certain that Dozha wasn't watching, Tet carefully wrapped his flint-pouch, striker, and coin bag deep in the heart of his discarded clothes before sinking down onto the wide bed. It was firmer than expected – just the right amount of give without being too soft. Tet twisted his shoulders and welcomed the crack of aching bone and muscle. His eyelids were heavy, and with each exhale it was harder to keep them open, to not let his body grow leaden.

A clatter of wooden drawers, a clink of metal and bone, but Tet was too lazy to raise his head. Only when Dozha seated himself beside Tet and pulled up the hems of the sleep trousers to reveal the twisted knees, did Tet force himself up on his elbows to watch. Tet didn't make a habit of showing strangers his scars, only the paid masseurs had that right. This was too intimate and his heartbeat skittered. *Why am I here, letting Dozha treat me like a pet?*

Because I need him? Because he was wrapped in secrets and Tet wanted to find a way to unravel them. That seemed right. A good story to tell himself.

Dozha knelt alongside him. 'I'll need your help for this part,' he said with a half-smile, and cupped his palm. 'Pour from the bottles, only as many drops as I say. From that largest, enough to fill a rich man's soup spoon.'

Tet leaned forward to do as Dozha asked. Massage might not heal the flesh but it did help, and Tet was grateful for anything that would bring him some relief. While he was counting out the drops of a second oil that smelled like sharp winter berries and dry leaves, the door opened and the girl from before entered with a water pipe which she set down to fill and light.

The heat of the small coal resting on the metal plate over the leaf-bowl seemed out of proportion, as though it were a fallen sun. The girl blew at it, turning it with her brass tongs. She did not pay any attention to the two mages, merely frowned as she sucked at the pipe. The thick smell of seven-petal. Want unfurled through Tet, closing up his throat.

His attention was turned by the sudden feeling of heat against his knee, like a brand marking. Tet jerked, shuddering at the unexpected slip into pleasure-pain. Dozha pretended not to notice, his fingers pressing into skin, easing the tightness. Tet willed the girl to work faster, and leave.

As if in answer to a silent command, she blew a deep grey cloud from her nostrils. 'I'll see you later,' she said to Dozha. He nodded in response, and then she was gone, her arms full of dishes, clattering like clay cymbals.

Tet's fingers fumbled for the pipe, and he grasped it blindly. The taste of chalk and visions was flat against his tongue, like licking a half-remembered dream. His inners began to unwind. The room was silent except for the sound of the pipe, and there was no need to talk and fill it up. Tet wanted this silence. It was safe. He could lose himself in the dream of seven-petal, imagine a heaven instead of his current hell. Imagine a universe not bound to the gods and their fickle games of chance.

Dozha worked on Tet's right knee first, where the scar was older, the curse deeper. His hand crunched and prodded, smoothed and stroked.

The room filled with the fragrance of seven-petal while Tet lay back and lost himself in the rhythm of Dozha's hand and the burble of smoke. He stared at the darkened ceiling and watched the play of shadows. He wanted – no, needed – to sink into a thoughtless drifting state. He had to empty his mind of Dozha's long fingers, the supple wrist, the slender arm, the curious fragility of his collar bone. He was just another human, nothing more than a bone cage that held his soul in place. This could be anyone Tet had employed to massage the pain out of his legs. He took a long pull on the stem of the pipe.

Empty your head, think of nothing. Dream of a world where you are the right-hand mage to a benevolent emperor. The thought was seductive. Himself, wrapped in power, healed, strong. A proud man, with no Nanak, Vitash, or Epsi holding their chains about his throat. And at his side, the shining Emperor that Sinastrillia predicted, a man who held the world in his grasp.

The thought stuttered, and he took another deep drag. What would make any emperors better than the White Prince? Even if that was the future Sinastrillia saw and wanted, it sat ill.

There was a better world than that, than kings of kings and mages of mages. A world where time was stitched in place, and where the gods were chaff, dream-things. Powerless. That was a vision that burned fiercer, that conflagrated in the chambers of his heart.

How do you kill gods, if they could even die?

Consume them, the thought came, clear and sweet as a lover's whisper in the dark.

'Not too much,' Dozha said, and paused to take the pipe from Tet's unresisting fingers. 'Just enough to take the edge off. Seven-petal makes mages useless.'

'And I am no mage.' Tet's mouth was filled with the ash and vanilla undertaste of petals. *But I am, and with my soul returned, and my true name, even the gods will fear me.* He remembered the little mountain dragon telling him that all the gods working together had not been able to heal time. A seed burst open, flame-flowered, new thoughts vining from it, growing a gleaming golden pattern of ideas. A plan so strange it could only have come from seven-petal. His fingers clenched briefly, a spasm, as though he clutched at some rope that would haul him out of darkness and into a new world.

Smoke layers floated around them like the ghosts of dragons, and Tet smiled grimly.

XXVIII

A CURIOSITY

For once, Tet would not have minded if time slowed to a honey-crawl, if it repeated that moment in endless golden loops. *Fuck the gods and their ruined time, let the world end now.* Dozha's palm was a curse that left no mark, one that brought pleasure instead of pain.

He sighed. The agony was slowly melting from his tightened muscles. But he couldn't hide his arousal; a half-mast stirring that chased after the warm pleasure of firm hands and sweet oils. *What a fool I must look to this mage, this man years younger than me, powerful. The son of a dragon.*

His face was hot, and Tet pushed his back down hard into the mattress, hoping to spark some distracting ache in the knots of his muscles, but the bed was too welcoming, and whatever reaction he had hoped for – this was not it.

Dozha made no comment, and Tet wasn't sure if that was more or less humiliating than the alternative. Despite Dozha's earlier warning to go slow on the seven-petal, Tet took a deep pull, filling his lungs with thick smoke. His head was wrapped in goat's wool softness, cushioned from the hard angles and bright points of reality. *Better this way, better to drown in sensation and disassociate myself from the lump of meat I live in.* Instead, he could fall into a dream, that one where he'd grown up in his family's tribe, where he was whole and healthy and had no magic. That one where he'd found love, a simple small thing that still somehow managed to smooth the rough skin of the world.

His eyelids fluttered closed, and he drowned. Here was his name – *Merithym* – like an anchor in the dream, and the person who lay next to him under the wooden arched ribs of their wagon, he had a name too. The dream strengthened, and Tet could smell the musk of raw silk from the South, the musk of love-making, the musk of the oxen outside. His fingers were twined in Tet's, and Tet knew his name as though he had cut it into his skin with a toymaker's scalpel blade. They whispered in the dark, and the gods did not hear them.

It was easier for Tet to lie to himself when his head was wrapped warm and soft with petal smoke, when the pain was leaching from him as though he were submerged in warmed fragrant oil, and the poison was pulled from his body like venom into amber.

Dozha's hand slid higher, and Tet twisted slightly to deter him.

Stop dreaming, he told himself. *Stop pretending.* This was not what he would be allowed to have. The gods had spread his future out on their board like the little bones fortune-tellers used in the market, and this was not what they had given Tet.

Fuck the gods.

Fuck dragons and monkeys and mages.

Still no words between them, and Tet kept his eyes shut tight. Pretended that he was not himself, that he was not there. Instead, he clung to the world where he was that Other-Merithym, the one who should have been. He was just a skin sack of meat and bone; these little pleasures were simple, they brought no complicated humiliations. He sank into an imaginary prism of oil, let the golden liquid close over his head. The world slowed and softened even as heat threaded through his body in a mapwork of fiery lines that converged at his groin. He throbbed. He ached. A pain that was sweeter than any others.

Tet had no idea how late it was when Dozha was finally done with his legs. All he knew were these things: he had a name, his stomach was full, his brain was foggy with wine and petals like a cloud of blossoms blown from peach trees. His legs no longer hurt as much and he felt stronger, more himself than he had in years.

Drugged, content, Tet threw off the shackling armour of all the people he had been. For a moment, he was his true self. He opened his eyes to a world that was subtly rearranged, and if he were still powerful, Tet would have been certain that it was his own fantasy become real. He was Merithym, and Merithym was just a man alone with another man. With Dozha, who was also just a man beneath his skin of magery and Underworld princehood.

Tet struggled up until he was cushioned by a mountain of pillows, and Dozha was lamp-lit, copper and gold and black. He felt remade. His fears and doubts were cast off by the drug and by Dozha's presence. It seemed natural to lean forward to taste the sweetness of seven-petal on Dozha's tongue, to touch skin that shone like new honey.

Dozha drew back out of Tet's grasp, and looked at him through lowered lashes. 'Unexpected,' he said.

'What – this?' Tet touched the mage's face, briefly, and dropped his hand. 'I'm also human, whatever your dragon thinks.'

Dozha laughed softly. 'I know that, Tet. But I've had people watching you, and what they told me...' He trailed off, uncertain.

Dimly, Tet considered being angry with Dozha for spying on him, but he couldn't be bothered. They all watched each other, and gods knew he was doing his own hunting. Dozha was simply better at it – fast and sly like a little fisher-cat from the islands – while Tet had blundered about like a dog on the scent of a deer. 'And what did these spies say?'

'That you were a man with limited appetites.' His hand spider-walked up Tet's leg, and stilled just below the groin. *So close. I no longer care about being rejected.* Tet covered

Dozha's hand with his own and shifted it higher, half expecting him to pull free. Instead, the thief mage closed his hand firmly around Tet's length, pressing heat through the soft material of his sleep clothes. A single pulse passed through Tet, like a wave of power at the first words of magic. He kept Dozha's hand pressed in place. 'I was raised a priest,' Tet said. 'I had to be.'

'And you're not a priest now?'

'I'm done with gods,' Tet said, and it didn't pain him to say it, not like it would have only a handful of months ago. Perhaps being without a soul had warped him beyond all redemption.

'Even so,' Dozha said. 'I don't think I'm going to be the meal that sates you.' He drew his hand free. His expression was troubled, and he looked half-angry. There was a rawness to that anger, an honesty that Tet found disconcerting.

'You cannot be sure.' Tet did not let his disappointment colour his voice. After all, Dozha was beautiful and powerful, a monster cut from red sandstone, and Tet was a mage who could do nothing, who stepped closer to death with each breath. He'd been a fool to think Dozha would welcome any advance.

'Truly.' The smile Dozha offered was weak, quickly gone. 'I'm not a whole meal.'

Tet shrugged. 'One arm, two. I do not care.'

This time Dozha laughed. 'Oh that, no.' He shifted forward like a cat wanting affection, and his jacket slipped from his shoulders. 'I'll humiliate myself, then leave, and you can feel better about being a mage with no magic.' He was bitter. An aspect of Dozha that Tet had not been allowed to see before.

Tet couldn't help reaching out to touch the thief prince's naked skin, flawless, beaten bronze, sparking under the dancing flames of the lamps, and Dozha did not stop Tet as he stroked down his body. Tet's heart bucked against his ribs, and Dozha's echoed, the beat rattling under Tet's palm. He pulled the jacket free.

Dozha's right arm ended at the elbow. Before, Tet had assumed that he'd lost it in some accident, or even had it removed as a punishment, but his fingers traced over no scarring, no healed wounds. 'You were born like this?'

'Yes. A bitter disappointment to my mother, who was certain the rest of her spawn would be similarly cursed.'

'Were they?' Tet's fingers encountered soft ridges on the skin, like weals.

'No. In fact, all of my sisters and my brother turned out to be perfect and beautiful. Perhaps Nyangist was trying to make up for me.'

'Ah.' Tet paused on the deepest of the ridges. 'What are these?'

Dozha shrugged back a little, out of Tet's grasp. 'I've tools for making certain jobs easier when I can't rely on magic. They're unfortunately painful to attach.' He shuffled back on his knees, just the slightest, but it was a clear sign that this part of the exploration was over. 'The marks will fade.'

Tet understood that he would hear nothing more about it, but he was uninterested in Dozha's little jobs and thieveries right now. Instead, he trailed fingers down from Dozha's collarbone, skirting one nipple and sliding lower down to his hip bone, catching it. Dozha did not resist when Tet pulled him closer, moved lower, untying the laces of his trousers and sliding his hand under the soft raw silk ready to meet heated skin, hard and hot as an iron brand.

'What—' Tet paused his hand.

'A curiosity,' Dozha said. 'Are you satisfied?'

Tet pulled at the trousers, revealing Dozha's truth. Slender as a finger and split down the underside like the cleft of a lily's stem. A curiosity indeed. And, Tet suspected, an aspect of Dozha that he kept hidden from others, from everyone. So why show him now, and how was Tet to respond? He needed clean brutality; Dozha was not a coddled child craving pat words, false flattery. 'And you charmed a witch of the caravans with this?'

Dozha snorted. 'It's a simple thing to keep the shape of a prick long enough to seduce a maid,' he said. 'But you know as well as I do that we have to return to the truth. No magic is permanent.'

Tet ran a finger along the cleft, to the tight bud of its head, and the stem trembled, made his own skin sing with answering heat. 'The ultimate inadequacy of mages, we are always at the end, revealed.'

*

The lamps had drowned themselves, the room was dark grey and it afforded both a brittle armour. Tet explored his unbound mage, his thief-prince, every curve and angle of him, and let Dozha return his ardour in equal measure. They made space for each other in spaces that they had not realised existed. It was heat, and sweetness, and rage, and tenderness. Storms and sighs. Tet pushed against his constraints, kissed fiercely, and remade his nameless dream lover in Dozha's image, until he could almost imagine the wagon's wooden bows above him, smell the stretched material, feel the rocking of the bed beneath.

For a moment, he let himself feel something like desire, affection. Trust. As each breached each, and taught the other new dances.

Afterwards, Dozha lay against Tet, oiled fingers drumming on his rib cage. He said nothing. It was a strange and uncertain time for words, and Tet knew better than to talk of what they had done, what thin webs they'd spun between them now. Sex was another kind of magery, another way to gain a measure of control. It was not predictable – never knowing if the threads were going to be sticky and strong as the golden silk of an orb-weaver, or fragile as desiccated cobwebs. Mages didn't trust to it. They trusted in names.

Tet was not so foolish as to think this baring of skin and mutual revelation of their vulnerabilities and brokenness meant that Dozha would do whatever it was Tet asked of him. *No. And do I want that kind of power over him anyway?* He knew exactly what it was like to have the whole world thinking that they owned him.

He was put in mind of Kani. Dozha hadn't mentioned her or his progress in getting the beetle and Tet was loathe to bring it up directly again. His free hand stroked down the hills and valleys of Dozha's spine, pausing in each small dip. His skin was velvet, furred like a white peach, and Tet considered waking him again just to taste him, lick the sweetness from him.

Dozha murmured, something sleepy and unintelligible.

'Kani comes to me in her dreams,' Tet said to the ceiling. Under his hand, Dozha's muscles tensed. He was not sleeping, after all.

'Does she now,' he said after a long, gloomy silence had passed.

In a manner of speaking – certainly it was what she believed. It was safest to leave it at that. Tet had no desire to start explaining to Dozha about the flint-pouch and the dogs. Sex or no, he was not going to hand over every weapon he had to a man who could prove to be as false and deceitful as any other.

When Tet didn't respond to his flat inquiry, Dozha pushed himself up onto the stump of his elbow and glared down at him. In the darkness, his eyes were black pools, no starlight reflected in their hidden depths. 'Tell me about these meetings.'

'Curious?' Tet shifted, cupped Dozha's cheek in his palm, ran his thumb along the curves of his mouth. The flesh was soft, still slightly damp. His skin smelled of a new musk now, the mingled essences of spendings, of oils and sweet wine.

'Yes. Stop trying to distract me.'

'She came to offer me bargains.'

Dozha breathed out, and his expression turned flat and wary, reminding Tet of a fox caught in the early morning light, uncertain if it had been spotted by an enemy or something worse. 'For your soul?'

'Yes.' Tet should end this conversation now, silence it with kisses, and pretend that nothing more was said. 'But they're just dreams.'

'I'm also a mage,' Dozha said. 'Or have you forgotten? Dreams are never *just* anything. Don't talk to me like I'm some fool of a, of a pot-maker. What does she want of you?'

'My name.' Tet dropped his hand. It was an act of surrender, though he wondered if Dozha realised it.

Dozha managed a twitch of a smile, forced and awkward. His eyes stayed hard and deep. 'And do you plan on giving it to her?'

'I can't,' Tet said simply. What was once the truth was now a lie, but Dozha didn't need to know that. Not yet, not until Tet was sure he could trust him. 'I don't have one to give.' A laugh jolted out of him, as unexpected as a robin bursting from a bush. 'Maybe she should have tried seducing me instead – I would at least have had a cock to bargain with.'

Dozha shoved at him. 'Fuck off, old man.' He sat up, drawing his knees to his chest. He stared off to the shadows of the underground room. Tet could just make out the furrows of his brow, but little more. Strands of his hair had escaped from his neat plait, and he looked almost vulnerable. A strange and uncomfortable thing. Tet saw the child he might once have been, damaged, turned out of his family for things he had no control over. Tet had no idea what paths had led to Sinastrillia taking the mage child as her own, raising him to be her thief-prince. What it might have been like for Dozha to be a human brought up under the talons of a dragon.

Tet's heart stuttered, and he cursed himself for falling to sentiment. Dozha was no longer a child, and he was a dangerous man to have as an enemy, and perhaps, even more dangerous to have as a friend.

Dozha turned his head suddenly and Tet was stabbed by the brightness of his eyes, like a little moth pinned, still fluttering, to cork. 'I don't believe you,' Dozha said. 'You were supposed to have been great once. How did you do powerful magic with no name to guide you?'

'Maybe I was not as great as people have led you to believe.'

'Shoom believes it. More so, Sinastrillia does.' He frowned and lunged forward to grab at Tet's newly disfigured hand. His grip was tight enough to make Tet wince. 'What did my mother want of you?'

'She wanted to offer me something.' Tet sighed. 'Another bargain. Bargains on top of bargains.' He closed his eyes and said softly. 'You're hurting me, Dozha.'

'She gave you your name.'

A thorn-prick of caution jabbed at Tet. 'And tell me how a dragon would do that,' Tet said. 'How would she even know to offer?'

Dozha released Tet's chalk-white hand. There was silence, then. 'Sorry,' he said. 'I am not used to...' A feather-touch on the white fingers, Tet's hand lifted, the soft warm wetness of a mouth. He kissed Tet's fingertips, nipped at the base of the thumb. An apology with something that could be a playful warning. A reminder that they were not just two men, but two men of power, and already they were giving too much to each other.

He pulled Tet's fingers from his mouth. 'What will you say the next time you see Kani in your dreams?'

If Tet looked at Dozha, he would not be able to do this next thing, this last test. But was Tet testing Dozha or himself? Or was he testing a woman who wasn't even in the room, a figment they had created between them? A third corner in a triangle, a mannequin who was nothing more than a collection of masks and magic. Tet squeezed his eyes tighter, until behind the lids in the watery darkness an explosion of fireworks began to play. Perhaps he owed Dozha a truth, even if it was a foolish risk. 'I will tell Kani that I have back my name. That I am ready to bargain.'

He opened his eyes.

Dozha nodded.

He would say nothing, and neither would Tet. Already they had spoken too much truth between them. There could be no

more of that. Tet closed his fingers around Dozha's and
dragged him back down.

*

After, because they would not talk of names and power again,
Tet asked something from the prince of the Underpalace. 'The
girl who came to kill me,' he said softly into the dark. 'Why did
you send her?'

Dozha didn't move when he answered. His breath tickled
against Tet's collar bone. His words hummed against Tet's
skin. 'I didn't send her. Shoom hired her, maybe to test you. I
don't pretend to understand the fat man's mind.'

'She died,' Tet said.

Dozha sighed, damp and warm. 'We know. And it was her
decision to take the contract and she was bound to whatever
end it brought her. We also have honour in the Underpalace,'
he said. 'We serve out our contracts to the best of our abilities,
and if we fail, we return the hire-coin. We don't steal from our
clients.' He was quiet for a little while, before saying, 'But you
gave her a sacred funeral and honoured her. It's more than
others would have given.'

Of course Dozha knew what had happened to the girl. Tet
pondered this while his one hand smoothed along Dozha's left
arm, stroking along from shoulder bone to elbow, from elbow
to wrist, wrist to fingertips.

Dozha trapped Tet's fingers with his, a small game in the
endless night.

'Do you not hate me for her death?'

Dozha did not answer.

Later Tet woke to a chilled room, and pulled the woollen
blankets and silk covers up and over the curve of Dozha's
shoulder, and though he seemed barely awake, the mage slid
one leg between Tet's and said, 'Should I?'

'I think so, yes,' Tet said, as the guilt clawed up his throat.

'Will my hatred grant you absolution?'

The answer was silence.

'Then no,' Dozha said. 'I will not hate you. Your guilt is your own choice.'

*

The morning lamps were lit, this time by a woman older than both mages combined, and they clawed their way out of sleep. If Tet had spent another night screaming, Dozha at least pretended not to have heard it. Tet's skin was tacky, but he did not feel the gut-wrenching exhaustion of another night clogged with bad dreams.

He was sated, after all.

The old woman set out breakfast trays on the table and took the dead water-pipe away. When she was gone, Dozha sat up and the blankets fell from his shoulders. His hair had come unbraided in the night and it fell to his waist, black as the wings of cranes. He pushed it back with his one hand and before Tet could offer to braid it for him the way a lover might, he whispered. A zephyr lifted Dozha's hair, dividing it as easily as a mother, and twisted the strands in place. 'I'll be busy for the next few days,' he said. 'You can rest here.'

'I must return to Peniki's,' Tet said, thinking of how he needed to be able to use the flint-pouch, of Ymat's man watching, and what he would report of Tet's absence. He leaned forward to count the bones of Dozha's spine, to press a kiss against the place where shoulder and neck met. When he drew back, Tet noticed a smear of white behind Dozha's ear. It matched his unearthly hand. Tomb-marble white. The same shade as the White Prince, as that witch Kani.

Soon they were both dressed and Dozha called for yesterday's sapling girl to lead Tet back home. Before they parted, he leaned close enough that only Tet could hear his whisper, as his hand slipped beneath Tet's jacket, fingers tickling along the white undershirt. Tet felt a sudden visceral desire -- not for sex, but to tell Dozha his name, to trust him entirely. It was a moth flit of emotion, a spasm. A name would not tie ribbons between them.

'Shoom is growing impatient,' Dozha said, 'and I have to make my move soon – before the prince takes his new clockwork elephants into the war.'

A dangerous move. Tet thought of that body tied to the white donkey by its own entrails, the little clockwork hunting monsters sent out by the court toymaker. But he also understood the urgency. The prince was now completely beyond the control of the voices of men, of little city-speakers who tried to temper his excesses. Eventually, he would bring the whole world down in flames around him in Nyangist's name.

Tet's throat closed. This could be the last time he saw Dozha. 'You will be careful,' Tet said, instead of all the hundred other things he could, all the questions he was desperate to ask.

'I'm always careful.' But the smile that accompanied the words was tired, a little strained. 'Tet,' Dozha said, and pulled him closer, kissing him once, pressing his closed mouth to Tet's like a benediction. He stayed like that for too long, their breaths mingling. Tet could feel the slight flicker of his eyelashes against skin, before he drew away. 'When I was born,' Dozha said, soft as goose down, 'my mother called me Oshaketri.'

A daughter's name.

XXIX

AND NOW THE DEAD

The girl led Tet back down a new route, but he'd begun to layer these passages over each other like skins worn to translucency, and the map was growing in his mind, matching itself to the more complete map of the upper streets of Pal-em-Rasha. He was not surprised when his sapling guide took him to an area near where Tet had met the failed toymaker Yulikiya.

He tucked his white hand into his jacket so as not to draw attention, and found a small pouch secreted there. It had been returned to him as softly as it was taken, and Tet closed his fist around it.

Dozha had given him back the hire-coin. An admission of failure. More than that – much more, Dozha had also given Tet his true name. He said it under his breath. *Oshaketri*. It felt right. Wrong and right. Right because it *was* his name. That much Tet could tell. It made him more real.

Wrong, because it was the name of a first-born daughter. Tet did not like what any of this meant. Dozha had with one act both betrayed himself and won Tet's trust, had shown him up. He had done something freely that Tet would never have done, and he knew it. Dozha assumed he knew Tet well enough to trust he would never use his true name – too burnt by his own dealings with men and princes to try do the same.

Or perhaps it had been a truly innocent, honest act. How was Tet to know what small loves Dozha had been allowed in his life, what pleasures he mistook for intimacy? He'd been honest enough to reveal himself. Or herself. Tet wondered how Dozha or Oshaketri or whoever he was saw himself, how they saw their own shape. Perhaps he shifted it as easily as he turned from man to dragon.

Oshaketri. By giving Tet this power over him, he had with one word revealed Tet's true nature. Dozha had shown his honesty, and Tet's lack.

He had also effectively withdrawn from the contract to steal back the *oresh*-beetle. Perhaps because he knew Tet would now be able to fulfil Kani's bargain. *Damn that serpent-hearted little shit. I don't understand him or his motives. I need the full picture of Dozha and all I have are slivers of glass.* When Tet put the shattered mirror together, what was he going to see?

He had an uncomfortable suspicion that he already knew, and he liked it little.

Now Tet was left with only one option to regain his soul, and with it his power. He had what Kani wanted, and such a simple trade it would be: his name for his soul. He would have his magery back. And Kani would have him on a leash. Was she the Emperor that Sinastrillia had seen in the currents of time?

What was to become of Tet once he was a mage again – there were gods hunting him down, and they would not be slow to deal out their punishments. Nyangist would settle for little less than his heart, of that much Tet was certain.

He was torn in so many directions. Threads were stitched under his skin, and each tied him to a different death and a different life. If Tet followed one, he must snip the others. And while the thread tying him to Dozha was silver-black and fine, it was also as easily broken as the silk of a spider's web.

Kani at least offered him back his power, and perhaps he would find some other way to escape the teeth and claws of gods. Even if it was a madness spurred by too much seven-petal, a dream where he ate the damn things, power and all. Tet had his true name, and Dozha's, and Sinastrillia had told him that the power of the gods was passing.. The word of a dragon was a dangerous thing to pin his hope to, but it was all he had.

*

The day was still bright. There was no chance of using the flint-pouch now and Tet was not ready to go back to hide in his attic room. He bought wrappings to bandage his hand, then walked through the city until hunger drove him into a small Imradian restaurant. At a corner table, half-hidden in the shadows, Tet listened to the cant and rhyme of the servers and chefs as they spoke to one another in their native tongue. He immersed himself in it, trying to find the flow.

I'm already planning to run. With a grim acceptance of the kind of person he was, had always been, and would remain, Tet knew he had given up on ever returning Nanak's eyes and freeing himself from her curse. He knew now that he would forever be a coward, crawling from the messes he made, as the curse slowly turned him into a mutilated wretch.

Dozha survived one-handed. Men came back from the war with stumps instead of legs. What was Tet afraid of? At the very least Tet could still play his lute and earn his coin that way. Just another beggar in a world lice-ridden with them.

Only, what hope could he have when Kani had him under her control, his name in her mouth like a word of power. There would never be a leash long enough.

Tet buried his head in his hands. Each way he turned, the threads knotted and tangled and he was tied tighter into an ending he did not want.

*

The afternoon sun sunk low. Tet had wasted his time picking at strange foods and softening his self-pity with pegs of cashew liquor. The shirring wave of sound from outside the little restaurant had grown louder, high as cicadas, and finally it was enough to pull him out of his self-pitying haze.

'What's going on?' He motioned toward the servers who were standing at the open glass doors and chattering at each other, their dark hands jabbing the air.

One turned to him and sucked on his little paper tobacco twist, and grimaced. 'Thief,' he said.

'Eh?' Tet bristled, his drunken mind turning the unexpected answer to an insult.

The man sucked viciously on his cigarette again and spat the rest of his sentence out with the smoke. 'Some fool thief, caught in the Pistil. He was caught by the monsters. The White Prince is displaying the body now.' He muttered something to his colleague, and the younger one continued, softer, slower. 'He wants to show the people of Pal-em-Rasha what will happen to those who think they can go against him.'

Dozha.

Tet threw a handful of Dozha's hire-coins on the table, enough to pay for his drinks and meals many times over, and ran out past the staring servers and into the heat-wet streets, following the drone and trumpet of the crowds. He wove through the massed people, pushing his way past bright silk shoulders, through the heat of bodies, the shimmer of gold and brass and white teeth like stars.

The death-procession wound through one of Pal-em-Rasha's grandest streets and though this parade mimicked the stomp and finery of the prince's engagement procession, it had none of its solemnity, none of its grandeur. Ignoring the pain whipping through his legs, through his heart, Tet pushed his way to the front of the crowd, cold sweat slicking his back, his sides.

What was left of the body had been crucified on two wide planks. The cross was held high by marching soldiers. Tet couldn't tell if the corpse had one arm or two. All its limbs had been chewed into ragged red and bone-splinter stumps and the entrails hung like tired bunting in loops of pink and grey. The face was a grinning skull. All meat eaten away.

The only thing that remained to give the body any identity of its own was the black flag of its hair, long and dark and bright as crane's wings. The body was marched past Tet, towards the lowering sun, and the crowd followed it like the tail of a snake.

Tet stood in the emptying streets, sound buzzing in his head, his hands clenched. Sweat ran down his face. His skin felt as though it no longer belonged to him, his hands the body parts of a stranger. The noise of the processions faded, replaced by the screaming of the striped geese passing overhead, echoing over the towers and domed roofs of the city. The streets stank of ox and meat, sweat and smoke.

Bells rang in a nearby store, and the murmur of trade returned as people went back to their day-to-day world. Tet stumbled forward like a man caught in the suck of a dream-tide, following the tug of strange currents. His feet lifted without his command. His head was empty, thoughts fine as dust. *I cannot think.* There was nothing for him to hold on to, to understand. A black ache settled into him, fat and cold as a coiled pit-viper.

It took Tet a while to catch up again with the crowd, and longer still before he was able to fight his way clear to where the corpse was now hoisted on display in the temple square. Nyangist's domed halls were rubble and ash, but this was still a sacrifice, and the priests and lions were there to see the blood drop slow and cold onto the thirsty stones.

Tet waited for the sun to shed its crown and the crowds to thin before he was brave enough to get a closer look at the body.

It was even harder now to tell anything about the corpse. People had spat on it, thrown spoiled fruit and handfuls of fire-blackened pebbles gathered from Nyangist's fallen temple. Even the black hair looked ragged, like the pennant of a conquered enemy.

I can't tell if it's him. The corpse looked to be the right age. Tet glanced around. The square was far from empty. It was not as though he could check to see if the thief sported a curiosity.

Laughter spilled out of him. A cold flat sound in the green-black of the lengthening shadows. Tet clapped his hand over his mouth and made himself breathe slowly. The smells of the city became overwhelming, making him want to fall to his knees and puke.

This is the first pattern, the one we call Dragon Mountain Breath, came the voice of the abbess, and Tet remembered the cold halls of the temples, the steady breaths of the priest-boys. *Calm. Silence. Power.*

Finally, he was able to reach forward and touch the cold skin. He could not smell seven-petal and incense and skin-sweet-sweat and almond oil. There was only the metallic tang of blood, the putrid sweetness of shit and death.

It could be him. But it could also be anyone else. Tet held on to that. Dozha was a mage and no mage should die like this, like meat.

Because Dozha was clever, and cleverness shouldn't be rewarded with this sewer-ending.

Because he was not dead. He had wrapped himself in shadows and shifting shapes, and he knew that the way to the prince was guarded and he wouldn't take a stupid chance.

'It surprises me to see you here,' said a voice so familiar and soft and spidery. It chilled Tet, and he turned slowly to look at Ymat Shoom. The Monkey was dressed in his city-speaker finery, in his embroidered white boots and his wide-sleeved robes of office. His bald head was shining with the swirls of indigo tattoos.

'Should you be speaking to me?' Tet asked. They were in the middle of a public square, and though he still wore soldier's rags and his face was thatched with a scraggly beard, people might draw unpleasant conclusions.

Ymat lifted his hands palm-up in mute apology. 'I hardly think it matters.' His one sleeve bulged, and his pet monkey peered out. It was not grinning now.

'What do you mean?'

Ymat took a small dancing step back as though Tet were a leper. 'For what little it's worth to you, I am genuinely sorry. I hadn't meant for things to go this way.'

Tet looked about, expecting soldiers, expecting to be arrested and hauled before the White Prince before being torn to pieces by clockwork animals, before his corpse was raised in warning alongside this poor dead fool.

There was no one. No uniforms of the palace and no ornamental helms, no shining swords and muskets and shields.

Ymat frowned at his confusion. 'Your death,' he said. 'It has settled on your shoulders. And I have not been able to retrieve your soul from that witch Kani.'

'My death.' It was not a question, but Ymat answered him anyway.

'It's in your eyes, the blackness.'

The square went red and sticky, covered in a layer of blood. Tet blinked, and Ymat Shoom was gone. The blood remained. Everything was still. The breeze caught a tendril of the corpse's hair and Tet reached out to touch it. The hair was cold, stiff. The silence pealed around him as Tet waited for time to restart. The gods were fainter this time, hazier than the smog of distant cities. The strands of hair moved under his fingers as the breeze gusted and the world burst into chatter.

'It surprises me to see you here,' Ymat said.

This time. This time our conversation will be different.

Tet turned slowly to face him. 'Does it? When you were the one who set me on this path?'

'I did not mean for you to die,' said Ymat. 'I only meant for you and your soul to be parted for a few days.'

'I'm not dead yet.'

'Your death has settled on you,' Ymat Shoom said, his voice suddenly lowered, gentle. 'I can see the blackness of it in your eyes.'

Tet felt it. He'd thought it to be the weight of his despair, but now that Ymat had named it, he knew. Sinastrillia's plan for him to go into the cavern of shades had pushed him closer to death, and Tet had reached that final border before time.

There was nowhere to run now.

'There will be others,' Ymat said. 'Other plans I'll have to make, other mages and thieves to hire.' He looked tired. 'Or perhaps, like you, I should also accept defeat. Be quiet and small and live out the life allotted to me. Wait for the White Prince to die of old age.' He looked up at the sky as though he studied the hidden stars for futures. 'It's my right to retire after my years in service. The prince won't even care. What am I after all, other than the youngest son of a minor family, with no chance to win land and influence in the art of war.'

Even the Monkey was giving up.

The city-speaker snapped his head back and stared at Tet. 'It is time for you to set your affairs in order,' Ymat said, and he was not unkind. He seemed genuinely concerned and Tet nodded, turned his face away from Ymat's empty pity. His lead heart shrunk, dull and slow as a trinket made by a third-rate toymaker.

'Don't run from your death like a coward,' Ymat said. 'Face it. Have a good end. It's all we have left to us.'

He was right. Tet knew it. Already he could feel his insides turning to putrefaction, and tasted the rot in his mouth. And if this body before him was Dozha's, then what did death matter. 'Please.' Tet caught at Ymat's sleeve with numb fingers. His tongue felt heavy and awkward, the words ill-shaped. 'Look after Hast for me.'

Ymat paused, eyes searching. Finally he nodded. 'It's the least I can do, friend.'

XXX

A NAME OR TWO

Tet's death crawled closer as he made his way home. There was no point left in pretending. He paid a rickshaw runner to take him right to Peniki's door, uncaring of who might see him.

Peniki was sitting on her stoop, red-raw hands braiding razor-edged leaf blades together and she raised her eyebrows as Tet stumbled out of the rickshaw. 'Not feeling well, Sai?'

He grimaced, holding on to the rickshaw with one hand to stop himself from falling over. His stomach clenched, and though he tried to swallow the feeling away, the next moment Tet was doubled up, vomiting a blood-laced mess of half-digested Imradian food onto the dust of the road. 'I just, just need to lie down,' he said as he wiped the spit from his face.

A wave of dizziness slammed into him and the sun-stained late afternoon went white, then empty.

*

Tet woke to find Peniki and the annoyed rickshaw-runner heaving him up the stairs.

'—hardly just leave him there, and what did you expect me to do – carry him myself?' said Peniki.

'It's not my job to drag drunkards to their beds,' the runner grumbled back. 'He smells like he bathed in a vat of cashew wine.'

Tet's back thudded along the narrow spines of the steps, and he grimaced, twisting himself free. 'I can walk,' he slurred. He wasn't drunk, though it felt like it. Like the worst part of an evening of too much millet beer and not enough food. He retched again, and they dropped him.

'Not all over my house,' said Peniki. 'Who do you think must clean?' There was a shrill note of fear under her lecture.

'Leave me.' Tet's mouth filled with the rotten metal taste of blood. He made himself swallow it, thick as old milk.

Peniki grunted in something that could be irritation or concern, and was probably a grudging mixture of both, but her skirts swished and her steps creaked away, fading as she left him lying only a few feet from the attic door. The runner clicked his tongue and called Tet a few choice words, then he too went. Tet lay with his cheek resting on the wood, watching the tiny cracks in the grain, counting the dirt grains gathered in the corners. The smooth-worn steps were cool against his temple.

After a few slow breaths, he pushed up from his palms and began to crawl laboriously. The distance seemed like miles. When he finally made it to the little pallet bed, he felt vaguely relieved. Even with the full enormity of his death and the nothing that was coming after, Tet still clung to petty things like not wanting to die on the floor with his face smeared in his bloodied spit.

He curled up onto his knees. The sun filtered in bloodied streaks through the chinks and cracks in the timbers, and there was a half hour or more before full dark. Tet could not allow himself to fall asleep, terrified that if he closed his eyes and lay down his head, then he would never wake.

And what if I can hold on till the night and call Kani – what if she's changed her mind?

It didn't help him to dwell on what-ifs and maybes. Tet refused to think of the body in the square and what it could mean. Perhaps there was no more Kani left. Instead, he dragged out his leather satchel and found his small round bronze mirror and razor. The beard was another mask belonging to Sektet Am, and if Tet was to die tonight, he wanted it to be without hiding under layers of anonymity. It seemed a fitting and honest desire to face his end as nothing but the person he had never really been allowed to be.

His hands trembled, there was no lather, and the blade was dull. Tet cut his face, scraped his skin raw, but at the end, under the trickles of blood and the rash, he saw himself again, dimly in the half-light, in the beaten bronze.

'Merithym.' His breath clouded the dull surface. His chest ached.

The light was fading. The cramping in Tet's stomach came and went with a vicious regularity, each wave longer and more painful than the last. His lungs were withered as last-year's leaves and each breath scratched raw. He coughed, over and over, a thin harsh sound.

Soon I will be a corpse too. Another body gone cold because of the White Prince. Perhaps Tet's end would not be so public, and it could be argued that it was all his own damn fault for making any kind of bargain with Ymat Shoom, but it was the White Prince who held Nanak's opals, who pulled the wings from his enemies and scattered his people like dry grains into ill soil.

It was almost dark and Tet closed his hand tight around the little flint-pouch. As soon as the blackness had draped itself completely over his room, he struck the first shower of sparks, and Epsi appeared, small as a rabbit. Then Vitash, wolfish and all bared teeth and snarls. Nanak, who regarded him with tea-bowl eyes brimming with the knowledge of his approaching death.

Now was the final spark of hope, the chance of truth, revelation, life. 'Bring me Kani, bring me my soul again.' The words barely sounded above a whisper.

Nanak faded away and Tet was left with the other two. They looked nervous, tasting his death in the room. Vitash whined and growled, and Epsi crawled onto Tet's lap to nose at his badly-shaven face. She licked the dried blood from his chin, and her tongue was warm, alive.

*

Kani did not come to him in raw silk pyjamas, half-asleep and narrow-eyed as a winter fox. Instead she was dressed in all her finery, the sweep of her hair held back with a single pin, eyes fresh-kohled and darkened.

'I am not dreaming,' she said from her high perch on Nanak's back.

t was true. The night had only just fallen, and there was no magic mystery of dreaming for her to pretend otherwise. She'd always known. He'd always known. It had simply been another part of the game they played.

'No.' Tet coughed into his fist. 'You never were.' He was relieved to find her alive, and not a dismembered corpse, spat on in a public square.

'Of course not.' Kani was white-faced as a devil, her gloved hands tight in the thick ruff of Nanak's fur. 'Only this time you've pulled me not from a bed, but from my duties. I'm to attend another of the prince's grand parties tonight. He will wonder at my absence.'

'I won't keep you long.'

She stared at him and shuddered. 'You're already dying,' she said, and there it was again, the fish-flash of her true voice. Her scent of burning syruped-petals, her scent of the prince's incense, of dragon scales, of sweet-almond and musk. Her breath like winter, her cold, cold hand and her black hair, loosened now from its braid. 'I thought we had more time.'

'I'm ready to bargain.' Tet felt like laughing or crying. It was hard to decide. Perhaps it was neither, and death had taught him a new emotion, one there was no word for. Maybe it was hope; he hadn't had enough to learn the feel of it.

'You will give me your name?' she asked softly, as though the question pained her.

'In exchange for my soul.' It was swinging on its chain, resting below her throat, beetle black and full of magic.

A slow relaxed feeling passed through Tet; the wind had changed direction and was bringing warmth from the south. He stroked one hand down Epsi's small head, fur silk-soft under his fingers. It was over. He smiled weakly. 'Merithym.' He threw the name between them as an offering. 'And now I suppose I must trust you.'

Kani's throat moved. 'I have my own honour, Merithym.' She took the beetle in one hand, sliding the chain up and over her head, and held it out to Tet from Nanak's back. 'By your name, I hold you to do me no harm.'

It took all the strength Tet had left to lurch off the bed and cross the tiny space to Nanak, to touch that small thing Kani held out to him like a scrap of dried meat offered to a starving dog. He closed his white fingers around it, and the pulse of magic boomed through his palm and shuddered up his arm. In moments, Tet had the chain over his head and the *oresh*-beetle against his chest, its claws already breaking through the skin. He could feel it taste it hear it, as though the whole world had suddenly brightened back to life.

It was not everything it used to be, but it was enough to drag him back from the mouth of death. A few day's respite, but Tet had a plan now, one where he would take a chance that would free him from gods forever. And he had the breathing space he needed.

'Don't release your soul yet, Merithym,' said Kani. 'Or every damned god in this city will come hunting you down. And I need you for the moment.'

Tet had no choice but to do as she said, he felt the constraints of it, a fishhook under his tongue. And Kani had a point. He was not yet ready to face down the three gods of his temple, and certainly not Nyangist, who would be eager to tear him limb from limb, slowly.

But Tet was not unarmed, his teeth had not been quite ground down. He stood straighter. He was almost a whole man again. His name was now his own, and if Sinastrillia was right, he would one day be stronger than he could ever have dreamed or wanted.

'And what is it you need me for,' Tet studied her familiar ambitious face, her tired and whitened face, 'Oshaketri?'

Kani's mask remained expressionless. When she spoke again, when her mouth parted like a split plum, the voice that came out was familiar as the taste of skin, and Kani was obliterated.

'How did you know?' Dozha inclined his head, the only sign of his calm curiosity.

Tet shrugged, pressing his transmuted hand against his chest as though he could push his soul back into place, right through his ribcage. 'A fleck of white.' A lucky guess. A desperate guess. All the times he had seen Kani and yet not seen her, the shift of her magic, the shift of Dozha's skin under his palm. The smell of temple incense and dragon's smoke in his hair. The jut of their chin, the twist under their words.

'A fleck of white,' Dozha repeated, the words so slow they could be made of frozen honey.

'Behind your ear.' Tet smiled thinly. 'Among other things. The shape of your face, the way you turn your head, the things you say. You hid yourself with fictions I did not expect— mummer's acts, false limbs, painted masks, but there were still tells.'

'I'm clearly not as good an actor as I'd thought.'

'No.' Tet shook his head. 'You are a very good actor. And a very good mage. But you should never let the audience see behind the curtain.'

Dozha snorted in wry amusement.

'You can shift your shape, but you cannot hold it for long. Therefore, if you needed to be the prince's bride, you had to have more tricks than magic.' And how that thought rankled— how far had Dozha gone in his deception, had he magicked his curiosity into a cunt for the prince, received him like a lover? It twisted at Tet's throat.

'A bride for one night only,' said Dozha. 'But that's not enough. I used magic to hold the illusion together, to misdirect you. There should've been no way for you to see through it.'

Tet pushed the image of Dozha/Kani under the White Prince out of his mind. 'In truth, I didn't.'

'What?' Dozha frowned.

'I didn't see through it. Kani was an expert fabrication. I only saw Dozha beneath her skin because I had to.'

'You make no sense.'

Tet was admitting too much. He almost laughed at his own sentimental dreams. He had fallen, and for a man who was a trickster and serpent's son. It didn't matter what Dozha was, only that he *was*. That he breathed, that his heart still moved blood through his body. They both still lived, and that was no small thing. What was an admission of love next to that? Let Dozha know how he felt, it didn't matter. 'Kani had to be you, or you were dead. I chose to believe that you were not.'

The glow from the dogs lit the attic room, leaving the two mages no shadows where they could hide from each other. Deeper and stranger than that – each held the other's name like a talisman. For the moment, Dozha was the stronger, and Tet was hampered by the threat of the gods' revenge, but the future would come when he swallowed his soul back and had power beyond dreaming.

If this was a maket game, it had ended in a stalemate. There was only silent truth between them. Though Dozha was dressed in the mask of Kani, in her armour and arm, Tet saw him clearer than ever before.

'The body in the square,' Tet explained. 'If you were Kani, and Kani came to me tonight, then that corpse could not possibly be you. I did not want it to be you.'

'She was an assassin,' Dozha said. 'The girl the White Prince caught. Shoom does like to throw around the money he claims not to have.'

'I couldn't tell, not properly. And I needed to know before I died.'

'I see,' Dozha said, but he sounded confused.

Tet's soul thrummed against his chest and he took a deep breath, feeling magic curl through him. It would be nothing now to strip Dozha's wardings from him and finally see exactly who he was. Instead, Tet asked a question. 'Why did you give me your name?'

Dozha shrugged, and Tet caught a hint of darkening flush in his cheeks under the white make-up as he ducked his head. 'Perhaps I did not like the idea of controlling you.'

'Then why not tell me all the truth?' He was truly curious. Dozha was too full of contradictions. A typical mage.

'Habit,' Dozha said. 'We can talk of this another time, and since we are at a deadlock, with neither being able to control the other, I'll have to break the first of many habits and ask you for your help.' He looked up, and there was that sly grin, that fox's grin.

'My help?'

He nodded. 'I can get to the prince tonight and I can get the breastplate, but I cannot leave without your assistance. It will need to be finely timed.'

'What will?' Although he was asking Tet, Dozha had already assumed obedience. As though he could still make Tet do whatever he wanted simply by saying his name in the right way. Perhaps he was right. Not because he knows my name, but because he gave me his, gave it freely. Under the many masks of the thief prince of the Underpalace was a man of honour, a man who paid his debts.

Dozha's expression of thoughtful concentration was remarkably his own, despite that painted, perfect face. 'Time, my Merithym. I'll need a moment.'

Tet tested the limits of his magic, letting the boxed-in power flow through him from toes to fingertips. He might not be able to stop time as he was now, but he could, if his soul was truly his own again. Would. When the moment was right. 'Ymat Shoom told you what I can do.' The power pushing through him was honeyed wine, sweet and dizzying. 'Or Sinastrillia did.' That seemed more likely.

'It was her idea.' Dozha let go of Nanak's ruff and dropped down to the ground as supple and smart as one of the city's cats. 'She's a master game-player, and she sets her board in her favour.'

Dragons could see futures and they loved their strategy games, but Tet did not like to know how neatly he had been placed and manipulated on Sinastrillia's Grand Board. And who exactly had she been playing him against? And why? 'She wants to set up a new empire, and a new emperor to lead it.'

'I know that,' Dozha leaned back against Nanak's flanks, and the dog turned her immense head to lick at his face. 'What piece do you think I am?' He returned Nanak's affection by stroking behind her vast ears, cooing at her as if she were the fat pup of a free-dog, and not a monster made of magic.

Oshaketri the Emperor. The greatest piece on the Grand Board, a rival to the White Prince. And Tet may have been a wind tile, but now he was Merithym, the Emperor's Mage. This was the future Sinastrillia saw, the one where Tet lived.

The future where he healed the cracks in time he'd made as an arrogant, terrified and drunken youth. 'You want me to stop time, Sinastrillia wants me to fix time. She wants me to follow this future where I walk at the heels of her Emperor like a slave-dog. And what kind of emperor would you be—'

'A one-armed one, with a working brain, and no desire to smash my armies uselessly against the city walls of men who should be our friends and not our enemies.' Dozha gave Nanak a final pat, stepped up to the edge of the bed, and knelt on the mattress, his hands catching Tet's wrists.

One hand firm and flesh, the other cold, heavy. Metal under silk. A clockwork hand. 'And what kind of mage would you be?' Dozha said it with a laugh and answered his own question. 'One who would destroy the gods and perform miracles. One who is loyal and expects loyalty in return. Merithym.'

And maybe Tet was thrice-damned, but he heard it in Dozha's voice, and he believed. 'Then that is what you'll have,' Tet said. He closed his eyes, and felt Dozha's forehead press against his own for a moment. He angled his head to kiss the plum mouth, to taste Dozha the way the prince had tasted him.

'Do we have time for this,' Dozha said, half-laughing, but not pulling away.

'I'm the Lord of Time,' Tet reminded him, but the mage was right. Even so, he couldn't bring himself to let go. They could die tonight. This could be the last time they touched each other's skin, breathed the same sweetened air. 'Dance with me, Osha.'

Dozha sucked in a sharp breath, then nodded.

XXXI

THE GILDED PISTIL

The two mages made their plans between biting kisses, soft gasps. They were ready but for one thing; Dozha wanted to say goodbye to someone before he made his way back to the White Prince's side.

'You think we will fail?' Tet ran his fingers through Dozha's hair, marvelling at this last moment. Perhaps he was dreaming, taking him here on the pallet bed was not real but just some final vision before death. 'Who is so precious to you that you risk making the prince wonder where you are?'

'Laketri.' He smiled wryly.

Of course. More fine shards carefully placed in the correct order.

'Jealous?' Dozha prodded him with one metal finger. 'Don't be. She's my sister. I'm not that depraved, you know.'

'Hush,' Tet said, and kissed him goodbye.

*

The Pistil played host to another of the White Prince's parties. Tet was no guest, but he walked through the crowds of merchant-queens and -princes, city-speakers, and rich women, wise women, old men who were saved from war by the armour of their stored goods. The deer-headed women and the clockwork birds, the chemical globes and the sweet stink of seven-petal.

He had been here before, wearing a rich man's face, with a false daughter to sell to the White Prince. He'd had a sackful of jewels and coin and Ymat's word to pay for his mask.

This time Tet carried everything he planned to keep. A small satchel, a handful of coin to see them safe when they ran. *If they ran*. The flint-pouch tucked behind his wide belt. The rest Tet had left behind for Peniki to discover. She'd be a wealthy woman and her smile would be brighter for it. *I wish her well.*

And now Tet stood cloaked in shades and shadows, using his weakened magic as easily as though they'd never been parted. He walked through the crowd and no person noticed him deeply wrapped in his power. Tet stayed far from the prince though.

The White Prince was with Kani, holding her hand like a metal ring about the foot of a bird, and his clockworker with their wide-brimmed hat and their fall of white veils stood near him; a movable pillar.

Kani was well-protected by her proximity to the prince. He thought her no threat.

All Tet had to do was wait and remember the route Dozha had drawn on the sloped wall of the attic room with charcoal. It was an easy enough thing for him and he passed the time imprinting the image into his head, following the passages in a prophetic dream.

Dozha would call him once he had the prince's breastplate and then they would have to hope that the gods would not be able to sniff Tet down before his work was done. A grass-head of hope, easily destroyed. His heart quickened, and he trembled with a fever of fear and excitement and anticipation.

Soon all his magic would be his again, completely, but until that moment, Tet had to be patient; watch Dozha play his part and charm the prince, whispering promises into his ear, sweet and poisonous while the musicians played songs from fallen empires.

The White Prince ran his fingers down Kani's throat, tilted her head so that he could press vicious kisses against her neck and mouth, consume her tongue.

Tet kept himself still, and tried to see only the figment of Kani, and not the truth of Dozha. The crowds throbbed around him, their voices a murmur, a moan. The dim stars spilled milky, adding their light to the soft globes the clockwork birds carried this way and that.

The party reached its climax and the music softened and slowed. Women and men drifted off back into the night, their deals made, their alliances strengthened or clean-broken as a twisted arm.

Dozha and the prince had gone now up to the apartments hidden in the heart of the labyrinthine passages. Only a few dregs still remained, and Tet spotted Ymat Shoom, his hands waving as he conducted some new enterprise, blackmailed another idiot.

Tet looked right at him and Ymat saw nothing.

Merithym.

The voice snaked through Tet's head like the whisper of a lover. Dozha was where he needed to be, and all that was left was for Tet to play his part in Sinastrillia's stratagem. Slowly as a man walking in his sleep, Tet raised his chalk-hand and touched it to the beetle. The clockwork thrummed, eager, and he pressed, fingers cracking the stone carapace against his chest as though the trinket were nothing more than the hollow egg of a thrush. It broke into his skin, the magic spiralling in like the drills of glass-winged cicadas. The power flushed through Tet's flesh, sloshing through his blood: a liquor, potent and sweet and fiery.

Tet closed his eyes against the fading stars, the fading party, and stretched his magic open, feeling the world spill around him in a bright quilt of potential. He could touch the minds of men like soft bumbling moths, the cool tooth-sharp mind of the dragon far below in the underground river, the firefly emotions of the gods scattered throughout the city. Here was the truth Sinastrillia tried to make him understand – that gods were no greater than men. They burned brighter and fiercer, they tore through the universe robed in magic and power, they snapped at each other, at men and monsters.

But humans built towers.

We spread our seed through the ripe earth and we swarm across the crinkled ground. We stretch our little wings and though our lives are brief, we change the face of the world.

We build towers.

And the gods are out of time.

Tet remembered what it was like to stretch out his mind until it touched the edges of time, like a wasp in a soap bubble, until the great stone door in his mind cracked along its seams and split open to the darkness and the chaos behind.

He took a breath so deep it never ended.

A wasp sting, a movement that was precise and controlled and nothing like the unleashed rage of his youth. The stone door opened, wide as the mouth of hell, and the universe froze in place. The last of the music snapped silent, and slowly Tet opened his eyes to a world caught in amber. The air vibrated against him but Tet walked through it as though the strange consistency of this timeless frozen universe was his true element, and he a little fish pulled from a hook and thrown back into the river.

Ymat Shoom's mouth was half open as he pointed at a small clockwork bird. The woman he spoke with looked sour, her eyes narrowed as she calculated what she could win from Ymat. Like him, she wore city-speaker's robes. If not Ymat, it might have been her or a thousand other minor players like her who tried to catch Tet in their fragile web.

The moth-wing minds of men might have stilled, but the raging fireflies were still out there and Tet had to move. The gods would find him soon. He could feel them waking, burning brighter. Perhaps they would try and restart time as they had before, or think it better to hunt him down first.

With his knees protesting every step, Tet raced through the web of passages Dozha had mapped out, following them with eyes-half closed, trusting in the remembered scrawl. The palace was a twisting knot, a tangle of mating serpents.

The only sound was the hard slap of leather boots on the Imradian marble, the tapping echoes from walls leafed in gold, and the harsh pant of Tet's breaths. Another mind moved slow and deep below, a silver-dark gleam that put itself in the way of the fireflies converging on the palace. It took a moment before Tet realised that Sinastrillia had engaged the hunting gods, buying him more time in a timeless world. He laughed, and the sound cawed through the passages and up the towers. He followed the black wings of laughter, up and up, drawn to where Dozha and the White Prince were waiting for him.

*

The doors to The White Prince's chambers were unguarded. Or at least, they were guarded, but the beasts were frozen in a perfect delicate balance like the spinning wheels and rods of the Clock of the Tower of the Floating University. Tet had to admire the intricacy of their craftsmanship. It pained him a little that there would never be a chance to talk mage-to-mage with the remarkable person who'd made these.

There were tawny gold lions and leopards cloud-marked, red wolves and even a small jade-scaled dragon. Their teeth were daggers, their fur made of individual silk threads stitched into metal as if it were woven cloth. Jewel eyes watched Tet, unmoving, and he reached out to touch the long fur of the clockwork toy nearest to the door. A red wolf, so life-like that Tet could almost believe he felt it breathing beneath his palm. He drew his hand away and stalked past the motionless guardians to open the door into the prince's sanctum.

Frozen time was pressing against him. Tet understood what Sinastrillia meant about the cracks. They sliced in jagged angles. Everything was static for now, but the pressure was building behind it and Tet was enveloped in a sudden dizzying fear of what would happen if he was not able to soften these weak points and push them together like torn dough. He rushed through a series of rooms that opened one from another, a coiling spiral of boxes, and in the final room found Dozha and the prince.

The air in the room was splintered, fracturing frozen light in a strange rainbow. Each movement Tet made split time further, the universe shredding into a cold black emptiness.

I need to end this soon.

Dozha was still Kani, exquisite and imperious, and he made a beautiful statue. Tet kissed his cold mouth and pulled him out of one element into another, pulling him outside of the stalled river of time. Dozha woke like a drowned man, and stepped back, eyes wide in a flare of distrust. Then he blinked, shook his head.

'You—' he began, then cut himself off with a sharp rueful grin. 'Sinastrillia said you could.'

The prince's breastplate lay at their feet, unbuckled, gleaming like the inside of an oyster. On the front of it were two opals, each one the hand-span of a grown man. Wards were etched into them, and they glowed with a mage light older than anything else in this city. Older even than the prince's gilded Pistil. His protection, the stolen eyes of gods.

It seems that I have always been a fool.

Dozha stripped off the long gloves still covering his arms. The right was revealed, a silver beauty that must have cost a small fortune. He pressed the top, and whatever magic and tricks kept it to the stump of his elbow released, and the metal arm dropped free. He caught it easily, well-practiced, and tossed the limb into the ship-wide bed where it lay like a dead fish.

Dozha gathered the prince's precious armour and put it on over his embroidered robes. 'You'll have to do the buckles,' he said.

Here then is my new emperor; a black-haired queen, a thief-prince, a shape-changing mage. Tet's fingers trembled as he did the buckles. He would not lose him, not now. Not when he finally had found the sheath that fitted his steel heart.

Around them time cracked and splintered, and the gods flared and flashed.

It was too late.

They arrived one after the other, like birds bursting through the high canopy of trees into the sun-bright sky: Epsi, Vitash, Nanak, Nyangist.

Three vast dogs, nothing like the little magic sendings Tet struck from sparks.

A lioness so huge she could swallow the stars.

And perhaps Tet was a mage who could burn the world to cinders, freeze the ash into a sculpture created solely for his own amusement, but he was not a god.

I'm just a man who knows my own name. He turned to Dozha, to Kani, to Oshaketri aand pressed a fierce kiss against Dozha's forehead, another against his mouth, his cheek. Goodbye and goodbye. Dozha was protected by the White Prince's breastplate, but it was still a thing of the gods and Tet didn't trust that it would always keep him safe. He needed to be in a place where they could never reach him, or this whole farce would have been for nothing. If Tet failed now, then Dozha was as good as dead.

There was only one way that Tet knew for certain he could keep Dozha safe, at least for a little longer. No matter what happened to him after this day.

'Run,' Tet said, and used his magic to do something Sinastrillia hadn't seen in her rivers and currents. 'Oshaketri.'

Dozha's eyes widened as Tet snapped the command into place. 'Run, Oshaketri, run. Run south until you find me.'

With a force of magic that was almost sickening, Tet pushed Dozha into a new place in time where the gods would not find him, pushed him into a future where the gods were gone, and when Tet had lost him completely, Tet pulled all the strands of broken time together and into himself.

It would not be enough. Never, but there was one small thing he could do.

Sinastrillia had given him a gift and then asked a favour in return. For once, someone had not told him what to do, nor forced him into service with threats and chains. *If Ymat had known my name he would have.*

While Sinastrillia had used him as a game-piece, she had also allowed him at least the pretence of being a man who could make his own decisions. Tet grinned, a death's head grimace of black humour. *Well-played, dragon.*

She'd known what he would do.

Tet was still a mage and he would one day be a great one. One that the world would remember. This was how he would fix what he'd fractured, how he would erase Dozha's tracks from the hearts and desires of little gods. He took a deep breath.

'I'm here,' he said to the gods. 'Come and get me.' He'd dreamed their deaths in his seven-petal visions. Let them come to him.

Like a slow carnival, the gods moved in a pageantry of giant monsters, their power sparking through them in rainbow shimmers of light. Tet opened his arms as the gods drew nearer, their magic lacerating his skin, leaving cat claw trails of blood.

With a final scream of rage and triumph Tet sent his magic clawing into theirs, tangling it into the threads of his own power.

The gods, slow to understand, began to pull back, but Tet bit down harder, reeling the power of the gods through his own soul, feeling the strangeness of it crack his bones, boil his blood. And with their power, with his own, he gathered the shattered splinters of the universe and spun them to him, a magnet drawing in a scattered handful of iron filings. He was not a god, and time was not something men were meant to bring into their own skin. The cracked bones, the broken glass joints of Tet's legs were nothing to the pain that rode his body now. He gritted his teeth, felt them shatter in his mouth, and he stitched and pulled at time until there were no more ruined edges and mirror-cracks and webs of brokenness.

He consumed the gods, and time was remade.

*

When time started again, Tet was emptied. Just a man. The power he'd had for a few long moments had all been used up to set right the things he'd done. Not only his power, but the gods'. They too had dwindled.

His head was a hollowed gourd, brittle and weak, and he lay where he'd fallen before the feet of a prince whose treasured protection had been whisked away; before weakened gods who would want their revenge slow. They might have been diminished, but they were not yet dead, and they would take Tet with them.

His fingers scraped the floor and even that small movement was enough to send sparks of agony through Tet's entire body. The universe and all of time had left his nerves flayed, his insides torn. *At least I saved Dozha.* A blue-blackness swelled behind his eyes and he struggled against it.

I will not go to my death like this, giving in. No matter what. Tet shuddered. This time the White Prince would not leave him in a cell underground to starve to death. He would want the city to see what happened to those who go against him.

And I want them to see it too. Another bit of entertainment for the loyal citizens of Pal-em-Rasha, but for others a reminder that their prince was a demon. Those people would find their way to the Monkey, or to men like him.

Right to the end it seems I will work for Ymat. I hope the bastard appreciates it.

*

They cut out Tet's tongue, because they thought it still mattered.

The White Prince wanted the city to watch Tet die. His clockworker would break Tet for him. They faced Tet with their toy beasts, their perfect beautiful beasts, and all across the temple square, the crowds were silent as the dead in the cavern of shades.

I am halfway there already. Over the heads of paltry humans were the looming shapes of the watching gods, thin and gossamer weak; the shifting smoke trails of the twenty-one First Men.

The toymaker walked closer, a pillar of fluttering white, and their creatures made a path for them, attuned to their every unspoken command. When they were so close that Tet could almost see the faint shape of them through the veils, they raised their hands and parted the material, enveloping him in their small white world.

There was only Tet, aching and thirsty and ready to die, and the broad moon face of the toymaker. Where the White Prince was sharp angles and handsome as a knife, the toymaker had a head like a puffball, her mouth a small slash, her nose just two flared nostrils. Only her eyes were like his; one clouded, one grey.

The sister-monster. Always loyal to her prince, always at his heel. The younger sister who had never died. *Which just goes to show how much rumour is worth*.

'You stopped time,' said the White Prince's sister. 'You stole my brother's treasures.'

It was not as though Tet could answer her. Frothy blood dribbled from his mouth, itched down his chin.

'It's impossible.' She pressed one hand to him and shuddered. 'No, no, you have no magic. You are a nothing.'

Tet coughed in answer, and the whole of his body was racked as his broken ribs made every gasped breath torture.

She drew her head back, and a single wrinkle appeared at the centre of the smooth expanse of her forehead. 'You are not a mage. Not anymore. So why are the ghost-dragons waiting?' Confusion tripped through her voice. 'The twenty-one First Men. I did not call them for you, but they came anyway.'

Of course they were waiting for him. They knew what he'd done, right there at the end, and so did the gods and the dragons. Even if stupid royal brats with candle-bright lives did not.

'You humiliated my brother. Do not think I will make your death easy.'

I suppose it would have been too much to ask.

The sister's veil closed and she drew away from him. Her clockwork beasts advanced and the sudden fear that grasped Tet's heart almost made him try to call out for mercy. Not that he could make the words. Not that anyone would listen.

Tet raised his head and stared out into the waiting mass of people. Sunlight glinted off the clockwork animals, half-blinding him, and tears sprung to his eyes. He blinked furiously and tried to focus on something, anything that would help him through this. Tet sent his mind back to childhood, back to the patterns of the meditation halls. It brought a momentary stillness. *Remember this, remember this*, he wanted to scream it at the waiting masses. He clung to the shape of his name, his true name, and the way it had fallen from Dozha's mouth like a blessing.

Laketri was in the crowd that gathered to watch the final tortures. Right at the front, like a beacon in a storm. She held her head high, unblinking. She was fiercer and more beautiful than a mountain leopard, and now Tet could see her resemblance to her sister-brother.

Ymat Shoom had also come to watch him die, but he did not smile, and even while they would flay Tet's skin and crack his bones, Ymat would understand that the war was turning and the prince's reign was almost over. Ymat had saved Tet from his first taste of death at the White Prince's hand, though he could not save him from this one.

And though Tet had stolen the breastplate away from the prince and Ymat, he would at least die with one debt paid. The prince would fall, as Ymat Shoom had wanted

I am, after all, an honourable man.

In my own way.

Laketri raised a hand as the first beast stepped up to Tet's stomach, and Tet kept his eyes wide, staring at Laketri's fingers, still gloved in drying clay.

Let it be quick, even though he knew it would not be. The toymaker had given her word and the prince had face to regain. As the first terrible pain ripped through Tet, the dragon ghosts surged forward, and Tet let go, falling through the world, from this darkness to another.

*

The temple square was cast in shadows and across the sky, the gods faded like flickers of ashy mountains. Tet stood next to his corpse. The dim shadows of humans were thick as flies about him. A faint strand of silvery ether connected him to what was left of his body. The heavens were a bright darkness, the sun a black hole as though all the colours in the words had inverted themselves.

'And that was me,' he said softly. A ruin. His voice was the only one he could hear in the feathery silence of death. Though the ghost people talked and moved, Tet heard nothing. An insistent tug pulled at the edges of his spirit-self, and the urge to snap the thread grew stronger.

'So it is.'

Tet had never heard this voice before, deep and rich and green with life. Slowly, he turned to face his companion.

The dragon was bigger even than Sinastrillia, her jade back arched, her great eyes like golden swamp-globes, whisker-filaments curling about Tet, caressing his spirit-skin. He'd never seen her. Or rather, he had only ever seen her spirit

A final proof that Tet was truly dead.

'Mil.' He bowed.

The First Dragon blew smoke from her nostrils and it smelled like seven-petal and autumn bonfires.

'Where do I go now?' Tet asked.

A dragon's laugh was never a comforting thing, but Tet felt no fear now. No sadness, no loss. Only a fading curiosity as to what happened next. When she was done laughing, Mil said, 'Most choose to follow me.'

'Most?' Tet cocked his head. 'There's a choice?'

'Some stay to cling to loved ones, or things.' She shrugged, and it rippled down her scaled back, a prolonged shiver.

'I don't want that.'

'Of course not.'

The crowds had thinned, the entertainment over. Tet's body would be left to be picked apart by pigeons and starlings. By feral dogs with no true pack. He bent down to touch his broken remains. The image was grotesque, but he had no stomach to be turned. Most of his stomach was currently lying around his feet. Tet wondered if this thought would have amused him, were he still alive. His fingers closed around the silver thread binding him to life and he tightened his grip, ready to snap it and follow Mil, when a dark figure came forward and dropped to her knees alongside him.

Peniki.

Tet paused. Why was she here now?

'What's she saying?' Tet asked Mil, and the sound filtered back, muted and crackled with a high whine like cicadas in summer.

'Idiot,' Peniki said to Tet's corpse. 'And how am I supposed to get you back? I'm an old woman, you know.' She began scraping all his body parts into a sheet, careful to leave not a scrap behind. Even the blood she rinsed away. No one stopped her. She was just some widowed woman, cleaning up the dead.

XXXII

GHOSTING

Mil didn't stop Tet from following Peniki and his corpse back to the house in the eastern quarter. She didn't come with him either, merely warned him that if he stayed, he ran the risk of ghosting. If he was trapped as a spirit in this world, it would prevent him from moving on to the cavern of the dead and journey to the Green Lands, and from there to rebirth.

'I don't plan on staying long.' That faint curiosity had gotten the better of him. He wanted to know what she was going to do. After all, she'd been his landlady, nothing more. Tet had left her only the remains of his money, the last of his possessions. A paltry thank you. There was no reason for her to gather the pieces of his corpse and ready him for burial. They were not relatives or lovers, or even friends.

Peniki pulled Tet's body in the hand cart she sometimes used when she took her spare brooms to the market to sell them herself, grumbling the whole way, lurching it up the small step to her front door.

A man came out to greet her and help carry the bundled cloth inside. A man Tet recognised.

'Is that all of him, Sai Broom?' he said.

'Enough that no one will be binding his ghost to the world,' she replied. 'Sai Tiger.'

Head ringing, Tet passed through the slammed door and watched as the Tiger dumped the remains, enclosed in their sheet, on the stone floor in front of the kitchen fireplace, before the feet of Ymat Shoom.

Ymat prodded at the bundle with one booted toe. 'Well,' he said. 'At least the arrogant little shit did manage to strip the prince of his power, if nothing else.'

'You're certain of that?' snapped the Tiger. 'Because from where I'm looking, we have no proof, and that damn thief Dozha has tucked tail and run like a scared dog. No one's seen a single hint of him. Gods-damned Underpalace was like an ant-nest that someone kicked open.'

'I have been reliably informed,' drawled Ymat Shoom, 'that the prince's magical protection has definitely gone. There's no sign of it in this world.'

'I don't like it,' the Tiger muttered. 'And I don't like that your pet here limped straight into the palace without consulting us. We were keeping him safe until you could get that bitch Kani to cooperate.' He scowled. 'No sign of her either. It's all very convenient. All these thieves and mages scattered to the wind.'

'No,' said Ymat. 'It's all very *inconvenient*, but we are resourceful people, and we will use what we have.'

'And what do we have?' Peniki's voice was unexpected, she'd been watching the men, her arms folded. 'I kept his trail clear, swept his traces from my house every morning to keep the dogs from finding him, and the damn fool decides to go walk to up to death and greet it instead.' She gestured at the bloodied bundle. 'And now, instead of a mage, we have *this*.'

'This is still a mage,' Ymat said, and a terrible shiver flickered through Tet's spirit. Ymat looked up at Peniki, frowning. 'Bring me everything he owned, no matter how small.'

While she went upstairs to fetch Tet's meagre wealth, Ymat busied himself by pouring a circle of mountain salt about the body. Southern sorcery from Utt Dih.

I should have seen Peniki for what she was – another of Ymat Shoom's pets. And now Ymat planned to perform some other trick and bind Tet to him, even in death. Tet would not let that happen.

'Mil!' he screamed, and the dragon was there, filling the room, more real than the dark shadowy figures of the Monkey and the Tiger. 'What is he doing?'

She glanced down.

Ymat was piling Tet's goods on the bloodied mound: his clothes, his lute, his coins, his flint-pouch.

The flint-pouch. It had still been on him when he died.

'Oh, Merithym,' said Mil. 'I am so very sorry.'

Ymat poured oil over everything, muttering in the language of the South, and Tet was frozen in place, unable to go on to death. 'No!' he screamed but no one heard and the ritual continued.

'You have work still to do, Tet,' Ymat said as the flames devoured everything that was once the mage Tet, that obliterated the man that was Tet-Nanak, Ohtet Maynim, Sektet Am. 'Come back to us, Sai Hound.'

I will not.

Did Ymat not understand that Tet was useless to him, that all his magic had been torn from him in order to restart time? Ymat was forcing him back when there was nothing for him to come back to. Dozha was long gone and far away, centuries away.

'No,' Tet said again, just as the tinder-pouch caught fire. The three dogs flickered into view but they were thin as shadows at midday, powerless to do anything. No living person in the room could even see them.

So the dogs were not fully-manifest, and they could do nothing physical. But Tet was not of this world, and a spirit could surely carry a spirit. 'Vitash, Nanak, Epsi,' Tet said, desperate that they would help, though he could see no way to break the strands of Ymat's craft. 'Take me from here. Anywhere. Take me to death.'

The ghost-dogs, those little fragments of some ancient witch's soul, her *oresh* split and made tangible, loomed and grew, becoming stretched and vast, liquid as living smoke. They flowed into Tet. A feeling bright and cold. The spirits of the three dogs swelled, filling Tet's spirit with theirs. The strand holding him to the corpse snapped. Ymat Shoom's fire shot bright green and orange sparks, then turned to a column of thick black smoke.

Tet heard their distant screams.

And then he was gone.

If I live again, it will be because I fucking chose it, not because some men told me I had to.

XXXIII

THE MERITHYM

My name is Merithym and I have known who I am since I was born. I did not speak when they cut the caul from my face, not like the first rebirth. That was a short life. Still, a valuable lesson to learn.

I have served three more lives since then, and whatever name the mothers and fathers give me, it falls from my soul like dead leaves. I keep my true name and each time I reach the cavern of shades again, I call the first of the dragons to me and tell her I will keep this name, these memories, through this death and into my next life. For she *will* give me another.

Mil has stopped arguing.

It's my fifth life since I died stretched out on a rack of blades before the White Prince. So now I'm on my *alm*-life. Or my *sek*-life, if you count that wasted one too. It's my first where I am not born into the crumbling ruins of Pal-em-Rasha. This time I am in a fishing village in Utt Dih. I have been here before as an old woman because I wanted to see the sea. I did not pass through this village, but took the Green Road to the grand city of Dih with its white marble walls and golden streets, its flower-garlanded bears, and temples filled with monkeys.

This time I was born at the sea's white-hemmed skirts, in a village poor as fish scales. I have grown up weaving nets, casting lines, sailing the boats out on the night tide, catching the lamp-fish that burn bright as the reflections of stars, learning my father's father's craft. It amuses me now to learn all these new things. I no longer play the lute, but a similar instrument that the women here use to sing to each other in a secret musical language that sounds remarkably like the love songs of dragons. I know their language. Born into it this time. Inducted into it with monthly blood.

Tonight is a feast-night, poor as such a thing is in my village. We have a guest and guests are never turned away, though we have mostly forgotten why. Something to do with the laws of the old priests in their decaying, empty temples.

Instead of doing my duty and helping the other young men and women of my village, I am sitting on the edge of the dock, watching the lights flicker on in the hall. My feet are in the rising water, and the moon tugs at the magic under my skin. I lean forward and dip my white hand into the water, swirl it in a complex pattern like rising and falling notation. The lamp fish skitter and flash, chasing my pale fingers through the saltwater.

In every life, my right hand had been as white as the belly of a toad. Fingertip to wrist. I don't mind, it helps me remember.

The night slides across the sky, the stars slipping toward the horizon, but I wait, letting the tide rise to lap against my knees and the fish swim bright around my legs.

Sinastrillia's head finally breaks the surface, and though I have felt her making her way south for days now, my heart dolphin-leaps. I always know where she is. I can feel her moving through the universe like a blade. In this life, I haven't spoken to her often, and this too, I don't mind.

It helps me forget.

'Merithym,' she says in her river-voice, so black and deep. 'A final move, before we set the board again for a new game.'

I splash a little water at her, like a child. Perhaps I am one; this body has only seen eighteen years, after all. 'There's a guest in the village house,' I tell her, though she already knows. I was too scared to go see him, scared that because I have a new face he will not remember me. *Oshaketri. Oshaketri and Merithym.* I wonder if there is a future where people will write songs about us, will turn the painful reality into a story garlanded with lies to make it more beautiful. I cough. *The Love Song of Oshaketri and Merithym.* How ridiculous. I don't even know if he will forgive me for what I did.

'Bring him here,' Sinastrillia says, 'We will need to talk.'

I nod and get up, my wet feet slipping a little on the old wood. There is a guest in my village hall and it was the way of our people to show their respect because as my mother once said, guests could be gods or ghosts.

Or emperors.

*

He looks up when I come into the room in the village-house, and my heart leaps like a snow-trout. He is still beautiful Dozha, with his crane-black hair and star-eyes. He looks exhausted, his clothing travel-worn and outlandish. I can see the stolen breastplate under a woollen jerkin, just hints of it. At least he's still protected. Dozha has collapsed into the most comfortable seat in the house. He tilts his head back to stare vacantly at the low ceiling.

One sleeve is pinned up, and his hand drums an impatient nervous message against his knee. He does not recognise me.

'My mother sent me to see if you have enough to eat.' I am carrying a covered tray. Dried fish, pickled fruits. I wonder if he will like them – they were not common in Pal-em-Rasha.

'I think I've had food enough, thank you.' He laughs gently. 'Your people seem convinced I was starving.'

I set the tray down on a small dining table. 'You've travelled far.' My hands are shaking, and the tray clacks against the wood.

He turns his head at the noise and frowns. 'I have. Further than you might think.' Dozha stands and walks toward me. 'What happened to your hand, girl?'

Of course, girl. Not the man he knew, not even the mage. I have magic but it's not any he would recognise. I hug myself. I have no breastplate to protect me. Come, I can do this. What are men but skins stitched over spirits? I am still Merithym. Carefully, I tilt my head, and allow myself a small smile. 'This?' I raise my hand out to him. 'It was a gift.'

'The gods are strange.' But he cannot stop staring at my hand.

'This one was from a dragon.'

His head jerks back, eyes narrow and wary. Dozha says nothing, but he waits for me like an actor ready to say the right responses, if only we are performing the same play.

'It was part of the price for giving me back my name,' I say. 'The rest of the price turned out to be a little higher than expected, but,' I shrug, 'you know how these things can be, Oshaketri.'

'You bloody shit,' Dozha says. 'You shoved me through time and told me nothing. I thought you were dead.'

'Yes.' I lower my arms. I do not need armour. 'There was that.'

He makes no move to come closer. But he's also not walking away. 'Do that again, Merithym, and I'll not forgive it.' He smiles thinly. 'And the retribution of mages can be terrible.' He has invoked my name. I'm not even sure what he's ordering from him. We could play at this game for lifetimes. Or we could stop.

'Terrible indeed,' I answer and step forward to put my white hand against his chest. The breastplate hums with subtle magic, weakened now in this time and place, but it still calls to me the way Dozha does. 'Take that stupid thing off.'

Beneath my palm, his heartbeat drums harder, and when he smiles, I think for a moment, for *now*, we have won.

-Fin-

ACKNOWLEDGEMENTS

When I was a child, I owned a huge fat, illustrated collection of the stories of Hans Christian Andersen, given to me by my grandmother Inga. While that book has long since been lost by family upheavals, I still remember the cloth cover, the illustration plates with their depth and detail.

And of course, the stories. I love so many of the Andersen stories, though I also love to twist them, strip away the Christian lip-service, and permeate the tales with my own queer takes. Which is how Thief Mage, Beggar Mage came to life.

If you know, you knew the moment the dogs appeared, but if you don't, Thief Mage, Beggar Mage is me playing with the story The Tinderbox, about a soldier who returns from war, and ends up with the stolen treasure of a witch – one part of which is a magical tinderbox that summons three dogs "with eyes as big as wagon wheels." And yes, there's a princess and the soldier gets to marry her in Andersen's version, when the soldier is saved from his death at the stake by requesting a final pipe (where he strikes the tinderbox and is rescued by the giant dogs).

Initially, I did try to have the ending offer the same "happy every after, final rescue moment", but I only got there in the most convoluted of ways. And I'm fine with that, I think it suits the Love Song of Merithym and Oshaketri better.

As always, my thanks go to my support network of fellow writers – the Musers, Nerine Dorman, Xan van Rooyen, Jenny Rainville, and all the people who helped work on edits and beta reads. Your support and help are how we got to this place. Special thanks to EM Faulds for constant sanity checks and cheerleading.

ABOUT THE AUTHOR

Cat Hellisen is a South African-born writer and artist living in Scotland, where they survive on blackberries and pakora.

You can follow them on twitter @cat_hellisen

Previous works include

When the Sea is Rising Red

House of Sand and Secrets

Beastkeeper

Empty Monsters

Bones Like Bridges

King of the Hollow Dark

Cast Long Shadows